Scotl

As the Graham and Maxw… feud, a lone warrior sets out to find the treasure that can grant his family victory. . . .

Fayth Graham's first and fiercest loyalty is to her clan and their unending fight against the hated Maxwells of Scotland. But when her cruel brother attempts to marry her off to a horrible old lecher, she disguises herself as a boy and escapes—right into the hands of her worst enemy. . . .

Alex Maxwell recognizes her immediately, despite her outward appearance. He would never forget the redheaded firebrand who had tempted him to his very soul—only to betray him to her vengeful family. Now, as he searches for the elusive Blood Stone, she is finally his to command. . . .

On their journey, they slowly discover an overwhelming passion that tames the hatred that once burned between them. But when Fayth is recaptured, Alex must choose between the treasure he can hold in his hand, and the treasure that he already holds in his heart. . . .

Praise for
TEMPTED BY YOUR TOUCH

"A tender triumph that tempted me to
keep reading all night long."
—Teresa Medeiros, author of *A Kiss to Remember*

Books by Jen Holling

Tempted by Your Touch
Tamed by Your Desire

Available from Pocket Books

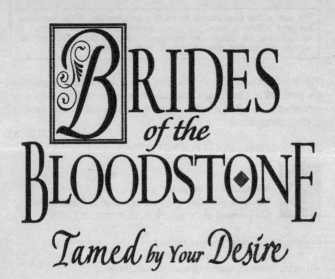

BRIDES of the BLOODSTONE

Tamed by Your Desire

JEN HOLLING

SONNET BOOKS

New York London Toronto Sydney Singapore

An *Original* Publication of POCKET BOOKS

A Sonnet Book published by
POCKET BOOKS, a division of Simon & Schuster, Inc.
1230 Avenue of the Americas, New York, NY 10020

Copyright © 2002 by Jennifer Holling

ISBN: 0-7434-3803-5

First Sonnet Books printing June 2002

10 9 8 7 6 5 4 3 2 1

SONNET BOOKS and colophon are trademarks of Simon & Schuster, Inc.

For information regarding special discounts for bulk purchases, please contact Simon & Schuster Special Sales at 1-800-456-6798 or business@simonandschuster.com

Cover art by Lisa Litwack; Photo credits: Marcus Brooke/Getty Images; back cover illustration by Gregg Gulbronson

Printed in the U.S.A.

To my daughters, Bridget and Sierra,
my strength and my sunshine.

Acknowledgments

A special thanks to Lauren McKenna
for insisting that Alex's story must be next.
And to Jennie Patterson, for rushing to my rescue
with her red pen. You're the best!

PROLOGUE

❧

ANORA MUSGRAVE WAITED in the shadows for opportunity to present itself. She'd been in and out of this bedchamber for hours, keeping guard over the Clachan Fala, the Blood Stone she was sworn to protect with her life if necessary. Musgrave witches had always been the keepers. Anora had been chosen for this duty as a child and had never known aught else—had never known the touch of a man, the love of children—and never would. And still her calling was unusual. She was the first in hundreds of years to seek the Blood Stone and remove it from hiding.

But it was wrong, Anora knew that now. She'd watched the bride, Elizabeth Maxwell, the new Lady Annan, giddy with excitement as her women dressed her for her wedding night. The Clachan Fala had been on the bedside table then, at rest. Anora had receded deeper into the darkness when Elizabeth's brother, Richard Graham, entered. They'd argued. Richard wanted the stone. Elizabeth threatened to tell her husband, so he left. She was angry then, slamming things around, muttering to herself. The women serving her shrunk away, afraid.

Another man entered. He made threats and slapped her. She tried to run, so he bound her hand and foot, and forced her to lie in the bed with the furs up around her neck. He told her if she stopped fighting, they'd let her husband live. Anora slipped away then, to warn the husband. But he was like the rest, frightened of an old woman and greedy for power, so she returned by the castle's secret ways to protect the Blood Stone. Elizabeth Maxwell lay silently in the bed, her eyes frantically sweeping the room. The man had not left; he was hidden in the folds of the bed hangings.

Anora's heart pounded with terror. She knew what was coming—she'd carried the Blood Stone close to her heart for a fortnight and its effects lingered in the *Knowing*. It wasn't the same as when she held the Blood Stone—then she could hear others' thoughts as if they whispered them in her ears. This was only a feeling, but she knew it belonged to the hidden man—it was dark and murderous. Elizabeth was desperate, afraid. Anora wished she could help. But it wasn't her place. She was only the keeper.

She heard men coming, laughing and shouting. Drunk. As soon as they entered, Anora knew there was no hope, that they'd failed yet again. The brother, Richard Graham, was with them. His eyes were sly and knowing—his heart was black, seething with hate and envy. Anora pressed hard against the wall, waiting. She wished again she could stop this, but it was not possible. Her sole purpose in life was to guard the Clachan Fala. Nothing else mattered.

Anora closed her eyes, turned her face away when Richard Graham plunged his sword into Elizabeth's husband, but she couldn't shut out Elizabeth's cries of horror and disbelief. When Anora opened her eyes, Richard Graham stood over the dead body of Malcolm Maxwell, Lord Annan. Another Graham yanked the sword from the door that held Malcolm's brother, Kinnon, impaled, and he, too, slumped to the ground. Richard nodded and one of the others swung the door wide.

"A Graham! A Graham!" he shouted and rushed through the door as shrieks and sounds of death filled the air.

Anora's body shook with sobs, her hand clamped hard over her mouth. Must it always end this way? With death? Her heart was not strong enough—she feared she would die here, her duty unfulfilled. Elizabeth, still prone on the bed, seemed to have turned to stone. She stared blankly ahead, her skin sickly pale, her eyes round and sightless. That's when Anora noticed the Clachan Fala was gone.

Richard strode over to his sister, his gaze moving to the empty bedside table and back. "Where is it? It was just here!"

Elizabeth did not speak, only stared like a dead person, eyes glazed, mouth slack.

Richard grabbed her shoulders and shook her. "Tell me! Where is the Blood Stone? Did one of my men take it?" When her head only bobbed with his shakings, he thrust her away, against the bolsters. Anora looked away as he ran his hands over his sister's body, looking for the Clachan Fala. Elizabeth made no sound.

Finally he swore and after staring about the room, strode to the door, muttering, "That old witch . . ."

Anora heard no more, but knew herself to be the old witch he cursed. If he found her, he would kill her. Moments after he was gone, the blank look disappeared from Elizabeth's eyes.

"You—hiding in the shadows. Come. Quickly."

Anora stepped forward, relieved. Elizabeth did have the stone, otherwise she'd be as ignorant of Anora's presence as the others had been. Another lingering effect of the stone: to become *Unseen.* If the keeper wished to be unobtrusive, then those around her failed to notice her—unless she spoke, or touched them.

Elizabeth threw back the bedcovers and slid off the bed. It had been beneath her body. Anora had not seen her hide it. There it lay, like a shivering drop of blood. The Clachan Fala. The Blood Stone. The cause of nearly a thousand years of hate and murder between the Maxwell and Graham clans.

"Untie me first—then take it," Elizabeth said, her gaze resting on the dead men. "So long as I live, Richard will never possess it."

Anora loosened the cord binding Elizabeth's wrists slowly, her gnarled and aching fingers clumsy. The tall young woman had no patience and untied her ankles herself. Anora gathered the stone in its bag and slipped it into the folds of her cloak. She turned to thank the woman. Elizabeth was on the floor, clutching at the bloody corpse of Lord Annan. It had been a love match. Anora knew this because it was the only way the stone could be brought from hiding. A love match betwixt a Maxwell of the Annan grayne and a Graham of the Eden grayne.

"Malcolm," the woman whispered, his face between her hands, his blood staining the pristine white of her shift, the silver blond of her hair. Her tears soaked his beard.

Anora hovered about, uncertain what to do. Now that she possessed the stone, she heard the whispers of others' thoughts all around her, like ghosts. But strongest was Elizabeth's pain. Though Elizabeth grieved silently, her mind screamed *No!* She couldn't accept it, even with his body before her, cold and lifeless, her mind refused to believe they'd been given such joy, only to have it ripped from them by her own brother. Anora couldn't bear to watch, knowing Elizabeth touched him, stared at him, somehow believing she could get through to him, bring him back.

Anora backed away, disliking the black void of nothing that emanated from the dead men. Malcolm Maxwell was long gone from his bride. Anora murmured her thanks, even though the dowager Lady Annan was beyond hearing.

The carnage outside Lord Annan's chambers turned Anora's stomach. Men and women were being beaten and tortured to reveal the Blood Stone's location. Anora clutched the stone to her heart, sickened that she could end it by turning the stone over to Richard, but also knowing that would only bring greater misery to many more people than these Annan Maxwells. She had a duty, and sentiment must not interfere.

Why me? There was another one, her successor, waiting outside the castle gates. She must know by now that all had gone wrong. She must be frightened, thinking Anora dead and the gauntlet fallen to her. She would be relieved to see the old woman emerge quite alive and in possession of the Blood Stone.

Anora groped along the wall, asking the stone to make her *Unseen.* At the door, she nearly walked right into Richard Graham. He held a torch and a dripping sword. Anora shrank back, pain numbing her arm, radiating across her chest. His face was splattered with blood, his lips drawn back from his teeth. He halted just inside the door, his head swiveling toward her, as if he smelled her.

Anora bit her lip until her teeth broke the skin, trying not to cry out as her heart convulsed. Her heart was dying! She panted, eyes squeezed shut, praying to hang on long enough to make it through the gates. When she opened her eyes, Richard was gone.

She staggered out of the keep and across the bailey, stepping around the corpses that littered the ground. The portcullis was down and the heavy door beside it shut. The porter was dead. A single Graham knight guarded the door. He wore a breast and back plate, no mail or shoulder coverings. Anora removed a short sword from a dead man's grasp. She moved to the side of the knight, who was oblivious to her presence, and slid the tip of the blade into the armhole of his armor. He tensed, as if he sensed something amiss, but before he could act, Anora plunged the sword into his chest, putting all her weight behind it.

He fell against the wall—seeing her now. Eyes wide with shock quickly glazed over as he slid down the wall. The door was not barred or locked and Anora slipped through, into the night.

Merry waited in the woods, her limbs frozen from the cold, her throat tight with fear. She'd seen the army of Grahams enter, had heard the screams from her hiding place. *Where was Anora?* Merry tried to remember everything she'd been taught. She'd been apprenticed to Anora a year ago. It had happened by chance. Anora's apprentice was murdered and the old woman had been frantic to find another, fearing she would die and the secret would die with her. Merry was a Musgrave and so had offered herself, eager to escape an unsavory marriage to the toothless tanner. Even living in the woods with an old witch—and eventually becoming one herself—was better than that.

Anora was a merciless taskmaster, too conscious of her own mortality. Merry had spent days and nights reciting the history of the Blood Stone, as well as its hidden location. These things were never to be written down, Anora had said, they remained always in a Musgrave's head. It mattered little, as Merry could not read or write. She was to choose a successor upon Anora's death and train her. It was like a river, constantly flowing, never dying, never ending.

Until tonight.

Or so they'd thought. When they received word of the wedding between Malcolm Maxwell and Elizabeth Graham, Anora had hoped their reign as keepers had finally come to an end. After tonight, their duty would be to watch until a son was born. But when they had arrived, Anora had sensed danger and instructed Merry to wait. The old witch had also advised that if she didn't return, Merry was charged with entering Annancreag and recovering the Blood Stone.

Merry's gaze sharpened, her mind returning to the task at hand. Someone stumbled away from the castle, down the winding dirt track. A small hunched figure that Merry immediately recognized as Anora. The old woman left the track, staggering through the tall grasses toward the trees where Merry hid. She hurried forward just as Anora collapsed.

"Anora! Are you hurt? What has happened?"

Anora didn't respond. Merry rolled her over. The black eyes stared back at her, the mouth turned down in a grimace of pain.

"Are you wounded?"

Anora shook her head, impatient. "I have it . . . take it . . ."

The blood roared in Merry's ears as she stared at the old woman, too terrified to move, to act. This was it. The duty had finally fallen to her and all she could think was that she was not ready. She was not competent enough to be the keeper. After a thousand years of keeping the Clachan Fala safe, she would be the one to muck it all up.

A gnarled hand came up and smacked her, hard.

"This is no time for fear!"

Merry found the Clachan Fala in the folds of Anora's cloak and clutched it to her belly.

"The iuchair . . ."

Merry removed the small curved beads strung on a cord about Anora's neck. The map. She fingered the smooth beads, unable to resist. Each was in the shape and color of a specific landmark. Merry sought out her favorite—a circular bead, red brown and pointed at the top. Its hole was larger than the rest—wide and gaping. Immediately images filled her mind. Heather-covered mountains. Standing stones. Wind-swept cliffs. Wind blasted her skin. The taste of salt water was on her lips. A standing stone loomed before her, just like the one in her fingers, but enormous, taller than a large man. She could see through the cleft as if she were before it, could nearly feel the heather beneath her feet . . .

Anora's gnarled hand clamped over Merry's, forcing her back to the present.

"Go—make haste, they'll soon be after you."

"I can't leave you," Merry said, pulling the old woman's head onto her lap.

Anora shook her head. "I'll be fine. I'm just tired. I'll be at home when you return."

The breath left Merry in a whoosh. The Blood Stone seemed to pulse against her belly—and she knew that Anora lied to her. Anora's heart was dying. She did not think she'd live through the night. But Merry also knew she was determined to die in her own bed.

The old witch's eyes softened, seeing that Merry knew. "Go, child. It's in your hands now."

The beads of the map bit into her hands, each tiny landmark carved and polished to look like a witch's bauble. She stood slowly, her eyes to the north, her heart swollen with purpose. The images swam at her again, mingled together now, but she knew how to use them, to call on them as needed.

"I won't fail you," she whispered to both the Blood Stone and her mentor, and raced into the night.

1

West March, England, 1542, 60 years later . . .

THE LITTER, PILED high with pillows and blankets, creaked and swayed as the horses made their way inexorably west to Lochnith and Fayth Graham's betrothed, Lord Ashton Carlisle. It was late September and the weather was mild; even so, Fayth sweat, stifled by the closed curtains of her litter. But they shielded her from the sight of the heavily armed guard surrounding her. The guards were more than protection. They ensured she'd not escape her fate.

Fayth leaned back against the pillows, loosening the laces of her bodice, untying the throat of the linen shift and spreading it wide. But that brought no relief. The air was thick. The stench of unwashed men and horse sweat permeated the heavy brocaded curtains. She was accustomed to the smell, if not to the elaborate garments her brother dressed her in. Since she was a bairn she'd dressed as a lad to train with her father and brother. And when she wore gowns, she favored simplicity—and no stays. The tightly laced wooden busks choked her and limited her range of movement. They scraped the healing stripes across her back, courtesy of her oldest brother, Ridley. He'd tried to flog her into agreeing to wed Carlisle. As of the present, he'd still not obtained her acquiescence. But apparently it no longer mattered.

Unable to bear another moment of inaction, Fayth parted the curtains slightly and peered through. A wall of armor-clad muscle and horseflesh surrounded her. Yet that did not deter her. She *must* escape. The alternative—marriage to a cruel old man—was unthinkable.

Mona had warned her what her life would be like if she wasn't able to extricate herself from this marriage. Fayth shook her head, angry, frustrated, refusing to accept her fate, even as she moved toward it. This was not how her life was supposed to be! Before Papa died there had been love, joy, friendship, family. Now there was nothing in its place. Fayth squeezed her eyes shut, pushing the memories away. Nothing would be gained by dwelling on what could not be changed . . . for now. But there was still hope . . . there was always hope.

Behind her eyelids new images spun. *Fire eating through tapestry and flowers, blood spilling, bodies twisting in agony.* Fayth's head jerked, as if to flick away the visions like an insect, but they gripped her. She didn't want to remember what she'd done—the pain and horror she'd caused. *Caroline screamed and screamed. Arms imprisoned Fayth, stifling, suffocating. Fayth fought his embrace, struggled for air as he squeezed. But he was too strong for her.*

Enough. Jaw clenched with new resolve, she pushed the errant memories away and peered through the slit in the brocade. The guard beside her was preoccupied, his helm-covered head at an anxious tilt, scanning the surrounding trees. Fayth's gaze tipped upward. Sunlight streamed through the branches like shafts of gold. They were in a forest, in Scotland. The West March was covered with forests and bogs, so she couldn't be sure exactly where they were or how much farther until Lord Carlisle's castle of Lochnith. She searched the trees, looking for a means of quick escape. A glimpse of something in the trees above caught her eye. A glint of metal? Or her imagination, weaving her desperate hope for rescue into fanciful visions? She strained her eyes, but could discern nothing.

She parted the curtains further, easing her head out. There were men before and behind the litter, but no one paid overmuch attention to her. Fayth wished fervently for a pair of breeches and a tunic. A cap to pull low over her hair and eyes. But alas, she would make do with gem-encrusted velvet and ribbons.

She would have to be fast, there was no room for hesitation or misstep. Someone shouted at the head of the cavalcade. The guard beside her tapped his horse's side and the horse stepped it up a bit, prancing forward as the guard strained to hear what was being yelled. Fayth paid no attention to the yelling—the guard was in front of her now.

She slid out of the litter, her feet dangling over the ground, and jumped. She rolled away, so the horse bearing the litter from behind didn't trample her, wooden stays digging furrows into her hips, and leaped to her feet. She was spotted immediately.

"She's escaped! Mistress Graham has escaped!"

The nearest guard yanked on his mount's reins, trying to turn sharply. The horse fought, rearing onto its haunches. Fayth darted into the trees. The clank of metal followed as her brother's knights dismounted to give pursuit.

Fayth tried not to panic—she had no idea where she was going. Well, she did—she was returning to England, to the village her father had kidnapped her stepmother, Mona, from—but currently, she was lost. Stones and sharp twigs pierced her feet through her delicate silk slippers. Damn, what she wouldn't give for a pair of boots!

The pounding of feet grew distant and Fayth chanced stopping to get her bearings. She leaned against a tree, her breath heaving in her chest. She could barely hear anything over the pounding of her heart, the roar of blood in her ears. She placed a lace-gloved hand over her chest, closed her eyes, and inhaled deeply, willing calm to settle over her. She couldn't think in such a panic.

After several such deep breaths her heart began to slow. The breaking of a twig and the soft crunch of leaves behind her set it hammering all over again as she whirled around.

But it wasn't her brother or his knights behind her. It was something far worse. Her throat closed and she couldn't speak—could only stare into the terrifyingly familiar face.

"Red" Alex Maxwell smiled, a cold curve of his lips that didn't reach the frigid blue eyes. "I've been following ye since ye left Graham Keep, but never did I think ye'd make it so easy for me."

Why are you following me? The horrified words formed in her head, but her voice was lodged somewhere in her chest, all tangled up with her furiously beating heart.

He wore no helm or cap, his dark reddish brown hair caught at the nape of his neck, holding it away from his face. Her eyes slid over the strong boned face to his temple. The red scar stood out, twisted and ugly. She'd given him that mark, slammed a jug of whisky over his head. Jesus wept, why hadn't she killed him? He'd murdered her betrothed! He'd ruined her life! Why had she lost courage? Had she the daring then, she wouldn't be standing here, caught between two enemies. She would be racing to freedom.

His utter stillness broke and he advanced. Fayth's paralysis gave way to terror. He would not be tricked again. He would rape and murder her this time—and from the grim determination etched on his face, that was exactly what he planned. She whirled to run—forgetting there was a tree at her back. She smacked into it and stumbled backward. He caught her arm, swinging her around.

Fayth hadn't spent half her life training with men for naught. Before he could catch her other arm, she ducked, grasping the dirk hilt that peeked from the top of his boot.

He reacted quickly to stop her, but she wedged the blade between them, pressing the tip to his leather-and mail-clad belly. A foolish act. She hadn't the strength to penetrate his armor. The top of her head barely reached his shoulder. But there was little else she could do.

He knew it well. He grabbed her other arm with his huge hand and yanked her hard against him. The blade skidded off the leather, pinning her hand and the blade between them.

She could taste her own fear as the scent of him surrounded her. Leather, sweat, and the faint fragrance of soap. He would kill her now for what she'd done to him, to his people—to her own sister, whom he now claimed as kin. Her body chilled with abhorrence, wondering if he would kiss her again. Like he did at Annancreag . . .

"Fayth!"

Fayth's head jerked around. Her brothers were near. They would rescue her from Red Alex. Then what? Take her to her old man husband. She looked up at her captor. He stared over her head, in the direction of the voices. His gaze dropped swiftly to hers, his hand sliding between their bodies and grasping her wrist. He forced the dirk from her hand and slid it back into his boot.

Securing both her wrists in one hand, he dragged her deeper into the trees. Fayth dug in her heels and fought him. He was so huge and she was so small.

An amused smile split his face. "Och, ye want to be carried, eh?"

Fayth shook her head frantically, but it was too late, he tossed her over his shoulder. She kicked to little effect, as his entire body seemed to be formed from granite. A scream lodged in her throat. Perhaps Ashton Carlisle wasn't so bad? So he was a cruel old man? So he had sick lusts? He might die soon, leaving her a rich widow. Compared to whatever abomination Red Alex had planned for her, that seemed quite satisfactory. And suddenly, decision made, she grabbed the long auburn hair trailing down his back and yanked as hard as she could as she let loose a shriek that resounded through the forest.

"Help! Help me!"

Alex growled like an angry bear and dumped her on the ground. Fayth kept hold of his hair, pulling him down with her—ready to take a hank of it as a war trophy—until she realized he'd released her. She scrambled to her feet. He was after her immediately, but this time she kept watch for trees and ran, not looking back. She could hear him pursuing her, could practically feel his hot breath on her neck. Terror gripped her, lending power to her legs and she ran faster. It was her gift in lieu of strength, her father had always said. She was no match for a man, but she was faster than any could hope to be and had the stamina to leave them coughing in her dust.

A grim pleasure came over her as she heard him fall behind. She resisted the nearly overwhelming urge to taunt him as she sometimes did her brothers. So intent was she on her escape, that she stumbled when her brother, Wesley, appeared from the trees.

"Fayth!"

She veered away, stopping short to find herself confronted by her oldest brother, Lord Ridley Graham. She turned frantically as men-at-arms materialized from the trees to form a circle about her. Red Alex was nowhere in sight. Of course, he wasn't stupid. They'd string him up from a tree if they got their hands on him, no questions, no trial. He was one of the most hated and feared reivers on the borders.

Ridley advanced on her, his pale blue eyes icy with fury. He'd removed his helm and sweat plastered the thinning golden brown hair to the sides of his head.

"Just where are you off to, little sister?"

Fayth blinked innocently. "I had a female concern." Her smile was strained. "It is now resolved. Come, we must be on our way." She lifted her skirts, shaking off the dead leaves and dirt clinging to the fabric, and started back toward the track.

Ridley caught her arm, turning her back to examine her. "Look at you!"

Fayth glanced down again, seeing the tear in her skirt and the missing gems. His gaze was on her hair and Fayth patted the plaits self-consciously. Her infernally wavy hair was escaping to bush about her face.

"How can I present you to Lord Carlisle like this?"

"Perhaps his eyesight fails. He's an old man after all."

"Goddamn it, Fayth, I should flog you for this!"

Fayth raised her shoulders in a resigned sigh, as if she really didn't care. But she did. Papa had never struck her. She'd taken some blows on the training field, but that was different. Since Papa died six months past, Ridley had taken to slapping her or even flogging her with a strap when she displeased him. She'd fought back at first. But he was her brother and knew all her tricks. And besides being larger and stronger, he never hit her with an audience—appearances were everything. So she'd taken to clenching her teeth and enduring his abuse. It was over quicker that way.

They passed Wesley, who stared at her with a bewildered expression. Poor Wesley, he simply couldn't fathom why she refused to accept her fate. Why she couldn't be the bootlicking lapdog he was. No, Fayth didn't even know Wesley anymore and that hurt worse than aught else.

After giving orders to the men, Wesley joined them. "You yelled for help. I heard you."

"I saw a wild animal. A boar, I think."

"A boar?" Wesley's expression brightened and he turned, hand on sword hilt. "It's been years since I've seen a boar."

"Not now, Wesley!" Ridley barked.

Resentment clouded Wesley's face, but he complied, falling into step beside Fayth, who was being dragged along roughly. Wesley was only a year older than Fayth's two and twenty years, though at times he seemed much younger. He should be his own man now, not Ridley's reluctant servant. But Papa had left him nothing and Ridley promised rich rewards.

Wesley elbowed her sharply.

Fayth frowned at him.

He shook his head meaningfully, his mouth a thin, hard line, the scar on his cheek standing out darkly.

Fayth knew this was his way of begging her to behave, but she would have none of it. "What's the matter, Wesley? You want to chase the boar? Then just do it. Why do you need Ridley's permission?"

Ridley came to an abrupt halt and looked between the two of them. He was not ignorant of Fayth's games and so he eyed her accusingly. He squeezed Fayth's arm so hard she gritted her teeth to hold back a groan.

Wesley stared incredulously at Ridley's gloved hand. "Christ, Ridley, are you trying to break her arm? Let her go!"

Ridley's hand tightened so Fayth gasped, rising on her tiptoes to somehow contain the pain. Just as Wesley's eyes narrowed and he stepped forward, Ridley released her. Fayth stumbled against Wesley, who caught her, cradling her abused arm in his hand.

They both stared at Ridley's retreating back. "Move!" he shouted, not even turning.

Wesley led Fayth forward, muttering under his breath.

"Help me, Wesley."

Wesley shook his head, avoiding her gaze. He'd left his helm with his horse and the mass of brown curls shone in the sunlight. Fayth wanted to touch him, to shake him until he was her Wesley again.

"What would Jack think of you now?"

Wesley looked at her then, his face closed in anger. "Much has changed since Papa and Jack died. You're the only one who doesn't understand that."

"I don't understand why it has to change," Fayth persisted, praying she was getting through to him. "You promised me I wouldn't end up like Caroline—you promised!"

"You knew what was at risk when you botched the Maxwell raid. Ridley advised you of the consequences. There's no one to blame but yourself." Seeing her mutinous expression, he said in a softer tone, "I just don't understand. What else is there for you? You *must* wed. Why not Carlisle? At least you'll be rid of him soon. Why must you fight us?"

Fayth shook her head sadly. "You're no different than Ridley. Don't forget how Papa shunned his methods—said he was without honor. You had honor once."

"Ridley makes things happen."

"Ridley speaks naught but falsehoods. How do you know all he promises you is truth?"

His hand that had been cradling her arm steadily tightened until he squeezed her as tightly as Ridley had.

"I know," he ground out through clenched teeth, as if trying to convince himself.

Fayth tried to yank her arm away. "Let go! You're hurting me!

Wesley released her abruptly, his face paling as he looked from her arm to his own gloved hands.

They reached the dirt where Ridley awaited them. He sent Wesley away with a look and shoved Fayth into the litter so she fell facefirst into the mound of pillows. She lay still, contemplating what she would do next. Should she tell them Red Alex was in the forest? There was a time when Wesley had wanted to avenge Jack's death as much as she did. He might still want to hunt Red Alex down. Though she'd happily dance on Red Alex's grave, it was unlikely they'd find him. Half the men on the borders were after Red Alex's hide and none had come close to snagging him. She toyed with the idea of setting Ridley on the outlaw as the cavalcade began its slow snaking journey through the forest. She sighed. Ridley probably wouldn't believe her anyway. He'd accuse her of creating yet another diversion to aid her in more escape attempts. And he'd be right.

An unusual sense of hopelessness washed over her. Her whole life since Papa's death seemed a series of near escapes. All she wanted was for life to return to normal—as it had been before Papa died. Fayth's eyes drifted shut as fatigue filled her in heavy waves. A strange lethargy settled over her and her mind became blissfully blank. No thoughts of her brother, who forced her into this union; no thoughts of Jack, the man she almost married, or his murderer, the black-hearted Red Alex; no thoughts of her sister, Caroline, whom she'd betrayed and hurt . . .

Caroline. No, even in sleep Fayth could not escape what she'd done. The memories oozed through the thick haze of her mind. *The fire again, the screaming.* Fayth gasped, forcing her eyes open. Sweat stung them. Icy fingers trailed down her spine, even as her body swelled with an inexplicable restlessness. Bile soured her throat and she pushed a curtain back, securing it open. The cool breeze couldn't sweep away the lingering feel of Jack's murderer, holding her like a lover. And he'd almost had her again, there in the wood. *I've been following ye since ye left Graham Keep.* Why? Why would he follow her? Was he bent on revenge for what she'd done? The thought that *he* might possibly want revenge—after all he'd done to ruin *her* life—made her seethe with contempt.

The body of an enormous—and gaudily arrayed—stallion suddenly blocked her field of vision. Fayth's gaze rose until she met Ridley's winter blue eyes and bearded face. His plumed helm rested on his knee.

He glittered like a jewel. A green velvet surcoat covered his heavy mail sark. A thick gem encrusted chain spanned his chest, holding the ermine lined cloak in a graceful fall off his shoulders. He'd not forgone his passion for indecently short breeches. The slashed green velvet barely covered the tops of his thighs and an obscenely large codpiece covered his groin. His horse was no less adorned, its mane and tail braided with ribbon. Feathers, tassels, and bells jingled and bobbed with every step.

The assessing gaze that raked her found her wanting. He was still furious. "Can you not at least try to do something with that hair?"

"What's the matter, Brother? Are you afraid Scratchton Carlisle of Louseland won't take me if I'm not perfectly arrayed? Surely he's used to scurvy-ridden women, being a Scot."

Ridley shook his head, sighing. "We're not so different, you and I—if only you could see it."

Fayth scowled. "And is your betrothed an old hag?"

Ridley laughed. They both knew the earl of Dornock's daughter was barely seventeen. "I care naught for her, just as you loathe the idea of Carlisle. Oh, it galls you to admit

it, but it's true. You lost your love and now you must make
do with what's left. Just as I lost mine—"

"Mona was never yours! She was Papa's and he'd beat
you to a bloodied pulp if he knew how you pawed at her!"

He looked around, annoyed, to see if anyone overheard.
"Enough."

Fayth smiled slightly. Nothing could get to him like the
mention of Mona. Everyone loved Mona. She was kind,
beautiful, wise. But Ridley loved their stepmother in a
most unseemly and incestuous manner. His fury had been
immense when she'd helped his prisoner, Sir Patrick
Maxwell, escape—and left with him.

"Godspeed her for escaping your sick lusts," Fayth said.

His face was a rigid mask. She might pay for her words
later, but he would not strike her now, not in front of everyone. Never in front of Wesley, who watched them, frowning, several horses behind. *Wesley.* Once Fayth and Wesley
had been inseparable. Fayth's betrothed, Jack, had been
Wesley's closest friend. It had seemed the three of them
were destined to be thick as thieves their whole lives.

Ridley smoothed a hand over his beard, visibly trying
to compose himself. "When we arrive at Lochnith, you
will wed Carlisle. If you stay put and be a good little wife,
I promise you, things will turn out well for you in the
end."

Fayth knew much of what he planned from listening at
closed doors. The Graham host accompanying Ridley was
enormous, swollen to several hundred men-at-arms and re-
tainers. It was necessary, as they traversed the lands of
many sworn enemies. Although Ridley had obtained safe
passage from them all, he took no chances. He also
planned a bit of a foray after the wedding. Fayth's betrothed was gifting Ridley with an estate at the southern
end of the Rhins of Galloway—Gealach, it was called.

Currently, however, Carlisle did not hold it. It had been taken by a band of outlaws several years ago and he had been unable to oust them. Ridley was determined to eradicate the outlaws, or destroy the tower trying.

It was all very tiresome to Fayth, being the instrument of men's doings and yet excluded from even discussing them. She sighed, weary of her brother and his plots.

"I want no part in your evil deeds."

"Just like Mona, eh? Well, don't think for a minute that she's free of me. You think she *escaped?*" He laughed, an ugly, unpleasant sound. "I let her go. I know precisely where she is—she and her dunderhead knight. And when I'm ready, I'll have them both back."

Fayth said nothing, her stomach shriveling up tight. How had he become so powerful? His reach so far? Mona must be warned. His words strengthened her resolve to escape. She must find Mona and warn her. Unfortunately she had no idea where her stepmother was, but a plan had been forming for weeks now. She would seek out Mona's family. They lived in a little hamlet in the English West March. If Mona wasn't with them, hiding from Ridley, then surely they would have some clue as to her whereabouts. Ridley believed she was the keeper of the legendary Clachan Fala. It was true Mona was a Musgrave and a healer, but Fayth thought it unlikely there was such a thing as the Blood Stone, so why would there be a keeper?

First, she had to escape. She slid a look at Ridley. He still stared at her with extreme displeasure. Fayth retreated inside the litter and drew the curtains, preferring no view at all to his face.

Fayth had been unable to orchestrate another escape before they arrived at Lochnith and she was imprisoned again. She prowled her chambers, her desperation grow-

ing. Guards were stationed outside the door. Since Fayth
had a proclivity for enlisting the help of servants, she'd not
been allowed any attendants. She wasn't even allowed a
lady's maid until after the marriage had been consum-
mated.

At the thought of the approaching wedding night, Fayth
recalled Mona's warnings about Carlisle. *He's a cruel
man, with evil desires. Your wifely duties will be unbearable—and will quite possibly kill you, if you don't kill
yourself first. Should you be forced to go through with this
union I will prepare poisons for you that will kill him
slowly, make it look as though he succumbed to an ailment.*

Fayth patted the pocket sewn into the underside of her
kirtle. The poison Mona had given her. It was meant for
Carlisle. Fayth didn't know if she could do it. If she
couldn't even kill Jack's murderer, how could she hope to
poison an old man?

Fayth clutched the vial through the silk of her skirts.
The very idea made her ill. She knew her brothers had
something dreadful planned for Carlisle, that this marriage
and peace were a ruse. She was sickened she'd been made
a pawn in it. Just like Caroline. Only somehow, Caroline
had found love and happiness, foiling Ridley in the end.

Fayth stared at the door, gripping the vial so hard she
was in danger of shattering it. What if Carlisle wasn't
cruel? What if Mona was mistaken? Fayth knew he had a
son, several daughters, and an assortment of bastards. Back
at home, before she'd been barred from speaking to the
servants, she'd heard talk of Carlisle and his children—of
beatings and incest. Of them running away, only to be
caught and tied to poles like animals. There was even a
rumor he'd killed one of his bastard sons for fancying lads.

Fayth surveyed the room. The gleaming walls were
paneled and hung with Turkish carpets. A huge canopied

bed dominated the room, set on a raised platform. Fayth shuddered and backed away.

She went to the door and opened it. The guards were Grahams, not Carlisles. *Damn.* The Grahams were well versed in Fayth's ways and immune to her wiles.

"Get back inside," one said.

She ignored him and tried to walk between them, but they crossed their lances, barring her way. She ducked beneath the lances. One of them planted a huge hand on the top of her head. He turned her and shoved her back into the room. The door slammed shut behind her.

"By God, you're a knave!" she shouted at the door. How dare he handle her so! Her pride stung from the indignity.

She scanned the room, her gaze falling on the narrow window deeply recessed in the wall. Fully aware of the multiple flights of stairs she'd been forced up, she threw open the shutters and stared down at the people milling about below, worrying her already ragged fingernails with thoughts of lashing sheets together and scaling the wall. Her shoulder ached with the memory of the last time she'd attempted that feat, pulling her arm right from the socket. She rubbed her shoulder, grimacing.

A sharp knock on the door startled her from her contemplation of the ground. She turned her back to the window, knowing whoever it was would not wait for permission. The door opened and Ridley entered, his insouciant gaze finding her. He was so pleased with himself these days. Fayth's mouth curled into a sneer that only grew nastier when Wesley entered behind Ridley. Wesley's gaze bounced off Fayth before wisely looking elsewhere. The angry redness was gone from the wound on his cheek, though it was ugly and twisted where Red Alex had cut him. He'd not had it tended immediately, so it had festered. When finally lanced and drained it had grown far beyond the original cut. Though it finally healed, the process had left him disfigured.

Fayth's sarcastic greeting died in her throat when a third man entered the room, leading a large, furry dog. He was a formidable man, barrel-chested and stocky—solid as a stone wall. His thick iron gray hair waved over his shoulders. He was shorter than both her brothers, though twice as wide. She found herself unable to form a sentence, frozen by the hard gray eyes that inspected her body with possessiveness. She'd been told he was three score, and though the youthful color had been leeched from his hair and eyebrows, they were as lustrous as a youth's, shining like highly polished armor. His dark craggy face was lined, but from a hard cruel life, not from the ravages of age. And the lust in his eyes . . . he looked perfectly capable of acting on it.

"Oh, aye," he said, his voice rough and abrasive, his Scots broad. "She'll do."

Deep in her belly, Fayth knew at that moment that everything she'd heard about Carlisle was truth, felt it so strongly she had to restrain herself from bolting.

The dog yipped, drawing Fayth's attention away from the soulless eyes. The dog was not a breed she was familiar with, so tall it came nearly to its master's waist and lean with muscle. With its thick black and white fur, and long narrow snout, it looked part wolf. Its eyes were clear and healthy; one a dark brown and the other a blue so pale it was almost white. Fayth realized vaguely that Ridley had been making introductions and that she'd been correct in assuming this was her future husband, Lord Ashton Carlisle.

"You fancy her?" Carlisle asked.

"The dog?" Fayth asked hesitantly.

"Aye. Do you like her?"

Fayth nodded. "She's beautiful. What breed is she? She looks somewhat like a wolf."

Carlisle contemplated the dog. She sat on her haunches and gazed up at him, whining softly. "I know not her breed, though I believe her too pudding-hearted to hiv wolf in her. I came by her . . . accidentally." On the borders, that translated to "I stole her." His smile was smooth, well oiled, exposing a rack of strong, white teeth. "I give her to ye." He released the leather leash binding the dog to his side. As soon as the tension was relieved from the leash the dog left Carlisle and came to Fayth.

Fayth held her hand out for the dog to sniff, then rubbed its ears. "What's her name?"

"I was told she was the finest sleuth dog on the borders, but thus far she's proven herself useless. So, that is what I call her—useless, worthless mongrel. If ye dinna want her, I'll probably kill her—she eats too much."

Fayth held the dog's head against her thigh. "Thank you, my lord. I like her very much."

They all stared at her with open suspicion; even Wesley's eyes narrowed in disbelief. They'd been expecting defiance, sarcasm, rudeness. She still had the capacity to surprise them, of that she was thankful.

Carlisle crossed the room, coming to stand before her. The scent of ale and peat smoke drifted from him. He wore no beard, only a thick silvery mustache. "Ye promised me a wildcat, Graham. She's meek as a mouse."

Fayth lowered her eyes submissively, though her hands kneaded the dog's fur. So he didn't like meek? It was too much to hope Carlisle would call off the betrothal and wedding because of her "meekness," but Fayth would keep it up, just in case.

Ridley didn't respond immediately, but his footsteps echoed across the wooden planks as he joined them. " 'Tis an act, nothing more." He took her face in his hand, forcing her to look at him. He smiled slightly. "She'll not be able to keep it up long, mark me."

"Unhand her," Carlisle said, frowning. "She's mine now and no one shall touch her."

Ridley dropped his hand and stepped away. "Of course."

A spark of hope ignited in Fayth. Carlisle had given her a gift, however coarse he was about it—he was a Scot, after all, and couldn't help his poor manners—and he appeared to be shielding her from Ridley. Perhaps he only treated his children poorly? Could it be that he would be a good husband?

On impulse Fayth asked, "You have children here? I'm looking forward to meeting them."

Carlisle stared at her a long moment, unblinking. "Dinna get yer hopes up—a more worthless, ungrateful, selfish group of brats ye'll niver meet. Even the bastards think o'er much of themselves."

Fayth's heart sank. He was estranged from his children. Never a good thing.

Carlisle grasped her chin as Ridley had. His fingers were harder, rougher as he turned her face this way and that. He yanked at the ties of her shift, pushing the collar wide. Fayth gasped, trying to cover herself, but the hard look he gave her made her lower her hands.

Wesley tensed, mouth thinned, hand on his sword hilt. The scar on his cheek darkened above the fine whiskers of his golden brown beard. Ridley put a hand out, calming his younger brother. Fayth gritted her teeth, keeping her eyes averted, as if she deserved no better than this. The idea of killing him was becoming more palatable every second.

"What is this?" Carlisle asked, yanking the collar off her neck, baring her to the shoulder. He gripped her neck, pushing her head awkwardly to the side to reveal the weal marking her skin.

She flushed with humiliation.

"Oh, that," Ridley said slowly. "A bit of discipline."

Carlisle turned Fayth so her back was to them, his hands pulling at her shift, shoving her stiff bodice downward. The welts, though healing, were scabbed and swollen, and the rough handling caused her some pain. But more than discomfort was mortification. That this abuse should be exposed—that he should handle her like an animal that must be inspected before purchase.

There was a long silence, then Carlisle asked, "Did she scream?"

"Not a sound. She glared at me and spat. Had she a dagger she would have cut my heart out." The sound of rustling fabric. "She gouged my arm—see?"

"Indeed?" Carlisle said in a voice thick with pleasure.

Fayth's breath caught. Her skin crawled from his touch.

The door slammed. *Wesley.* Fayth knew he couldn't bear to watch Carlisle handle her in such a fashion. So he left. There was a time when he would have thrashed a man who touched her with such familiarity. Everything had changed.

"He's suffering from the flux," Ridley said in explanation. "Let's hope he makes it to the privy."

Carlisle didn't respond.

Fayth closed her eyes, her hand curled into the dog's nape to hide the trembling. *Oh God help me.* She would throw herself from the window before she married this man. Carlisle turned her around. She kept her gaze on the floor, face hot with anger and desperation. His hands were on her face again, forcing her to look at him. He scrutinized her, as if trying to determine the truth.

"I like you, little pretty. I think we'll get on fine."

He released her and turned to leave.

Ridley followed him to the door, but paused after Carlisle passed through. He craned his neck, as if watching the other man disappear along the corridor, then turned back to Fayth, his hand on the door latch. "You're a lucky one, methinks. Blessed by fairies or some such."

"You're the only one who believes in childish stories, Brother."

He ignored the bait. For years Papa and Ridley searched for the mysterious Clachan Fala—the Blood Stone—thought to be thousands of years old and imbued with magic. It was the reason Papa had married Mona, hoping to get the Blood Stone for himself. And now Ridley was carrying on the quest with a passion that far exceeded Papa's.

"He's not quite right in the head, is he?" Ridley said, still standing in the open doorway. "Mona had said he was sick of mind, but I didn't believe her. I thought it yet another ploy to save your skin."

"At least someone tried."

He made a moue of mock sympathy. "Poor Fayth, even Mona has abandoned you. Freed the big knight and followed her loins, eh?"

Fayth ignored him, wanting him to just go away.

Seeing she wasn't going to play his game today, he sighed and said, "Oh—about the poison hidden in your kirtle, I replaced it with berry juice some time ago, in case you decided to use it on me."

He laughed at her shocked expression. By the time she ripped the vial from its pocket and hurled it at the door, he was long gone. Fayth went to the bed. The dog climbed up beside her and lay its head in her lap.

"What shall I do?" she asked the dog, stroking her fingers through the silky fur. She couldn't give up hope. There had to be a means of escape. No castle was impenetrable, from the inside or out—her father had taught her that. And once she was free, she'd find Mona. Ridley would stop at nothing to get the Blood Stone. And that's what he believed Mona to be doing—fetching the Blood Stone out of hiding to deliver to Caroline and her new husband, Robert Maxwell.

If he was truly following Mona's movements then she must be warned. And besides, Mona was all Fayth had left. Like Fayth's sister Caroline, Mona had been mother and friend to her. Fayth had lost Caroline, but she would not give Mona up. She chewed at her thumbnail, certain that if she thought hard enough, she could overcome this obstacle and find her stepmother.

2

RIDLEY LEFT HIS sister's room for the fine chambers Lord Carlisle provided for him, fists clenching and unclenching all the way. He was impatient for action and worried Fayth would ruin everything. She was more trouble than she was worth. He could hardly wait to be rid of her.

"Wine," he said, lowering himself into the chair before the fire. His servant, Gilford, was there seconds later, pressing a goblet of his finest claret into his palm. Ridley had brought his own, as most Scots wine was swill. He drank deeply. His belly calmed, filling with warmth. He sighed, wiping his hand across his lips.

Gilford hovered behind him, anxious to please. He'd been servant to Ridley's father, secure in his position. With Hugh not even a year in the grave, Gilford's position was now precarious. He was loyal and trustworthy, but he was a constant reminder of Father, a man Ridley strove to forget. Both his mother and father had been cold and unloving creatures—unfit to parent rats. Well, to him at least. It still cankered that his siblings had been so coddled and himself, ruled with an iron fist. He was nine years older than Caro-

line, his closest sibling in age, so he'd never felt any true
kinship to anyone. Father had claimed he was hard on Ridley because he was heir. But Ridley knew it had been more
than that. In Hugh Graham's eyes Ridley lacked most of
the essential qualities he valued in men: honor, integrity,
and loyalty. But Hugh had never looked hard enough.

What did it matter. Ridley had stopped caring long ago.
It only troubled him now because it was his father's fault
that his siblings were so damn contentious. Ridley sighed,
needing release.

"Find me a woman," he ordered Gilford. "And be certain she is not a toothless trull this time."

"Yes, my lord," Gilford murmured and left the room.

He needed to forget. More than his nasty sister, he was
haunted by the memory of his stepmother. He'd tried, with
little success, to put Mona's betrayal from his mind and his
heart. And sometimes he was successful. It was difficult to
be unhappy when all his carefully laid plans were beginning to bear fruit. Even with such incredibly willful sisters,
he was still achieving his dreams.

But dreams could be an empty thing, when you faced
them alone. He stared at the flames, his jaw set, rigid. He'd
loved his stepmother. He'd given her everything, his heart,
his body, his fortune, laid at her feet. And it was not enough.
It had been the same with his father—never enough.

And Fayth constantly rubbed salt in the wounds. Refused to let them heal—always throwing in his face how
Mona abhorred him, would rather throw herself from the
highest precipice than endure his touch. At least he would
soon be rid of Fayth. His sister could vex him, but she
could not divert destiny anymore than Mona could.

There was a scratch on the door. Ridley bid them enter,
unhooking his doublet. He turned, expecting a woman and
finding instead, his brother.

Ridley stood, disgusted. "What is it, Wesley?"

Wesley's jaw was rigid with tension. He was a slight
man, but not one to underestimate. From experience Ridley had learned the smaller they were—the meaner. And
every bone in Wesley's body was cantankerous. He had
once worshipped Ridley, tagged after him like a puppy.
But, of course, like everything else, that had changed. He'd
become greedy. But he could still be bent to Ridley's will.
Wesley had fought him on marrying Caroline to Lord
Annan, but in the end, he'd been obedient.

Wesley seemed to be framing his words in his mind,
trying to find the right phrase.

Ridley raised his eyebrows in expectant impatience.

As usual, finding nothing adequate in his common little
brain, Wesley blurted out, "Carlisle—I cannot abide him. It
makes me ill to think of him with Fayth."

"Then do not think on it." Ridley held his goblet out for
a refill.

Wesley stared at the vessel belligerently, then looked
about the room. Seeing no servants, he snatched the goblet
away. "I cannot help it." He strode to the table and poured
the claret.

Ridley sighed and accepted the goblet thrust into his
hand. "Must we go over this again? Fayth is to wed
Carlisle—there is nothing else for it."

"You're wrong. We follow Red Alex's lead and take
Gealach. I'd like to see Carlisle oppose us!"

Ridley's irritation won over. He set the goblet aside and
advanced on his brother, pushing him hard so he stumbled
backward. "Do you hear yourself? Alexander Maxwell
holds Gealach by no more than his sword arm. Were
Carlisle dead, he still has no claim to the land. Until he
owns it outright he will never stop fighting to hang onto his
pathetic little tower. He has less than three score men; he

does not stand a chance against me. When I take something, it will be mine beyond doubt. Do you understand? I will not wage constant battle just to survive. I am more than a simple thief and reiver."

Wesley jerked his head away, hating the truth.

"Now. The tower is yours, as I've said. And you have the pleasure of wresting it from the outlaw. But I need this marriage for more than the tower—you know that well. Should there be a war, I will be first in line to claim the spoils of my many kinsmen."

Wesley turned back, another defiant question in his eyes. "What of Lord Annan? He will be furious when I kill his brother. Will that not ruin all your other plans?"

Ridley smiled. "The deed, you fool. I'm merely taking what is mine. What can Lord Annan say? Alexander Maxwell holds Gealach by will alone. The land belongs to Carlisle and will soon pass to me. No one—not even his brother—can fault me for taking what's mine." He pointed a finger at Wesley before turning away. "Even Lord Annan understands that."

Wesley was silent. Ridley took up his wine again, impatient for the woman. He was about to send his brother away when Wesley said, so softly Ridley almost didn't hear him, "But . . . is it worth it?"

Ridley hurled the goblet at Wesley. It caught him in the temple and drenched him in crimson. Wesley's teeth were bared, his lips peeled back, but he made no move forward.

"Is it worth it?" Ridley came at Wesley, grabbed handfuls of his doublet and shook him. "Father left you nothing. He provided dowries for your sisters—but you, he left *nothing*." That wasn't entirely true, but with the help of Ridley's expert forgers, that's what Ridley's version of Hugh Graham's will read.

Wesley's hands came up, gripping Ridley's wrists

tightly. His control was tenuous, Ridley could see that. It was becoming tiresome, keeping Wesley in line. Each encounter became more impassioned, more violent. Soon Wesley would not be swayed, might even strike back. And so, soon, Ridley would rid himself of his brother. An accident. But for now, he was still useful.

"*I* am giving you land and power. Why do you doubt me?"

"I'm not doubting you." Wesley jerked away, rubbing his hands over his forehead. "I simply don't understand why we must give our sisters to monsters. There must be another way."

"Do you truly believe Carlisle is a monster?"

Wesley opened his mouth to answer, but Ridley held up a silencing hand. "I recall you returning from Annancreag less than two months ago, ranting incessantly about what a monster Lord Annan was."

Wesley's mouth snapped shut.

Ridley smiled. "You see? And when you tried to rescue her, what happened?"

Wesley looked away, his skin flushing. Ridley knew the incident still infuriated Wesley, that he hadn't forgiven Caroline for what to him was the ultimate betrayal—falling in love with the enemy, Lord Annan.

"She didn't want to be rescued. She'd fallen in love with her monster and his monstrous ways." Ridley shook his head. "Really, Wesley, give it up. It's beginning to reek of something incestuous."

Wesley's jaw jutted out until it popped, his eyes narrowed dangerously. "I've killed men for less than what you accuse me of."

Ridley blinked innocently. "You think *I* say these things?" He shook his head. "Nay, nay, Brother. 'Tis what the men whisper. You love your sisters *too* dearly. I'm only warning you. A leader who inspires disgust is no leader at all."

Wesley looked away, his head bobbing in a sharp nod.

"Good," Ridley said as the door opened and a female servant was led in. "Tomorrow, you will ride on Gealach."

"Yes, my lord." Wesley's gaze was on the woman, his expression inscrutable. She stared at her feet.

Ridley approached the woman and circled her. She was a pretty thing—in need of a bath, but young and ripe.

Wesley watched them.

Ridley gestured to the woman. "When I'm finished, shall I send her to you?"

Wesley averted his eyes, shaking his head. "No. Good night." He left the room, pointedly looking away from the woman.

Ridley stared at the closed door for several seconds after his brother was gone. How very odd. He'd never seen Wesley with a woman—or even talk about bedding one. Perhaps this would be useful, once he understood what Wesley wanted. Perhaps he wanted a wife? Or his own woman. Or mayhap he didn't like women at all, but boys. Ridley rubbed his beard thoughtfully. Yes, this could be very useful.

He turned back to the lass. She wore a starched cap, but he noted black locks escaping to curl at her nape. Ridley snatched the cap off her head. Waves of ebony cascaded down her back.

Ridley darted a look at Gilford, who smiled and nodded hopefully. The fool! He thought he was being clever. Ridley gripped her chin, forcing her to look at him. Her eyes were blue. The tension drained away. Not black, but blue. And she looked nothing like Mona, whose hair shone almost blue it was so black. This woman's was like a piece of coal. Her skin was rough and chapped. Not creamy and silky. She smiled hesitantly and the stained teeth repulsed Ridley.

"Bloody Christ. Take her away."

The girl's face fell and Gilford shoved her roughly from the room, speaking harsh words to her. Ridley went to the fire, rubbing his hands over his face. It was always this way. He wanted a woman, wanted release. And yet he could find none. There was only Mona.

His hands curled into fists as he thought of her, her head fallen back as that bone-headed knight rutted on her; small, pearly teeth, gleaming between soft lips. She'd chosen the filthy Scots prisoner over him. And he would kill her for it. But first, she would get him the Blood Stone and then she would pay for her perfidy.

But bloody hell! It enraged him that the knight had her. No one but Ridley should possess her—ever. They would both die. The entire Maxwell clan would die for her lusts.

"Forgive, my lord. Should I find another lass? One more pleasing?"

Ridley turned slowly, his eyes narrowing on the servant who had tried to bring him a Mona imposter. "Why do you keep bringing me these hags?"

"My lord . . . I found her pleasing—"

"You brought me your slut?"

"No-no! My lord, I only meant I thought her pretty as do many others—"

"I am no common rustic, you fool! I cannot rut on a dumb beast simply because it is female!"

The man cowered now, his face bloodless. Ridley was tempted to beat him, but there was dinner with Carlisle later and he needed this man to ready his garments.

"Prepare my doublet for dinner—go! Get out of my sight."

When the man was gone, Ridley turned back to the fire, his heart an empty void.

Fayth was relieved when the meal she was forced to share with her future husband, her despised brother, and several others, was finally over. Not that anyone had paid much attention to her. Oh, Carlisle had groped at her beneath the table and Ridley had stomped on her foot a number of occasions, but mostly the men had been engrossed in discussions about the impending war and Red Alex. Fayth was heartily sick of both subjects. If there was to be a war, then she wished the men would just go fight it and stop blathering about it so much. It was especially repellent to hear Ridley's silver tongue wax on about how he would ensure Lord Carlisle's lands were spared any English incursions. And Carlisle, gloating like a swollen toad, believed him. Fayth promised herself that if she were actually forced to marry him, she would endeavor to convince him of Ridley's perfidy.

But she wasn't ready to concede defeat just yet. She'd made another escape attempt while being escorted to Carlisle's chambers, but it had failed. She'd almost made it to the great hall when she tripped over a cat and was hauled back to dinner.

Fayth sat on the bed, mulling over the meal. The dog, which she'd named Biddy, climbed onto the bed and lay her big head on Fayth's lap. Fayth stroked the silken fur absently. She'd been tempted several times to tell Ridley and Carlisle of Red Alex and what he'd said to her in the woods. Why she hadn't was a mystery that currently nagged at her. Red Alex was the worst sort of scoundrel and she would do well to rid herself of him. But who would believe her? Besides, he was the outlaw that held her bride price—Gealach, and therefore an obstacle to Ridley. And Fayth would do nothing to aid her brother. If anything she would work to construct as many obstacles as possible to thwart him.

Her mind turned back to the encounter in the woods. Following her, indeed. He obviously wanted to revenge himself on her for what occurred back at Annancreag. Her skin flushed at the memory. It was his own fault. Had he been doing his duty, rather than imbibing and looking for a whore, it never would have happened.

With great effort Fayth forced her mind to other matters, such as escaping before she was forced to say vows. She chewed her thumbnail, reviewing what she'd been able to discover about the castle's floor plan.

She was staring blankly at the far wall when the enormous carpet that covered the paneling bulged outward. Fayth leaped off the bed, Biddy right behind her. The dog's hackles rose and a low growl rumbled in her chest. Fayth scanned the room for a weapon, but before she found anything, the bulge moved. There was a clicking sound, as of a lock engaging, then a girl emerged from the side of the carpet.

She looked about until her gaze rested on Fayth and Biddy—who had stopped growling and now sat calmly on her haunches beside Fayth.

"There's a door there. It leads to my father's bedchamber." The girl smiled, a wide and worldly grin. "No doubt he'll be using it to visit ye tonight."

Fayth's belly gripped. *Not if I can help it.* "You're Carlisle's daughter?"

The girl nodded, coming closer. She wore a simple bodice and petticoat, but the fabric was an expensive violet damask, imported or stolen.

Fayth smiled slightly. "Come to get a look at your new stepmother?" She would do everything in her limited power to make certain she was never the mother of Carlisle's children, but she couldn't say that. Besides, she remembered when Papa brought Mona to them. They'd been wary and curious, but Mona had been so very kind to them all they couldn't help but love her. Fayth's heart ached sharply. The backs of her eyes burned. She swallowed hard and forced a tight smile.

"I'm Diana," the girl said, coming to stand before Fayth. Carlisle's daughter was taller and several years younger. Her black hair hung loose down her back, her blue eyes framed with equally thick sooty lashes.

Fayth inclined her head. "I'm Fayth Graham."

"I know." The blue eyes studied her. "You'll not last long. He'll break you in a fortnight."

Chilled, Fayth asked warily, "Break me?"

"Oh, aye, it's why yer here, after all." Her expression instantly changed to meek submissiveness, nearly cowering. "Just say, 'Aye, my lord, whatever pleases you, my lord,' and he'll tire of you quickly." Diana smiled again, the facade gone.

Fayth didn't know what to say. It seemed Carlisle's daughter confirmed her worst fears.

Diana's lips curled. "You'll learn soon enough how to become invisible. And if ye dinna, he'll get rid of ye, like he did my brother."

The coldness seeped deeper into Fayth's bones. "How many brothers and sisters do you have?" Why was she asking? She shouldn't care. She would be gone from this place tonight—no matter what.

"Nine."

Fayth nearly swooned.

"But only five of us live with Father." Diana reached out to pat Biddy and the dog cowered, ears laid back. Diana shrugged, her hand dropping back to her side. "Two of my sisters and one of my brothers are married."

Fayth forced a smile. "That makes three."

"Aye. The other my father sent away to the Church, to be a monk . . ." Her eyes narrowed with pure hate and a thin smile of satisfaction curved her lips. "But he's an outlaw now."

Fayth raised her brows. "An outlaw?"

Diana raised her chin a notch, her smile widening. "Aye. He rides with Red Alex."

Fayth rolled her eyes and turned away. "Splendid."

"Father was wrong about Laine—and he's proved it now. He does for Red Alex what he refused to do for Father. And it's eating at Father."

Diana followed her to the window. Fayth was hoping to avoid any further conversation about the notorious red reiver. She'd had more than her fill of the man. But it was obvious Diana took great pride in her brother riding with Maxwell spawn and would not abandon the subject so quickly.

"My father hates Red Alex. But he hates my brother more."

Fayth shook her head, confused. "Is that what you want? Your father to hate you?"

Diana shrugged one shoulder with forced nonchalance. "I care not."

"Well, I suppose I might be a bit angry, too, had such a villain corrupted my son."

"He's not a villain."

Fayth turned to the girl. "You don't know that. He seems like a hero to you because he got your father in a lather, but he's naught but a common outlaw."

Diana's cheeks flushed, but she held Fayth's stare. "He saved my brother from hell."

"I see. Your brother apparently was not a good monk. You think riding with an outlaw will get him into heaven?"

"You dinna ken him. *I* do."

"Ah. So that's the way it is. Will it be a virgin birth or do you plan to tell Lord Carlisle who the father is?" Though she wouldn't be the first girl to claim such a thing, it was doubtful Ashton Carlisle would believe it. But telling him Red Alex was the father might be more dangerous than lying.

Diana gasped, then laughed. "I'm not pregnant! And if I were, my father would never let me marry Red Alex!" She laughed again, twirling about the room so her skirts belled out. She stopped, hands on hips. "I dinna want to marry him anyway. I just wanted . . . well, I was curious . . ."

Fayth had to smile—it sounded like something she might have done. "You laid with him just to defy your father?"

Diana's knowing smile faded. "Will you tell Father?"

"Do you want me to?"

The girl chewed her lip thoughtfully. Fayth could see she didn't quite know what she wanted. She obviously loathed her father and wanted to hurt him, but this was not the way to go about it. She might find herself in dire circumstances, indeed, if he ever discovered the affair—a consequence the girl had obviously belatedly realized.

Fayth went to her, trying to smile gently, as Mona always did. "You don't want me to tell your father. Who knows what he'll do? He might even make you marry Red Alex." That elicited a strange shudder from Fayth—disgust, surely. "Let me tell you about Red Alex. I *do* know him."

Diana frowned.

Fayth nodded sagely. "Yes. He murdered my betrothed."

"Really?" Diana was not at all appalled. It was the way of things on the border, so Fayth strove to strengthen her statement.

"My father said I could wed how I chose or not wed at all. And so I chose Jack Graham. He had no titles or lands . . . but he was what I wanted."

Diana smiled sadly. "My father would never say that. He believes marriages are for alliances."

"No wonder he and Ridley get on so well."

"Why did Alex kill Jack?"

"Red Alex was holding him for ransom. My brother, Wesley, had collected the money but before he could deliver payment Red Alex wrote that Jack was dead."

Diana's eyes lit up. "Alex gave *me* a letter." She dug in her bodice, her tongue poking between her lips.

"I see you keep it close to your heart." Had the girl heard a word she said? Her lover was a murderer!

"Oh, I canna read it, nor can I ask our priest to. He would just tell my father." After groping inside her chemise for an interminable amount of time while Fayth watched with raised brows, Diana produced the missive. "Will you read it to me?"

Fayth looked from the wrinkled and soiled parchment to Diana and back. "Ah . . . I really don't—"

"Och, ye canna read either." Diana sighed.

Fayth didn't correct her misconception, though she was sore tempted to satisfy her curiosity. Diana stuffed the parchment back into her bodice dejectedly. What was it? Was he telling Diana to meet him for a tryst? Or some ridiculous poetry?

"Oh, very well! I can read it."

Diana fetched the letter back out. Fayth took it gingerly, unfolding it with her fingertips. She scanned the strong black scrawl, frowning. It was not written in English or Latin.

"What does it say?" Diana asked, anxiously gripping her skirts.

"When did he give this to you?"

"He gave it to me several months ago. He said if anything happened to him, I was to see that the abbot at Dunfermline got it."

"Is that where your brother was, when Red Alex rescued him?"

Diana shook her head emphatically. "Oh no—Alex would never send anything *there*. The abbot of Dunfermline is a good monk—not evil."

Fayth blinked. "What did these monks do to your brother?"

Diana swallowed, clearly troubled by the thoughts. "I'm not supposed to speak of it . . . and I dinna really know, anyway."

Fayth suspected the girl was not being entirely truthful. She waited patiently, but apparently the subject was closed. Fayth shrugged, folding it and handing it to Diana. "I can't read it. I think it's French."

Fayth was wondering why Red Alex would be writing to an abbot when Diana said, "So you don't really know him. He just killed your betrothed."

Fayth cleared her throat. "Well . . . actually, I do know him. My sister is married to Red Alex's brother, Lord Annan. I was . . . visiting my sister at Annancreag and one night your lover, completely sotted, I might add, accosted me. Tried to molest me like a common whore."

Fayth felt a pang of guilt. So that wasn't the complete truth. Still, he *had* consumed a prodigious amount of whisky. And he *had* molested her . . . sort of. It didn't matter. Diana was a young innocent and must be warned away from such devilment.

Rather than becoming appalled, as Fayth had hoped, Diana seemed amazed. "And ye didna like it?"

Fayth let out an exasperated sigh and Diana giggled.

"He said my name meant the moon—that I was his moon."

"Well, Diana is a moon goddess," Fayth said. How odd that Red Alex knew that. Most borderers, those of gentle and common birth alike, could barely sign their own names, let alone read a book. But, of course, that single

piece of knowledge meant nothing. He probably learned it
from some priest before slaying him and stealing his
rosary. The letter, however, was something of a mystery.
He probably didn't even write it. It was likely lifted from
one of his hapless victims. So then, why worry about delivering it to the abbot?

Diana's voice cut through her thoughts. "He never
comes around anymore. Not since I refused to marry
him."

"You didn't really want to marry a murdering, lecherous
outlaw, did you?"

Diana shook her head. "Of course not! I would never
marry so low. But still . . . He's so very handsome and he
makes me laugh. Did Jack make you laugh? Is that why
you wanted to marry a commoner?"

Fayth was suddenly eager for the girl to leave. She did
not want to discuss Red Alex or Jack Graham anymore. She
didn't even want to think about them. She had other, more
pressing matters to contemplate. The door behind the carpet could mean freedom if she could get rid of her visitor.

"Well, yes. He was often amusing. But that's not why I
wanted him."

"Ye keep saying *wanted*. Why did ye want him? Did ye
love him?"

Her questions annoyed Fayth, so she busied herself
pouring water in the basin to wash her face, pretending she
hadn't heard. Then she made a big show of yawning.

Diana took the hint and stood. She wandered to the
door, rather than the hidden panel, and Fayth turned to
frown at her.

"Aren't you going out the way you came?"

Diana shook her head. "Not now. Father will be occupied in his bedchamber. He'll be vexed if I interrupt."

Fayth's shoulders slumped. *Damn.*

Diana turned a speculative eye on her. "You're not thinking of running, are ye?"

Fayth blinked. "Of course not!"

Diana scowled. "Well, ye should."

Fayth stepped forward eagerly. "Will you help me?"

Diana blinked in horrified amazement. "Lord, no! He'd beat me dead. I'm just saying ye should try. It would vex him so if you succeeded." Smiling at that thought, Diana left.

Fayth paced the room, stopping when she spotted the glass vial she'd thrown at Ridley earlier. She picked it up and squeezed it angrily, her eyes on the carpet-covered door. If not for Ridley, she could administer enough poison to incapacitate Carlisle and then escape.

Fayth pushed a heavy trunk in front of the hidden door, though she doubted that would keep him out if he were determined. The sky was already darkening, though full night was still some time away. Fayth scoured her room, hunting for a weapon to use against her betrothed when he arrived. There was nothing. She emptied the juice from the vial and broke off the top, so she had a sharp edge. She could ram it into his eye or throat.

Fayth sat on the bed, waiting, alternately chewing her fingernails and stroking Biddy. The anxiety was making her ill, but the dog helped soothe her. She fell asleep and the dream returned. Red Alex pawing at her. Except now she was Diana and she wanted it. She pressed herself against him like a wanton, putting her tongue in his mouth.

She was ripped awake by screaming. The candles had gutted and she was damp with sweat, her chest heaving as she labored for air. The screaming grew louder and more voices joined in. Men shouted. The thunder of pounding hooves was deafening. Metal clashed violently. The acrid scent of smoke made her nose twitch.

Lochnith was under attack.

3

FAYTH ROSE FROM the bed and looked out the window. The bailey was alight with torches. More of Carlisle's men poured into the bailey, engaging the raiders. Fayth spotted Grahams among them, though they fought with considerably less enthusiasm than the Carlisles who were defending their home.

Her blood surged. It was a perfect night for a raid. She ran to the door and swung it open. The guards were still there.

"What's happening?" she asked.

"We're being raided."

"I can see that. Are you just going to stand there? Or help?"

"I have orders, Mistress Graham."

She slammed the door and returned to the window, peering down at the fighting below. Even with the numerous torches and the outbuildings ablaze, she couldn't make out the raiders. Probably broken men. More people rushed out bearing buckets of water and wet blankets to fight the fire.

Carlisle and Graham men dominated the fight and the raiders were retreating. Fayth saw her betrothed, wearing a leather jack and wielding a huge sword. He lost his targe when his opponent's sword hammered it to splinters, but still he fought on like a man half his age. She turned away from the window, slightly queasy. He would be randy tonight. Men always were after battle.

Her gaze went to the rug where the door to his room was hidden. If he was out there, then he wasn't . . . She ran, pushing the trunk away and throwing the rug aside. She pushed on the paneling until it popped open. The narrow stairwell was unlit. Fayth felt along the wall until she reached the bottom, the dog snuffling at her heels. She was faced with a wall. She ran her hands over the surface before her until she encountered a latch. The wall sprang open.

She found herself in a bedchamber, even more elaborate than her own. The bed was enormous and hung with heavy brocaded curtains. A bust of Ashton Carlisle stood beside the bed. There was a small room, just off the bedchamber, where Carlisle's attendants slept. Fayth rummaged through their meager belongings until she found an extra set of clothing. She shed her gown and shift and slipped into the hose, fumbling to tie only the most strategically placed points. When she was fully dressed, her hair tucked into a cap and pulled low over her eyes, she slipped out of Carlisle's chambers.

Carlisle's device was sewn prominently on the shoulder of the tunic she wore, so she wasn't worried about being mistaken for a raider. She was, however, worried she would come across one of the raiders who would slay her with no questions. The keep was fairly deserted and those not fighting were too busy hiding the valuables to take much note of her. In the kitchen, a man filled a sack with food. Fayth's heart stopped when he turned around but then she saw the device on his arm, matching hers. Her relief was short-lived. He came after her—to shut her up with his fists no doubt—and she sprinted into the bailey.

She was just outside the stables when the man grabbed her and shook her. "Ye tell no one what ye've seen."

Fayth shook her head vigorously—she didn't care that he was pilfering his master's larder. But she was afraid he would realize she was a woman. A figure loomed behind him. Fayth's mouth dropped open, but before she could say a word, the man struck her attacker in the back of the head with a sword butt. He crumpled to the ground.

Fayth shrunk against the wall. Her rescuer's broad, heavy shoulders were encased in chain mail, covered with a leather jack. A small, light crossbow—a latch—and a bundle of quarrels hung from his belt. He carried an enormous two-handed sword—that he wielded with one hand. His metal helm had no nose guard, so his face was visible. It was a face she'd never forget, one that had been branded in her memory by his hands and his mouth.

Alexander Maxwell—better known on the borders as Red Alex.

Not again! she wanted to cry. She'd escaped him once today, she prayed luck was still with her. She shrunk farther into the shadows, hoping he couldn't see her face.

"Carlisle's bride," he said, his dark eyes freezing with purpose. "Where is she?"

He thought she was a servant. She pointed to the castle and started to edge away. His scowl was fierce as he came after her.

"I know she's in there—*where?*" He grabbed the front of her tunic, dragging her out of the shadows. "Take me to her."

She fought him, kicking, scratching, punching. But he was a rock. Her cap fell off in the struggle. His breath hissed between his teeth. "Well, if it isn't the wee whore herself." He leaned over, pulling her onto her toes by the front of her tunic. His face was inches from hers. "In yet another disguise." His eyes were dark, dark blue. She had noticed that before, but then they'd been hazy with drink and desire. They froze her now, made her bowels watery. This man would kill a woman without a single ounce of remorse. Her gaze went to the ugly wound on his temple.

Fayth knew the price for that bit of work would be heavy. She was rarely at a loss for words or a plan of action, but she found herself scared to immobility, her mind frozen with fear.

He sensed it, his eyes roving over her face. His wicked smile was smug. "You're not getting away this time, little one." He picked her up under his arm, as if she were no more than a sack of grain, and carried her into the stable.

She squirmed and bucked silently. She didn't scream. Carlisle might come to her rescue. She didn't know whom she feared more, Carlisle or Red Alex. She'd left her broken vial in her gown and had nothing but her wits to save her.

A thick candle rested on a wooden table, illuminating the interior and casting an orange glow over his chain mail and the blade of the sword as he sheathed it. He pushed her against a wall and ripped off the band sewn around the sleeve of her shirt, removing Carlisle's device. Biddy appeared with Fayth's cap in her mouth. Red Alex took it from the dog.

"Good lass," he said, scratching the dog between the ears. Biddy's tail swished vigorously through the dirt.

Fayth scowled at her newfound friend turned traitor. Biddy watched the proceedings with her long pink tongue lolling out the side of her mouth.

Red Alex put the hat firmly onto Fayth's head, pulling it low over her face and stuffing her hair under it.

He stepped back, keeping a hand on her, but looking her over. "I cannot believe ye almost fooled me again—you look nothing like a lad." He met her gaze and shook his head. "You're a stupid, stupid girl, out here, alone, dressed like a boy."

"What do you want with me?" She was almost afraid to hear his answer, but he wasn't inclined to talk. He merely stared down at her, hands hard on her shoulders.

Fayth returned his look boldly, refusing to show fear, her mind speeding forward. She'd been working on how to get out of the gates unnoticed and he just solved that problem. If she left with him, as a raider, she'd get out safely. But what then? At least Carlisle didn't plan to kill her—not right away, at least. And who knew what Red Alex had planned before he murdered her? Torture? Rape?

Once outside the walls of Lochnith she would be free. All she must do was escape Red Alex and run. He'd never catch her on foot, encumbered with his armor and weapons. And Red Alex was but one man. Here at Lochnith she had scores of Carlisle's and Ridley's men-at-arms to worry about. The odds of her living and seeing Mona again were far better if she let Red Alex kidnap her.

"Are ye going to scream?" he asked.

She shook her head.

He gave her a suspicious look, as if attempting to gauge her honesty, then took her wrist, dragging her from the stable. He moved swiftly along the wall until he neared the gatehouse. Fayth saw that the raiders were gone. Only Red Alex remained. Her heart sank. He'd never get out alone—he didn't even have a horse. Carlisle's men were gathering near the keep entrance, Carlisle at their center. Fayth spotted Ridley, just stepping outside, his armor unscathed, having missed the entire battle.

Red Alex whistled, a low and musical sound. A horse appeared from the shadows, reins trailing the ground. Red Alex mounted, with Fayth under his arm, and flung her across his lap. She tried to sit up, but he was loading a quarrel into his latch on her back.

"I can't ride like this—what are you doing?"

"Shut your mouth and keep your head down." His helm dropped onto her head. She quickly secured the strap under her chin. His thighs tightened as he spurred the horse forward. Fayth closed her eyes and held on. Men began to shout. Fayth heard arrows whoosh by, pounding feet pursuing. Someone grabbed her leg, trying to drag her off. Fayth clawed at Red Alex's thigh, clinging to stay on. She heard the click of Alex's latch releasing the quarrel, followed by a scream of agony. Her leg was released. And then there was the hollow clop of boards beneath the horse's hooves. Moments later, the horse was in a flat run, Red Alex's hand firmly on her back, arrows filling the air around them.

Fayth thought she might vomit. Her stomach and chest and thighs were battered from the ride. When the arrows stopped, he didn't slow the horse, though he slid his arm around her waist, lifting her so she could swing her leg over the horse's withers.

They sped through the darkness, his arm a solid band around her waist, pressing her hard against his chest. If he was going to kill her, she reasoned, she'd be dead by now. So it was punishment he had in mind. She refused to even consider how he planned to extract vengeance from her hide and focused instead on the advantages this gave her. Escape was possible.

After a time, he slowed the horse to a walk. Where were his men? Why had he no plunder—except her? Then she remembered the question he'd asked when he thought she was a servant. *Where is Carlisle's bride?* And earlier today, in the forest, *I've been following ye.* Her heart dipped down to her toes, urgency and desperation filling her anew. She had to get away from him.

Full dark had fallen. The moon rose high above them, huge in the cloudless sky. They rode for an hour before he finally stopped. Fayth had been cataloging all the ways she could escape from him and none of them seemed likely. After the last time, he would be too diligent, too suspicious. He dismounted, dragging her down with him, never releasing her. They were at a burn. The horse's hooves crunched on the stony bank as it went to drink.

Fayth unhooked the strap under her chin and dragged the helm from her head. Her cap fell off with it. She kept hold of the helm—it was a good weapon.

As she glowered up at him, memories of their first encounter flooded her mind. She'd deceived her sister and pretended to be a whore so she could let in Wesley and his band of broken men. Unfortunately, Red Alex had been utterly taken in by her ruse and had been all too willing for a tumble. He must hate her—not only for tricking him and wounding him, but for making him the weak link that let in a swarm of raiders. Raiders who murdered his people and stole his sister-in-law.

Fayth seemed to shrink even smaller under the heat of his stare. She was significantly shorter than Red Alex, who was a giant of a man. The top of her head barely reached his shoulder. Her eyes were currently trained on his leather-clad chest. His hands dropped away from her shoulders. He began to remove his gloves. Fayth let her eyes trail upward, over wide shoulders and a neck thick with muscle. His chin was dark with whiskers, his mouth a hard, unforgiving line. His hair appeared brown in the moonlight, but she knew it was roan dark and threaded with blond and copper. His gloves off, he held them both in one hand, and folded his arms over his chest.

Fayth met his eyes finally, a fist squeezing her heart. His gaze was steady and thoughtful.

She swallowed hard. "Well . . . what now?"

"I believe, the last time we met, we were transacting some business."

She blinked up at him. "What . . . ?" *Transacting business?* She'd been pretending to be a whore . . . Her eyes widened and she took a step back. "You can't mean . . ."

His mouth curved wickedly.

"You know I didn't mean it . . . it was a ploy, nothing more."

He followed her, the smile softening the hard line of his mouth. "Ah, little one—that was your first mistake. You don't play games with me. You started it and I mean to finish it."

4

ALEX HAD SPENT much time imagining this moment, playing it over and over again in his mind. Now that the time had come and the vixen stood defiantly before him, he found he could do none of the things he'd imagined. Oh, he wanted to strangle her—and ravish her. But damn it all if she didn't look like an innocent, incapable of the acts she'd committed. And she was as bonny as he'd remembered. More so perhaps, as his memory did her no justice. He felt foolish for having believed her fiction. No whore was ever so finely kept.

His men awaited him in the wood, he knew. His cousin Eliot probably stirred them up for another raid—anything to take command. And Skelley, the voice of reason, was rarely heard when Alex was absent. But Alex could not go on, not until he had it out with her. Though she looked a sweet maid, he knew she wasn't. She was a temptress and a witch. She'd bewitched him that night, insinuated herself into his thoughts, his dreams. He would not let her get away with it.

He took another step toward her, intimidating her. She took a step back. She was afraid, but a brave little thing.

She didn't run, or cower. She held his gaze and he could see the wheels turning in her head, calculating. She was wily, this one. She'd escaped him once today and he'd discovered she ran swift as a deer. He would keep her within arm's length at all times.

"You'll have to rape me then," she said. "I'd rather die than allow a beast like you to rut on me."

"A beast," he mused. How apt. He felt like a beast of late—single-minded, obsessed. He could not banish her from his mind. He knew of only one way. To have her and be done with it. He caught the front of her tunic before she could back any farther away. In a flash of silver, he saw his helm arc upward, toward his head. He pulled back and it grazed his cheek, opening the skin.

She tried to swing it again, but had lost the advantage. He caught it and yanked it from her grasp, tossing it into the darkness. She clawed at his hand, kicked at his booted ankles, but was strangely silent. No screaming. No calling for help this time. Only the harsh sound of her breath, panting with fear and exertion.

He caught her chin, turning her face up. "Why don't you scream?"

Her warm breath puffed over his hand and the desire coiled deep in his belly. He had to get her out of his blood.

"Out here you don't know who will come to your rescue."

He smiled at her logic. "Carlisle might come for you."

Her gaze darted upward, tangling with his. *Oh, she didn't want that.*

His smile grew. "It seems you're in a difficult situation."

She pulled her chin from his hand. "What do you want? To rape me? Kill me? Torture me? Turn me over to your brother for imprisonment?"

"Hmm . . . They all sound good. You choose."

She stopped struggling and looked up at him. Her throat

worked as she swallowed. Even dressed as a boy he wanted her. Her tongue darted out, small and pink, wetting her lips. "If I . . . give you what you want, will you let me go?"

Alex's breath stilled. He could see the moon in her dark eyes. Her hair curled wildly around her shoulders, the soft breeze disturbing it, sending a ringlet fluttering across her parted lips. He saw his hand reach up and push it away. His fingers shook. She didn't flinch.

"Will you?" she asked, her voice soft as the air.

She was playing games with him again. But then so was he. He could never have her—not the way he wanted. He knew this and yet still, he hesitated. His cheek stung. He touched the wound and looked at his fingers. Blood smeared them.

"What do I want?" He still held the front of her tunic, crumpled in his fist. It looked so harsh, his enormous hand, grabbing at her.

She took a step closer, placed her small hand on the leather that covered his belly. "You want me . . . willing."

His knuckles touched her chest and though there was coarse homespun between his skin and hers, his imagination was a living thing. It was another trick. But what could she do? No jug of whisky was present for her to smash over his head. If she possessed a weapon hidden on her person she'd have used it by now. Perhaps she planned to take one of his weapons, or scratch his eyes out. None of these things would be easy for her, small as she was.

And, of course, he could not let her go. So much depended on her value to others that he had no choice but to use her. To pretend he would release her simply to satisfy his base lust was disgusting. And yet his body was perfectly willing to be disgusting and more.

He unbuckled his sword belt, tossing the weapons in the grass several feet away. He had a dagger strapped to his thigh and another in his boot. He discarded them both. Bear, his horse, had finished drinking and wandered over to nose at his weapons.

She had stepped away while he did this, her eyes sweeping the landscape.

"Hoping for rescue?"

Her gaze inspected him from head to foot, an eyebrow raised in derision. "I'm wondering how long this will take and thinking you won't delay me overmuch."

He laughed softly at her insult. Could she truly be so worldly or was it an act? He suspected a great deal about Fayth Graham was a facade. "You're a slow learner, lassie. I tend to take insults as challenges to prove myself."

She blanched slightly, the sarcasm draining from her expression. "Will you let me go?"

He slid his arm around her waist, pulling her against his body. He closed his eyes, inhaling the scent of her hair. Her smell had haunted him. That and the taste of her mouth. She rested her hands on his arms. He ran one hand up her back, to her neck. She was so small, so fragile. She trembled, but she turned her face up, her eyes large pools of darkness.

"Will you let me go?"

"Mayhap. If I find you pleasing." Another lie. He tried not to be repulsed by what he was doing. After all, she was an expert deceiver. Why should he feel a shred of guilt for playing her game?

Her eyelids fluttered shut. Her lashes fanned against her cheeks. Her skin was not the pure white that most women coveted, but lightly tanned. Pale freckles clustered across the bridge of her nose. She was no whore, though he'd called her that and worse in the past month. He hesitated between desire and conscience. She was not truly willing. She was bartering her body for her life.

His father wouldn't have hesitated. He'd have nailed her

to the ground by now, screaming for mercy. He'd see her brutally punished for all she'd done and hope she lived through it so he could ransom her.

Alex swore and she opened her eyes. He couldn't do it. After all his planning, he couldn't harm her. One look at the uncertain fear in her soft eyes and his fury petered away.

He *would* steal another kiss. He told himself it was the least he could do to chastise her. Her mouth was parted to speak, but he kissed her. She struggled, her hands fisting against his chest and pushing. Her mouth was soft beneath his, sweet. Her breath sighed into him, filling him . . . and then she went limp in his arms. He examined her slack features, annoyed at himself. He'd frightened her into a faint.

This was not his finest moment. He'd never even paid for women before and here he was, forcing himself on this wee thing and scaring her into insensibility. He looked around, trying to decide what to do. His experience with women was minimal—nonexistent when it came to swoons and suchlike. He lowered her to the ground and untied the water skin from Bear's saddle. Perhaps a drink would revive her. He knelt at the burn, filling the water skin.

He heard nothing until the quarrel landed in the water with a plop, barely missing his head. He rolled aside, splashing through the water and reaching for weapons that weren't there. His first thought was that Carlisle had found them, until he saw Fayth Graham, astride Bear, latch leveled at his heart.

He straightened, water dripping from his hair and chin.

"You raping murderer," she said, her lovely face twisted with hate and disgust. "I should kill you for ruining my life."

The bitch had tricked him again, this time with a false faint. He ground his teeth, furious with himself for becoming giddy-headed over this woman, and came after her. She had already reloaded the latch. At such close range, the quarrel would punch through his jack and mail, perhaps even through his body.

She lowered the latch, aiming the quarrel at his crotch. "Or mayhap I'll put an end to your lechery . . . Forever."

"Do that and you'll not find me so merciful."

"Merciful!" She spat on the ground, her mouth curved unpleasantly. "I wonder if Jack found you merciful." With one last glare of hatred, she dug her heels into Bear's sides, yanking the reins to turn the horse. Bear bounded forward.

Alex whistled.

Bear turned and came back, despite Fayth's kicking and sawing on the reins, and her promises to personally geld the horse if it didn't obey. She was enraged, her eyes burning, her mouth a thin line.

"You're not a very good horse thief, lassie."

"Let him go!"

He advanced on her, reaching for Bear's bridle. "I'm not finished with you just yet. You can try to ride away, but Bear's well trained. He obeys me over anyone else."

The latch came up again, the steel bolt head a few feet from his nose. "You won't be able to whistle at all if I shoot you in the face."

Alex held up his hands, as if surrendering. "Then do it. You think me a raping murderer. Punish me."

Her finger trembled on the trigger, her mouth a thin white line. Bear had stopped a few feet from him, waiting for his next instructions.

"Let him go or I will shoot your eye out!"

"Which is it? Heart? Mouth? Eye? Or . . . ?" He waved a suggestive hand at his crotch. "Let me prepare for the forthcoming blow." He cocked a brow at her angry stare. "It is forthcoming, is it not?"

She tapped Bear's sides and the horse came forward, toward Alex. He tensed, wondering what she would do. He didn't believe she would shoot him. Oh, she was a vicious and clever little thing, but not bloodthirsty, of that he was certain.

She kept the latch trained on him. "You killed my betrothed—and now you try to ravish me. You don't deserve to live."

"Carlisle is alive and well. I've not harmed him."

Her lip curled. "You don't even remember, do you? Not Carlisle. Jack Graham. My betrothed. You murdered him."

Alex went still. In his thirty years he'd killed many men but never murdered one. He'd killed Grahams—and likely she was right about this Jack. But he'd never killed a man who wasn't trying to kill him. But that truth would mean naught to a woman who'd lost her love. Perhaps she *was* capable of murder. He must tread more carefully.

"No great loss to you, little one. You've a far bigger fish in your net with Carlisle."

"I don't want Carlisle! I wanted Jack!"

They stared at each other for a long time. The wind puffed behind her, sending her hair in a shimmering dance about her shoulders.

"Well? Are you going to shoot me?"

Her face was tight with indecision, her finger flexing on the trigger. Finally she dug her heels into Bear's sides and started to ride away.

Alex whistled again. Bear stopped and turned around.

"Goddamn you!" She let the quarrel fly.

Alex tried to dodge it, but the bolt punched through his jack and mail, tearing into his shoulder. The impact sent him reeling backward. He yelled, grabbing the shaft and trying to yank it out. Too deep.

She had loaded another quarrel and aimed it at his face. "Whistle again and I'll ruin that pretty face."

This time, when she urged Bear forward, Alex let her go, no longer doubting she would follow through with her promise.

Alex rode back to the forest on a stolen horse, his shoulder throbbing with every jolt. Skelley waited for him at the edge of the clearing, shifting from foot to foot. Alex dismounted as the older man took the horse's reins.

"Where were you?" Skelley asked, handing the horse over to another man. "And where is Bear? I canna believe ye've lost that horse again."

"He'll be back." Alex moved to the fire and began peeling off his blood-soaked jack. He had tried repeatedly to pull out the quarrel, but it was too deep and his armor only hampered his efforts. He'd only been able to break off the shaft; the head was still embedded in his flesh.

Skelley helped him out of the jack, shaking his head and muttering about fools getting their due. Skelley was an English Musgrave, but had wed an Annan Maxwell a lifetime ago and had been closer than blood ever since.

Eliot appeared, one empty sleeve tucked into the belt of his tunic. He stroked his black beard, inspecting Alex's wound critically. "Can't take it off if it becomes putrid." He shook his head as if that were a damn shame. He'd be well pleased if Alex also sported one arm. "And no little lady. So what now?"

Alex didn't feel like having this conversation. He'd been fond of Eliot once. They were cousins and had fostered together. Red Rowan, Alex's father, had loved Eliot like a son. Alex wished he understood what had soured his friend. Perhaps it was the loss of his arm—though it had been removed when he was a lad and he hadn't seemed the worse for it for more than a decade. It was later that Eliot changed, became angry and sly.

Alex ignored his baiting question and shed his mail and shirt.

Skelley poked about the swollen skin. "We'll need some hot water and a probe—Laine, fetch the leech."

Laine's head popped up from where he'd been hovering uncertainly behind a cluster of bushes. With a brisk nod the lad darted across the clearing, his silvered hair glinting in the firelight. At the age of fifteen the boy's hair was liberally streaked with gray. As a favor to Laine's sister, Alex had rescued the lad from a monastery where he'd been a most reluctant novice. Afterward, the boy had refused to return home. Not that his father wanted him. Laine was bastard born and had shamed his father by leaving the abbey. Ashton Carlisle cared nothing about the atrocities the boy had endured at the hands of a depraved priest.

Laine vanished from Alex's view, disappearing behind the flames. Alex stared into them, unseeing.

"Well?" Eliot asked. "I thought the plan was to kidnap the lass. What happened? Did you kill her?"

"No."

Skelley inspected Alex's bloodied shirt, tongue probing at his missing teeth. "Go away, Eliot."

"Did ye rape her?" Eliot persisted, waggling his eyebrows.

"No."

Skelley ripped the shirt into strips, separating them into clean and soiled piles. "Did you even see her?"

Alex's grin contained no humor. "Aye, she shot me with my own latch."

"Did she, now?" Skelley said, not looking up from his task.

Eliot, hooting with laughter, strolled away to share the news.

"Aye." Alex looked at his hands, curled into fists. "I had

her in my hands for the second time today . . . and she tricked me again."

"Have ye learned yer lesson? Have ye had enough of her? There are some women who are simply better left alone and this poison lass is one of them!"

Alex ignored the older man's harping. Skelley was as skittish as a woman sometimes. Skelley was another of Red Rowan's men who had chosen to follow Alex rather than the oldest son and heir, Robert. It wasn't that they didn't respect Rob, but he was peace loving. He refrained from fighting unless necessary. If it became necessary, Rob was as fierce as any of the Maxwell boys.

Alex held a different view. If their enemies felt the need to redress every slight, real or imagined, why should he be any different? There was little sense sitting about writing letters and trying to arbitrate peace when the adversary kept stealing your kine. And those that saw Red Rowan in Alex had joined him, along with many others he'd picked up along the way, like Laine and Davie. In all, he had nearly two score men.

Alex peered at the older man bellowing at Laine to hurry it up.

"Skelley, do you recall Jack Graham?"

Skelley frowned, scratching his beard and twisting his mouth awkwardly as he tongued the gap in his teeth. "Och, the lad we held for ransom nearly a year past? Eliot got to him, aye?"

"Ah . . ." Alex remembered him now. "She was going to marry him."

Understanding dawned in Skelley's eyes. "Well now. No wonder she hates ye."

Davie the leech, as the men had taken to calling him, arrived, probe gleaming in the firelight. The enormous man knelt beside Alex, his intense gray eyes inspecting the wound. He met Alex's gaze again and nodded shortly, indicating he could get the bolt head out.

Alex grit his teeth and looked away as Davie began silently digging in his shoulder. Davie had been with them only a short time, but he hadn't spoken a word. He didn't hear either, though he understood others if he looked at them when they spoke. He had a good sword arm, was deadly with a longbow, and knew much of healing.

Alex fixed his gaze on Skelley as Davie worked, talking to keep his mind off the pain. "Who was Jack Graham that her father would let her wed him?"

"He was Hugh's man," Skelley said. "Wesley had been willing to ransom him. He must've been worth something."

Alex gasped as Davie slowly pulled the quarrel tip from his shoulder. Skelley was there with water and whisky. Alex drank deeply, the fiery liquid burning his throat and belly, but easing the pain.

"If he were a Graham of any significance I would know of him."

"You canna ken everyone's business," Skelley said, dousing Alex's shoulder in wine.

Skelley was the peacemaker. He'd stopped Alex more than once from making grave mistakes when his temper got the upper hand. Alex watched the older man as he wrapped his shoulder tightly in the remnants of his shirt. Davie cleaned the quarrel tip for reuse. These men had been good to him, loyal and true. He couldn't let their home be taken from them. Gealach belonged to them all.

"I know Graham business," Alex insisted.

Alex didn't know why it troubled him so, but it did. Fayth Graham was the kind of woman Alex could never have. Her father and brother would wed her for alliances and power, never to an outlaw lacking lands and titles. Women such as Fayth were destined for lairds and heirs, not second or third sons. Alex would never have looked at Fayth, let alone touched her unless she were a whore. He'd been a fool for believing her ruse, but he'd wanted her from the moment he saw her and had let himself be deluded.

"Lucky for you she's no a verra good aim."

Alex looked up at Skelley, his brow furrowed. "I think she's likely an excellent shot. She didn't want to kill me . . . I goaded her into shooting me."

Skelley said nothing for a long time, inspecting Alex consideringly. "Twice she held your life and spared it. And her a Graham."

Alex felt that strange tightness in his chest again. It had come and gone ever since he'd met up with her in the forest. He'd felt it when he saw her, seemingly running for her life, in an exquisite gown that encased her small form like a suit of armor; and again at Lochnith, dressed as a lad, trying to escape fate; when she was between his thighs on Bear, pressed against his back; when he'd looked down on her, the moonlight on her face. When he'd let her ride away.

Alex shook his head, seeing her hair in the flames. "Why would the daughter of Lord Hugh Graham promise herself to common Jack Graham?" He looked up at Skelley. "She doesn't want to wed Carlisle, either. A fine match, that. Land, titles. And she likely brings him a substantial tocher. He's an old man; she'd be a rich widow soon enough." He expelled a breath. "And yet she'd prefer life with *Jack Graham*."

"Perhaps she loved him." Skelley wagged his eyebrows. "Or perhaps it was something more . . . mayhap he compromised her?"

"Perhaps . . . if so, my opinion of her slips for he was worthless and a lecher."

Skelley chuckled. "Och, lad. Love lends a fog to obscure the truth of one's character. She likely saw only the good in him and ignored aught unpleasant."

Alex shook his head. "I still cannot see it."

He tried to shrug off the strange mood that had descended on him. Nothing had been the same for him since Fayth Graham bashed him in the head with a jug of whisky. It was as if she knocked something loose and, now, he was filled with discontent.

"So she's out there—alone?" Skelley said, stroking the thick pelt of his beard.

Alex snorted. "Dinna fash on her. I worry for the hapless men who cross her path . . . besides, she's dressed herself as a lad and has my weapons."

Skelley regarded Alex oddly. "So is it over? Since she's escaped, there's no marriage, no business transaction. Carlisle still holds the deed to Gealach."

Gealach. Carlisle. Ridley. Alex hoped, that for now, the tower was safe. Ashton Carlisle's estates were scattered about the West March. Lochnith was his largest and finest, but he also held the tower of Gealach on the southern end of the Rhins of Galloway, a location considered remote and uninhabitable by many. Gealach had been a small tower in complete disrepair. The fields untended, the inhabitants gone to corruption, finding it easier to raid their neighbors than work for sustenance.

Alex had seen Gealach some four years ago and been much taken with it. As the third son of Rowen Maxwell, the ninth Lord Annan, he had gained no lands or titles upon his father's death. After amassing a goodly bit of coin and beasts from his personal endeavors, he'd offered to purchase Gealach from Lord Carlisle, but the laird had refused. Alex had then offered for his daughter, Diana's, hand, a bonny lass with a waspish tongue, on the condition that Gealach came as her dowry. Carlisle had laughed in his face. And so Alex took the tower by force and had thus far held it safe from harm—and Carlisle.

He'd put the inhabitants to industry and began repairing the tower. Three years he'd worked to restore the tower and lands. Damned if he would lose it now. With Fayth Graham's marriage to Lord Carlisle, the laird was gifting Ridley Graham with the estate of Gealach. And Lord Graham had come to Scotland in force to take it.

Though Lord Carlisle had been rich in land, he'd not been rich in men and so his few forays to recapture the tower had been failures. Lord Graham was a different matter. There was no clan on the West March—with the exception of perhaps the Armstrongs, when they quit their squabbling amongst themselves and came together as one—that could raise more men in a saddle, armed to the teeth, than the Grahams. It was a force Alex could not contend with. And so he'd been forced to find his advantage in other ways, such as taking Carlisle's lovely bride-to-be and holding her until he agreed to sell Alex the land.

But now neither of them had Fayth and Alex didn't know what was to become of his home. He rubbed his bandaged shoulder. "Aye. For now I think Gealach is safe. But I dinna trust Ridley Graham. This isn't over. He didn't drag a hundred men into Scotland to turn around and leave because his sister decides she doesn't want to wed. But for now we wait. I've a lost brother to fetch and stolen kine to unload. On Tuesday, take Laine and Eliot to Liddesdale and get rid of Carlisle's kine. That should give my shoulder time to mend."

Skelley left him with his thoughts. Alex found himself watching Davie meticulously clean his instruments. He would have liked to question the man about his unusual methods of healing, but Davie couldn't answer. Neither could he read or write; Alex had tried to communicate with him that way, to no avail.

Alex waved at the gleaming instruments laid out on the piece of cloth, capturing the mute's attention. "Your sister taught you this?"

Davie nodded, rolling the cloth up and tying it securely. He walked away before Alex could ask another question.

Alex's thoughts whirled with the throbbing of his shoulder. She'd shot him. But she hadn't killed him. She'd been ready to marry a commoner, was prepared to fend for herself in a harsh world that spared no sympathy for a woman's plight. And there was Alex's brother, Patrick, missing for weeks. Perhaps with Fayth loose on the borders, Ridley would be occupied enough to leave Gealach alone. At least long enough for Alex to head north and find his brother. Alex's hand was drawn to the bead hanging from his neck, secured by a leather string. His only clue to Patrick's whereabouts.

Skelley returned, bearing a wooden cup that he proffered to Alex. "Something from the leech."

Alex took the cup. He wrinkled his nose at the pungent smell, but drank it down. Skelley nodded with satisfaction and took the cup, turning to leave.

"Skelley," Alex called at his retreating back.

Skelley looked back.

"Be careful in Liddesdale."

"I always am."

"Nay—I mean it. If the Great Harry wants a war, we'll give it to him. But until that day, I need you here."

Skelley's eyes crinkled as he smiled beneath the fur of his beard. "Ye ken me. Besides, I'll have Eliot."

Alex looked skyward. "That's what I'm afraid of."

5

AFTER HIDING IN a deserted hut sitting forlorn on the seething bog of Solway Moss for several hours, Fayth finally felt it was safe to venture forth. Surely Red Alex had gone to have his wound tended or simply dropped dead. Either way, he wouldn't trouble her again for a day or two—enough time for her to cross back into England. She had to travel east through Scotland, to avoid Ridley's border lands, then head south when she hit Liddesdale to the White Lyne. There she would find herself in Musgrave lands.

Though she had never done this alone, she had no fear. No lone traveler was safe on the borders, but she was considerably less conspicuous disguised as a boy than if she traveled openly as a woman. And besides, she'd spent half her life masquerading as a boy. There was a sense of comfort and security in it, reminding her that perhaps some things didn't have to change.

She stopped for the night at a cottage. The couple was kind enough to share some gruel and hard bread with her and let her sleep in a corner. They told her they were tenants of the earl of Dornock and that his castle was due east—the direction Fayth was traveling. The earl of Dornock's daughter, Lady Anne Irvine, was betrothed to Ridley. A plan began to form, so that by the time Fayth started out again in the morning, she'd decided to stop off at the earl's castle for a brief rest before continuing on to Liddesdale.

Fayth forded the Annan and made the slow treacherous trek through the desolate moors until she came upon the earl of Dornock's lands. It was easier than Fayth had expected to get into the earl's stronghold. His castle was loosely guarded and when she asked the porter why, she was informed it was Tuesday, as if that were explanation enough. And so it was. Fayth had lost track of time, but now recalled that every Tuesday was Liddesdale market day. Fayth was pleased to hear this news, as she would have to pass through Liddesdale anyway. The bustle of the market would ensure little notice was taken of her, even with such a conspicuous mount as Bear.

The horse was a good one, but as she led him to the castle stables she noted the curious looks the horse garnered. He was too fine a steed for a lad in rags to be in possession of. He was a magnet for thieves and anyone who'd ever seen Red Alex on him would remember. The only sensible thing to do was sell him at the market and buy a lesser mount that would not draw unwanted attention. She had no wish to court more disaster. Besides, if she ever did meet up with the blackguard again, all he had to do was whistle and the horse would come running. The whoreson likely would, too, even though the last time she'd put an arrow through him.

The vision caused her to close her eyes, forcing it away— which was most troublesome. Why should she care if she maimed or killed him? He was her enemy—the sworn enemy of her family for as long as she could remember. Maxwells and Grahams had been slaughtering each other in one of the bloodiest feuds on the border for hundreds of years. The hate went so far back most couldn't recall how it had begun. But Mona knew. *The Blood Stone,* she'd said, *greed and lust for the Clachan Fala began it. Pride and retribution gives it power to continue.* The border officials rarely intervened, as they were more likely to find themselves in the crossfire than do any good. Even the Scots and English kings, both known for violently punishing those who displeased them, chose to ignore the ancient squabbling.

At the stable, Fayth dug through Red Alex's small leather pouch until she produced a penny. He had various implements tied to his saddle: a rug, a small sack of oats, a flat metal pan for cooking the oats into bread, and a leather pouch containing coins. Fayth had already inspected them thoroughly. She gave the stable boy the penny for watching Bear and headed back into the bailey.

A few discreet questions earned her Lady Anne's whereabouts: walking in the gardens. Fayth followed the wall, staring gape-mouthed up at the enormous castle. Ridley's ambition struck her afresh. He was so very clever, much cleverer than any of them had understood. And he was rapidly gaining power and prestige. Lady Anne was a Scot and the earl's youngest daughter, but still, she was the daughter of an *earl.* That Ridley had aimed so high and hit the mark was a frightening prospect.

She came to a gate that blocked her way. The river entrance. Boats rowed by, into the arched opening leading to the bowels of the keep. Fayth turned back and entered the keep. She managed to locate the kitchens and there found a scullery maid willing to give her directions to the gardens. On her way out she snatched a crust of bread. She slipped into an alcove and quickly devoured it, her stomach cramping with want for more.

When finally Fayth entered the sunny atrium at the cen-

ter of the castle she paused. The flowers were in bloom
around her, their colorful heads bobbing in the breeze. An
interesting array, considering it was nearly autumn. There
were orchids and irises, but also harebell and thistle, its
spiny bulbs and purple flowers oddly charming clustered
about the edges of shrubs and trees.

Several women in lacy gowns walked about the paths,
ribbons in their hair, and hanging from the arms of fine
men. Though not the daughter of an earl, Fayth was nevertheless a gentlewoman, raised on fine clothes and horses,
scented baths and maids to plait her hair. She could read
and write and play the lute.

And most of her life she'd eschewed it, choosing
breeches and daggers to gowns and sewing. But she realized now that she'd always wanted it to be there for her,
that she somehow wanted both worlds. That was impossible now.

Fayth looked down at herself. She looked like a common ragged boy. It seemed the best she could hope for was
to be pawed at by a landless outlaw. Her cheeks burned as
they did every time she thought of Red Alex. He hadn't
hurt her and she'd shot him. She *must not* think of it!

"Wool gathering?" a soft voice asked. "Care to share
your thoughts?"

Fayth whirled, searching the thick bushes beside her. A
girl straightened from where she crouched among the foliage. She wore a green velvet gown, once fine, but now
well worn and frayed at the edges. She peeled off her
leather gloves, caked with dirt, and ran the back of her
hand across her forehead. Her thick dark hair was piled
atop her head, mahogany curls escaping to twine against
her damp cheeks.

"I'm looking for Lady Anne," Fayth said.

The girl straightened, smiling strangely. "Well, you've

found her. In a most undignified state. My father would be appalled. I can only personally tend my garden when he is gone."

"My lady," Fayth said, pulling on her cap and bowing like an awkward lad. "I have come with important information about your betrothed."

Lady Anne became very still, gloves dangling from her pale hands.

Fayth rubbed her own roughened fingers together self-consciously. When dressed as a boy she always felt comfortable among men. Females, however, made her nervous. They were more perceptive and Fayth felt they saw through her disguise on some level.

Lady Anne scanned the garden quickly before inclining her head for Fayth to follow. She disappeared into the bushes. Fayth hurried after her. Lady Anne led her through winding trails until they came to a tiny clearing, paved with slabs of flat gray slate. A stone bench sat in the center. Faint light filtered through the branches, but it was otherwise secluded.

"A favored rendezvous for lovers," Lady Anne said, smiling. She sat on the bench, patting the empty space beside her. "Is it a love letter from Lord Graham?"

Fayth hesitated. The girl's eyes glowed with anticipation. Fayth hadn't expected this. She'd assumed Lady Anne would be as horrified as both Caroline and Fayth had been when they were forced into marriage. Lady Anne appeared . . . excited.

Fayth sat beside her, smiling gently. "How old are you, my lady?"

"Seventeen . . . well, almost. I will be in a fortnight." She grasped Fayth's hand. "Tell me, did he send you to look upon me? And come back with a report? Will he find me beautiful, think you?"

This was not going as Fayth had planned. "He will find you very beautiful . . ."

The girl clasped her hands to her breast, her face aglow. "But that is not why I'm here. I'm afraid my news will not be welcome."

Lady Anne's hands slid to her lap and she blinked at Fayth. "You're not a boy."

Fayth laughed self-consciously, touching the hair she felt escaping from her cap. "No . . . I'm not. I cannot tell you who I am. But you must know about Lord Ridley Graham. It's imperative that you have all the information before you decide to wed him."

"Are you his lover? Do you carry his child?" Lady Anne's face flushed, but she held her chin up, proud daughter of an earl that she was.

Fayth shook her head, becoming exasperated. "No, no! Please my lady, no more questions. I must give you this information and then be on my way."

Lady Anne nodded reluctantly, some of the redness fading from her skin.

Fayth took a deep breath, unsure how to begin. She wasn't certain she knew all of what Ridley planned. It had become difficult to eavesdrop near the end and Wesley was distressingly tight-lipped. But at least she could tell Lady Anne what she knew.

"Lord Graham has been securing strategic marriages for himself and his sisters—"

"Strategic?" Lady Anne raised a skeptical eyebrow. "My father has praised his effort to end the blood feuds."

Fayth found a stick and knelt. "Look, here is the firth." She drew a horizontal V to signify the Solway Firth. "And here is the land surrounding it." She drew rough circles. "These are various estates. Lord Graham's Eden estates, his debatable land estates, his coastal estates. Now look, here are Ashton Carlisle's lands. Lord Graham tried to marry m— I mean, he tried to marry his youngest sister to Carlisle. See this?" Fayth drew a footlike peninsula off the far southwest of the Scottish side of the firth. She circled an area at the southern tip of the peninsula. "This is Gealach; it will go to Lord Graham immediately when the marriage takes place. Now look here. This is Annancreag, the estate of Robert Maxwell, Lord Annan. Ridley married his oldest sister to him. Here, and here, he has purchased land from the Carruthers and Bells—whom, incidentally, he raided to near ruin. I happen to know the Douglases won't budge. They're too strong for him to chance any major raids and they refuse to sell their land. But still, Gealach gives Ridley a good position on the coast." Fayth looked up from her map, meeting Lady Anne's shocked expression. "Now, what is left?"

The color had drained from Lady Anne's face as she stared at the crude drawing. Fayth's stick pointed to the area along the Sark, one of the earl of Dornock's estates.

"Do you see? He is amassing this land, in preparation for an English invasion."

Lady Anne shook her head in disbelief. "He will not receive this estate when we wed—"

Fayth grabbed a handful of the girl's skirt. "No. He'll receive this estate." She pointed to a spot north.

Lady Anne's eyes widened. "How do you know these things? Twice you called him Ridley. Who are you?"

"It doesn't matter," Fayth said, annoyed at herself for lapsing into using Ridley's first name. She tried to bring Lady Anne back to the point. "Lord Graham doesn't want to marry you for that estate. He wants you for the alliance. The English king is planning an invasion and Ridley means to make sure it happens. Are you aware that King Henry claimed ancient English suzerainty over Scotland some thirty years ago?"

Lady Anne shook her head.

"Well, he did and he is using that as an excuse to invade Scotland. When the English win and annex Scotland Lord Graham will be the first in line, as kin, to be awarded these lands."

Lady Anne stood, prying Fayth's hand off her skirts. "This . . . what you claim is preposterous! Leave you— Now! Before I call the guards!"

Fayth stood, staring sadly at the young girl. "I'm sorry, my lady. I only meant to help—"

"Leave off!" she cried, hands over her ears, eyes squeezed shut.

Fayth needed no more prompting and sprinted out of the garden. She made it to the stable, fear and anxiety twisting her gut into knots. But it seemed Lady Anne alerted no one. Fayth was allowed to leave Dornock unmolested.

When Fayth was a good distance from the castle, she stopped, looking back. It irritated her she'd wasted time trying to rescue the silly girl from Ridley. The girl didn't want to be rescued. Fayth sighed and spurred Bear forward, toward Liddesdale. She wouldn't be making any more charitable stops after that fiasco. Let them learn the hard way. Fayth only wanted to find Mona.

What if Mona was on some mysterious quest, as Ridley claimed? As unlikely as it seemed, she *had* released Sir Patrick from the dungeons and escaped with him. If Fayth traveled all the way to Musgrave lands, only to find out Mona had never even gone there, she might never find her stepmother. But if Mona were chasing after the Blood Stone, then it was possible someone in Liddesdale had seen her. People came from all over the west and middle marches for market day. It was a nest of reivers so corrupt and violent the area warranted its own personal keeper, apart from the west and middle march wardens, to handle the lawlessness: the Keeper of Liddesdale. Fayth had heard he did little to curb the criminal activities and, in fact, partook in them more often than not. And though Mona and Sir Patrick would likely be lying low, trying not to draw too much attention to themselves, there was an excellent chance someone there had seen them anyway—perhaps even spoken with them.

The very idea that she might be close to finding Mona made Fayth impatient and she urged Bear to a gallop. Tired and hungry, Fayth rode into the village with a handful of other travelers. Stalls extended past the village's main street, fanning out with merchants displaying their wares. Fayth dismounted, leading Bear past a woman shoving candles in her face and a man waving a bolt of canvas.

Fayth patted Red Alex's coins. Had there been more, she would have bought the soap now being held enticingly out to her by a little boy. There was only enough for food and perhaps a bed in someone's stable. Once she traded the horse for a pony, the difference might purchase her a few luxuries.

A group of men stood near a fence housing a dozen goats. They eyed Bear appraisingly and her, suspiciously. Reivers. Likely wondering how such a young lad came by a horse like Bear and calculating how easy it would be to snatch him. She'd best guard her mount well else she'd be on foot.

The villagers went about their business, trying, with little success, to steer clear of the outlaws that swarmed the village. They came to sell their plunder and spend the proceeds on a hot meal, some gaming, and a bit of pleasure. And because of them there was never a shortage of gossip. Even now, as Fayth passed stall after stall, Lord Wharton's name was on everyone's lips. Rumor had it the warden of the English West March was urging the English clans to raid the Scots, and promising to turn a blind eye to their warden's protests. Borderers needed no encouragement to plunder each other's lands. An open invitation, free of reprisal, was a thing of dreams. But he was also offering money to certain treacherous Scots clans to raid their neighbors.

With so much information being bandied about, Fayth was optimistic about discovering intelligence on Mona and Sir Patrick. The thought put a spring into her step. Fayth longed to hear her stepmother's soothing voice, feel her comforting touch. She alone loved Fayth with no reservation, never asking her to change, never reproaching or disapproving. Mona had never been ashamed of Fayth.

Warmed by thoughts of a reunion with her stepmother, Fayth stopped at a stall where a man sold cheese that he claimed came from the King of France's own larder.

"Royal cheese," he cried, seeing he'd caught Fayth's eye.

She joined him at the stall. "How much?"

Bear poked over her shoulder, snuffling the man's goods, then snorting with something strangely close to derision.

"Royal cheese doesna come cheap."

Fayth inspected the half dozen rounds of cheese critically. "How did you manage to lift the French king's cheese?"

"Think you the king guards it himself?" The man scowled. "Go away, unless you're buying something."

"How much cheese will this get me?" She held two pence in her palm.

The man cut her off a large hunk.

Fayth dusted the filth off it and asked, "Where might I go to trade a horse?" The covetous stares directed at Bear made her anxious to sell him quickly.

"The Dragon's Lair." He pointed to an alehouse down the street. The sign over the door was painted with a green dragon breathing fire.

He grabbed her sleeve, pulling her close, and lowering his voice. "For two shillings, I've a bone from Saint Francis's thumb—will keep you safe." He opened his hand, revealing a gleaming finger joint.

Fayth shook her head, disgusted, and crossed the street. She considered what to do with Bear while she was in the alehouse. There was probably a stable nearby for boarding beasts but she didn't have enough coin to spare for such luxuries, yet she couldn't just leave him outside, unguarded.

Bear nudged the back of her head, picking at her hat with his lips as if urging her to get on with business. Fayth put her hand on the horse's nose and approached the alehouse. A young girl stood outside the Dragon's Lair. Her mother sold bread, her arms full of a basket overflowing with rolls and loaves and sticky buns. Fayth's stomach growled and she took a bite of her cheese.

Fayth offered the girl a penny.

She took it, gazing up at her benefactor.

"Watch my horse and I've another for you."

The lass looked up at her mother, who nodded. She took Bear's reins with a smile and led the stallion into the narrow wynd between the alehouse and the adjoining building. Fayth stared at the open doorway of the Dragon's Lair. She could see nothing inside, only shifting, smoky darkness. She'd never done such things alone, always with Papa, Wesley, or Jack. But she was not afraid. The disguise was like a shield, lending her courage and strength.

It took a moment for her eyes to adjust to the interior. The stench was horrific, a mixture of sour ale, sweat, roasting meat, and garbage. The establishment was packed. Men sat at tables, shoulder to shoulder, and more men stood behind them. Fat candles burned in the center of each table and torches lined the walls, but did little to dispel the windowless gloom. Fayth edged her way through the crush of bodies. She was forced to press up against a woman in a soiled red gown. It looked to have once been fine silk, but was now worn and ragged. The woman turned. Her bodice was so low her nipples showed. The woman saw her staring and winked, trailing a long finger-nail down her cheek. Unnaturally orange hair flowed down the whore's back. Her cheeks and lips were smeared with crimson paint.

"Oooh, not e'en a beard . . . want a tumble, laddie? Half price, for ye."

Fayth pulled her head away, her cheeks burning. "Uh . . . no. I'm looking for a horse trader. I was told there was one in here."

The woman pointed to a table near the back where three men sat. "That's Armless Eliot. He sometimes trades horses, or kine . . . or other things."

She started to turn away, but Fayth caught her arm. "I'm looking for someone else. A woman—with black hair and eyes."

The woman stepped back, giving Fayth some room, and placed her hands on her hips. "Oh, we have dark ones—"

"Not a whore. A gentlewoman . . . she was accompa-nied by a knight. A big blond man. A Scot."

The whore's interest waned and she shrugged. "I see dark ladies and blond Scots everyday."

Fayth thanked the woman and made her way to the trio. She picked out Armless Eliot immediately. He wasn't com-pletely armless. Only one arm was missing, the sleeve of his tunic tucked neatly into his belt. The other hand was wrapped around a wooden mug. He had a thick black beard that hung down to his chest, but was well groomed. His long black hair was tied back into a sleek lovelock. A set of black eyes roamed over the crowd until finally settling on Fayth. He didn't smile when she stopped beside his table. His companions, noticing his preoccupation, twisted around to look up at her.

One was an older man with kindly brown eyes and a graying brown beard. He didn't smile, either, though the thick brows were raised in question. The third occupant of the table was a lad—and yet his hair was gray as an old man's. The glossy black was still visible, but it was so streaked with gray that his fair, unbearded and unlined face was a shock to see beneath it. On closer inspection, fine black down coated his upper lip. His gaze was clear and blue, and somehow reminded her of an angel. He, of the three, smiled, displaying fine white teeth.

"Good day," the boy said.

Fayth cleared her throat and lowered her voice to sound male. "I was told you purchase horseflesh."

"Aye," the boy said, nodding. "Sometimes we do."

"I have a horse for sale."

"What kind of horse?" the kind-eyed man asked.

"I'm uncertain of the breed. It's a stallion and huge. Well trained."

The men exchanged glances. Armless Eliot's black gaze rested on her. "Is he stolen?"

Fayth tightened her lips. "Of course not. Are you calling me a thief?"

"A fair question," the kind man said, "in a nest of thieves such as this, aye?"

The gray-haired boy stood. "Where is he? I'll have a look."

"Just outside, in the wynd between the buildings." Fayth started to follow, but Armless Eliot propped his leg on a nearby bench, blocking her way. She stared down at the thickly muscled thigh, at the boy's retreating back, then into the black eyes.

"Have a seat, lad. Laine knows his business."

Fayth took Laine's empty seat. She didn't particularly want to join them for either ale or conversation.

"What's your name?" Armless Eliot asked.

"Hugh," Fayth answered. She always went by her father's name when disguised as a lad. And it always sent a pleasant surge of pride through her.

"I'm Skelley," the kind-eyed man said. "And this is Eliot. We're only passing through. It's not likely we'll buy your horse, though Eliot is always looking for a good mount, him being crippled."

Fayth glanced at the empty sleeve and back to the black eyes, which on closer inspection proved to be very dark brown. Though he had only one arm, she didn't believe he was particularly challenged. He appeared perfectly capable of inflicting considerable harm.

"I think you might like this horse." Fayth scratched at herself, leaning back on the bench. "As I said, he's extremely well trained. My . . . father left him to me and now I find myself short of funds and must sell him. But he's not very old, maybe four years."

"Did your father train him?" Skelley asked.

Fayth nodded.

Eliot leaned toward her, an amused light in his eye, as if this were a game to pass the time. "Who was your father?"

Fayth hesitated. Though these men were Scots, she had yet to determine their surname. But Eliot's question gave her an idea of how to introduce the subject of Mona and Sir Patrick. "Is. He's not dead. Sir Patrick Maxwell. He ran away with a black-haired witch, Mona Musgrave. I'm trying to find him. She bewitched him." A foolish story, but the version Ridley spread.

The men were both silent, their faces expressionless. Skelley dug at his ear. Eliot stroked his beard.

"How old are you, lad?" Eliot asked, letting his fingers come to rest buried in the black waves.

Though Fayth was actually two and twenty, she had no trace of a beard and was very small, so she said, "Fourteen, sir."

Eliot looked at Skelley, who shrugged and said, "Aye, 'tis possible."

Excitement surged in Fayth. Perhaps they knew Sir Patrick! "Do you know my father?"

"I might," Eliot said. "Do you?"

Fayth wasn't sure how far to take this farce. She didn't know how well these men knew Sir Patrick, if they did at all. Didn't know if they could catch her in the middle of a lie. So she said, "I know some things. Things my mother told me, things he told me the few times he visited. And I know what I've heard from others."

Skelley grinned. "And still ye think he's worth finding?"

Fayth nodded. "He's my father."

Skelley's smile faded and he dropped a heavy hand on Fayth's shoulder. "Then I know someone who can help ye."

Laine returned. He leaned over and whispered something to Skelley. Eliot still showed no signs of emotion. He stared fixedly at Fayth, dark eyes somehow both cold and hot. She could see his mouth in the thick waves of his beard, sensual, smooth.

"We might be wantin' yer horse," Skelley said. "The man who knows of yer father—methinks he'll want it." Skelley stood. "Will ye come?"

Fayth looked at the trio hesitantly. "I have to go with you?"

"No," Skelley said. "But unless ye do, no sale and no information."

Fayth looked from one man to the next, her gaze resting longest on Laine. She could probably find someone else to buy her horse with little effort—and it would certainly be easier to purchase another here at the market. But if the intelligence on Mona proved useful it might save Fayth a great deal of time.

"Where is this man?" she asked.

"To the north a bit."

"I was hoping to trade the horse for a pony, or buy one with the proceeds of the sale. Will this man have a pony for me?"

Eliot leaned forward, eyes gleaming, hand planted on the tabletop. "Oh, I think he'll have just what ye're looking for, laddie."

Fayth's eyes narrowed, but she knew not what else to do. The thought that she might actually be a step closer to locating Mona had her nearly trembling with excitement that she fought not to show.

"Very well. Take me to this man."

After two hours on horseback, Fayth was beginning to get nervous. She rode Bear, who was not alarmed by their new companions. The three men surrounded her—one on either side and Laine behind. Eliot rode well for a one-armed man, Fayth noted, and didn't doubt he could catch her if she bolted. Was she a prisoner? She wasn't clear on that, since Skelley had told her she didn't have to come. Of course she didn't have to! She was free now. A man—or male, at least—afforded much more freedom than a mere woman. They were simply riding as men do, rather than catering to womanly needs.

Skelley seemed to think his friend could help her and for some reason she trusted Skelley, as well as the boy. It was Eliot who made her uneasy, but for now, she was willing to go along with it, holding apprehension at bay, since their goals currently aligned. But if this man proved useless, she might be in trouble. A frightening thought occurred to her. What if Sir Patrick had a son? One who had committed some atrocity against their friend? Surely this mysterious man would know as soon as he set eyes on her she was not whom he sought? What if he didn't? What if it was Sir Patrick who had offended him and so he expected the son to pay for the sins of his father? Her mind churned with possibilities, none of them encouraging.

"Uh . . . what's your friend's name?" Fayth asked Skelley, since he was the most likely to answer.

"He'll be tellin' ye that himself soon enough."

Fayth frowned. "What? Is it a secret?"

"It's not for us to say," Laine said.

Fayth looked over her shoulder at the boy. He was grinning.

"Why? Have you nothing good to say about him?"

At that, they all chuckled foolishly, but said nothing more. Fayth was becoming irritated. They reminded her of little boys hiding a toad behind their backs, plotting to thrust it in their sister's face.

They reached a wood and traveled into the shelter of its trees. Half a mile inside they stopped. Skelley whistled three times. An answering whistle came immediately. Bear's ears pricked; his muscles bunched beneath Fayth's thighs. He tried to start forward, but she held his reins hard.

Eliot gazed at the horse, then at her with black half-lidded eyes. "He seems a bit . . . anxious, wouldna ye say?"

Fayth licked her lips. "Yes, well, he responds to whistles . . . one of the means my father used to train him. But I don't whistle so well."

"I see," Eliot said and started forward.

Fayth gritted her teeth as they trod single file deeper into the wood. She was certain now things were not as they seemed. They knew she lied. Did they know she was female? Her stomach lurched. Could they be luring her into the forest to rape and murder her? Were they taking her to share with their companions?

Fayth's heart hammered in her ears, her breath coming short. This was yet another of her stupid, impulsive mistakes. Reckless, thoughtless—that's what Ridley always said, and others, too, though with kinder words. Even Red Alex had called her stupid. Her teeth clenched. She would not think of that man. She could not think of him without becoming infuriated. She needed calm, clear thought now. Her hand sought the dirk she'd stolen from Red Alex, fingers gripping the hilt.

A clearing lay ahead, filled with scattered fires. She didn't know whether to be relieved that they'd finally arrived, or even more frightened that her fate was finally upon her. A tall man approached from the clearing. Fire backlit him, making him a black shadow, moving stealthily through the trees. His build, his very walk, was vaguely familiar to Fayth.

Bear became excited again, snorting and striking the ground with his hooves. He jerked his head, as if testing her hold on the reins. The man stopped and his stance sent a chill of alarm along Fayth's spine.

"We brought ye a wee gift," Eliot said, his eyes alight with humor that Fayth had not believed possible in such a hard countenance. "Yer nephew wished to return yer horse."

The air seeped out of Fayth's lungs as she understood why the man seemed so familiar—more than familiar. He neither spoke, nor came forward. His hand went to his shoulder, which he rubbed absently. Fayth felt faint and clutched the dirk's hilt tightly so the sharp edges dug into her palm. She *would not* swoon before him.

"My nephew?" Red Alex said, walking closer.

Soon his face was visible, if shadowed, and Fayth wished again she'd killed him when the opportunity had presented itself. She kept her head down, prayed he would not recognize her, knowing that for a fool's wish. When he was beside Bear's withers, she drew the dirk up, to threaten him. His hand clamped down on her wrist, twisting and squeezing until her fingers sprang open, dropping the dirk to the ground.

He did not release her. She met his blue eyes, burning into hers. He was smiling and she mimicked it, her lips curling, her breath hissing between bared teeth.

"Ah, of course," he said, his voice thick with satisfaction. "My nephew."

6

His grip didn't lessen as he dragged her from Bear's saddle, then pulled her into the clearing. Several crude shelters had been erected in the border manner—thatch and mud, easy to construct, no great loss if destroyed. She guessed there were maybe two dozen men, but didn't have the opportunity to count. He shoved her into the largest of the shelters. She stumbled several paces, rubbing her arm. He let the rug that served as a door fall shut. The one-room shelter was lit by a candelabra—stolen, she was certain. There was a pallet and blankets, the remains of a meal, and a wad of bloodied linen. There was also a wide array of weaponry.

Fayth lunged for a Lochaber ax leaning against the wall, but he was quicker, grasping the neck of her tunic and jerking her back. She swung, her balled fist making contact with stubbled jaw. His head snapped back, but he held fast. She swung again. He caught her wrist, twisting it behind her back. She clawed at his face with her other hand, but he caught that one, too. It soon joined the other, pinned to the small of her back. She kicked at his ankles and shins. He held both her wrists in one hand, hauling her up against his body, oblivious to her struggles. He yanked the cap from her head and buried his hand in her hair.

Her heart slammed against her ribs, certain he would now finish what he'd begun back at Annancreag, then later beside a deserted stream. And he would be angry, too, that both times she'd bested him—wounded him. Unmanned him. He would be brutal, punishing. She braced herself for the worst. She would not make it easy for him.

He tugged at her hair, pulling her head back so she was forced to glare up into his face. Into his calm, measured stare.

"And still, no cries for help," he mused. "Not even a whisper."

She stilled at his unruffled expression. He was not burning with lust for vengeance. Whatever punishment he planned to administer, he would do it with his wits intact.

"Who would help me here?"

His eyes narrowed slightly, though he didn't seem angry. "They think you a lad?"

She stared at him, uncomprehending.

His grip on her hair tightened. "Skelley, Laine, Eliot? They believe you a lad?"

Fayth nodded. The fingers tangled in her hair relaxed, though didn't release.

"Good. 'Tis better that way."

"What's better?" He opened his mouth to reply, but before he could, she said, "You like the boys? Is that it?"

To her surprise, rather than strike her in fury, as Ridley would have, he smiled. A wide-eyed, genuine smile, and laughed.

"God, but you've a wicked tongue." He lowered his head, his smile becoming wolfish. "I told you before, little one. Dinna seek to insult my manhood or I'll be forced to prove my virility. And you're the only lass in miles."

Her skin felt overhot, tight. She was suddenly unable to

swallow properly, her mouth dry as sand. Unbidden, the memory of when he kissed her at Annancreag intruded. She'd let him do it, had been forced to play along, act a whore. But for a moment . . . for a small, isolated moment, she'd forgotten entirely that she was acting. Had felt every inch the wanton in his arms. And had hated him for making her betray Jack's memory in such a way. Even now her body quickened, pressed against him, his fingers massaging her scalp, just as it had back at the stream, when he had stolen her breath with wanting. It repulsed her, this traitorous response to him.

She turned her face away, staring at the wall. "Do what you will and get it over with. I'm sure it won't take long."

Again he laughed and, to her surprise, he released her hair. "I'll let you go now but it's only so we might talk. Will you behave? If not, I'll have to bind you."

She nodded and he stepped away. She sighed, relieved for the distance he put between them. She rubbed her wrists, though he hadn't hurt her. She wanted him to think he had. Best if he underestimated her. He stepped back to the doorway and peered out. She was struck again by his incredible size. His broad shoulders blocked the doorway. He had to bend his head to look through the opening. Why had he still not harmed her, after all that had happened? He was Red Alex, notorious reiver. He was as responsible as Wesley for keeping the feud between their clans alive this past year when others had tried for peace. He'd murdered dozens of Grahams, stolen hundreds of Graham kine and horses. He loathed her family as she did his. Why was he now so mild with her? It made no sense.

"Talk then," she said.

He dropped the rug back in place, turning to her, his hands folded over his chest. "Twice now, you have spared my life."

Fayth blinked. This was unexpected. But she didn't particularly care to examine why she'd been unable to finish him.

"Why?" he asked, moving closer. "Twice I've been at your mercy. Twice you've chosen to let me live."

When she didn't respond, he took another step. "The first time, I thought it was a mistake, that you meant for me to die, and thought I was dead. But fortunately my thick head thwarted you. Bigger foes than you have tried for my life and thought they won it." He was before her now; an arm's length separated their bodies. He looked down at her, his brow troubled. "But now, I'm not so sure. You could have killed me back there and you didn't. You even gave me the opportunity to come out of it unscathed—short one horse. And when I forced you to shoot me," his hand went to his shoulder, "you merely wounded me, when you could have sent the bolt straight through my heart."

He regarded her steadily. A scabbed line marred his jaw where she'd cut him with his helm. Candlelight glinted off the copper whiskers hugging his chin and jaw. The room was too small, too close.

"Why, lass?" He wagged a finger at her, as if something had just occurred to him. "And in the forest, I thought for certain you'd set your brothers after me. But you didn't tell them, did you?"

There was no explanation for why she kept sparing him—she wished there was, so she could reconcile it in her own mind. She didn't lower her gaze from his, though she longed to. His hair was roan dark inside the shieling, tied at his nape. His eyes were so blue, dark, dark, like rivers. He really was very bonny, a fine face, with strong features, a wide mouth, made for smiling and laughing—or kissing.

She did look away then, her cheeks hot. How could she have such thoughts? Was that why she'd let him live? Because he was so very bonny? The thought was so disturbing she dismissed it and instead tried to imagine him murdering Jack. Jack, bound hand and foot while Red Alex bludgeoned him to death. Or Jack, running into the trees, trying to escape, but shot in the back with an arrow.

"What shall I do with you?" he asked softly, dispelling her imaginings. "I cannot let you go—"

"Why not?"

His mouth tilted into a smile. "She speaks—or he? Tell me, how shall I address you in the company of my men?"

"Must you address me at all?"

"Oh, aye. As I was saying. I cannot let you go. Your brother might catch you and take you back to Carlisle. I cannot have that."

"I swear he will not."

His smile was condescending, though not unkind. "You are a braw, brave lass, but forgive me if I dinna think you a match for Lord Graham, a hundred men-at-arms, and a few fine sleuth dogs."

"I spared your life—twice! Don't you owe me something?"

He grinned. "Oh, I owe you something . . . but I'm not sure what. Not just yet, that is."

She bit back the vile comments that sprang onto her tongue. "You could take me to Caroline," she said instead. "Surely your brother will devise some punishment befitting my crime."

Alex shook his head thoughtfully. "He's besotted with your sister and she's a soft, kind woman, nothing at all like you. She'll not allow him to punish you. What would they do with you? Neither of them want you there. You've proven yourself thoroughly disloyal. Your presence will cause discord, discord neither of them desires. Rob would probably send you back to Ridley."

"What makes you think Ridley or Carlisle would have me now?"

His smile was tight. "Do you know why Ridley wants you wed to Carlisle?"

She nodded cautiously, wondering if he truly did, or if he was referring to something else entirely.

"Do you know that I currently hold Gealach?"

She nodded again. She had convinced herself it was the reason she'd not told Ridley about their forest encounter. Ridley wanted Alex dead to ease his way into Gealach. So long as Red Alex lived, the tower would be difficult to secure. Of course, that went against her own tumultuous feelings about Red Alex, but if there was anything Fayth could do to thwart Ridley, she would do it. And quite suddenly, she relaxed, relief washing over her. She'd spared his life, not because she'd felt something other than complete loathing for him, but because he was an obstacle Ridley wanted to eliminate.

Alex folded his hands behind his back, his expression grim. "Gealach is not mine by right but by force. However, I have offered for it, through coin and marriage. Lord Carlisle will not sign over the deed. Your brother has resources and men Carlisle could only wish for. When Gealach is deeded to him, he will descend on my land and there is little I can do to stop him."

"What about your brother, Lord Annan? Will he not come to your aid?"

Alex shook his head, turning partly away from her. "My brother's loyalties are divided. Ridley is his brother-in-law, and though he doesn't trust him, he will not jeopardize the peace or his marriage."

Fayth was silent, wondering why he told her these things. Did he want her to understand why he kept her prisoner? Perhaps his reason was a valid one, from a border perspective, but she couldn't help him. She *had* to find Mona.

He turned back to her, giving her a narrow look. "Skelley told me who you were asking after. Sir Patrick. You're his son, eh? My nephew . . . What is this fiction? What business have you with Patrick? Or is it your stepmother, the witch, you seek?"

The urge to gnaw her fingernails with worry was great, but she kept her fists balled at her side. Should she tell him? It was her first impulse—to trust him. And she heeded her first impulses far too often, mistaking them for some kind of silly intuition. But trusting him was folly. No, she must think this through.

"What is your business, lassie? The same business you went to Annancreag for? The same business responsible for the death of Annan Maxwells?" When still she didn't answer, he shrugged. "It matters not since you won't be able to complete your business. Perhaps, in time, you'll decide you want to share your purpose."

In time. She didn't like the sound of that. A desperate, clawing urge to be away gripped her. She couldn't stand being confined. Being kept. "What will you do with me?"

"You'll travel with me to Gealach as my prisoner—my *male* prisoner, until Carlisle agrees to sell me the land."

Her lips curled in disgust. Just what she needed, another man deciding her fate. "What makes you think Carlisle wants me that badly?"

He grunted, but didn't answer. He took her cap from the ground and dropped it back onto her head. "So? What shall I call you? Mickle? Wee lad? Fair Willie?"

He tried to tuck her hair beneath the cap but she slapped his hands away. "Hugh."

He stepped back, a look of mock surprise on his face.

"Named for your father, eh? The great Hugh Graham . . . hmm, well, let us leave off the Graham, lest it cause bloodshed in my camp. And despite what you believe, I want you whole, laddie. What say, Hugh Bell?"

"Bell?" she spat. "I'm no Scot!"

"You're a Graham, and therefore part Scot, by my calculations."

"I only claim the English half—the better half."

He laughed again, his eyes nearly dancing. He found her delightfully amusing—that much was clear. It made her itch to scratch his eyes from their sockets.

She looked away. "They think I'm your nephew . . . so I must be a Maxwell."

He burst out laughing. "Oh—I'd forgotten that!" He laughed so hard his eyes streamed. He bent over, clutching his side.

"It's not that funny," she said, scowling at him.

"Oh, aye—it is. It really is."

"My sister is now a Maxwell. It's not as if it couldn't happen."

His laughter died and his gaze turned speculative. A sharp knock sounded on the outside of the shieling, then Laine poked his head in. "Sir? Is aught amiss?"

"No, no," Alex said, looking away from her finally and wiping his eyes. "Please, feed my nephew. He's to be under constant guard, but extend him every courtesy due a Maxwell guest." He flashed her a wide, white smile. "I cannot have you question my hospitality."

He caught her arm before she reached the door. "If you try to run, I'll break your leg."

Fayth jerked her arm away and he laughed again. She saw Laine's guarded look and knew the boy had heard Alex's threat.

Alex's voice rang out over her head, loud enough for the

entire camp to hear, though he was speaking to the boy. "He's a fast one, see that he doesn't get away."

Fayth followed Laine out, glad to be away from Alex's infuriating presence. He was unbearable! How could he see any humor in this awful situation? But, of course, she was his prisoner, at his mercy. He could afford to laugh.

"If you're really Sir Patrick's son," Laine asked, "why'd you try to attack Alex? He's your uncle!"

"I thought it was a trap. You and Skelley and especially Eliot were acting so odd . . . Besides," Fayth said, becoming more comfortable with the web of lies she was weaving, "I've never seen my uncle before. Red Alex doesn't look like my father." That much was true, for she had caught a few glimpses of Sir Patrick before he was moved to the dungeons. Other than sharing Alex's unusual height, the two brothers looked quite different.

"So . . . you're really Sir Patrick's son?" Laine asked when they were several paces away from Alex's shieling. His expression was skeptical.

Fayth shrugged. "My mum says so." She grinned up at the boy. "Well, she says he's one possibility."

Laine looked slightly horrified.

"What? You never met a bastard afore?"

His face reddened. "Of course I have. What do you think *I* am?"

Skelley appeared beside them. "That does sound like Sir Patrick. Only staying long enough to sow a few bastards."

"Och, aye," Fayth said, warming to the game. "And I hope to be just like him. Why, I had me a wench just afore I met up with you. She's probably breeding already."

Skelley just chuckled, but Laine's skepticism returned. "You're a liar and a thief. I suppose one begets the other."

Skelley threw an arm around Fayth's shoulder, his hand dangling dangerously near her unbound breast. "Dinna mind Brother Laine. Had he a wench, he wouldn't know what to do wi' her."

"That's not so!" Laine protested, the red blotches on his face spreading. "I've had countless lasses. I simply choose not to boast of it."

Fayth hunched her shoulders and dragged her feet. Skelley took the hint and removed his arm. She would have to bind her breasts as soon as possible.

Skelley pushed the side of Laine's head playfully, messing up the graying ebony locks, and strode back the way they'd come, to Red Alex's shelter. Laine's grin seemed to have permanently fled. His mouth was a thin, mutinous line and Fayth regretted her stupid boasting. It was what her father and brothers often did, and Jack, as well.

"Why did he call you Brother Laine?"

"It's not what you're thinking. I told you, I've had lots of women."

He was a virgin. She felt like a coarse half-wit for embarrassing him. "Then what did he mean?" she asked, following him across the clearing.

He stopped in front of a pile of canvas sacks and turned to her, hands on his hips. "I was to be a monk. My father gave me to an abbey even though I begged him to let me be a knight." His mouth twisted bitterly. "He said every father in his family gave a son to the church and since I was the weakest sack of shit he'd begot, I was the chosen one."

Fayth stared back at him solemnly, not knowing what to say to such a revelation. This was Diana Carlisle's brother, the one Red Alex had saved. It had meant nothing to Fayth when Diana had told her the story, but now, faced with the young man, she felt strangely unbalanced, as if things were not quite as they seemed. She tried to recall what Diana had told her about Alex rescuing Laine, but could remem-

ber little. She glanced over her shoulder, catching Alex's
dark gaze on her and swiftly looked away.

"There's food here." Laine gestured vaguely at the canvas sacks. When Fayth made no move toward them, he
opened one and began rummaging through it.

"This is better to you than a life of contemplation?
Crawling about the woods like an animal?" she asked,
scanning the campsite for a means of escape. She was
being watched closely. Eliot sat on a boulder, his thick leg
propped on a log, staring at her. His eyes looked black
again. He patted the latch hanging from his belt and
smiled.

"We're only in the woods right now to raid," Laine said.
"Gealach is remote, not a good place from which to stage
raids, but it's where we reside, mostly." He gave her a hard
look. "I owe Red Alex my life, as do most of these men."
He went back to the bags. "There was very little for me to
contemplate at Rees . . . except perhaps a quick death."

Fayth frowned at him. "That's the coward's way."

His mouth flattened but he didn't raise his head.

"How did Red Alex save your life?"

The silence weighed heavy. Fayth thought he wouldn't
answer, but finally he said, "Alex knows about the
monks . . . not that Dunfermline was anything at all like
Rees Abbey, where I was. He says most of the monks at
Dunfermline were good men . . . but he understood that
some of them . . ." He swallowed hard and met Fayth's
steady gaze. "Like Father Rae, aren't very godly."

"Not godly?" Fayth was more confused than ever. This
was not what she'd expected from a band of outlaws—
from Red Alex's band of outlaws. "Who is Father Rae?
What did he do?"

When it became clear Laine would say no more about
his time at Rees, or Alex rescuing him, Fayth asked, "Does

Eliot owe Red Alex his life?" She glanced back at the one-armed man. His eyes were still fixed on her.

Laine gazed at Eliot for a few seconds. "Aye . . . but it was long afore I came to be with them. Eliot is a Maxwell and kin to Alex. Red Rowan took him in when his father was murdered. By a Graham, of course."

Fayth fought her scowl of irritation. *Of course.* As if only Grahams went about murdering Maxwells.

"He lost his arm in a hunting accident. He would have lost his life, if not for Alex."

If not for Alex. Fayth found her gaze drawn to Alex again, but she resisted. "Why does Eliot keep staring at me?"

"Red Alex probably set him to guarding you."

Fayth noticed another man loitering nearby, but he wasn't nearly as vigilant.

"He certainly takes his duties seriously."

"We all do, Hugh. We're not merely a band of outlaws. We have a home and we mean to keep it." His head jerked back to the bag.

Fayth studied the lad. He didn't speak in the rough border accent of the others. Though he was certainly a Scot, this speech bore the mark of education. He'd spent a good while at the abbey.

Laine finally pulled dried meat and a loaf of hard bread from the sack. "You'll want to watch out for Eliot, he's not fond of strangers. It took him some time to tolerate me. He can't abide Davie."

"Davie?"

Laine broke the loaf, offering half to Fayth. He pointed across the clearing to a pale-haired man, sitting beneath a tree, grinding something with mortar and pestle. "Aye, Davie's our leech. He's only been with us a few weeks. He doesn't speak and cannot hear."

Fayth accepted the flagon of beer Laine passed to

her. "If he can't speak or hear, how did he learn to heal?"

"His sister was one of the finest healers on the border. The villagers hated him—thought he was a half-wit. She took care of him after their mother died. But she drowned one day, no one knows how or why, though her husband, an angry man who wanted nothing more than to be rid of the dullard, accused Davie of murdering her. When we came through the village Davie was being tried for murder."

Fayth looked again at Davie, frowning. "How did you convince the villagers he was innocent?"

"We didn't. Red Alex and Skelley sat through a bit of the trial, for it was a public thing, and not much of a trial at all. In the end, took him at sword point." Laine took a bite of his meat and spoke around it. "And so here he is."

Fayth stared for a long time at the fair-haired leech. This was all so troubling. She wasn't sure she wanted to hear any more of these stories. She looked away and noticed several men had joined Eliot and his attention was now on them as they played cards.

Laine gnawed at his bread, following her gaze. "Stay clear of Eliot and you'll do fine, lad." He grinned suddenly and Fayth was relieved for some unfathomable reason that he was no longer annoyed at her. "If you prove yourself worthy, Alex might even let you stay."

Fayth wouldn't be around long enough for that to happen. "Is that what you did? Proved yourself worthy?"

"You ask a lot of questions."

Fayth smiled blandly. "I'm curious about my uncle, is all." Laine grunted.

"So . . . what did this Father Rae do that was so bad?"

Laine stopped chewing abruptly, piercing her with a hard stare. "That's none of your business."

Fayth's eyes widened as she suddenly understood. She'd

heard stories about the corrupt monks, buggering boys, girls, animals, anything that moved. "Did he—"

"He didn't!" Laine reached beneath the sacks and grabbed his latch. He stood. "I wouldn't go far, if I were you."

He crossed the clearing and came to stand by Eliot, watching the game over the one-armed man's shoulder. Fayth set aside her rock-hard oatcake and chewed on her fingernail, wondering how she had offended the lad. It was clear he didn't want to speak of his time at the abbey, but why? Had the priest really violated him? And Carlisle refused to help him? But Alex *had* helped, when Laine's own father had abandoned him. Fayth's head hurt from thinking so hard. What did she care? Why did it matter that Alex had helped Laine or Davie? It changed nothing. She wasn't staying. She had to get away and find Mona.

Alex had been directing the men to break up camp. They would be leaving soon. He would probably make her ride with him and she would have no opportunity to escape.

No one seemed to be paying attention, so Fayth stood idly and wandered toward the trees. She stopped at a birch and leaned against it, as if that had been her destination all along. Laine turned away from the game, but he hadn't spotted her yet, though she saw by his sudden alertness that he noticed she was no longer where he'd left her. Fayth pushed away from the tree and walked quickly into the woods.

"Hugh!" Laine shouted.

Fayth glanced over her shoulder and saw that two men had started after her, one of them Eliot. She hesitated, noting their size. They were large men, bulky with muscle. Their thighs were swollen with it. But she was small and light and fast. She could outrun them.

She sprinted into the forest, dodging trees and branches and brambles, not looking back. An arrow whizzed past her leg, almost causing her to trip. She caught herself, then pain seared through her arm, sending her sprawling forward into a tree. She looked down, horrified to see a bloodied arrowhead and gore-streaked shaft protruding from her upper arm. *At least they hit my arm and not my leg.*

She kept running, gripping her elbow to hold her arm tight against her side. The pain was sharp, burning, but she kept going, even when she no longer heard them crashing through the forest after her. Her vision was beginning to cloud when she finally stopped.

There was a roaring in her ears. Air sawed in and out of her lungs and her arm—it was fire—molten lead, dragging her down. She leaned against a tree, trying to catch her breath. She stared upward, at the sunlight streaming through the canopy of branches and leaves, dazzling her eyes. Something dripped nearby. Fayth couldn't remember the last time it rained. Her hands felt sticky. She raised one hand in front of her face and stared uncomprehendingly at the red glove she wore. Her stomach lurched. Blood. So much blood.

When she no longer labored for air, she examined her arm, ripping the sleeve off to expose the wound. The arrow had gone straight through. She reached around, felt the fletching bristling out of the back of her arm. Blood streamed down, splattering onto the leaves beneath her. The dripping. The ground seemed to tilt beneath her feet and her stomach heaved again. She slid to the ground, shaking uncontrollably. Had the bone snapped? She couldn't tell, couldn't move her arm.

She stared down at her hand, lying open on her thigh, and willed herself to make a fist. The fingers curled and tightened in a weak grip. Relieved, she closed her eyes, meaning only to rest for a moment.

She woke to something wet lapping at her cheeks. She stared blearily at the furry face filling her vision. One brown eye, one winter blue. Biddy. The dog sat beside her, panting, its tail swishing noisily through the blanket of leaves.

"Biddy . . ." Fayth said, her voice cracking and weak. Where had the dog come from? Fayth raised her good hand to pat the dog's head. When she returned her hand to support her hurt arm, she noted that the ragged flesh around the wound was red and swollen.

Biddy closed her mouth and whined softly. She began to wash Fayth's face again. Blood from Fayth's hands streaked the dog's coat.

"How did you find me?" Her arm throbbed dully. It felt as if a weight stone were tied to her shoulder, pulling her arm off.

Biddy barked several times. Fayth turned her face away, trying to shush the dog, but was too weak to be effective. She had to get up, get moving again, or they would find her. She frowned, momentarily uncertain from whom she was running . . . Ridley? Red Alex? Both? She shook herself, recalling the men at the Dragon's Lair, her lie, and being confronted with Red Alex.

The last was all the impetus she needed. She rose to her knees, cradling her wounded arm tight. Her mouth was so dry. She needed to find a stream—to drink and clean the wound. Slowly, she rose to her feet, feeling like an old woman.

She turned in a circle, swaying all the while, trying to decide which way to go. The forest swirled around her, a bright whirlwind of green and gold and brown. She closed her eyes, shuddering violently.

A sharp whistle sounded to her right. Fayth jerked toward the sound, eyes snapping open, and stumbled. She caught herself on a tree, bumping her wounded arm against the trunk. Blinding pain sliced through her arm. Fayth's mouth opened to scream, but no sound came out, only a desperate sobbing.

Biddy was hysterical. The dog danced about, yipping and barking excitedly.

"No, no!" Fayth said. "Quiet!"

The dog only became increasingly agitated and started to howl. Fayth staggered away, abandoning the dog. It was clear her wound, though in her arm, was affecting her whole body. She felt slow, weighed down. Every step jarred her arm so badly she bit her tongue. Lights burst behind her eyes. A metallic taste filled her mouth.

The blood still streamed down her arm, leaving a trail behind her. Biddy followed, whining and barking. It was hopeless, she'd never escape.

She tried to yell, "Go away!" but it came out in a tortured breath. She clenched her teeth and pressed forward. It was an arrow wound to her arm, damn it! Not to her head, or heart, or belly—or even her leg! A minor wound that would not hamper a man, would not hamper Red Alex.

She heard shouting and another whistle. Biddy went wild, yipping and chasing her tail. Fayth forced herself to run. She felt heavy and lumbering, but kept at it. Biddy's barks stopped and the voices grew faint. Hope began to grow, giving her a spurt of strength. She chanced a look over her shoulder, seeing nothing but trees. Then her foot tangled in a root, turning painfully, and she was falling.

The ground smacked into her jaw and she bit her tongue again. She landed on her arm, twisting the arrow until she felt the skin tear. She tried to scream, but only moaned pitiably. Her eyes were open, yet she could see nothing but blinding light. She trembled uncontrollably. Her lips moved in a silent prayer. *Oh please, Lord, just this once, let me faint.*

7

LADY ANNE IRVINE, youngest daughter of the earl of
Dornock, was a bundle of nerves and doubts as she waited
to meet her betrothed. She'd been so happy just a few short
days ago. She'd exchanged portraits with Lord Ridley Graham and been well pleased with her intended's appearance.
He had written her lovely letters, proclaiming her beauty
and his impatience to wed her.

But since the visit from the woman disguised as a boy,
Lady Anne had been filled with nothing but misgivings.
Part of her was convinced that the girl must have been a
spurned lover, out to have her revenge on Lord Graham.
But mostly, she remembered the earnestness and sincerity
in the woman's face.

Anne had spoken to her father about it but he dismissed
the woman's visit. He said it was probably a kinsman of either the Irvines or the Grahams, intent on keeping the feud
alive.

Perhaps.

But Anne, though young, was not a fool. Her father
knew this, and so gave her leave to break the betrothal with

Lord Graham if, after meeting him, she found him not to her liking. Anne had written him straightaway, telling him she wished to meet him before they agreed to wed. As she expected, an answer had been quickly forthcoming. He was most distressed, as he'd thought the marriage was already agreed upon. He promised to leave Lord Carlisle's stronghold of Lochnith immediately and would arrive at Dornock soon, to set her mind at ease.

His desire to satisfy her was a point in his favor, Anne had to admit, but at the same time, she was wary. Peering into the looking glass, she plucked at the yellow ribbons in her hair and adjusted her bodice.

There was a scratch at the door and then her maid entered. "Lord Graham has arrived."

Anne wrung her hands, searching the room as if for an escape. "Did Father send you to fetch me?"

Her maid shook her head. "Nay, but he sends his man up."

"Good." Anne began to calm. "Tell them I am in the gardens. Have them join me there."

She hurried from the room. This would give her the opportunity to observe Lord Graham before they met. In the garden, she slipped through the bushes and waited.

After an interminable amount of time, she spotted her father, short and squat, looking like a stuffed hen in his silk and velvet coat and feathered cap. Beside him walked a tall man, dressed in elaborate finery. His golden brown beard was well groomed, his legs, encased in tight hose, were long and muscular. He chatted amiably with her father. His gestures were wide and confident, his laugh full and pleasant.

Anne chewed her lip, trying to decide what to do. He was more handsome than the miniature he'd sent her. And yet, something raised the hair on her neck and arms.

"May I ask what you're watching?"

Anne nearly screamed and whirled, her hand pressed to

her bosom. A young man stood before her. How he'd found her, she didn't know, as this path was hidden from sight.

He was about five years older than she and of average height—taller than herself by nearly a head. He wore no hat. Dark curls framed his head like a cap. His eyes were large and brown, a fine brown beard hugged his jaw, almost covering a ragged scar on his cheek. She found herself transfixed by it, wondering what had caused such a wound. His jaw tightened and a gloved hand went self-consciously to the scar before falling away just as suddenly, as if trying to convince himself he had nothing to be ashamed of.

His gaze moved over her, taking in everything, and yet not offending. "You're not a servant. May I ask again what you were watching?"

Anne realized she still clutched her chest as if her heart had failed. She dropped her hand and began working at the finger of her glove nervously. "I am Lady Anne Irvine and I was hoping to catch a glimpse of my betrothed before I met him."

Something sparked in his eyes. Humor? He moved closer. She held her breath, heat climbing her chest, and then he went past her. She closed her eyes briefly, trying to recapture her wits. She turned to find him peering through the break in the branches.

When he turned back, his expression was somber. "Did you get your glimpse, my lady?"

She nodded.

He was so straight, so serious. He seemed coiled, ready to spring on a foe at any moment. A strength emanated from him that she found fascinating.

"And did the glimpse please you?"

"He is . . . comely."

He raised a brow, noting her hesitation.

Anne shrugged. "But what does a pretty face tell you? Nothing, except it masks the truth better."

"What is the truth?"

Anne's cheeks colored. She didn't even know this man. Why was she saying these things to him? She started to back away, but he reached for her. His hands closed into a fist before touching her and drew away. But it was enough to stop her. She looked back at him.

"I should go . . . they'll be looking for me."

He stepped back, putting his hands behind his back. "Of course . . . I'm sorry."

She knew she should leave immediately. But his eyes held her. She couldn't look away. She saw sorrow and darkness there. But there was warmth, too, simmering below the surface.

"Who are you?" she whispered.

Before he could answer, she heard her father. "Anne! Where are ye, lassie? Come out!" And then to someone else, "She knows all the little trails. Designed the gardens herself."

The man looked around their little clearing with new interest. "This is your doing?"

Anne nodded.

"It is the finest garden I've seen. I was drawn to it immediately—I had the urge to hide myself within, as if it were another world, a fairy kingdom—"

"Aye! That is just what it is!" Anne said, clapping her hands, thrilled that he'd understood her intention so well. "I come here oft, to forget things . . . for a little while."

He cocked his head slightly. "And what must a fine lady like you retreat from?"

Why did she keep saying these things to him? She shook her head, shy suddenly. She knew she should go but couldn't leave without knowing who this man was and if she'd have the opportunity to speak with him again.

"What is your name, sir?"

"Wesley."

She repeated his name, smiling slightly.

He stepped forward, his hand reaching for her neck, hovering over the pendant she wore. She lowered her chin, but could not look away from his face for long.

"It's lovely," he said, pulling his hand away quickly.

"Thank you." She fingered the seashell strung on a yellow ribbon about her neck.

"Do you like the sea?"

"Aye . . . I swim very well. My father says I'm surely a selkie that shed her skin."

He smiled and her breath caught. "I can see that. You are very beautiful. Lord Graham is most fortunate."

Her cheeks burned. Other than her father, no man had called her beautiful. Well, Lord Graham had, but that was only in a letter and based on the miniature she sent him—which she feared had deceived him, as she'd asked the painter to make her pretty.

"What of you?" Anne asked. "Did you come with Lord Graham?"

He nodded, then gestured with his chin. "You should go."

Anne didn't move. "Will I see you again?" It seemed very important that they finish their conversation, that she have the opportunity to learn all about him.

"I'm afraid so." His expression was regretful and she wanted to ask why, but he said, with more urgency, "You really should go now."

She didn't want to leave and meet her betrothed. She'd rather stay here, in this secluded garden, and talk to this strange young man. Of course, that would be ruinous and so she hurried down the path, stopping once to look back at him over her shoulder, but he was gone.

Ridley was annoyed that the girl kept him waiting, playing games with him. He had no wish to wed a child; his preference had always leaned to mature women, not innocents. Her father, puffed up with pride over the silly garden his daughter had designed, chattered inanely about it. Ridley fixed a smile of interest to his face, all the while wondering where that damn girl was so he could be through with this and leave.

He'd left Carlisle in a state of agitation that could put all Ridley's plans at risk. A handful of Carlisle and Graham men were currently searching the march for Fayth, but if they didn't find her soon, Ridley would be forced to mount a costly and time-consuming sweep of the borders. But it was necessary. Carlisle had been most insistent. No Fayth, no deal. He was a sick bastard and Fayth would pay dearly for the trouble she'd caused them all. One bright spot was that Ridley wouldn't have to mete out the punishment himself. Marriage to Old Scratch was precisely what she deserved.

Lady Anne appeared suddenly, surprising a laugh from her father. He held his hands out to her. She was pleasant enough looking, if not a bit plump. Her hair was an unappealing shade of brown. Her hazel eyes regarded him warily. What had changed her mind? For until her last letter, all those before it had been filled with childish sweetness. He hadn't bothered to read them through.

"Lady Anne, your portrait did you no justice. You are a rare beauty." He smiled and reached for her. She placed a gloved hand in his. Fresh dirt dusted the fingers, leaves clung to the lace, and the glove wasn't even on properly; several of the fingers hung loose and empty.

Ridley didn't allow his smile to falter, though he

cringed inwardly. He barely brushed his lips against her hand. He was only too glad to release her when his brother joined him.

"Lady Anne, this is my brother, and captain of my guard, Wesley Graham. Wesley, may I present Lady Anne Irvine, daughter of the earl of Dornock."

Wesley murmured a greeting, his gaze barely registering the woman before jerking to the side. God's wounds, he was an oaf. Every day Ridley became more convinced his brother was a sodomite, for he seemed to detest the company of women.

"Good morning . . . Wesley," Lady Anne said. She stared at him for an unseemly amount of time.

Ridley glanced at Wesley curiously and noticed how red his scar was. Of course, Wesley was an eyesore and she was horrified by his disfigurement.

"That will be all," Ridley said, and Wesley retreated stiffly.

"What happened to his face?" Lady Anne asked, staring after him.

"Anne," her father admonished softly, taking her hand and patting it affectionately.

"No, no," Ridley said, "she may ask questions without fear of giving offense. He was in a fight with an outlaw, Red Alex. You know of him surely? He's brother to your neighbor, Lord Annan."

"He fought with Red Alex?" she asked, eyes wide.

Ridley sighed. "Yes, and he would do it again, given the chance. An angry man. I'll not make you suffer his company, my lady. You have my word."

Her gaze followed Wesley until he disappeared, then met Ridley's. "He's your brother."

"Aye, and so I must suffer it, eh?"

He laughed, but she didn't even smile. A dour one, like

his sister Caroline. Ridley bit back the groan that threatened to erupt and forced his face into a pleasant smile. He
held his arm out. "Shall we walk and get to know each
other?"

Wesley sat very still, listening to his brother rant end-
lessly about what a stupid little swine Lady Anne was and
what a doddering old fool the earl was. He didn't know
how much more he could take of Ridley maligning these
good people. He wanted many things from life, and Ridley
held the key, but he was beginning to think the price required of him was too high.

"She is ruining everything!" Ridley hissed—referring
to Fayth. "When I get my hands on her she will think marriage to Carlisle a sanctuary. I vow it!"

Servants packed trunks in the next room. They were
leaving to go after Fayth. Normally, Wesley would be in
the gatehouse and stables, making sure everything was
ready to leave when Ridley was. But the pull of finding
Fayth and finally making Gealach his own dimmed in light
of this new development that so aggravated Ridley.

Lady Anne had refused Lord Ridley Graham's suit. Red
faced and flustered, the earl had relayed the news to them.
When asked why, the earl said, quite apologetically, that
she simply didn't like him. He babbled about some common lass, dressed as a boy, warning Anne against marrying
Lord Graham. Would Lord Graham please give her more
time? Perhaps she would reconsider. Ridley had barely
kept his temper about him. He'd asked to speak with Lady
Anne, but she'd refused.

"Everything I plan turns to shit on the whims of women,"
Ridley ground out, throwing his goblet against the wall.

Wesley fought not to wince, remembering that not too
long ago Ridley had slammed a goblet upside his head. He

clenched his teeth, forcing the anger away, and said, "Might I speak with her?"

Ridley whirled, as if noticing him for the first time. *"You?* What could you possibly say to her?"

Wesley truly did not know what he would say, didn't even know why he'd offered, especially when the very idea of Lady Anne wed to his brother filled him with seething bitterness. But since he'd begun, he said, "I could speak well of you and discover what Fayth said that so offends her . . . And see if it can be rectified." When Ridley only stared at him, he said, "I'm your brother, after all. Perhaps she'll believe me."

Ridley seemed to consider it, then shook his head. "Nay. You offended her sight. It certainly will help nothing if I force your countenance upon her."

This information was like a knife stabbing quickly into Wesley's chest, then withdrawing, leaving behind a numbing burn. He averted his eyes, unable to formulate an adequate response.

"Besides," Ridley said, turning away and lowering himself behind the writing table. "You are a buffoon when it comes to women. You'd no doubt muck things up worse." He pulled out a sheet of parchment and began writing. "However, I will write her a letter. You may deliver it for me. Then we must find Fayth before she destroys everything."

8

FAYTH HAD NO IDEA how long she lay on the forest floor, but it seemed like excruciating hours, in which she promised herself repeatedly she would get up, yet never moved. Stones and twigs bit into her cheek. She was so thirsty. There was a loud snuffling in her ear. She tried to turn her face away, but found she couldn't move.

Biddy licked her ear, whining. Footsteps approached, then stopped. They'd found her. She couldn't remember who—didn't care.

Someone stood over her. "Christ," he muttered.

Leaves and needles crunched beneath his feet as he shifted. She felt his hand on her shoulder, moving toward her wound. She flinched, trying to move away, fearing he would try to remove the arrow and knowing she would probably faint if he did.

"Easy, now." His hands turned her body, moving her onto her side, laying her arm straight, elbow resting on her waist, forearm on hip. She whimpered, then bit her lip to stop the pathetic mewling sound.

"Cry out, lass, your arm is in sorry shape. It must hurt like hell."

His words were a key, unlocking the screams of agony. But still she tamped them down, furious at him for weakening her, for making it harder to hold the tears at bay. She forced her eyes open. Red Alex squatted beside her. He was alone, except for Biddy. He visually inspected her arm, a deep frown pulling his brows together.

"It's not so bad," she insisted.

He turned his head slightly, to meet her gaze. "I ken ye're strong, Fayth, ye dinna hiv to prove it to me." His Scots was broad. She'd heard it that way once before, at Annancreag, when he'd been drunk on whisky and full of lust. Now, he was sober and surely far from lust. His gaze moved back to her arm and he stared, his mouth tight and thin.

She realized, with a mixture of disbelief and wonder, that he was worried. About her. Blackness edged her vision. Her eyes fluttered shut.

"That's it, Fayth, just rest."

Fayth. He'd said her name twice. Somehow it sounded different falling from his lips, as if he infused it with new meaning. *Fayth.*

When he yanked the arrow from her arm, she let out a scream that resounded through the forest. She wanted to faint—prayed for it. Instead, her stomach heaved until she vomited.

He murmured things to her, wiped her mouth and the tears from her cheeks, then moved her away from her mess. Why did it have to be Red Alex that found her? Why did it have to be *him?* And yet when his voice stopped or he moved away she panicked, frightened and alone, until he returned and spoke softly to her. Reassuring her.

He pressed a cup to her lips and she drank. She slipped in and out of blackness. They hadn't returned to his camp and they seemed to be alone, except once when she became aware of her arm being dressed by another man. She stared at him for a long time. His hair was white blond, his eyes like dirty ice. He didn't speak. She knew him . . . and she didn't. He met her eyes once and nodded, then went back to his work. She woke again and it was dark. She was wrapped in a rug and Biddy was pressed against her belly, sleeping. A fire crackled nearby.

She tried to raise her wounded arm. It moved slightly, her fingers flexed against her belly. She let out the breath she'd been holding. She hadn't realized until that moment that she'd expected them to take the arm off. Of course, it was still a possibility.

She rolled onto her back, relieved to find her good arm free. Biddy sat up, yawning loudly. Fayth reached beneath the rug and touched the wound. It was wrapped in linen and strapped to her side to hold it immobile. It still throbbed dully, but her head was clear. She stared up at the moon, nearly full, and tried to piece together what had happened.

"Hungry?"

The voice came from behind her. She twisted her neck to look back.

Red Alex sat against a tree, long legs bent, arms folded across his knees. How long had he been there, watching over her, caring for her?

"No." Her voice was thick from sleep.

"You really should eat. You look near starved. Doubtless that's why you nearly died from an arm wound."

"I didn't nearly die," she scoffed. "Where are we? Where are the others?"

"We're in the woods, near to where I found you lying in a pool of blood. I couldn't chance moving you far, and besides, with you being wounded it's more likely my men will discover you're a woman—something I dinna want, at least not until we get to Gealach. As for the others, Skelley and Eliot are nearby, keeping watch. The rest are packing the camp and preparing to return home in the morning."

"You shot me."

Alex shook his head. "Not me—one of my men. But he was only following orders."

"You ordered him to shoot me?"

"No, I ordered them not to allow you to escape." He shrugged. "Doubtless they thought an arrow in the arm or leg would slow you down."

Eliot. Fayth was sure he was the one that shot her. He'd been itching to maim her since he laid eyes on her.

Fayth fell silent, oddly annoyed Alex hadn't been the one to shoot her. When did he plan to punish her for tricking him, beating him over the head, shooting him in the shoulder, and stealing his horse? It irritated her further that he also had been recently wounded by an arrow and was so obviously weathering it better than she was. Her eyes went to his shoulder but she could see nothing of discomfort, only the white linen of his bandages peeking out of the open falling collar of his shirt. He'd shed his mail and his leather jack hung open. The notorious red reiver was a mass of contradictions that left her head fuzzy and confused. He was hated and feared by so many, and yet in his little world, he was kind and fair and . . . well, she didn't want to think of what else.

"I have to ask a question," Alex said, breaking into her thoughts. "It's been troubling me since you ran into the woods."

She didn't respond, looking away.

"Why did you run?"

"I'm a prisoner, being held against my will by the enemy. What would you have me do? Sit around patiently, waiting for you to have your revenge?"

"No . . . I understand why you ran. What I don't understand is why you chose that moment to run. Everyone was awake and alert. I'd just told them to keep you under guard and so they were at their most vigilant. Rather than bide your time and lull us into believing you're not a runner, you dart into the forest as soon as you leave my shieling . . . It's as if you wanted to be recaptured!"

Fayth made an incredulous noise and struggled to sit up. "Wanted to be recaptured! I couldn't bear enduring another moment in your vile camp."

He was beside her, helping her to sit. She tried to shove him away, but he ignored her feeble resistance. Her head swam when she was upright, her stomach queasy. She felt drained, weak, like a newborn kitten, incapable of the slightest defense.

"Besides, you were packing up the camp. I had a feeling that once we were moving you wouldn't be letting me out of your sight."

He remained kneeling beside her. "Well, you've the right of it." He shook his head, smiling slightly. "Still, it was thoughtless, lass. Reckless and incredibly—"

"Yes, I know! Stupid and foolish! I'm lucky I wasn't killed!" She knew the speech. She'd heard it plenty of times, mostly recently from Ridley shrieking about her incredible stupidity. Red Alex was the last person she wanted to hear it from now. The idea of him chastising her left her hot with humiliation.

He looked taken aback. "Well . . . aye, though Eliot's a fine shot and wouldn't have killed you." His face tightened slightly, as if he didn't quite believe his own words. "What I'm trying to say, if you'd let me finish, is that it was thoughtless, reckless—"

She scowled at him, waiting to see what new insult he meant to add.

"And incredibly courageous."

She blinked. The hot resentment that filled her dissolved into something else that fluttered deep in her chest and belly as he held her with his dark blue gaze.

He laughed, though not at her, but in amazement. "My God, lass, I've never seen the like. You just ran, arrows flying around you. Even when you were hit, you kept going." He shook his head. "And you, naught but a wee lass."

His praise made her uncharacteristically flustered. Her face burned and she averted her eyes, shrugging with one shoulder. "The moment presented itself, so I seized it. I knew I could outrun Armless Eliot and the other man. No one was attending me, except Laine, and I didn't think he'd shoot me."

He regarded her for a long moment, increasing her discomfort. "Is that what you always do, Fayth Graham? Seize the moment?"

"If I think there's a chance of success . . . then, yes."

He tilted his head slightly, snagging her gaze again. She forced herself not to look away, though she desperately wanted to. His gaze was warm, admiring even. For an odd moment he reminded her of her father. Hugh Graham had been tolerant, indulgent even, but rarely proud. Fayth's dearest memories were those times his eyes shone with pride, that his voice was rich with it.

Fayth was on fire, even her scalp tingled with it. "Stop looking at me like that."

His gaze dropped to her arm. "How does it feel?"

Relieved at the change of subject, she looked down at her bandaged arm. "Fine, I suppose. You tended it?"

"Aye, Davie and I. I didn't think you'd make it, to be honest. Couldn't rouse you for a bit. But you're a stubborn lass. I suppose you just refused to die."

She frowned. "It's only an arm wound. How could it be so bad?"

"There are places on the body—here," he indicated the inside of his biceps, "here," he pointed to the inside of his thigh, near his groin, "where a wound is fatal if not staunched. You had already bled so much . . ." He shook his head. "Well, I know men who've lost less blood and not lived . . . and here you are, speaking to me."

"There was another man . . ."

Alex nodded. "That was Davie. He'll be back to check for corruption later. He's staying behind to see to you."

"Staying behind?"

"Aye—the others are going on ahead, to Gealach. We'll follow when you're ready to be moved." He looked into the trees, as if his tower were in sight, his eyes strange, faraway. "Ridley and Carlisle might be headed there now, looking for you. I need all my men there."

"So it's just you, me, and Davie?" she asked uneasily.

Alex grinned slightly. "And Skelley and Eliot. Probably Laine. Laine is sore upset that you escaped and almost died on his watch."

"It's only an arm wound!"

Alex laughed softly and shook his head.

He found her protestations amusing! She wanted to get up and hit him just to prove how strong she still was, but he was right. She was too weak. She didn't think she could stand without assistance. Damn it! It burned to be so dependent on someone else, particularly when that someone else was her betrothed's murderer, a fact that kept slipping her mind for some reason.

"Come, you must eat something to regain your strength. We have a journey ahead of us."

He fetched a sack and returned to sit beside her. He removed a bundle that upon unwrapping revealed dried meat and an oatcake. He held the meat to her lips as if he planned to feed her. She jerked her head back and almost toppled over when her vision clouded. His hand was there, on her back. His face swam into focus. When he tried to feed her again, she snatched the meat from his fingers.

"I can feed myself!" He held his hands up, as if to show he meant no harm, and lay the oatcake on her knee. Fayth inspected the meat critically before taking a bite. He left her, disappearing into trees.

"Good riddance," she muttered. But when he didn't return immediately, a sense of panic began to invade. What if he didn't come back? What if he decided to leave her here to rot?

So what if he did? She tried to convince herself that it didn't matter, that she could fend for herself. She'd wounded her arm, for Christ's sake! But it only took an attempt to stand to prove how helpless she was. She needed him, at least until she got her strength back. As she recovered, she would determine if Red Alex had any idea where his brother, Sir Patrick, was. Then she would escape and find Mona. She would not be reckless this time. She would consider every possible outcome of her actions and choose the wisest course. She would give no one reason to call her reckless or stupid.

Having a plan of action gave her some comfort. She continued scanning the surrounding forest until she sighted Red Alex, returning with Skelley. Only then was she able to settle down to eat and rest.

Alex struggled to get comfortable on the hard ground. He'd slept on it often enough, wounded even, but still preferred a bed. His shoulder ached where Fayth had shot him. It had seemed fine at first, but he felt the poison now, the fever, creeping into his limbs. Making his body ache. But it wasn't bad yet, and it might not be. He'd battled the fever before and often enough it barely interfered with his doings. It was Fayth he was concerned with. If the fever took her, she wouldn't have the strength to fight it.

He didn't want to worry about the woman sleeping an arm's length away from him. She was responsible for countless problems, had a nasty temper, loathed him, and yet still, even now that she was firmly in his possession— she was going nowhere with that arm—he could not rest. It was concern for Patrick, he told himself. Patrick had been missing for a month now. His trail, if Alex could even find it, was growing cold. He'd sent a messenger to his other brother, Robert, to discover if he'd learned anything new. Robert's reply would be waiting at Gealach when he arrived. Alex had in his possession a clue to Patrick's whereabouts, but as long as the Grahams remained a threat to his lands, he could not pursue it.

Fog rose from the ground around them. Skelley sneezed in the distance. Alex wondered how long they could keep up the charade that Fayth was a boy and didn't know why he cared. As a female she'd be a distraction to the men, as she already was to him. And he did not like the idea of others being distracted by her. Some speculation had already arisen at his decision to tend "Hugh" personally—alone. He'd merely stated it was because the boy was family. The other men, excepting Skelley and Eliot, had been satisfied with that. Skelley knew better. Though Alex trusted Skelley, this was a secret he was unwilling to share. He'd had to share it with Davie, but that was out of necessity. They'd had to remove her shirt to tend the wound. But Davie never spoke. The truth was safe with him. As for Eliot . . . well, nothing much satisfied that man.

Alex heard the crunch of footsteps and tensed. Eliot emerged from the fog, as if he knew Alex was pondering the particular problem that was Eliot.

"Get yer rest, man," Eliot said. "I'll watch him till morning."

Alex shook his head. "Nay."

"I ken why ye're doing this," Eliot said, hand braced on hip.

"Why am I doing this?"

"Bloody hell, Alex! I shot him in the arm, no the chest or back." Eliot pointed an angry finger at the sleeping form. "That is not Patrick's son. I dinna ken what he wants, but he's too pretty to be a Maxwell."

Alex only stared back, refusing to be drawn into this again. He'd already given Eliot such a tongue-lashing for shooting Fayth—and giving orders for others to fire upon her—that he was astounded the man would seek him out again so soon.

Eliot sighed. "This isna aboot the lad, is it? It was an accident, before. The Graham was a murderer and a bloody cheat, besides—he had it coming. No great loss."

"I'm sure the Grahams beg to differ," Alex ground out, his gaze darting to Fayth, glad she was still asleep.

"Ye're vexed because of the ransom. I said I'd—"

"Eliot, I am finished discussing this with you."

Eliot's face grew dark. He hated being dismissed by anyone and yet Alex had taken to doing just that far too frequently of late, as the man frustrated him beyond reason. He knew something must give soon, but now was not the time.

Alex sighed, scrubbing his hands over his face. "It's over."

"Aye, but I know ye dinna believe me." He jerked his head at Fayth's sleeping form. "Christ, Alex, he's but a bairn. Ye think I'd hurt him?"

Aye. Alex didn't know why he didn't trust Eliot with Fayth. After all, thus far Eliot had only brutalized sworn enemies of the Maxwells. But these days, Eliot made him uneasy and it saddened him. Alex wished he understood what had soured his friend.

"Just the same," Alex said, "I'll watch over him."

Eliot stalked away and Alex's shoulder slumped in relief. At least Eliot didn't suspect Hugh was a woman and a Graham, at that. Jack Graham, and several other prisoners, had been killed on Eliot's watch. Alex allowed his prisoners relative freedom of the keep. Gaming and whoring tended to escalate into fighting. Alex understood this. Only it happened a bit too often when Eliot was in charge. After the last incident—when several prisoners were brutally murdered in what Alex refused to believe was the mere accident Eliot claimed—Alex had punished him. He'd gotten off easy, as most men would be expelled or killed. But Alex let him stay, hoping for change. He'd stopped giving Eliot authority. But rather than forcing Eliot to reign in his temper and try to prove himself worthy, Eliot bitterly resented it.

Alex closed his eyes, trying to ignore the deep throbbing in his shoulder. He planned to depart this clearing tomorrow. If Ridley were looking for Fayth, then they must keep moving. Gealach was two days' ride, but with an invalid it might take as much as a sennight.

After a moment Alex sat up and leaned toward her, to check her color. When he'd found her yesterday, she'd been lying in a puddle of blood. Her skin, dusky and pink normally, had been nearly gray, her lips tinged blue. He'd been angry with her for running, frustrated that she kept slipping from his grasp. And more than a little disgusted with himself for groping her before. She probably ran because she feared he would rape her, despite her bravado and bold insults. He'd taken her to keep Gealach, not ravish her. And yet it would be a lie to say he hadn't contemplated it. Contemplate, hell—he'd imagined having her naked beneath him for weeks. Lain awake wishing to God he was alone so he could relieve himself. He was thirty, not some untried, beardless lad. This was what she had reduced him to.

But when he'd seen the blood, all that had faded. His sole concern became staunching her wound. He'd thought her dead or at the very least in that realm of unconsciousness where one was oblivious to the world around them, the deep sleep that some never woke from. But no, she'd opened her eyes, pinned him with a glare, and insisted she was fine. He smiled at the memory.

His smile faded as he acknowledged that her wound complicated things further. And he could not keep her. He would give her to Carlisle if the old man cooperated. If not, Alex would eventually return her to Ridley. And she did not want either of them. She had preferred to let Red Alex kidnap her than stay and face her fate.

He inhaled the damp air, and sighed, wondering again why this woman had such a hold on him. His gaze was drawn to her, as it was so often. In sleep, she was an angel. She'd not regained her color, but it was no longer grayish. Her lips were pale, but pink. Yes, she would recover so long as the wound did not corrupt. Alex poked at the bandage, looking for signs of seepage.

She swore, her jaw tightening as she clenched her teeth, holding in any other moans of pain—signs of weakness. After a moment she opened her eyes, turning her head to look at him.

"How long have I been sleeping?"

"Not long."

Her eyes drifted shut again. "Then why are you bothering me?"

"I'll be waking you every few hours, at least tonight. Davie said we must not let you sleep too long." Well, the leech hadn't exactly *said* it. He'd gestured at the moon, tracing a track across the sky, then pretended to shake Fayth awake. Alex assumed he was indicating the passage of time and saying she should be wakened periodically. He'd tried to verify this with Skelley, who had been watching the show with his tongue working busily at the gaps in his teeth, but the older man only shook his head, bewildered.

"Davie . . . ?" she said.

"Aye, our healer."

"Oh yes." She sighed again, but her eyes opened, staring blankly before her. "What will you do with me?"

It disconcerted him that he'd just been contemplating that very subject. He was not ready to discuss it with her. "It depends on Carlisle. You know that."

"No."

"You would rather stay with me?"

She darted him a dark look.

"I'm confused then, because I can see few other alternatives for a woman alone."

"Yes, I'm sure you see very little."

Alex smothered his smile. She was most contentious. "Why all this trouble to escape Carlisle? It's a woman's lot to wed. Your sister went to the altar readily enough, and she had misgivings. But she knew her place."

"Caroline's place was in a nunnery. She spent her entire life preparing to be a nun. You have no idea what her place is. Or mine!" He opened his mouth to respond, but she wasn't finished. "And as for your place, it's the gallows, with the other outlaws and murderers, waiting to hang!"

"I might say the same about you since you're responsible for the death of many Maxwells."

She quickly averted her eyes, her mouth thinning. She shook her head and seemed about to speak, but she said nothing. However, her expression was unmistakable. Regret. She regretted what happened and the pain she had caused.

"What's the matter?" he asked.

"I didn't know that so many would die . . . I thought—"

"You didn't think! Otherwise it would have been obvious!" He was angry suddenly—at himself, at her. Had he not been so eager to bed her, believing her absurd fiction about being a whore, no one would have died. He would have stayed alert, she would not have knocked him in the head with a jug, and no Grahams would have penetrated Annancreag.

Her regret vanished, replaced with resentment. She stared into the fog, silent, stoic.

Alex's anger dissolved. Well, he'd lost that opportunity. She wouldn't speak to him when he was raging at her and he didn't blame her. After a pregnant pause he asked, "When I came upon you in the forest and again at Lochnith . . . you were trying to escape. Surely you had a plan for a new life. Or will you pretend to be a boy forever? Riding alone or with outlaws?"

"I have a plan." Her voice was stiff and she still refused to look at him, staring instead into the swirling darkness.

He nodded thoughtfully. "Very well. What plan were you advancing when you proclaimed yourself my nephew?"

"I was hoping to discover my stepmother's whereabouts."

"Your stepmother . . . ? The dowager Lady Graham?"

She slid him a sideways look. "Yes. The one who ran away with your brother, Sir Patrick."

"The one who bewitched my brother."

Fayth made a disgusted sound. "She did not bewitch him."

"Oh, aye, she did. I've proof."

"Proof?" she scoffed. "Please, share. I'm beside myself."

"After you and Wesley kidnapped Caroline, we went to

Graham Keep, hoping Caroline was there, as well as
Patrick, since Ridley had promised to release him when
Rob and your sister wed. But he never did. Ridley swore he
had neither of them and let us search Graham Keep to
prove it. I found a small sack in your stepmother's chambers. It contained nail parings and a lock of Patrick's hair."
It contained another item that Alex was not about to share
with her, that he'd shared with no one but Rob. "What else
could it be but bewitchment?"

"Your brother had been a prisoner for nearly a year. Why
would it be necessary for Mona to bewitch him? Wouldn't
he already be indebted to her for helping him escape?"

"Perhaps. But Patrick hates being beholden to anyone
and I have a hard time envisioning him selling his sword
arm to protect a woman."

"Who says she needed him? Why must women always
need men?"

"The Clachan Fala."

She rolled her eyes. "Not that rubbish again."

"It's not rubbish. Well, at least your brother doesn't believe it is."

"What about you?"

Alex shrugged thoughtfully. "I don't know what I believe. Legends are oft based on truth. Even if she's not the
keeper, she might believe she knows where it's hidden and
she'd need protection in her quest. So she put a spell on
Patrick that made him her servant."

Fayth let out an incredulous breath. "What a fantastic
story. I would never have thought it of you."

Irritated, Alex said, "Obviously you believe them traveling together, otherwise you wouldn't be asking after
Patrick. What's your theory?"

"Oh, I don't doubt it has something to do with that
cursed Blood Stone. Sir Patrick is probably just like Rid-

ley, obsessed with that stupid legend and determined to find the *Clachan Fala.*" She spat the last, as if it were a dirty word. "Your brother probably kidnapped Mona. I can't imagine her going with him willingly. Just like my father, and Ridley after him, he will use her and hurt her as if she were a tool, rather than a person."

"That's why he married Caroline to Rob, isn't it?"

She nodded. "According to the legend, there must be a marriage between a Maxwell and a Graham to bring the Blood Stone forth."

"Doesn't it seem odd to you that after Rob and Caroline wed, your stepmother runs away?"

Fayth's mouth thinned. "Not at all. You know not what it's like, living under Ridley's rule. And Mona's lot was far worse than mine . . . Ridley lusts for her . . . is obsessed with her. He held her prisoner, trying incessantly to bed her."

Alex inspected her color. She was paler than when she first woke, her lips taking on a whitish cast. He should make her rest again, but he was learning much from this conversation and was loath to end it. He supposed her skepticism over the legend was warranted, and yet, Alex wasn't so sure. Somehow, he felt there was something to the tale. Perhaps it had been embellished over time, but he was certain there was a grain of truth in the story. He wore one of the grains around his neck. He placed a hand on his chest, feeling the stone bead through his shirt.

"Well . . . my brother has never needed to kidnap a woman," Alex said. "They go with him willingly, as I'm sure Lady Graham did."

"Clearly you don't have the same effect on women."

Alex scowled at her and leaned forward, so his face was close to hers. Her eyes widened, but that was the only indication he unnerved her. "But you're not exactly a woman, eh, Hugh? Not the best judge of my effect on proper females."

Her lips clamped shut and her cheeks reddened. "I may not be a proper female but plenty of men find me acceptable. More than acceptable." Her chin tilted defiantly. "You certainly didn't hesitate to paw at me."

Alex shrugged, leaning back nonchalantly. " 'Tis true, I'll admit. But I thought you were a whore—not the finest class of women. You get what you pay for, eh? And I don't remember rendering any coin."

The air left her in a whoosh. "I took my fee from your scalp, you filthy toad! I wouldn't stoop to pleasure the likes of you! You—you're beneath me!"

Alex rubbed the scar on his temple, which ached at the memory of their first meeting. He knew she was lashing out in anger and humiliation—humiliation he had caused—but her barb stung. As a third son and an outlaw, with nothing to his name but what he'd taken by force, he *was* beneath her. And suddenly, he didn't know why he bothered with her. He'd been through this before and come out with his pride in shreds. And this one had a more finely honed tongue than the last.

After a fitful silence, she said, "You didn't deny it."

"That I'm beneath you? Why bother? You'll believe what you must."

She looked surprised and slightly embarrassed. "Uh, no. That's not what I meant. You didn't deny that your brother seeks the Clachan Fala."

"Oh . . . no, I don't deny it."

"Well? Where do you think he's looking?"

Alex gave her a narrow look. "Doing your brother's spying again? You think I'd tell you so you can run back and inform him?"

"I don't think I'm running anywhere for a while."

"You'd think, aye? But with you . . . well, I'd not be surprised if you sprouted wings and flew."

Her face reddened. He'd angered her again. He sighed and started to stand, ready to give up on this impossible woman, when she burst out laughing. The laughter stopped abruptly as she clutched her arm and grimaced, but when the pain apparently subsided, she glanced over at him and chuckled softly, shaking her head.

"What?" he asked, trying not to return her smile, inordinately pleased she couldn't remain angry at him.

She shrugged. "I'm just wondering if I'd be a bird . . . or a butterfly?"

He snorted. "A bat. Most definitely."

She smiled and lay her head back down, turning her face away from him. She said nothing for a long time and he thought she'd gone to sleep. He was just thinking about trying to rest again, when she asked, "Is my arm . . . ruined?"

"What mean you?"

"You know what I mean. Think you it will corrupt? Will the scar be ugly?"

Alex paused, uncertain how to answer her question. It was not in his nature to be dishonest and yet women were so very vain. He didn't want to deal with a weeping female. But this was Fayth Graham, no ordinary female and not prone to fits of tears.

"You will certainly have a large scar . . . as for corruption, we can only wait and see. Sometimes it happens right away, sometimes it happens later."

Her head jerked in a nod. "And if it does?"

"Well . . . if it does, surely you know what must occur."

She gave a thick laugh that sounded choked. "I guess everyone can call me Armless Hugh, then."

Alex didn't know what to say. He reached out to touch her, then quickly withdrew his hand, annoyed with himself. He lay on his back, resting his hands behind his head. He inhaled sharply as the movement pulled on his wound, the pain radiating through his chest and shoulder. He stilled until it subsided, staring into the gloom, resisting the urge to say something more, to offer some comfort.

"What does Gealach mean?"

He started at her soft voice, but answered, "Moon."

"How odd."

"I thought so, too, until I saw it one night, from a distance. The stone the tower is built from is pale and seems to absorb the moon's light. It glows, almost as if it were made from moonstone."

She sighed softly and a whispered word drifted to him, "Beautiful."

"There is a story that says the tower was built by an Irish prince in order to find his way back to his love."

He fell silent, waiting to see if she would ask to hear more. She was quiet and Alex felt a pang of disappointment. He shouldn't be doing this anyway, talking such foolishness with her. He liked her far too much already.

"Yes?" came the hesitant word.

Alex smiled. "The prince was sailing to Scotland, to visit his uncle, the king of Galloway—"

"The king of Galloway? That must have been a very long time ago, indeed."

"Aye, indeed. Anyway, the prince's ship was struck by a storm—"

"Did the prince have a name?"

"Huh?" Alex raised his head to look at her, but she still faced away.

"His name? Surely he was the prince of something and had a name, at that."

"It's just a tale, Fayth."

"Still, he must have a name."

Alex sighed. "Prince . . . Shanahan, aye? That's a good

Irish name. And he was prince of all Eire. Now, may I proceed?"

"Yes."

"Now, a storm struck Prince Shanahan's ship and everyone perished save the prince. He was washed up on the Mull of Galloway. A young maid found him and brought him home. She nursed him back to health and they fell in love. But he was the prince, after all, and must marry a princess, not a commoner. So he built her a tower, from the most beautiful stone he could find, right there on the coast. He promised to come to her once a year."

Fayth snorted. "Stupid girl."

Alex quirked an eyebrow, amused. "After a year had passed, Prince Shanahan could not wait to return to his love. He'd married the ugly Irish girl his father chose for him but he thought of nothing but his Scottish lass."

"What was her name?"

"Umm . . . Firtha."

"No, I don't like that."

"Bonny, then?"

"Very well."

"So the prince set sail for his Bonny, bringing her great riches to prove his love and devotion."

Fayth snorted again.

"Unfortunately, a thick fog descended and he lost his way. Poor Bonny thought he had abandoned her, that he found another. So she cast herself from the battlements to the rocks below. But on the sea, the fog finally cleared and lo! The moon shone on the tower, making it glow like a beacon. He sailed into the secret cove and unloaded his treasure. But then he learned of his beloved's demise and joined her, throwing himself into the sea."

"I don't like that story."

"Aye, well . . . The villagers say their spirits haunt the

beaches, forever seeking each other, and the treasure has never been found, though many have searched."

"Have you looked?" Fayth asked.

"Ah . . . a bit, aye."

Yet another snort. She was most unladylike in her derision.

Alex scanned the sky. He'd been able to see the moon earlier, but the fog obscured it now. He remembered when he'd held her by the burn and had seen the moon shining in her eyes. He wondered what she was thinking. Did she think about the story or something else? About her own lost love? He didn't know why he should care. He tried very hard not to care. His eyes burned from the fever, so he closed them, resolving to think on her no more.

9

SHOUTING SLOWLY PENETRATED the haze of sleep. Fayth's entire body throbbed. It began in her arm, a deep, angry pulsing, and engulfed the rest of her body. The shouting grew louder. Her head was stuffed with straw. She couldn't think, couldn't understand what was happening. Couldn't even remember where she was, or why.

She heard Ridley's voice and panicked, trying desperately to wake, to rise and run, but found movement impossible. He'd found her. She'd never escape him. But then arms were around her, lifting her. And the voice, soothing her. Yes, she knew this man and it wasn't Ridley. Though he claimed he was trying to be gentle, she was jolted about and cried out several times.

She tried to open her eyes, but they burned terribly. "What's happening?" she asked. Her voice sounded far away and she wondered if she'd even spoken aloud.

They were moving. She was on a horse. Her hand curled, but held no reins. The arms were still around her.

"Grahams and Carlisles are nearby. My scouts sighted them. We must move."

Fayth forced her eyes open, found herself staring into a handsome face. It was scarred and furred with whiskers, but still quite beautiful and comfortingly familiar. Her throbbing arm was pressed between their bodies. She clutched at him with her good hand. "Please don't let them get me. Please." The effort was too much and she closed her eyes, her fingers slipping from his leather jack.

His voice cut through the encroaching darkness. "I won't."

"Promise me."

"I promise."

She somehow knew this man would not break a promise and so allowed herself to drift, relieved to let him handle it now. It was too much, worrying about Ridley and trying to remember where she was and who this man was that held her. The motion of the horse, however, was too violent to allow for thought, and soon she was moaning, holding herself stiff to contain the pain. Her entire world centered on the pulsing in her arm.

The man was breathing hard. Fayth's cheek rested against his chest and it heaved with effort.

"We've got to stop," the man yelled.

"Can't," someone else called back.

"It's too much for . . . him."

"Then leave him. He's dead already."

The movement stopped. "There's a cave not far. I'm going there."

"Damn it, Alex, at least take him to Gealach. There's women there to tend him. He's not worth getting killed over."

"He'll die before we get there. Send Davie back with supplies."

The horse was moving again. *Alex. Alex.* The other man had addressed her protector as Alex. She did know an Alex, of that she was certain. The name brought forth the image of dark hair and eyes, of arms embracing her. Tales of princes and fair maidens, living in far-off moon towers. The scent of leather and sweat and whisky. Yes, she knew him well. This comforted her and she stopped struggling for clear thought. He would take care of her.

She was jostled about some more, then she realized faintly they were no longer on the horse. He carried her, an arm under her knees, another curled under her back, cradling her against his chest. Cold, damp air enveloped her. She shivered, though her skin was on fire. He laid her down and his arms slipped away.

"No." She reached blindly for him, her eyes wrenching open. She caught his arm, but her fingers were weak and awkward and slipped away.

He didn't leave. He knelt beside her. "I'll be back."

"Don't go," she said. Her voice was thin and raspy, her breath hot across dry lips.

"I must fetch water. I'll only be gone a moment—"

"No!"

He hesitated, then sat beside her, taking her hand. "I'm here, lass. I'll not leave."

"You didn't leave me back there. They told you to."

He said nothing. Her burning eyes watered but she kept them open, gazing at him. Everything was so woolly in her head, so confusing. But he had stayed with her and that was her anchor. He understood what she did not. He would see to everything. That was enough for her.

They were in a dark place, but light originated from somewhere she couldn't determine. Enough light to see his face. Dark, reddish hair hung loose, sliding over his shoulders. His eyes were dark blue, deep as midnight. His jaw was shadowed with whiskers. His eyes were on her as well, studying her face. The thick reddish lashes fell. He pressed his eyes closed and sighed deeply, as if exhausted.

There was a flush to his skin. She untangled her fingers from his and touched him. The moment her hand pressed against his skin, his eyes sprang open. Her fingers were pale against his face. She'd expected his skin to be cool, soothing against her hot palm, but he was as hot as she was.

"You're ill?" she said.

He shook his head. "It's nothing."

There was something she had to tell him but she couldn't recall what. Something he'd done . . . or she'd done. She couldn't remember. His hand covered hers, holding it against his cheek.

"Davie'd better get here quick."

"Davie . . . ?"

"Aye, the healer. Remember?"

She should remember and she tried . . . Davie . . . Davie . . . ? She shook her head.

He frowned, concerned. "Let me get you water. It will cool the fever." He took her hand from his cheek and tried to lay it across her belly, but she wouldn't let go, tangling her fingers with his. He clasped her hand between both of his and leaned down, so his face was close to hers. "Listen to me, Fayth. I will be right back. I vow it."

She thought she might cry for fear of being alone in this strange, confusing place.

His hands tightened almost painfully on hers. "I've never known you to be a coward, lass. Dinna start now. I need your strength."

The tears and the desperation receded. Yes, he did know her. She could be strong for him. She nodded her head, licking her dry and cracking lips. "I won't be afraid—so long as you come back."

"Nothing could keep me from you."

His eyes transfixed her, she couldn't look away. He stayed that way, gazing down at her. She waited for him to leave, but he didn't. One hand came up, the fingers brushed across her forehead, pushed the cap off her head. Then he leaned forward and pressed a lingering kiss against her hot skin.

The air left her. She squeezed his hand, wanting him to kiss her again. She knew this. His smell, his touch. That's how she knew him. Her prince in the moon tower. They'd kissed. Did that make her a fair maiden? He started to draw away, but she turned her head, lifted her neck slightly, her lips brushing the corner of his mouth.

"Kiss me," she whispered, her hand squeezing, her eyes begging.

"You're not well," he whispered, so close she felt his breath caress her. "You know not what you're saying."

"I know you," she said. "I know this."

He drew back enough to search her eyes. "The fever has clouded your mind."

"Perhaps it has clouded yours."

One corner of his mouth tilted, but he did not kiss her.

"If I die—"

"You'll not die," he said fiercely, and lowered his head, his lips brushing hers, gently. She touched his face again and he deepened the kiss, his hand sliding beneath her head, his fingers hot against her neck. Yes, yes, she knew his taste, his feel. Craved it. He must be her husband, or her lover. Her moon prince.

Her tongue darted out, stroking his bottom lip. He groaned, but the sound was swallowed by their mouths, joined in a kiss so deep it touched something inside her, set it to quivering. She gripped his hair, urging him closer, but he pulled away, gently prying her fingers loose.

"I'd better get that water," he said hoarsely, "afore we both turn to ash."

Alex's hands shook as he fumbled with the laces securing his water skin to Bear's saddle. After carrying Fayth for the past two hours his shoulder throbbed. His head was beginning to ache in time with his shoulder. He pressed his forehead against Bear's withers, trying to collect his thoughts. After a moment he worked at the laces again, finally freeing the water skin. It was nearly empty. He needed more water—now—before he was beyond such simple tasks as fetching water. He prayed Davie would return soon. He had not thought his wound would fester, had thought it was mending and so had refused the healer's attempts to fuss with it.

He slid a hand inside his jack, touching his shoulder. The linen was damp. He pulled his hand away and inspected his fingers. Blood. Perhaps he'd only pulled the stitches loose. And perhaps there was seepage mixed with the blood. Corruption.

He bit down on his lip, willing away a sickening wave of dizziness. He must not succumb to the fever, to the delirium. He was stronger than Fayth, and she needed him, or she would die. He pushed away from the horse and scanned the area around the cave. He knew this place. There was a burn not far, if he could only remember which direction. Fog obscured everything. The raw edge of panic gripped him. He knew the west march, could find his way in the thickest fog, the deepest night. This disorientation frightened him.

Alex closed his eyes, envisioning this patch of forest in the daylight. There was a faint trail, to his right, left by animals. He opened his eyes and started forward. He couldn't discern a trail, but kept moving. Soon he heard the faint gurgle of water and he ran, relieved. He slipped down an embankment, lost his footing, and splashed into the water.

The freezing water stole his breath. He gasped, crawling from the stream. He shivered on the bank, trying to catch his breath. The water had braced him, cleared his head. Fayth. Alone in the cave. He quickly filled the skin and picked his way back through the forest.

Bear was at the cave entrance, his head inside, brown tail swishing anxiously. Alex pushed the horse aside, ducking to enter. The ceiling was low; he couldn't stand straight. But he'd placed her near the entrance. Wolf was there, sitting by Fayth's side. She stood when Alex entered, wagging her tail joyfully.

"Biddy?" Fayth said, her hand on the dog's side. Then her eyes found Alex, fever bright and fearful. He was undone by her wobbly smile, the relief in her face at his return. He sank to his knees beside her.

"Here, drink." He slid his hand beneath her neck, tilting her head to take the water. She drank deeply, some of it running down her neck. Several strips of linen secured Fayth's arm to her side. Alex removed one of the linens and soaked it in water, wiping the cloth over her face and neck. Her cheeks were flushed, her eyes red.

"Stay," she said.

He stretched out beside her. She lay her head on his wounded shoulder. He gritted his teeth until the pain subsided. He stared at the ceiling as Wolf—or Biddy, as Fayth called the dog—settled down beside him, and prayed Davie would not be long.

Alex didn't know how long he'd been sleeping. His entire shoulder throbbed with a dull sickening pulse, in time with the pounding of his head. He groaned, trying to roll over, but something pinned him to the ground. He raised his head, squinting. Sunlight streamed through the cave's opening. A cloud of red-brown curls rested on his shoulder.

Alex dropped his head back down. His saddle was beneath his head. He didn't remember doing that. That wasn't good. But he knew why he was here. He'd come here because Fayth could not be moved. She was mindless with the fever from her wound. He was waiting for Davie.

His eyes burned and he knew she wasn't the only one boiling with fever, but his wits were still intact and that was a good sign. He needed to tend her. Feed her, give her water, dress her wound.

With great effort he eased himself to sitting, moving her gently off his shoulder and resting her head on a rolled-up blanket. His stomach roiled and the pounding in his skull nearly blinded him. When his head cleared, he leaned over her, checking her color. She'd been so pale, before. Now she was flushed, her lips dry and cracked. He pressed the back of his hand to her cheek and drew back at the heat. She moaned softly, fidgeting, her brow creasing.

He reached for the water skin, pleased to find it full. He must've filled it last night. He slid a hand beneath her neck.

"Wake, lass," he said, holding the mouth of the water skin to her lips. She tried to turn her head away until he tipped it. Water spilled over her lips, running down her chin. Her eyes came open and then she was drinking, greedy, gasping for breath.

"Slow it down," he murmured, pulling the skin away.

She swallowed and grimaced. "More." Her voice was raspy, raw, her fevered gaze fixed on his. He gave her a bit more, then set it aside. He laid her head back on the blanket.

"Let me change your dressings, then we'll eat something, aye?"

She nodded, her eyes never leaving his face.

The sleeve had been ripped off her shirt, so it didn't impede efforts to monitor the wound. The dressing was stained with fresh blood. He kept his face impassive as he gently unwound the linen. She gasped, her breath shuddering in and out, but never cried out, or told him to stop. He saw, when the wound was exposed, that the bleeding had stopped and the stitches held. It was merely seeping. It was swollen and red, but the seepage was clear and didn't smell. That was good. Of course, it was early, the wound could still corrupt. He didn't know if or when it should be amputated and wished fervently for Davie.

He had no wine so he poured water over it and dried it with a clean cloth. As he rewrapped it, she said, "Why are you doing this?"

"Doing what?"

"Taking care of me. Dressing my wound."

"Someone has to." He tied it off and met her gaze. "And I'm afraid I'm all you've got right now."

"Red Alex is all I've got." She shook her head slowly, her eyes drifting shut.

Obviously she'd regained her mind, if she knew who he was. He supposed there was little chance now of coaxing another kiss from her. Ah well . . . He hoped she wouldn't become uncooperative—not that there was much she could do, other than be unpleasant.

When he turned to rummage through his bags he noticed the pile of hares in the corner and grimaced. He scanned the interior of the cave, but Wolf was nowhere to be found. Probably hunting up more food. The dog was highly obedient, but there were some things he had no way of communicating, such as, a pile of rotting animal carcasses didn't help matters.

His body protesting, he dragged the hares out, knowing Wolf would drag them back when she returned. Fayth watched him with a dull, glassy stare. Outside the cave the air was cool, but the sun had burned away the fog. He heard a rustling and turned. Bear burst from the trees at a trot, head shaking, vocalizing his displeasure at this extended stop.

Alex scratched the horse's nose, wondering how long they would be safe here. The Grahams might follow Skelley and the others, but then Skelley might have lost them. In that case, they could come back this way.

Alex sent Bear back into the trees and returned to the cave. He had nothing to feed Fayth but dried meat and oats. He didn't think meat would set well on her stomach, but he had no fire to make the oatcakes. With a grunt of pain, he got to his feet again.

"Where are you going now?" She attempted to roll on her side, her eyes wide.

He paused, surprised by her panic. "To gather wood and start a fire. You must eat and I canna make you an oatcake without a fire."

She lay back, her face and body going slack. She gave him a shaky nod.

He returned to find her watching the cave entrance intently, but her gaze followed him as he built the fire.

"I'll not leave you, lass," he assured her, glancing at her as he struck the flint.

"Why not?"

He shook his head. "Can you not see past my surname to the man trying to help you?"

"Yes, I can. But I don't understand it."

"Here's what I don't understand." The fire was crackling and he sat back on his heels, turning to look at her. "Why such a bonny lass would mask it with breeks?"

She smirked, a measure of her old self returning. "You wouldn't understand, because you're a man."

"Try me."

She eyed him suspiciously, then said, "Because men don't see me when I wear skirts."

Alex made a face of disbelief. "Oh, I don't know about that. I saw you fair well that night at Annancreag." He remembered that night, and her, vividly. Never had a lass roused him so deeply.

"That's just what I mean," she said, looking away from him finally, turning her face to the wall. "All you saw was a potential bedmate."

He felt hotter suddenly and was momentarily glad for his fever, to hide the blush. "Very well then, what is it you want others to see when they look at you?"

Her shoulder moved in a shrug. "I want to be spoken to as a person. Not ordered about, like an empty-headed child."

Alex said nothing for a time, contemplating her words as he mixed oats with water and spread the mixture on a greased iron plate. He held it over the fire. He had no response for her statement. He had no sisters and though his father had adored his mother, he had not treated her with the same regard as he did men. This troubled Alex. For his mother had been a fine woman. Intelligent, pious, kind. And she had been content in the role God made for her. This vision of womanhood collided with Alex's own experience with others' expectations. He'd once been destined for another life. A life his mother and father planned with great hope and pride. And he had been unable to conform to their vision of him.

So lost was he in his thoughts that her soft voice startled him. He stilled as she spoke.

"When I was very small . . . five, mayhap, I used to follow my father and brothers everywhere. They delighted in my presence—well, at least my father did. I'm but a year younger than Wesley, so he didn't begin to mind me until the differences between us became clear and then even he was uneasy with them, as I was. One day I was told that I shouldn't follow them when they trained or hunted . . . that it didn't become a gentlewoman."

Alex turned toward her, his boots grinding in the dirt floor, and removed the oatcakes from the fire. She didn't look at him. She was on her back, staring into the darkness above her.

"I ignored them at first. But soon my father sent me away. It was clear I . . . embarrassed him." Her cheeks, already ruddy from fever, flushed further. "I was very angry and envious of my brothers, of all the men able to be with Papa all day. And they did it because they were men—for no other reason!" She looked at Alex then, her eyes flashing with old indignation, mouth thinned. "And I was expected to sit upstairs and sew . . . and learn other such feminine things while they rode and hunted and became warriors." She looked upward again, exhaling loudly. "It seemed so unfair. So, one day, I borrowed some of Wesley's clothes and joined them in the training yard. Papa and Wesley recognized me at once."

"Did they punish you?"

She shook her head, smiling. "Papa laughed and Wesley, though he tried to appear disapproving, was glad to have me back. Papa thought it clever of me and wanted to see if the other men could tell. So he allowed me to stay."

"And no one ever knew?"

Her smile turned down slightly. "Ridley discovered me and tried to ruin it. But I became different, you see . . ." She chewed her lips thoughtfully. "These men, who had teased me and made jests, treated me different. They . . . *saw* me. They offered me advice, taught me to shoot a crossbow, to wield a sword, fight with a dirk."

Alex contemplated her in the muted light. "Do you wish, then, to be a man?"

She darted him a dark look. "I ken your meaning, I've heard it enough before. The answer is no. I wish to be a woman, but one who is seen."

"But nothing of womanhood interests you."

"That's not what I said." She sighed. "I don't know why I expect you to understand."

He wanted to protest. He did understand, but he would not give her that. Not now, not yet. Perhaps not ever.

He thought she was finished with him but she said, "It was a trial. Don't you see?"

"A trial?"

"Papa wanted to prove that I couldn't do it. That I couldn't pass as a boy and that I lacked skill and strength. And courage." From the jut of her jaw she was challenging him also to proclaim her inadequacy.

"You showed them, eh?"

"I did." She grinned to herself. "None of the men knew any different . . . except Jack . . ." She flashed Alex an obscure look, her mouth flattening.

Alex held her gaze, unwavering. Would she ask him what happened to her lover? Would he tell her? It was best if she continued to believe he was responsible.

But instead she looked down at her hands and said, "Jack kept his mouth shut. They all saw how well I did. Papa couldn't send me away after that."

"You must be miserable when you're not proving a point, aye?"

She scowled at him, but he saw the pull at the corner of her mouth as she fought a smile. Her oatcake was cool and he brought it to her.

"Can you feed yourself, or shall I?"

She took it from him, avoiding meeting his gaze, and her fingers brushed his. She jerked away, crumbling the oatcake down the front of her.

"Here. Have mine."

She tried to take it from him, but he held it out of reach.

"Nay, you obviously don't know your strength, Hugh, let me."

She colored furiously. "I knew I shouldn't have told you anything! Now you'll never stop teasing me!"

He merely smiled and held it to her mouth. She averted her head, mouth thinned mutinously.

"Prefer you to starve? Really, even men must eat."

Her smile was pure sarcasm. She leaned forward and took an enormous bite from the oatcake. He refrained from any further jests, pleased she was eating. He relinquished the oatcake. After she finished, and refused his offer to make her another, he put the small sack of oats away.

"Aren't you going to eat?"

He shrugged. "Later. I'm not so hungry." He handed her the water skin.

She drank, never taking her eyes from him. "Why are you doing this?"

He feigned confusion, standing and walking to the entrance of the cave. "If you feel better today, we'll set out for Gealach in the morn."

She was silent and when he glanced back she stared at him.

"I guess I owe you now, too."

He raised a brow in question.

"It seems like everyone owes you their life."

An ember popped. Alex thought about what it would be like to have her beholden to him. But she was like Patrick, loath to be in anyone's debt and eager to give recompense so she could be through with them.

Alex shook his head. "Nay, lass, you owe me naught."

"How did you save Laine?"

Alex turned to face her. "I cannot tell you that."

"He's Lord Carlisle's son. The one from the monastery."

"You've been talking to Diana." Alex didn't know why the thought filled him with dread.

"A bit, yes." Her smile was enigmatic, little more than a

deepening of dimples. Then she frowned. "How did they hurt him?"

Alex shook his head. He couldn't speak of it—Laine had made him swear—but even if he could, it was not talk for women's ears.

"What about Eliot?" she asked.

He resumed his seat beside her and leaned his elbow on his knee. "Eliot is my cousin. He's a year older than I. We were the youngest bairns in the family and always begging to hunt with my father and uncles and brothers. When finally they said aye, Eliot and I were determined to slay a great beast, a dragon or some such."

"Dragons?" She tried to sit up, but couldn't.

She was so very weak. An odd fist closed around Alex's heart as he watched her struggles. He took the saddle and blanket and arranged them so she could lean back. She did gratefully, a sheen of sweat on her forehead and lip from the exertion.

"Dragons?" she repeated. She didn't look terribly interested in his tale, but he sensed she needed to occupy her mind.

"Aye. We were verra young. We had no business out there with men, but my father and uncle thought it was never too soon to teach a lad to hunt."

"Did you save him from a dragon?"

"No, a boar."

Fayth raised her brows in surprise.

"Aye, I know. You rarely see them anymore, they weren't so plentiful then, either, though they were to be had. Anyway, we were becoming bored, as the others had all made kills and we were missing even the toads with our wee bows. We wandered away in our search for mice and birds. We heard grunting and growling, and realized right away what it was."

"Oh no," Fayth said, genuinely horrified.

Alex hesitated, then continued. "Aye, we decided to pursue it. We had great visions of Cook roasting it with an apple in its mouth and all the men slapping our backs and praising our great skill. It was rooting about in a thicket. It was my idea to block its exits. Eliot got off the first shot. Rather than run away, the boar charged at him." Alex shook his head. "It tore him up."

Fayth's hand was over her mouth, her question muffled. "You killed it?"

Alex nodded. "Aye. I was too scared to even shoot my bow, so I took after it with my dirk." Alex sighed, still feeling the regret after all these years. "But I wasn't quick enough. Eliot still lost his arm."

"But he lived."

"Aye."

Alex stared out into the daylight, recalling Eliot after losing his arm. He'd not been angry or bitter. He'd thanked Alex for saving his life, though Alex had been filled with remorse that he'd not been quick enough. And they'd gone on. Eliot had learned to do nearly everything he could do with two hands with one. When Alex had been sent to Dunfermline, it was Eliot, and sometimes Patrick, who visited him, sneaking in whisky and candles, books, warm underclothes—things which were eventually discovered and cost him dearly in beatings and the other vile forms of punishment monks devised in their solitude. The more Alex thought on it, the harder it was to determine exactly when Eliot changed.

Alex slowly became aware that Fayth stared at him, unblinking, chewing an already ragged thumbnail.

"If you're still hungry, I can come up with something, I'm sure."

She gave him a narrow look and dropped her hand in her lap, balling it into a fist.

"I know how you and Eliot felt . . . wanting to make your father proud."

"Aye?"

Her cheeks flushed, a lovely bloom of color, as if she wished she hadn't spoken.

"Did your dragon hunt win your father's approval?"

"Well . . . no, and I was quite a bit older than you were."

When she seemed disinclined to continue Alex prompted her, "Come now, I told you my dragon slaying story, now you must tell me yours."

"There's not much to tell, really. It was a year or so ago. Papa had just started allowing me to go on raids with him and Wesley—" She stopped at the look of horror on Alex's face. "If you're going to do that, I won't tell the story at all."

Alex forced a look of polite interest. Hugh Graham took his daughter raiding? Good God!

She settled back into her story. "He only took me on small raids, ones he was sure there was little chance of a skirmish. We were raiding the Musgraves—they'd recently stolen from Papa a hundred kine, his best horse, five sleuth dogs and an ox—when they ambushed us. Papa told me to ride away. I protested and begged him to let me stay." Her mouth tightened, her gaze on her hands which twisted the frayed ends of his wool rug. "In front of everyone he became furious and threatened to use his belt on my arse if I didn't go home."

Alex refrained from shouting, *Good for him!* and tried to look properly sympathetic.

"I was humiliated. He sent Jack with me, to see me home safe. The Musgraves pursued us, but we got away. On the way we passed Ned Storey's tower. The tower looked deserted and no one was watching the sheep penned just outside the barmkin." She grinned, her eyes sparkling with mischief. "So we took them."

"And Jack didn't try to stop you? Didn't he have orders to see you home safely?"

Her smile faded and she gave him a sharp look. "No, Jack never tried to tell me what to do."

He waited for the accusations to fly. She'd accused him of murdering Jack before and she'd been quite passionate about it. But she kept her peace with an obvious struggle. She must feel beholden to him, he decided, for she didn't seem one to hold her tongue.

"Anyway," she said with emphasis and a warning look, *Stop interrupting!* "Papa's raid was a failure. They came away with naught and lost two men. He was so surprised to see the sheep—you should have seen his face!" She wasn't with him now, her eyes shining, looking within. "Before that night, he'd not talked about me much. He told everyone about my raid. He made me tell him the story over and over, then nagged at Jack. And when he became very ill, just before he died and would drink too much, he would tell the story to anyone who would listen."

She smirked suddenly, coming back to him. "Ridley hated the story. You should have seen his face curl up into itself every time Papa would start telling it."

Alex laughed, delighted with the story. He'd loved his father's regard as well, though it seemed he'd felt it a good deal more than she had, so he could understand her pride.

They smiled at each other for a moment, then her smile turned to a troubled frown and she looked away. "I don't understand you. What do you want from me?"

"I want Gealach," Alex said, disappointed the warm moment had to end. "If I have you, Carlisle cannot marry you. It's that simple."

"Carlisle can't marry me if I'm dead, either. So again, why are you doing this?"

"Carlisle won't be eager to do business with his betrothed's murderer. This will be a legal transaction, completed by our solicitors. There will be no question that Gealach is mine."

"I see." She looked down at the blanket draped across her legs. "Well, that certainly makes sense."

Alex watched her curiously. What had she expected him to say? The truth? Not likely. And yet what he told her *was* the truth. At least it had been in the beginning. Maybe even that was a lie, because he'd wanted her since the first moment he'd seen her. He still wanted her, yet now he didn't know what he would do with her if she ever said aye—a more unlikely event he could not imagine.

He was staring at the cave opening when he sensed her moving toward him. He looked at her sharply. Her eyes were fixed on his gaping shirt front, her hand reaching toward his chest. Alex froze, eyebrows raised. What the hell was she doing? And where did she get the strength? She was obviously determined to do something and he didn't try to stop her until her hand curled about the bead that hung from a leather string around his neck. She tried to jerk it off, but he caught her wrist.

Her eyes snared his, her face damp with sweat. "Where did you get this?" Her voice harsh, angry.

She didn't release the bead and he kept hold of her wrist. "Let go."

"No. Give it to me—it's not yours."

"It's not yours either."

Her lips thinned and he knew the strain of her awkward position was draining her. But she was nothing if not tenacious and tried to yank it off again.

Gently, Alex pried her fingers loose and forced her back down. Her eyes remained fixed on the bead, now swinging forward from his shirt.

"That's Mona's bead. Where did you get it?"

"I found it at Graham Keep, in Lady Graham's chambers." Before she could ask what he was doing rifling through her stepmother's chambers, he said, "Ridley invited us to search the keep, remember? Rob was sure he hid Caroline and Patrick, and indeed, Patrick had been kept in the dungeons for nigh on a year."

"But they were gone," Fayth said. "So you stole an enchanted stone?"

Alex smiled, taking the bead between his fingers to look at it. "Hardly enchanted . . . it's a landmark."

Her brow furrowed, but she remained silent.

"It was in the small leather sack, along with the lock of Patrick's hair and nail parings."

Fayth's eyebrows raised.

"Now you see why I say she bewitched him?"

"I suppose . . . but why the bead?"

"Your stepmother knows Ridley wants the Clachan Fala and she is but a lone woman. What if she put a spell on my brother to protect her?"

Fayth looked down, plucking at the rug, trying to hide her annoyed amusement.

"Are you saying Mona Graham is not a witch? She is a Musgrave, after all. They are reputed to be the keepers."

"Yes, yes, I've heard all that before."

"Then explain it to me."

She shrugged. "I can't. All I can say is, if Mona really could do magic, she would have turned Ridley, or my father, for that matter, into a toad a long time ago. And if she could bewitch men, surely she could *un*bewitch them."

"Unbewitch? What mean you?"

"Well, Ridley is obsessed by her. It's unnatural. She has long tried to stop his nonsense, but he only grows more . . . infatuated with her."

Alex was thoughtful. "Then perhaps she paid him. All I know is they escaped Graham Keep together and neither has turned up. It is unlike Patrick not to visit between wanderings and tell us where he is headed next." His fist closed over the bead. "And this was in her chambers along with his hair and nails. What else could it all mean?"

"How do you know it's a landmark?"

"Have you been north? To the Highlands?"

Fayth shook her head.

"There are standing stones everywhere, more than on the borders. Do you see the unusual shape of this? It looks like a bead, but it's not, it's merely a stone with a hole in it. There is a group of stones, all of them are similar, some with clefts, some with holes. But see the markings? I think it's a marker and the Clachan Fala is buried there. Or it reveals another clue about its location. I would have investigated it already, but then I learned about your betrothal to Carlisle . . . and well, I had to take care of Gealach first."

Fayth gave him an obscure look. "If there really is a Blood Stone and you found it, Ridley would give you the deed—anything you wanted . . . in exchange for the stone."

Alex returned her look, frowning. "Just what are you suggesting, lass?"

Her skin was pale from her earlier exertion, but a feverish light—having nothing to do with her wound—lit her eyes. "Go get it! Don't you see? Ridley wants it because he believes it will make him unstoppable."

Alex snorted. "Impossible."

"It is said that the Blood Stone will protect whomever holds it from harm. If you possess it, he could never take your tower."

Alex smiled patiently. "Let's just suppose, for a moment, that's true. It would protect the bearer from harm, but his home could still fall down about his ears and all his men could still be slain before his eyes."

She sighed, shaking her head as if he were thick.

"I thought you didn't believe in it?"

"I don't—but Ridley does. If he even thought you possessed it, he would be wary of you—perhaps even leave you alone."

Alex didn't reply, still fingering the bead. She made a persuasive argument, but still, Alex didn't believe Ridley was that stupid.

She lay back against the rolled-up blanket and closed her eyes. "Think about it, Alex."

Alex. She had never addressed him with such familiarity. He stared at her a long time, eyes narrowed, but she didn't say another word and eventually fell into a fitful sleep.

By evening, the fever, which had abated during the long hours of the day, took hold of Fayth again. Alex himself felt trapped in a nightmare, his mind thick and sluggish. When the howls of wolves filled the night, Fayth shook in her sleep. Wolf returned to guard the cave's entrance, the fur on her neck bristling.

Alex didn't know what to do, couldn't recall how to treat a fever. It seemed he'd once known and the knowledge was still there, hovering on the edges of his memory, just out of grasp. He wrapped her snug in a blanket, then held her when she still shook so violently her teeth chattered.

She woke several times, her gaze darting fearfully around the cave until resting on him. It had been nearly ten years since Alex last prayed but he found the long forgotten words and whispered them until he fell into an exhausted sleep.

10

SKELLEY CRASHED THROUGH the forest, spurs digging into his horse's sides when it balked at the terrain. He had Davie, of course, but he'd also brought Eliot and Laine, the former for his sword arm and the latter because, with Alex absent, the lad was like an appendage. Grinding his teeth with frustration, Skelley searched the trees around him, looking for a familiar landmark. It wasn't the first time Skelley wished for Alex's innate sense of direction. To Skelley much of the bogs and forests of the marches looked the same regardless of the weather.

The sky had been boiling with a storm since they'd left Gealach. Skelley had wasted no time gathering everything they would need: food, blankets, fresh linens, water, Davie's wee box of herbs, a horse litter, and two extra horses. It wasn't until they had set out again that Skelley began to worry they might need two litters, for Alex had been unwell when they'd left him.

They'd been traveling one day and so far the storm remained no more than a threat. But now that they were almost there it looked as if their luck was changing. Thunder shook the heavens. Though it was afternoon, it looked more like dusk, but the lightning cracking the sky lit the path ahead of them.

"I'm telling ye," Eliot was saying, as he had been for the past two days. "We should kill the little bastard when we get there. This whole business stinks like a dunghill."

Skelley ignored him, though Laine gave the one-armed outlaw an angry, tight-lipped glare.

"I'll knock that look off yer face, ye gutless fart," Eliot said, raising his hand as though to hit Laine.

"That's enough!" Skelley shouted, reining his horse in. "The boy may be kin, Eliot."

Eliot snorted derisively. He yanked on his horse's reins, bringing it right up to Skelley's so their withers nearly touched. "What is wrong wi' ye, man? Ye've been with Red Alex, what? Five years? Seven? Every time he gets an itch in his arse we've got to take up wi' weans and half-wits?" He waved a hand at Laine and Davie. "He treats his lice better than us."

"If you dinna like it," Skelley said, his fists clenching in anger, "you can leave."

"Aye, so that Hugh bastard can take me share of land? I think not." Eliot leveled an evil look at Laine. "I canna understand his fondness for laddies. Methinks he's turned sodomite."

"Goddamn you!" Laine drew his sword and rode forward. "You'll take that back or I'll give you two stumps!"

A smile spread across Eliot's face, but before he could speak the sky sent down a torrent. Skelley adjusted his bonnet so the water streamed off the metal brim, keeping his vision clear. He was profoundly annoyed that the conflict that had been simmering below the surface for months was erupting now.

"Enough of your squabbling!" Skelley shouted to be

heard over the storm. "You can take up yer grievances with Alex when we find him."

"We must stop," Eliot said. "At least until the rain lets up."

"What if the Grahams found them?" Laine asked, still wielding his sword.

Skelley gestured for the lad to sheathe his blade.

"Then we're too late already," Eliot said.

Laine's hand still gripped his sword hilt. "You'd like that, wouldn't you?"

Skelley shook his head, wishing they'd shut up and trying to remember which way the cave was. Davie rode ahead, pointing, and the rest followed.

Eliot kept his mount beside Skelley, letting out the line for the horse he led so it wasn't between them. "What if we arrive at the cave and find Alex dead? What then?"

"We'll talk about that when it happens."

Eliot leaned close, black eyes burning. "Know this. As his nearest kin, Gealach is mine. And Alex's precious little varlet can be buried wi' him."

Skelley straight-armed Eliot right out of his saddle. He dropped into the mud with a splash. Skelley flexed his hand, ready to lay into him again. He'd been itching to do that for years.

Laine looked between Skelley and Eliot, wide-eyed. Davie reined in a few feet away, blocking the frightened horse's escape and capturing the lead. His pale eyes were devoid of warmth or expression.

Skelley kicked his horse forward so it pranced around the fallen Eliot. "By God, man, I've heard enough! You can be sure Alex will get an earful when we return. We have no use for knaves in our ranks. And if you lay a finger on Hugh, I'll kill ye meself."

"He's a thief and a liar and has caused naught but trouble since we found him."

"You're a thief! And that lad is Red Alex's nephew. I'll not hear of harming him!"

Eliot snorted derisively, swiping the blood and rain from his mouth. "Nephew! Ye believe that drivel? Methinks Alex is turning monk again and favors buggering the pretty lad's bum."

There was a hiss of metal as Laine drew his sword again, eyes blazing. Even Davie rode forward threateningly, his mount stamping the ground too near Eliot's mud hole for comfort. Such slander could not go unanswered, or unpunished, but Alex would be furious if Skelley took matters into his own hands, as he would love to.

"You've gone too far," Skelley said, barely able to speak through his fury. "Get on your horse."

Eliot ran his arm across his mouth, smearing mud across his black beard. It was quickly washed clean by the rain. He held Skelley's eyes for a long moment before nodding and getting to his feet.

Skelley knew this was far from over. Eliot had been a problem for some time, yet Alex was loath to send him away. He'd been a favorite of Red Rowan's and had once been as close to Alex as his own brothers. Alex kept looking for the good in Eliot, giving him chances to redeem himself. But Skelley believed the only kind bones in Eliot's body had been buried with his arm.

Eliot tried to catch his horse, a skittish mount that didn't particularly care for its rider, when an arrow sliced through the air, knocking Skelley's helm from his head. Skelley ducked and shouted, "Go!"

Eliot snagged his horse and tried to mount—a difficult task for a one-armed man at the best of times, no easy task when the horse was temperamental. But Eliot would spurn all offers of help, Skelley knew, so he rode past him. Davie was already gone, but Laine had turned, firing his latch into the forest.

Men burst through the trees and Skelley delayed no longer. With a final shout at Laine to *move,* he spurred his horse forward after Davie.

Laine started after Skelley, looking over his shoulder. Several men surrounded Eliot, who had stopped trying to mount his horse and stood with his one arm held up in surrender. Laine loaded his latch and fired at one of the men. It caught him in the throat, sending him sprawling off his horse in a funnel of blood. Laine's heart was racing. He'd never killed a man before and was sickened, but a fellow rider's life was at stake. Though that life might not be worth saving—or risking his own for—he could not face Red Alex if he didn't try.

Laine drew another bolt to load in his latch, but two men were bearing down on him. He abandoned the latch and unsheathed his sword.

He yanked on his reins, turning his horse to meet the attackers when something caught him across the back. He slumped forward, over the horse's neck. He caught a glimpse of Eliot, facedown in the mud, water plopping all around him, before another blow knocked him from his horse.

When Skelley was certain they were no longer being followed, he stopped. Eliot had definitely been captured or killed. Skelley couldn't say he cared, but knew Alex would not be happy. He waited, heart pounding, for Laine to burst out of the trees behind them. The rain had let up, was now a blanket of mist. Water dripped from branches and leaves. Skelley thrust wet hair off his forehead.

"Come on, lad," he whispered. Skelley turned his head slightly at the sound of Davie's approach. He came up alongside Skelley, placed a hand on his shoulder, and shook his head. Skelley knew he was right. They must go on. Alex needed them.

Skelley looked over his shoulder one last time before following Davie into the trees. They had lost the extra horses, the litter, most of the supplies and two men, but at least Skelley still had Davie and his wee box—that was something.

And Davie seemed to know the way, which was a relief to Skelley, who feared he was well lost. Davie picked his way around the jagged rocks protruding from the ground, Skelley close behind. He stopped and dismounted. Skelley followed, surprised to see the entrance to a small cave, hidden among the brush and trees. Davie had already disappeared inside. Skelley hobbled the horses and turned only to give a bark of surprise when confronted with Bear. The massive horse bobbed his head, nudging Skelley's shoulder, pushing him toward the cave.

"I'm going!"

The silence from the cave made Skelley uneasy. He ducked his head and entered. It took a moment for his eyes to adjust to the gloom. Davie had lit several candles and situated them around the edge of the cave. He knelt in front of his pack, rummaging through it. Skelley walked over to the two lumps against the wall, his legs stiff with fear. Wolf lay beside them. She lifted her head and whined, then lay it down again. There was a pile of dead hares in the corner, covered with flies and stinking horribly.

They must be dead. Skelley had taken too long. He had ridden as hard as he could, but it had still taken nearly three days to get to Gealach and back. Too long.

Davie returned to the two bodies on the floor, urging Wolf aside. The dog went to the pile of hares and sniffed at it, disturbing the black cloud that clung to it. Davie rolled the largest lump—Alex—onto his back. Alex moaned and tried to roll away. Skelley let out a sigh of relief and hurried forward to lend assistance.

Davie unhooked the jack and Skelley helped him peel Alex out of it.

"Alex!" Skelley said loudly. He pressed a hand against his friend's face. It was hot and dry. "Alexander Maxwell!"

Alex opened his eyes. "Skelley . . ." His gaze moved to Davie, then he jerked and struggled to sit up. "Fayth . . . Fayth . . ."

Skelley glanced at Davie, but he didn't seem to think this ranting was odd. Of course, Davie seemed to find nothing odd . . . or amusing, or vexing. Skelley reckoned Alex was delirious and tried to hold him down. But Alex was unexpectedly powerful and threw him off. He pushed himself onto his elbow and leaned over the form beside him.

"Take care of her first, Davie." He sat up, his eyes surprisingly clear, and gestured to the other lump.

Skelley frowned and finally got a good look at what he'd thought was the body of Hugh, but it was clear this was no man. Her hair was free of the cap and spread about her in dull curls. Damp ringlets clung to the sides of her face. Her skin was flushed and damp. The doublet had been removed and her shirt was open, barely covering her breasts.

"Christ God," Skelley muttered. "He's a lass."

"It's Fayth Graham," Alex said, never taking his eyes from her. "And she's dying."

Davie leaned over her and shook his head.

"What?" Alex grabbed his arm. "Is it too late? You can't help her?"

Davie rolled his eyes and shook his head again. Skelley wished the fool would speak, but they all knew he wouldn't. Often Alex had no problem understanding the man, but this was not one of those times.

"She's not going to die?" Alex asked.

Davie nodded.

Alex's shoulders slumped, his gaze still fastened on the woman. He leaned closer, then gently touched her cheek with the back of his fingers. Some of the worry cleared from his brow. "She's not so hot . . . and she's sweating." He looked at Davie anxiously. "That's good?"

Davie nodded, smiling slightly. He began unwinding the dressing from her arm. Skelley wanted to speak alone with Alex, to tell him about Eliot and Laine, but he was transfixed, watching Davie and the woman's arm. Skelley peered over Davie's shoulder to get a look at the wound. He'd only seen it when they found her and it had been sore nasty then. It was red and a bit swollen, but the stitches were holding and the wound was scabbed over.

Davie placed a hand on Alex's shoulder and nodded encouragingly.

"I think he means ye did well," Skelley said, since Alex stared blankly at the leech. "That ye took good care of her."

Alex swallowed hard, nodding his head and sitting back on his heels. He looked around the cave, his gaze lighting on the pile of hares in the corner. Wolf brushed past Skelley's leg on her way out of the cave.

"Christ," Alex muttered. "She's going to get more." He called the dog back.

She returned, wiggling enthusiastically at the sudden attention. Alex rubbed the dog's ears, speaking softly to her. He straightened and approached Skelley. He favored his shoulder.

"Did you run into any trouble?"

Skelley nodded and gestured for Alex to follow him to the mouth of the cave. "There's Grahams in the wood. They attacked us and took . . . or killed Laine and Eliot." Skelley looked away, ashamed he'd lost men. "We cannot stay. Laine or Eliot might talk, if sufficiently induced."

Alex looked over his shoulder at Fayth. "She shouldn't be moved."

Skelley grabbed his arm. "She must."

The whiskered jaw clenched as Alex pulled his arm away.

"That hurts, aye?" Skelley examined Alex's flushed skin and red eyes. "She might be mending, but you're getting worse. We must have a look at that shoulder afore we leave. Have you been tending it?"

"How could I?"

"What good will ye be to her or Gealach—or us, for that matter, if ye're dead?"

That seemed to give Alex pause. He looked again at Davie, where he leaned over the woman. Skelley had never seen Alex like this. True, he'd been acting odd ever since the Annancreag raid, but since Fayth Graham had shot him he'd been deeply preoccupied. It was unlike Alex to lose his wits over a woman. But Skelley couldn't say he was unhappy about the situation. It was about time the lad became witless with something besides anger. However, Skelley feared Alex would lose more than his wits over a woman like Fayth Graham.

"You're right," Alex said, returning to Davie's side to watch over the lass. "We'll head out as soon as my shoulder is tended."

Eliot was dragged to a camp several miles from where they'd been caught. It had been a highly uncomfortable journey. Since Laine had two arms, their captors had bound his wrists to drag him behind a horse. The boobs had puzzled over Eliot's one-armed state for a good ten minutes before looping the rope around his neck and dragging him that way. Most distressing when he stumbled.

By the time their captors had thrown down the ropes—not bothering to remove their bindings—Eliot was on his knees in the mud, the rope having cut a raw furrow in his neck. Laine's hands were in much the same condition, but the lad still came over and yanked the rope over Eliot's head. The boy looked positively indignant. Eliot felt an uncommon surge of wry humor and genuine affection for the boy. This was his first kidnapping, where he was the abductee, that is. Eliot had done this before. Since Eliot was a common outlaw, he'd be treated like rubbish. Laine, however, would warrant softer confinement if he revealed his parentage.

"Tell 'em who ye are," Eliot said, his voice a broken rasp. "They'll treat ye fine."

"Unless they're naught but a pack of broken men."

"Like us?"

Eliot scanned the clearing, assessing the enemy. He knew they were Grahams, but he knew not what grayne. He suspected it was the Eden grayne, as they were the ones Alex had most recently offended in his attempt to kidnap Fayth Graham. He grew still as he surveyed the encampment. It went far back into the trees, past the clearing. There were at least one hundred men, all with horse. His gaze came to rest on a large green silk tent, indicating a lord of some standing and wealth, and half a dozen smaller canvas tents.

The flap of the green silk opened and a man emerged, his gaze seeking them out immediately. Wesley Graham. Wesley strode across the clearing, sizing them up the whole way.

"I know you. Armless Eliot, they call you. You're Red Alex's man." He leaned to the side, viewing the empty sleeve belted to Eliot's side. "Don't look completely armless to me."

"Aye, and it's as good as two of yers."

Wesley turned to inspect Laine. "And who are you, little girl?"

Laine's face turned nearly purple with rage. "I am Laine. I'm also Red Alex's *man*."

Wesley was unimpressed. "Have you a surname?"

Eliot waited for him to reveal his father's name, but instead, he said, "I am a Maxwell, now."

"Oh are ye, ye little bastard?"

Even Eliot jumped when the man came out of nowhere and clouted Laine alongside the head. The boy fell over, clutching his face and rolling in the mud. Ashton Carlisle, Laine's father.

"Who is this?" Wesley asked Carlisle.

"I'm sorry to say this turd is me son. I gave him to the monks at Rees, but he disgraced me by running away." Laine was still writhing on the ground, trying to stand up. Carlisle grabbed the boy's hair, yanking him up to look into his face. "I been looking for you, laddie."

"That's enough," Wesley said.

Carlisle turned on him. "Don't you tell me what's enough, or I'll kick yer—"

"He's a prisoner," Wesley said loudly and with a note of boredom. "And therefore I want him fit for questioning. When we're finished, you may do with him as you will." Wesley gripped Laine's biceps and helped him to his feet. "Until then, stay away from him."

Carlisle looked ready to murder Wesley, but he said no more, stalking away and disappearing into the silk tent. Eliot deduced that Carlisle was not in command and that meant only one thing. Ridley Graham was here.

"Come on," Wesley said, and followed Carlisle into the tent, Eliot and Laine trailing along behind him.

The interior of the tent was decorated like a palace. Turkish carpets covered the ground, tall candelabras were placed strategically around the perimeter with mirrors to reflect the light, making it surprisingly illuminated. A camp bed was near the back, covered with fine linen sheets and furs and partially hidden from view by a white screen bearing a painted green serpent. In the center of the room, seated behind a table, was Lord Ridley Graham, partaking of his dinner. Carlisle had joined him and was gnawing on a haunch of mutton, glaring at Laine all the while. Eliot's stomach rumbled in response.

"This is your son?" Lord Graham said.

Carlisle nodded disgustedly. "Bastard born, but mine, if that swine he calls mother is to be believed."

Lord Graham stood, wiping his mouth and hands on a table linen. He circled the table, coming to stand before Laine, looking him up and down. "Looks like a monk's boy."

Laine's ears turned crimson, but he stood rigid, directing his blank gaze to the right.

Lord Graham stared at the boy a long moment before turning his attention to Eliot. "The one-armed rook. I've heard of you."

Eliot made an elaborate bow, flinging mud all over the fine furnishings and Lord Graham's hose and boots. "At your service, my lord."

Ridley came at him, grabbing his arm and twisting it. Eliot hadn't noticed Carlisle getting up, but now he was behind him, shoving him to his knees. Eliot's lips drew back from his teeth, hissing in pain. Terror knifed through him.

Ridley twisted his arm, pulling it up higher until Eliot thought it might twist right off. He ground his teeth together to stop from crying out. *Not my arm, not my arm!* His heart hammered in his ears, sweat sprang up on his face and neck.

"Think you life is difficult with one arm, Eliot? Would you like to find out what it is to live up to your name? To be truly armless?"

Please Lord, no. Eliot prayed to himself, ready to tell Lord Graham anything he wished if it would save his arm.

"Goddamn you, Father!" Laine cried, shoving Lord Carlisle so he stumbled backward. Eliot surged to his feet, relieving some of the pressure, but before he could strike out, Ridley knocked his feet from beneath him, sending him sprawling on his back. He'd thankfully released Eliot's arm.

Eliot held his arm up, to ward off any blows. But the blows didn't come. Wesley had stepped between Carlisle and Laine, stopping the old man from clouting his son again.

Ridley looked between Eliot and Laine, then said to Wesley, "Take the boy. Feed him and clean him up."

When they were gone, Ridley held out a hand, smiling apologetically. Eliot paused, his gaze darting to Carlisle, who had faded into the background, mutton chop in hand. Eliot gave Ridley his hand and got to his feet.

"The boy is of no use to me," Ridley said. "He's young, passionate, full of foolish courage." He smiled wryly at Eliot. "You, however . . . You can help me." Ridley returned to the table and sat, pouring two goblets of wine. "And perhaps I can help you. Come, sit with me and talk awhile."

Eliot didn't move, still shaken from Ridley's violent threat. The man was all manners and nobility now.

Eliot scanned the tent's interior suspiciously before starting forward. "I can't help you."

"Please, sit. Eat. You must be famished. Alexander Maxwell can't possibly feed you well."

Eliot was hungry and so sat down, only grabbing food he'd seen Ridley eating. "I eat well enough. Alex ain't me mum, after all."

"Of course, but it is beyond his means to care for his men in the same manner I care for mine." He gestured to the men-at-arms stationed at the back of the tent. They were braw, fat lads, well groomed and relatively clean.

Eliot said nothing, tearing into his chicken leg. It had been some time since he'd eaten aught but oatcakes, barley stew, and dried beef. The feast before him was heavenly.

He ate well enough when they were at Gealach, but they'd been in the woods for months, chasing after Graham scum.

"There are many ways I reward those who serve me. Tell me. How does Alexander reward you?"

Eliot stopped eating to stare at Lord Graham, laughter bubbling in his chest. He was being bribed. He could hardly believe it! A skilled extortionist himself, he was interested to hear Ridley's offer.

He leaned back in his chair, wiping his mouth and fingers on the white tablecloth. "Oh weel . . . Red Alex rewards me well. Coin, animals, insight."

"But what do you do with insight? Have you a home to put such furnishings? Or fields to graze your beasts, for that matter? And what spend you coin on, but women and game?"

Eliot grinned. "What better way to spend coin?"

Lord Graham smiled broadly. "Why, investing it in yourself, your land, of course."

"I have no land."

"Alexander hasn't rewarded you with land . . . ? Oh, I forgot, he owns nothing outright. Only that midden pile, Gealach . . ."

"Gealach is no midden pile. Red Alex makes a small fortune in port fees. And there's the traffic between Scotland and Ireland. And now that he's encouraged the tenants to cultivate the land, he's beginning to see some return. And Gealach has other . . . advantages."

"Advantages?"

Eliot smiled. "I canna be giving away our secrets, now can I?"

Lord Graham's brow furrowed in confusion. "But is it *your* secret, or Alexander Maxwell's?"

The man had a point. What was Gealach to Eliot? He'd helped take it and defend it and yet what did it afford him but a place to sleep and a few meals? Alex was the laird.

Alex reaped all the benefits of ownership. In fact, he refused to parcel out any land until he held the deed to the estate. Why should Alex be the one? They weren't so
different. Eliot's father hadn't been a laird, as Red Rowan
had been, but then what had that meant to Alex? Red
Rowan had left him no land or titles. He was no better than
Eliot. Why should everything go to Alex?

"Do you want it?" Ridley asked.

"Want what?"

Ridley smiled patiently. "Why Gealach, of course."

Eliot's pulse skipped a beat. This was unexpected. He'd
expected many things, but not to be offered an estate. He
shook his head slowly. "I'm no fool. No lord would give an
estate to a common outlaw."

"True . . ." Ridley leaned back in his chair, hands folded
over his belly. "Not right away, that is. I would first appoint
you warden of Gealach. You would guard it and protect it
for me, as master in my absence."

Eliot's heart grew swollen with desire. All his life he'd
known he deserved better and would've had better if he
were a whole man. It should've been Alex that lost his arm.
Instead he was heralded as a hero. And it had been as such
since. Alex was the best at everything. Only Eliot knew, if
he'd two arms, he could be better. Women wanted Alex and
men respected and followed him. Eliot repulsed them. Men
sneered at him and he had to buy his women. But to have
Gealach—to take Gealach from Alex—was a heady
thought.

But still he said nothing. Ridley was using him. Not that
Eliot minded being used, if the price was right. But he
must not appear overeager.

Ridley raised his brows, leaning forward slightly. "Is
this inducement enough for you to seek a new master?"

"Perhaps." Eliot picked his teeth idly, inspecting his discovery. "What would you require of me? I wilna kill Red Alex."

"Murder isn't necessary . . . well, at least not Alexander." Ridley looked idly over his shoulder at Carlisle, who peeked through a hole at the back of the tent, thoroughly engrossed in whatever he spied.

Eliot sat quietly, waiting for Ridley to go on. After a moment he did.

"Alexander Maxwell has kidnapped my sister away from her betrothed, Lord Carlisle."

Eliot raised his brows, interested. Apparently, Ridley didn't realize the kidnapping was unsuccessful and that Fayth Graham ran freely about the west march. Eliot wouldn't be the one to inform him.

"Does he still have her? She's slippery, that one—prone to escape. She likes to dress as a lad and call herself Hugh."

Eliot froze, his gaze riveted on Ridley. "Hugh, ye say?"

Ridley smiled. "I see that sounds familiar."

That rotten bastard. Eliot could barely contain his fury. So Alex thought to hide it from everyone, or did he? How many knew? Skelley certainly, the lack-wit leech, definitely. The little bugger boy, Laine, probably even knew. Everyone but Eliot. Alex trusted him with nothing. Which also meant he wouldn't share in the spoils of this endeavor. That lying, cheating—

"Well?" Ridley prompted him out of his thoughts.

Eliot held out his hand, his expression grim. "Aye, my lord. I'm in. What would ye have me do?"

11

FAYTH RESTED AGAINST the wall of Alex's chest as they traveled in silence across the bogs and forests. They didn't have another horse for Fayth to ride and even if they had, it was doubtful Fayth could have sat in a saddle all day. Alex was staying away from the firth, he told her, in case Ridley watched the most direct route to Gealach. They'd left the cave yesterday afternoon and ridden until long past dark, finally stopping to rest when Fayth was no longer able to suppress her moans of agony and exhaustion.

The short rest had done her some good, but they were back at it again today, and dark was falling. She hoped they would stop soon, though none of them seemed inclined to. Fayth's arm ached dully and she felt frail and empty, but her head was clear and she no longer burned and shook with fever. Her captor/protector, however, was another matter. She chanced a look up at him from beneath her lashes. His face was flushed with fever and he seemed ready to collapse. This was her doing. She'd shot him and now it would fester and he would die.

Her father would have been so proud.

Her teeth clenched at the thought. She no longer wanted to make her father, or anyone else, proud. Except perhaps herself. And she'd done nothing of late to earn even her own pride. Alex was not at all the man she'd expected and though she was still uncertain of many things, it was clear he was inherently a good, honorable man. She should tell him about Ridley and all his scheming. She owed him that much, but she was afraid he'd think it a lie or trick.

He felt the movement of her head against his chest and glanced down at her. "Do you need to stop?"

It set her heart fluttering every time he looked at her that way. She wished he wouldn't, it made everything that much more confusing. And why was he so gentle with her? She could not understand him. She was his enemy. Before recent events, had their roles been reversed, she could not say she would have been so charitable.

His eyes were fever bright, but still the deepest blue she'd ever seen. He hadn't shaved in days. Dark reddish-brown whiskers shadowed his chin and jaw and upper lip—nearly a short beard. She'd thought he was fetching, clean shaven, but the beard made him seem older, more worldly, accentuating wide, sensual lips.

She quickly lowered her eyes. She tried to speak, but her mouth was dry. She cleared her throat and rasped, "Could we stop?"

He called to the others. He handed her down to Davie, who settled her against a rock and left to tend Alex's shoulder. As usual, Alex tried to insist Davie tend her arm first. And, as usual, the leech pretended not to hear him. When Alex pushed at his shoulder to get his attention, Davie merely looked at him blankly, as if he didn't understand, though he appeared to understand most of everything else Alex said.

Skelley had disappeared into the trees with Biddy. Fayth turned her attention back to Alex and Davie. The leech had a fire going and was heating water to brew one of his concoctions. Meanwhile, he helped Alex out of his jack and shirt. Fayth wished she could see what was going on. She craned her neck, but Davie's back blocked Alex's wound. Only his good shoulder and a long muscular arm were visible. Like most of his exposed skin it was marred with twisted silvery scars.

Fayth didn't want to care about his shoulder. But he'd nursed her through a fever and stayed with her. He claimed he owed her for sparing his life. But she'd not spared his life. She'd never been able to take it. She frowned, thinking again of Diana Carlisle. The girl had been haunting her since her mind cleared. What had she meant to Alex? Alex had told Fayth that he'd offered for Gealach through marriage. Diana had said he'd called her his moon. Fayth pondered the meaning of these things, watching Davie as he dipped a wooden cup into the heated water and turned back to Alex. Fayth started at the strangled roar wrenched from Alex—abruptly cut short.

That's it. Grabbing the rock with her good hand, she pulled herself to standing. Her head swam and her stomach turned. She leaned against the rock until her vision cleared. Her stomach was still fluttery when she started toward the men, but she was determined to regain her independence. Her legs felt weak and wobbly, and she stopped three times to lean against a tree before she traversed the short distance to Alex and Davie.

She eased her way around Davie and what she saw sent her vision clouding and her stomach roiling all over again. She fell, landing with a plop on her backside. The ground was padded with fallen leaves and soft from rain, but it still sent painful vibrations up her arm.

She opened her eyes a crack and saw Davie scowling at her. He waved her away, then went back to his work, not waiting to see if she obeyed. Fayth bit her lip and forced herself to look at Alex's wound again. Fresh blood ran down his arm, mixed with a thick yellow discharge. Davie had cut open the stitches and poured his boiling mixture into it. What he appeared to be doing now, Fayth observed, quickly averting her eyes, was cutting away the rotting flesh. She pressed her hand to her mouth, praying she wouldn't be sick or faint.

When she could breathe again, she dropped her hand. Davie watched her critically and with a touch of annoyance.

"Is he going to die?" she asked. The thought of Alex dying should not cause her such alarm, just the same her heart pounded painfully, waiting for Davie's answer.

The leech shrugged, gesturing again with his bloody knife for her to leave.

Alex's eyes opened a crack. "Davie's working hard to ensure I do, it seems. It feels like he's cutting my heart out with his wee knife."

Davie began probing and cutting at his shoulder again. Alex hissed through clenched teeth and shut his eyes, jaw locked.

"What is he doing?" Fayth asked, panic entering her voice.

"I jest," Alex said, not opening his eyes. "He's trying to help me . . . since he cannot tell me what he's doing, I can only guess. I think he's cutting away the corrupted flesh before it poisons the good flesh."

"Oh . . ." Fayth's pounding heart began to slow. He was in such pain. The veins stood out in his temple, the cords and muscles in his neck and arm were bunched and hard. Perhaps she could take his mind from it. She decided to satisfy her curiosity about him and Diana.

"Which one of Carlisle's daughters did you offer for?"

His eyes opened and some of the tension visibly left him. "What?"

"You told me you tried to secure the deed for Gealach through marriage. Well, Carlisle has several daughters. Which one did you want?"

He eyed her suspiciously. "You don't know?"

"Very well," Fayth said, caught. "Diana blathered on and on about you so that I stopped listening—but I do think she mentioned that you wanted to wed her."

"Well, I did. Why? As her future stepmother, are ye assessing me as a suitor? Mean ye to put in a good word wi' Carlisle?"

Stung by his unexpected sarcasm she said, "If I'm ever her stepmother I'll warn her far away from the likes of you!"

He gave a soft laugh that ended on a choked groan. "She had a sharp tongue, that lass, but nothing compared to your poison sniping."

Fayth's lips clamped down hard. She hadn't meant to snipe at him. That's not why she came over. She began the labor of trying to stand.

"Wait, Fayth. Don't go."

She paused, looking down at him haughtily.

He sighed dramatically. "Sit and I'll tell ye."

She sat.

"I made the offer to Carlisle first, of course, after he'd refused to sell me the land. His reply was that he'd wed her to a Turk afore he'd wed her to me—which was no surprise, considering I'm a third son, but I had to try. I thought to myself, once the deed is done, surely he'll come to accept me. So I began visiting Diana in secret. She thought it great sport at first, but when I asked her to marry me secretly . . ."

Davie had finished cutting at the wound and was now applying a poultice of herbs to the raw flesh. Fayth noticed that it had stopped draining pus and the blood that still trickled from it was bright red and clean.

"She said no?"

"She said she was destined for better than the wife of a landless outlaw. When I told her of Gealach, she reminded me that it belonged to her father and that it was a rotting pile of stones unfit for the likes of a gentlewoman."

"Ah, love . . . Ain't it sweet," Skelley said behind them.

Biddy sniffed at Alex, then leaned against Fayth, tongue lolling from her mouth. The dog had been rolling in something. She stunk of dead animals and the coppery odor of blood.

Alex smiled wryly at the older man, but there was darkness in his eyes. *Love?* Had he truly loved Diana Carlisle? This troubled Fayth inexplicably. Why should she care? She didn't—not really. She was merely feeling grateful for all the care and kindness he had shown her. There was nothing more to it.

"Anyway," Alex continued, turning his attention to his shoulder as Davie wrapped clean linen around it. "When she realized my intent, she warned me that if I told her father about our . . . meetings, she'd claim I raped her."

Fayth stroked Biddy's fur, matted with mud, leaves, and other unidentifiable substances. Fayth wasn't quite sure what to say to Alex's story. Diana Carlisle was a very stupid girl. It was true there was no love between the Maxwells and the Carlisles, but neither did they have a deadly long-standing blood feud, as the Grahams and the Maxwells did. In Fayth's opinion, a lass could do a lot worse than Alexander Maxwell. Unfortunately, he was a Scot and a Maxwell, but he was young and handsome, and it was clear he would never harm a woman. Naturally, his landless/titleless state was problematic for fathers and upward-minded daughters, but that was not Fayth. She had other standards for a potential mate, and though the ability to provide was one of them, Alex met that and more.

Though he had yet to gain the deed for Gealach, his sheer determination weighed the scales in his favor. If he failed, as Fayth suspected he might, there were other lairds—allies of the Maxwells—who would sell him land. He must have the resources, otherwise he wouldn't keep trying.

Yes, he would make an excellent husband.

Davie finished with Alex's wound and turned to Fayth. Alex's weary but relieved gaze rested thoughtfully on Fayth. Uncomfortable with the direction of her foolish thoughts, she watched Davie remove the dressing from her arm, trying to ignore the intensity of Alex's gaze, though every fiber in her body burned with awareness.

"Mind you, lass," Alex said. "I don't fault her. I understand her desire to improve her station through marriage. After all, that's exactly what I tried to do. I had hoped, however, that the softer . . . womanly emotions might override her common sense."

Fayth questioned that Diana had any common sense at all and suspected more than her emotions had gone soft.

Skelley scoffed. "He means, he'd hoped she'd fall in love with him and defy her father."

"As usual," Alex said with a self-deprecating, one-armed shrug, "I overestimated my charms."

Davie apparently found her wound mending well, because he merely wiped it clean, applied the same poultice he'd put on Alex's wound, and rewrapped her dressings.

Skelley had been waiting for something; his tongue worked busily at the gaps where he was missing several teeth. He nudged Davie's shoulder so the young man looked up. "Finished?"

Davie nodded.

"Good. Come wi' me then. I've downed a deer. I canna bring it back alone."

Davie quickly put his things away.

"You two rest here and we'll have venison tonight."

And they were gone, Biddy loping along beside them.

Fayth wished she hadn't moved from her rock, for the way she sat now it was impossible not to look at Alex and he would know if she purposely avoided eye contact. Why couldn't she look at him? It was most troubling—she'd never before had a problem meeting a man's eyes and yet when she met Alex's all sorts of unnatural things occurred to her body. So she glanced at him several times, but he leaned his head back against a tree, the philter Davie had given him resting on his thigh, cupped between his palms. Fayth watched the steam rise from it.

"Where did you learn to train animals?" she asked.

"From Brother Gilbert."

When she didn't respond, he raised his head. "No more questions?"

"You think I'm intrusive."

"Nay, though I vow you ask more questions than anyone I've ever met."

"I'm just curious," Fayth said defensively. "You're some kind of hero to your men and I'm trying to understand it. And now you're Saint Francis to the animals."

Alex laughed. "Saint Francis? Brother Gilbert would love that."

"Who is Brother Gilbert?"

Alex sighed, turning the cup in his hands, eyes fixed on the rising tendrils of steam. "Brother Gilbert was one of my teachers at Dunfermline Abbey, where I trained to be a priest."

Fayth gaped at him. The letter he'd given to Diana. He'd instructed her to give it to the abbot of Dunfermline should anything happen to him. So he *had* written it.

"Aye, my mother and father had big plans for me. I was to become archbishop, or at least a great abbot, one day."

When she remained speechless, he raised his brows. "It's not as if I was ordained, lass. You can close your mouth. I took no vows."

"How long were you at the abbey?"

"Three years."

Fayth tried, without success, to imagine Alex in the flowing robes of priesthood, hair short and tonsured. "I didn't think it took that long to become a monk . . . or is it different, being a priest?"

"Oh, aye, it's different. But I failed at both. Most are novitiates for but a year . . . mine obviously went on much longer. The abbot said I lacked humility."

"That's all you lacked?"

Alex quirked a brow at her, as if to determine whether the question was sincere or sarcastic, then said, "There are twelve degrees of humility. I couldn't quite grasp them. But you're right, I failed in other ways. According to the abbot, I am unable to refrain from the desires of the flesh. I cannot banish evil and impure thoughts—thoughts of revenge. I drink too much wine, I talk too much, I laugh too much—and too loudly—I tell coarse stories that are deemed inappropriate for chaste ears, and," he grinned wickedly at her, "I simply canna love chastity."

"I see," she said, trying to look thoughtful, though her cheeks were heating up, vaguely remembering a fever-induced kiss that had been far from chaste. She forced the memory away and tried to imagine Alex in a monastery, drinking and laughing while the other monks frowned reprovingly. She smothered the smile threatening to form.

"What happened?" she asked.

"I didn't want to be a priest . . . I tried, for my mother . . . It was her deepest desire to have a son in the Church. Rob was heir and Patrick . . . well, it was clear from the start there wasna a pious bone in Patrick's body. That left me."

"Was your mother . . . disappointed?"

Alex became very solemn. "Aye." He inhaled deeply, thoughtfully. "She taught me all I knew of God, afore the abbey. Her vision of the Lord was a good one and I thought it was a worthy thing to serve Him. I lied to her, told her it was what I wanted." He shrugged one shoulder. "I thought it would be easy to conform and be a good priest. But my mum's God was not at the abbey. Oh, they were strict and chaste and verra good men, in their own manner, upholding what they believed to be God's will in the most literal sense." He sighed. "But I didn't see God there. And now I must wonder, if He's not there, where indeed, is He at all?"

He didn't seem inclined to say more. She watched him twist the cup in his hands, not drinking. His words troubled her. Was it blasphemy he uttered? She didn't know, not being well churched herself.

He glanced up, following her gaze. "Here." He offered her the cup.

"Oh, no." She shook her head. "You must drink it. It will make you better."

To her chagrin, he stood with little effort and sat beside her. "You should drink it, too."

She could feel the heat from his body. He was like a fire, blazing nearby, and she was so cold. His arm brushed against hers. She had the urge to press herself to his heat, let it engulf her.

She took the cup for something to do with her hands and sipped at it. She handed it back. "Thank you."

He watched her intently and finally she met his gaze with a challenge. "What?"

"I'm making you uneasy."

"No," she lied, shaking her head a bit too vigorously. "Not at all."

"You know not what to think anymore, eh? Now that you no longer hate me."

"How presumptuous of you."

"So you do still hate me?"

She refused to look at him. She *must* hate him. And yet, in her heart, she knew he was right, the hate had faded, replaced by something new, something she cared not at all to examine. But it was *wrong* that it should die! Jack's murder was still unavenged and she sat here sharing a cup of swill with his murderer.

"Do you hate me or not? It's a simple question."

Why couldn't she answer him? She tried to force herself to say, *Yes, I despise you.* But it was such an untruth she couldn't force it past her lips.

"I can't imagine why you'd care," she said finally.

"I don't."

"Good."

They fell silent, Alex sipping at his cup. He offered it again. "So . . . why do you still hate me?"

Fayth blurted out, "Because you killed Jack Graham, the man I was to wed."

"Aye, I think you've mentioned that—"

The anger surged forward fresh and she welcomed it. It was better than the giddy-headed confusion that seemed to grip her when he was near. "Because if he were alive I wouldn't be here now—I would be a wife and a mother. You ruined my life."

He gave her a puzzled frown. "You *want* to be a wife and mother?"

She didn't know what she expected, but not this. "Of course I do."

"Of course?"

"Of course!"

He mulled that over for an infuriating minute. She felt a

strange burning in her eyes. What did he think? She didn't like men, or children? That she didn't want a normal life?

"I like gowns and jewels and baths, but I don't see why I must confine myself to them, why I can't experience other things."

"And be seen."

"Yes! And be seen!"

She was nearly panting with agitation. How dare he assume things about her? He didn't know her! He couldn't know her.

"So . . . was Jack Graham one of those things you wanted to experience?"

"I loved Jack." She'd thought the anger would bolster her, remind her of who she was, but now she only felt like crying. Crying for the loss of her future, of all that could have been.

He seemed to sense her distress. "I'm sorry, lass. I didn't mean to make ye grieve again."

She choked back a small sob. She felt his hand on her back, urging her forward, to lay her head against him. She resisted, panicked at the idea of being enfolded in his arms again. The fever-induced kiss hadn't been a dream—the danger of it recurring forced her to finally acknowledge it. She was afraid for it to happen again, afraid she would forget everything she was in his arms. But he only pressed harder until her head fell against his good shoulder, his arm draped around her. She kept her eyes closed, her heart beating frantically against her breast.

Jack's murderer was comforting her! She would surely burn in hell for this. It felt as though she was already burning, deep in her belly, her chest, her neck. Would he kiss her now? Her mouth tingled in anticipation. God no, she could never hate him—not anymore.

He shushed her, though she made no sound, and slowly she began to relax. She didn't know why she was so frantic. She'd spent the past two days leaning against him, hardly able to lift her head for long moments. She lay on his shoulder in the cave, his arms wrapped around her to keep her warm. She found the heat of him, the familiar smell and feel, oddly comforting.

His fingers trailed across her jaw and chin and she opened her eyes. She knew it must be very painful to move his shoulder—she couldn't hold her own arm up for more than a few seconds—and so she leaned back from him slightly, to look into his face. She caught her breath at his expression. He did seem to be in pain, though she questioned whether it was the physical kind. His eyes clouded, as if he were concentrating very hard on something. On her.

"Are you well?" Hesitantly, she reached up and touched his face. He was still very hot, though she'd assumed from his conversation he felt better.

"No . . . I dinna think I am."

Fayth's gaze tangled with his and she couldn't look away. Her hand rested on his shoulder after touching his face, but she didn't move it, even though her arm ached with the effort of holding it there.

His arm slid more fully around her, drawing her near, supporting her weight so she didn't have to. His head lowered. He was going to kiss her. *Why?* Was it the fever? Had it affected his mind?

"Do you remember . . . before, when you kissed me?" he whispered, his breath hot against her skin.

Her breath caught and she gave a jerky nod.

"So do I. I canna stop thinking about it."

His voice, his words, disarmed her and she went limp. His whiskers brushed against her skin as he pressed a kiss against her closed eyelid. The kiss was as unexpected as his words and her breath hitched. He murmured something she could not understand. His hand slid up her neck, his thumb tilting her chin upward. He looked at her, she knew, though she could not look back.

His lips brushed against hers and the last of her strength was sapped away. His mouth was as hot as the rest of him, but she welcomed it, her own body always cold since her fever fled. Her mouth opened beneath his, pulling him deeper into the kiss. He dragged her against his chest, mindful of her arm. His tongue traced her lips and teeth before dipping inside. The wanting grew with each wild beat of her heart as he kissed her deeper still, sucking and probing her tongue and lips. No, the other kiss had not been a dream and nor had the fever been what had burned her to ashes—it had been Alex.

His hand, hot as coals, slid under her tunic, over the coarse homespun of her shirt, until he cupped her breast. It seared her like a brand through her shirt, startling her so she drew back in surprise.

He pulled his hand away, but held her close, pressing his forehead to hers, his hand cupping her head. "God help me, but I can do little more than kiss ye right now."

Her vision was fuzzy and she felt as though she floated. "Why?" Her voice surprised her, rough, breathy. She wanted his hand back, only under her shirt this time, burning her skin.

"I fear I might faint from the effort." But he kissed her again, his tongue swirling against hers, drawing her into him. She wanted to stay that way, her weakened body pulsing with his strength, his warmth.

He broke away. Her head fell forward against his shoulder, quivering with desire. She tried to burrow closer, her face against his neck. He smelled of the forest and of the herbal poultice and wine Davie used to cleanse his wound.

"You don't hate me," he said. She could hear the smile in his voice.

She stilled, wishing he would stop reminding her of Jack. His hands rubbed over her back and lower, skimming the curve of her bottom. Jack had never kissed her sense-less—and she'd never returned his kisses with such enthu-siasm. Shame filled her at the thought of Jack—that she would *want* to forget him, that she would compare him to Alex. He deserved better than this. She hadn't done her duty to him. As a Graham she was expected to avenge his death and here she was, lusting after Red Alex.

What if Alex didn't do it? Her heart faltered. He didn't seem the type to murder indiscriminately.

"Did you kill Jack?" Once she whispered the words, she wished them back, but they hung there in the silence.

His hands stilled. He said nothing for a long while and a fear filled her, fear that he didn't remember, that he'd killed so many prisoners he couldn't put a face to them all.

"I'm responsible for his death."

She stiffened, drawing away from him. "Responsible? Did you order him killed? Or did you kill him with your own hand?" She was aware that her voice rose in anger and agitation, and something else, despair. She'd wanted him to say no.

He sighed, trying to pull her close again. "Fayth . . ."

"Let me go."

He dropped his arms, putting space between them. She stared straight ahead, into the trees, aware that his gaze still rested on her.

"Aye, I killed him."

She was such a fool. She was disgusted by what she'd done, with how she still longed for him. "Get away from me."

"Fayth—"

"And don't ever touch me that way again!"

"Fine." He stood abruptly and paced away.

Fayth frowned hard, knowing that if she concentrated hard enough, she could turn the twisting ache in her chest into something else, something useful.

12

⌁

LAINE SEARCHED the Graham/Carlisle encampment for Eliot. The one-armed man was enjoying his captivity a bit too much. He constantly played cards and dice, gambling money on loan from Lord Ridley Graham. Lord Graham had even brought a whore into camp for them. Laine had declined, but Eliot was with her for several hours.

Eliot claimed his behavior was all a fiction, meant to lull Lord Graham and Lord Carlisle into believing he was their please man. He told Laine of the offer Lord Graham had made him and that if they played along, pretending to turn Judas, they'd be set free. Then they could join Alex at Gealach. Laine had been reluctant at first. It would mean being civil to his father, and therefore his father believing he'd won. But Laine's objective was freedom and so he eventually caved in.

As it turned out, he'd not had to worry about spending time in his father's smug presence. Lord Carlisle stayed away from him and Laine had been forced to suffer no more than his hard, disapproving stares from across camp.

The past few days had been spent listening to Wesley

Graham lecture him on their mission: the rescue of Fayth Graham. The man was a rigid taskmaster, testing Laine repeatedly and never satisfied. Laine had been shocked to discover Hugh was not Red Alex's nephew, but Fayth Graham, his father's intended. Why had Red Alex not told them?

"Because he means to keep it all for himself," Eliot had said, his beard dripping with grease from the feast he'd recently consumed. It appeared Eliot was not being subjected to the same level of training as Laine, a fact that troubled the boy greatly.

"He tricked us into helping him kidnap her," Eliot continued, "then pretended he wasna successful."

Laine shook his head at this skewed logic. "But we found her at the Dragon's Lair, remember? She was at liberty then."

Eliot picked a piece of gristle from his teeth. "Skelley was there. Skelley's in on it. Red Alex is going to reward Skelley and no one else."

But Laine thought this stupid talk and said so. Eliot had gotten angry and called him foul names. But he'd come back later, full of apologies and requests for him to pretend to believe the story so Lord Graham would set them free.

And so far Eliot was right. Wesley had just informed Laine they were free to leave. Laine would waste no more time in this nest of deceit. He finally found Eliot at cards again with two Grahams and a Carlisle.

"It's time to go."

Eliot didn't look up from his cards. "It's a bit late to be starting out."

"I'm ready to go."

"We'll leave in the morn."

Laine'd had enough of Eliot's behavior. He snatched the cards from Eliot's hand and threw them into the fire. "I'm going now. Without you if necessary."

Eliot stared at his burning cards. "I was winning."

The other men laughed and patted his shoulder as he stood. He faced Laine with an air of boredom. "Fine. Let's go, then."

Laine was relieved, as he didn't relish a confrontation with Eliot. Eliot could be particularly nasty. He'd been strangely friendly to Laine since their capture, and Laine didn't know what to make of it. They were in this together, however, and having no one else to rely on, Laine didn't question his civility.

Eliot joined him by the horses. Leather sacks were tied to their saddles, filled with provisions—courtesy of Lord Graham. Laine supposed Lord Graham's hospitality and kindness might have seduced him, had he not known his own father so well. Any man Lord Ashton Carlisle held in high regard was not to be trusted. Even Eliot, a man hostile to nearly everyone—and at feud with the Grahams, besides—had become docile under Ridley's touch.

Eliot mounted easily, waving his hand at Lord Graham and Lord Carlisle, who stood outside the tent, watching them. Lord Graham raised his hand in farewell, but Laine's father put his back to them, his lips curled in disgust.

Laine turned his face away, his throat tight with humiliation. *He abandoned me, as if what happened were my fault.* And suddenly it felt as though he were to blame, that he'd somehow allowed it to happen—encouraged it . . . Fiercely, Laine put all thoughts of Father Rae and the monastery from his mind. It was over, he would never go back. He must be thankful his half-sister, Diana, had cared enough for him to send Red Alex to his rescue.

He dug in his spurs and put this place, his deception, and his father, behind him. They'd been riding for nearly an hour when Eliot called for him to stop. He drew rein and scanned the forest around them. The air was heavy and chill from the recent rains. The mist of his breath blossomed around him.

"They're following us," Laine said.

"I ken." But Eliot didn't look overly concerned.

"Should we try to lose them?"

Eliot said nothing, but he was listening, his head cocked slightly. The snapping of twigs and branches, and the crunch of leaves followed them.

"They're not really trying to hide it, either," Laine said, puzzled by this behavior.

"Aye . . . they're no stupid. They're making sure I'm no playing them false."

Laine frowned slightly at Eliot's reference to himself, as if Laine hadn't been party to the whole farce.

"Well?" Laine said, becoming annoyed. "Shall we try to lose them, or—he lowered his voice—"ambush them? Then we can return to Red Alex with prisoners."

Eliot nodded and waved at Laine to follow him. He dismounted, leading his horse into a thick cluster of trees and bracken. When they were hidden in the foliage, Laine turned to peer through the leaves. The sounds had stopped, but no one appeared.

Laine shook his head, confused. "What are they waiting for?" When Eliot didn't answer, Laine turned his head to look at him and caught the blade of a dirk coming at him. He flung himself backward and the blade caught his neck, puncturing, but not slicing. Laine made a strangled scream, slapping his hand over the wound and struggling to back away from Eliot.

Blood oozed thickly between his fingers as he slid partly down the tree. Eliot stood over him, the dirk clutched in his fist, stained with Laine's blood. Laine had never liked Eliot, but hadn't thought him capable of such an act. He was cousin to Red Alex, had grown up with the

Annan Maxwells. Laine couldn't grasp this traitorous act and stared at Eliot in disbelief, gasping for air.

"Now I'll gi' ye yer first, and last, lesson on the nature of men." Eliot took a step forward. "Trust no one."

After the monastery, Laine should have learned that lesson by now. He edged around the tree, putting a bush and several jagged boulders between himself and Eliot. The one-armed man merely laughed.

"Ye still underestimate me, laddie. Ye canna get away. If I left ye now, ye'd die from that neck. Let me do ye one kindness, to repay ye for yer misplaced trust. Come here and let me end it quick."

The betrayal nearly choked Laine. He tried to speak, but to his horror nothing came out but a strange gurgling. The pain was sharp, burning, as if the knife were still there, blocking his words.

Eliot circled the stones, stalking Laine. "Lord Graham knew ye'd be a problem and suggested I get rid of ye. I wanted to be finished wi' ye right there in camp but Lord Graham wouldna hear of it. Carlisle's too important to him, it seems."

Laine wanted to cry. As if his father cared! His father likely would have wielded the knife himself, if asked.

"And then there was Mr. Wesley. He didn't want ta kill ye either. Lord Graham thought it best if I handled it."

Laine shook his head, mouthing, *Why?* His mind couldn't wrap around it. Eliot loved Alex, as they all did. How could he do this?

"Why? For Gealach, of course. Lord Graham will make me warden of it if I get him the lass."

Laine shook his head, wanting to scream, *Fool! He's using you! He'll never give you anything. He wants you to kill me away from camp so the blame cannot be pinned on him. You are naught more than a tool and a scapegoat.* But all that came out was a wheezing sound. Laine began to feel a spark of hope, even as his limbs grew weak and heavy. He could still breathe. Laine backed away, wanting to run, but his vision clouded and he knew he'd never make it if he turned his back on Eliot. He must conserve his strength. He must be clever.

Eliot cocked his head to the side. "Why do ye shake yer head at me? Ye dinna believe it? Well, I wondered that me-self, but if he tries to cozen me, he's playing wi' the wrong man. I'll slit his gullet as easily as I did yers." His smile was a white slash in his ebony beard. "Methinks he knew this. That's why he chose me, because I could be trusted, if compensated properly."

Something hit Laine's calves and he fell backward, over a stone and into a bush. The branches tore at his arms and clothes and the burning wound in his neck.

God help me, he prayed, as the world darkened and Eliot's shadow fell over him. But he knew it for a fool's prayer. God had abandoned him long ago.

13

ALEX COULDN'T HIDE his relief when Gealach was finally sighted in the distance. His fever was no worse and as he'd gotten little rest, he thought that was probably a good sign. His shoulder hurt like hell, but it was clean, with no trace of corruption. Alex hoped he was finally on the mend.

Their injured states had doubled the travel time to Gealach and they were all weary of their own stench. Fayth had said little to him since he'd kissed her two days ago and then took responsibility for her lover's death. There was no help for it. He *was* responsible for his men's actions, even if some of them were harder to manage than others.

His thoughts turned to Eliot and Laine. He regretted his inability to go after them. If they were alive, Alex would soon hear from the Grahams with a ransom request. It was possible Ridley would attempt to trade Eliot and Laine for Fayth, but Alex thought not. Laine was Carlisle's son, and though he'd turned his back on the boy, he surely wouldn't use him in such a manner. And Eliot . . . well, it was doubtful Ridley or Carlisle saw him as being of any value to anyone.

They'd managed to reive a mount for Fayth, a large pony, but it was better than holding her in his arms for hours at a time. His thoughts turned foolish, unable to ignore the soft bottom and slim, lithe back pressed against him. Besides, she'd insisted. Every day she pushed herself harder to recover. It annoyed Davie to no end, as he tried to communicate to her that she needed to be careful. Naturally, she pretended she didn't understand him.

Alex watched Fayth tilt her head to take in the view, the wind blowing dark curls from her face. He could almost feel her little intake of breath and smiled. Gealach had the same effect on him. He raised his eyes from the tangle of dark curls and flushed skin to view his home. They had left behind the soft heathered ground and moss-covered birch and rowans for the rocky uplands that led to the Rhins. He held much of the Rhins and the Machers. His current residence, Gealach, sat atop a sheer cliff face, looking down on the Northern Channel. Seated on the craggy peninsula that extended north and south, Gealach rose above the sea, waves crashing into the dark gray stone she was built on. On a clear day one could see the green hills of Ireland to the west and the Isle of Man to the south. He couldn't look at the tower without recalling the pride in his father's face when he'd learned Alex had captured Gealach. Red Rowan had been so overcome he'd been unable to speak, only grip Alex's shoulders hard and stare into his face, as if truly seeing him for the first time. It had been Alex's finest moment. But on the heels of that memory came that of his mother, watching her husband embrace his son. Her own expression had been desolate, realizing Alex would never be a priest, that he was a fighter, like his father. That none of her sons would ever belong to the Church.

Alex pushed away his mother's disappointment. Without a word spoken among them, they reined in to gaze at the tower. The mist hung over the world like a shroud, obscuring the tower at intervals. The pale stones were darkened with age and wear, but still striking against the stark landscape. Alex sensed no trouble. His banner still flew from the walls, snapping in the gusting sea breeze. He spurred Bear forward, eager to be home.

As they carefully climbed the slope, slick and green with moss, Fayth seemed to sit straighter, throwing off her weariness.

"It's beautiful," she breathed.

Alex's chest swelled with pride. "Aye," he said, his voice rough. "And she's mine. I'll not part with her."

Ahead of them several ox-drawn carts labored up the steep path cut into the rock by the comings and goings of the locals. The carts were loaded down with provisions for the inhabitants and supplies of wood and stone for the constant repairs. A villager and his wife led the procession. They waved as Alex and his men passed, calling greetings and well-wishes.

Fayth's head turned slightly, as though she wanted to look at Alex, then thought better of it. "There's something I must tell you."

"Aye?" He watched her cautiously, wondering what brought on the sudden truce.

She rode her pony close beside Bear. "There's more to Ridley's plans than merely possessing Gealach. That's only a small part of it."

Why did she tell him this? She thought him a murderer; she saw him as her enemy. And yet, he sensed she was coming to trust him. The knowledge closed like a fist around his heart, since nothing could come of it. As soon as they arrived, he would send a message to Carlisle, relaying his terms. The deed for Fayth. She would hate him then. But what was the alternative? Set her free? So she could be raped or killed? Keep her?

That possibility set his pulse thrumming, but she'd never stay. She'd run away from him as surely as she ran from Ridley and Carlisle. He wanted a willing woman, not a prisoner. No, there was nothing else for him to do. Lying to her about Jack had been the right thing to do. He'd not thought his feelings for her could go beyond lust—had never imagined hers could even go that far. It was best if he ended it with her angry and hating him over Jack.

Her voice drew him from his thoughts.

"He has been reinforcing Wesley's band of broken men with his own and sending them on forays across the border to weaken the Scots in preparation for an English invasion."

Alex already knew this. Many English lords had been raiding the west march heavily. Some Scottish lairds were in the pay of the English and purposely stirring up trouble. He even knew Ridley was party to it, though the viper denied any involvement, claiming Wesley operated independently of him. Everyone knew it for a lie, but none of the border clans were strong enough to oppose the Grahams.

"He has been arranging strategic marriages: mine, Caroline's, his own to the earl of Dornock's daughter, and buying up land from clans he raided into poverty."

She paused, chewing at her thumbnail again. He reached over and placed his hand over hers. She started, sending a shock of awareness through his own body. He pushed her hand down, resting it firmly on her thigh. She stared at their joined hands for a long moment before looking up at him. Her eyes never ceased to fill him with longing. Warm amber, shot through with liquid sunlight.

"I wish you wouldn't do that."

He removed his hand, sitting straight in the saddle. "Then don't chew your nails."

Her cheeks colored slightly. "Now you sound like Caroline."

"Then I am in good company."

She frowned, her eyes narrowing suspiciously. "You like Caroline?"

"Why wouldn't I?"

She looked away, gaze fixed on the tower. "Well . . . she's a Graham—"

"No, she's a Maxwell, remember? She married my brother."

She seemed slightly put out by his interruption and continued as if he hadn't spoken. "And she's so very perfect. She never does or says anything wrong. She never gets upset. Many men find it . . . unconscionable that a woman be so . . . well, so like a man."

"Luckily Robert doesn't. Me either, though I confess, she took some getting used to. I dinna think Patrick would mind, either."

She fell silent. As he watched her, he began contemplating things he shouldn't. She was to marry another man. Even if she wasn't, she would never marry him. And Alex didn't go about debauching virgins he had no intention of honoring, a fact that led to his having little experience beyond a few friendly widows. And Diana Carlisle. But then, he'd meant to marry her, not simply debauch her, though he suspected he'd not been the first to plow those fields.

He reminded himself that, at one time, he had meant to ravish Fayth as punishment. The idea still had merit. *Damn it all!* He must stop thinking about her. She had no idea how he seduced her in his mind, constantly. He gritted his teeth and forced himself to think of other things.

He cleared his throat. "Uh . . . Ridley, you were telling me his plans."

"Oh . . . as far as King Henry is concerned, war with

Scotland is inevitable. But Ridley is taking no chances. He's doing all he can to provoke the Scots. If there's a war, he means to distinguish himself in battle and take many prestigious prisoners. He's counting on these prisoners turning themselves over to him, because he is ally or kin. When King Henry annexes Scotland, he will be awarded their lands."

"*If* the English win, perhaps the lords will swear fealty to Henry. Then they keep their lands."

"The Scots can't possibly win a war against England," she said, a note of condescension in her voice. "You haven't the men, the resources, or the discipline."

"Scots are the fiercest of fighters—"

"When protecting their stolen goods, but fighting for a common cause? An idea?" She snorted. "Never."

"We'll fight to keep out the English."

"Really? I happen to know of several Scots clans that would welcome the English with open arms. Besides, you haven't won a battle against the English since Bannockburn."

"What about Hadden Rigg? That was but a month ago and we routed the English, taking many prisoners."

"A failed raid. Nothing more."

"Oh, I can see now why you thought you could best me, lass, as the Scots are gutless simpletons. I'm amazed we manage to feed and clothe ourselves."

She laughed, the tension draining from the set of her shoulders. "I didn't mean that. I'm sure if the Scots army was made up of naught but Annan Maxwells, you couldn't lose. But it's not. It's made up of Armstrongs and Carlisles—"

"Aye, and Johnstones. I see what you mean. It's unlikely the Armstrongs will even fight, mind ye. They're like carrion. They'll pick over the battlefield when it's over, never lifting their sword arm."

"That's what Ridley is counting on."

Alex sighed. "Aye, and many borderers will switch loyalties if it's advantageous to do so."

"Well . . . as Ridley's prisoners, it won't be. If they swear fealty, the king will likely restore their lands and titles. I think Ridley means to kill those who agree to swear fealty so that won't happen. Then he will control the entire firth and the western road into Scotland, as well as the traffic between Scotland and northern Ireland."

"An ambitious plan."

"Ridley is nothing if not ambitious."

She blinked up at him, eyes clear and earnest. "You will tell your brother, Lord Annan, this? Perhaps if he knows, he can save himself and Caroline."

Alex was strangely touched by her concern for her sister and warmed that she trusted him as the messenger of such sensitive intelligence.

"I will."

She looked away, jaw tight. "I also hope this information helps you defend yourself against Ridley . . . I owe you for saving my life; this seems meager payment."

Her trust was the most precious gift he'd ever received but he couldn't say that, so he just nodded his thanks and continued on in strained silence. They reached the thick wall surrounding the tower, an impressive greeting to the keep. He'd repaired the crumbling wall and gatehouse to its former splendor. The gate was open and the guards cheered at his return. The tower lay before them, its defects glaringly obvious. Alex resisted the urge to make excuses for the keep, to point out the repairs he'd already made, and lay out his plans for more. In the interests of defense, he'd made the wall a priority. Now that it was finished, the keep would soon be just as fine. He wouldn't apologize for what couldn't be helped.

He dismounted and held up his arms to help Fayth down from her pony. She hesitated and he waited for her curt reminder that she could dismount without his aid. But then she surprised him by sliding into his waiting arms. He wanted to hold her against him, but people were watching and she was his prisoner. She could stand and walk without aid, so he turned, offering his arm.

She leaned heavily on it as he led her across the courtyard. "Are you planning to send me back to Carlisle soon?"

His step faltered. "Aye, I'll be writing him with the terms of the ransom."

She stopped to stare up at the keep. It stood four stories, with a cellar. He had repaired the roof, but the stone crumbled in many places, and what was once a small chapel was now a blackened shell. The strong new boards of the stables were a stark contrast to the dark and rotting wood of the older buildings. His beasts were confined in crude pens, but they were healthy and plentiful, as were his people.

"So . . ." she said, her gaze sweeping across the bailey, taking it all in. "This, in exchange for me?"

The flush of his skin deepened. He nodded, knowing what she must think. That he thought her life and her future were worth less to him than a run-down pile of stones. But Carlisle was a good match for her. A worthy match for her.

"I think . . ." she said slowly, sadly, "you're getting the better end of the deal."

He frowned down at her.

She smiled apologetically. "But Carlisle knows that. He won't trade."

His throat had gone dry. He forced himself to swallow. She started forward, tugging slightly on his arm. He began to walk again, her words ringing through his mind. Carlisle not trade? He'd considered it but thought it unlikely. An alliance with the Grahams was extremely lucrative for Carlisle. Even if he thought it an uneven trade, Ridley, as Fayth's brother, would surely seek to even the score, make it worth Carlisle's while, to see his sister out of the hands of a scoundrel and married proper, if for no other reason than to seal the alliance. And Alex was still prepared to compensate Carlisle. How could he refuse?

Alex suffered through the greetings of his small staff, consisting of a steward, a cook, and their wives and children. They all stared at Fayth openly. They had anticipated a hostage, though they'd expected her to be dripping in silks and jewels. The cook's wife, Wynda, took Fayth's hand gently, patting it.

"Ye puir dear. Come wi' me. I've a room readied and clean clothes."

But Alex wouldn't relinquish her arm. Both Fayth and Wynda looked up at him curiously.

"I'll show her to her room," Alex said, leading her to the stairs at the back of the hall. "Send a bath up for Mistress Graham."

Wynda stared at him incredulously, hands on her ample hips. "A bath? *Up?*"

Alex hesitated. When baths were taken at all, they were done in the kitchens, so hot water did not have to be hauled far.

"I'll bathe as everyone else does," Fayth said, smiling at Wynda graciously.

"Gude," Wynda said. When she met Alex's scowl, she rolled her eyes. "I'll shoo the men oot and stay meself to help her, aye? Does that please ye, me lord?"

"Very well," Alex said, leading Fayth up the stairs.

"I'll fetch ye when it's ready," Wynda called after them.

Torches were placed at intervals, illuminating the narrow staircase. Alex glanced down at Fayth and noticed the small smile pulling at the corners of her mouth.

"You find it amusing that my servants are so disobedient? I'm sure you'd find nothing of the sort in Graham Keep."

"Oh no," Fayth said. "Ridley would flog the skin off a servant who took such liberties."

"Well . . . I cannot flog her. I mean, she does fine work, and your bath will be clean and hot, I vow it—"

Fayth's laughter filled the stairwell, bright and clear as bells. Her eyes shone, deep dimples shadowing her cheeks. "I think she's wonderful, Alex."

Her smile, completely uninhibited and utterly arresting, left him fumbling for words. They had reached the landing. He stopped and turned to her. "I was . . . concerned, because you're accustomed to finer surroundings and treatment. I mean to say . . . they are the finest of people, and I think Gealach is fine, but you probably don't, and you're not used to such common treatment—"

"I'm a prisoner, remember?"

"Aye, but that doesn't mean I cannot show you the hospitality owed to a lass of your station."

She stared up at him for a long time, her mouth set in a thin, thoughtful line. He took her arm again, leading her to a small room near his. He opened the door and let out a sigh of relief to see Wynda had cleaned it thoroughly. He had accumulated a great deal of insight—furniture and other such things lifted in raids—but as yet had used it little. They had been hauling what they didn't sell down to the tunnels beneath the tower, where it sat, covered in sheets. But Wynda had obviously set the men to hauling up one of the finer beds and bedding. A woven silk rug covered the floor. There was an ornate chest at the foot of the bed and a small table and bench beneath the narrow recessed window. The shutters had been painted green and trimmed with yellow flowers that left the shutters to circle the walls. Pots and baskets bursting with flowers of yellow, purple, blue, and crimson adorned every flat surface. They surely came from Wynda's personal garden.

The Rhins and Macher boasted an unusual array of foliage that bloomed much of the year, owing to the mild sea climate. Wynda had a special plot in the courtyard, protected from the strong winds, that was to be left alone upon fear of excruciating punishment. Alex was touched that she had raided her own garden to make Fayth's room comfortable.

"Will this do?" Alex asked.

Fayth looked around the room, her expression inscrutable. "Yes." She crossed her arms gingerly beneath her breasts, careful of her wound, and eyed him speculatively. "I assume you didn't show me to my room for the pleasure of my company?"

He nodded, closing the door behind him. "You truly believe Carlisle will not trade you for Gealach? I still intend to pay him generously—in addition to returning you."

She shook her head slowly, but firmly.

"What about Ridley?"

"No. I am worthless to him. He only cares about the Clachan Fala." She shrugged. "Had you that, well, then perhaps he would consider your offer."

"I don't have time to chase after a magical gemstone that might not exist."

"I'll help you."

Alex couldn't stop the laughter that erupted at her offer. "You must be truly desperate to offer me aid."

Her cheeks flamed and her eyes narrowed. "You think I'm of no use?"

Alex tried to temper his amusement. "Why are you so insistent about this? I thought you didn't believe in it?"

"What does it matter if I believe, or if it's even real? You planned to use it to find Patrick. Why not accomplish two things?"

"And you get nothing out of it—just the warm knowledge of knowing you helped me."

The old Fayth was back, scowling at him, arms crossed over her chest. "I would be reunited with my stepmother if you found Patrick. And if we did find the Blood Stone, then everything would be fine. You could keep Gealach and I could be free."

Alex shook his head. "Why would that be the result? Your stepmother obviously has plans for the Blood Stone. You expect her just to forget them so I can use it for my own purposes?"

Her head bobbed but not in an affirmative. She obviously hadn't thought this through and hadn't considered a possible conflict with her beloved stepmother.

"Fine!" she cried, throwing up her arms and turning away. "Just go away."

Well, her short-lived truce now made sense. She'd been planning to reason with him all along. He felt a pang of guilt that he was forced to be so unreasonable, but he couldn't be impulsive, not with Gealach at stake. He hesitated, wanting to explain himself to her. But then her words came back to him. She was just a prisoner. No matter what he told her, it would change nothing between them. He was still an outlaw, a Maxwell, and a murderer. Nothing he said or did would ever change those things. Not even Gealach.

"Don't try to escape." When she didn't acknowledge his words he said, "Fayth, I mean it. You'll get more than an arrow in the arm this time."

She whirled around, her face flushed. "Just what I need, another man telling me what to do!"

"I'm only trying to protect you—"

"Like you protect all your prisoners? Like you protected Jack?"

He deserved that, he supposed, though it made him furious to have it thrown in his face. Rather than stay and endure more of her abuse, he turned on his heel and left.

14

FAYTH STOOD ON the roof of Gealach Tower, hands resting on the parapet, gazing out across the North Channel at Ireland. She closed her eyes as the chill breeze blew against her cheeks. When she opened them again, Ireland was still there. Alex had been right, you could see for miles on a clear day and the view was breathtaking.

She was still annoyed she'd been unable to convince Alex to help her find Mona. She'd felt so sure from the way he looked at her and touched her that he would help her. He helped everyone else, why not her? His refusal had been bitterly disappointing. She still couldn't shake the odd feeling of betrayal, which was absurd! He was her enemy, after all; had she really expected him to join forces with her? To be her savior? What a simple little fool she was!

She turned at the sound of footsteps behind her, but it was only her guard, circling the roof idly. She turned back to the open air. It seemed her whole life had been a prison, constantly guarded. Only as Hugh had she known freedom. She was in skirts again, her hair plaited at her neck, her body cleaned of work and road dust. She wondered whose garments she wore. They were not servants' attire, but the clothes of a gentlewoman. The bodice was stiffened violet taffeta. The skirt was a fall of fine silk, marbled murrey and bice. Linen petticoats and silk undergarments. Everything was too big, of course. Fayth ran her hands self-consciously over the loose bodice, envying the woman who had once filled it out.

Far below, towering waves crashed against the jagged rocks, sending up white spray. Birds glided over the sea, diving to capture fish, then disappearing into the cliff the tower sat upon, where their nests were hidden. Was there a beach below? Hidden from her sight by the lip of the cliff? She would love to explore this place thoroughly, if only she weren't a prisoner.

Her guard was wandering again, his steps echoing off the battlement, but Fayth didn't turn. Her thoughts drifted to Mona and Caroline, her mood turning maudlin. Would Alex warn his brother of Ridley's plans? Would it be enough to save Caroline the misery of losing her husband and home? And Mona . . . Fayth was losing hope she would ever find her stepmother. She was useless to those she loved most.

"I see you didn't ignore my invitation from lack of interest."

Fayth turned quickly, hands clutching the parapet for support. Alex stood behind her, looking over her head to the distant shore. She moved away from him, his nearness sending a disturbing wave of awareness over her. She loathed this infernal fragility. Her wound no longer ached, but the arm itself was as weak as a piece of string dangling at her side. Just this morning she'd begun lifting things, to build her strength, and now her arm was sore as a result. It still angered her that a mere arm wound had so debilitated her, but at least she recovered, however slowly.

Alex stepped away, as if sensing he unsettled her. They'd been at Gealach two days and she'd seen little of him in that time. He'd invited her, via Wynda, to walk to the roof with him this morning. She'd ignored the invitation and waited until after dinner to venture up herself. Now here he was anyway.

She turned away to walk the perimeter of the wall. Her guard had been sent away, which meant she would not be rid of Alex easily. "It's unnecessary to spend time with my gaoler." She really thought that was best. When she was with him she had all sorts of stupid and reckless impulses.

He said nothing, nor did he follow her. She stopped at the opposite wall, no longer able to enjoy her outing. Annoyed, she turned toward him. He stood in the spot she'd vacated, looking out over the sea as she had, his head lifted as if smelling the air. He wore no hat and the sun caught the copper and blond strands threading his dark hair. He was tall and straight, with strong broad shoulders. Even now, when he was still—and at times he was so still and watchful he unnerved her—he reminded her of a tightly coiled spring, a force on the edge of release.

Though he kept himself neat, he had little regard for fashion. His leather doublet and breeches were well made and functional, his boots, sturdy but worn. His long, sleek hair tied back with a simple leather thong. And yet, she found him infinitely more attractive than any of the fops that paraded through Graham Keep.

Oh, why did he have to be a Maxwell? Why did he have to be Red Alex?

Drawn to him, she approached slowly, circling the wall. When she was several feet from him, she stopped. He glanced at her briefly, before looking back out to sea. He seemed distracted and Fayth felt free to study his profile. He'd shaved the beard away and his tanned skin was unblemished except for the scars he bore. Scars she had inflicted. A thin pink line where she'd cut him with his helm.

A jagged puckered scar on his temple where she had bashed him with a jug. And another, hidden from her view. A ravaged shoulder where she'd shot him.

Confusion churned in her belly, constricted her chest. Every time she gazed upon the wounds she'd inflicted she was blanketed with guilt. Even though he was a Maxwell and her abductor, she would take back every hurt if she could. Wesley would think her pudding-hearted, that she regretted maiming Jack's murderer. And he would be right! Fayth chewed at her nail, her gaze shifting between Alex and the view. What was the matter with her? Her heart was at constant war since she'd met him. He'd overturned everything she believed, thought she understood, so that she knew nothing at all anymore.

Alex shifted, leaning his hip against the parapet. He stared down at her, hands crossed over his chest. He saw where her gaze was fixed and he rubbed the scar on his temple. "Not too pretty, eh? Scarred as I am."

She flushed, lowering her eyes and clasping her hands together tightly. She'd been thinking the opposite, that he was a pleasure to look at, comely beyond words. "As I inflicted them, it would speak ill of me if I could not look upon my work." But she couldn't, not without remorse.

He kneaded the scar. "Your work . . . I'd never thought of it that way."

"Aye, I've been busy inflicting pain. At least the wounds I gave you healed."

"Whose wounds have not healed?"

Fayth shrugged. She'd said too much, more than she'd meant to. She'd been doing better, trying to rein in her impulsive nature—thinking before acting and stopping thoughtless words before they fell from her tongue. But somehow, when she was with him, she found herself saying things she never meant to give voice to.

"We've all done things we regret, Fayth. You must forgive yourself."

She looked up at him hopefully. "Have you? Done things you regret?"

"Aye. I have."

She leaned her elbows on the wall, at ease with him as she'd been with no one else, ever. Even Jack. She frowned at the thought, remembering Wesley's words. *You have no idea what Jack wanted. Jack was never any more to you than a way out.* Had she used Jack, as Ridley used her? A tool? She'd never exchanged as many words with Jack in all the years she'd known him as she'd already done with Alex. *Jack never kissed me until I could not breathe.* She trembled at the thought and quickly pushed it away. What did she know about Jack? She searched her mind, couldn't even recall if he had siblings, if he could read or write . . . who his friends were, besides Wesley.

She sensed Alex watched her. She asked, "Have you heard from Carlisle?"

"Not yet."

"Is that what you're waiting for?"

"Ah . . . aye."

"May I give you some advice?"

He raised a brow curiously and nodded.

"I know how Ridley's mind works. And though I can't anticipate exactly what he might do, I can give you some possibilities." She leaned against the parapet in the same manner he did, facing him. "He might tell Carlisle to agree but it will be a trap."

Alex folded his hands behind his back. "Why are you offering me advice?"

She straightened and strode away, toward the ladder leading into the castle. "Why do you think? To save my own skin. I'm the only leverage you have. No reason to give me up for nothing."

The air inside the keep stifled after the fresh breeze on the roof. The idea of returning to her room to sew or wander about left her deflated.

"If you feel strong enough, I could show you the cellars."

Fayth couldn't imagine what there was to see in the cellars, but anything was better than her room, so she took the arm he offered.

As he led her down several flights of stairs, he said, "I know you're not as thoughtless and self-serving as you'd have me believe."

"Do you?" Fayth was glad for the gloom, it hid her furious blush.

On the ground floor, he led her through the hall to the kitchens, where Wynda and her daughters watched them with raised brows, but made no comment, then on to the larder. He removed a candelabra from its wall sconce and handed it to her. He pushed aside crates and casks, revealing a square of wood cut into the floorboards. Slipping his fingers in the cracks, he pulled upward. The door creaked on leather hinges, releasing a damp, molding smell.

Fayth wrinkled her nose, but handed him the candelabra when he reached for it.

"I'll go first," he said, and disappeared into the hole.

Fayth stepped gingerly to the opening. She'd never been afraid of heights, but in her current state, she found the distance to the shining candelabra daunting. Alex held the candelabra higher, illuminating his face.

"Come on," he encouraged. "I'll catch you if you fall."

Heart racing unnaturally, Fayth lowered herself into the hole. Her arms and legs trembled as she climbed down the ladder. Halfway down, Alex grasped her hips, then her waist, anchoring her the rest of the way. His grip loosened when she was on solid ground, but remained on her hips as she turned.

The candelabra rested on the ground at their feet, leaving his face in shadows. Confronted with his overwhelming presence, surrounding her, supporting her, the myriad of reasons why wanting him was so wrong fled. She raised her chin, trying to glean something from his expression. He wanted her, too. She knew it. Could feel it in the flexing of his fingers, as if he fought the same urges. This little excursion, alone, in the dark, was so very dangerous.

The war continued raging in her heart. She'd vowed to be more thoughtful, to not act recklessly. And here she was, exploring the bowels of Gealach with the one man she could not resist. She was a reckless fool. But none of that seemed to matter when her heart pounded and her skin tingled, when all she wanted was for him to kiss her again. She longed for these feelings she didn't understand, the passion and excitement she hadn't known existed until Alex. She wanted to gorge herself on it, as she sometimes did on sweetmeats, until she was sated. And why not? Soon enough she would have none of those things, no matter what her fate.

His fingers slid away as he reached for the candelabra. When he straightened, he held out his hand. Wordlessly, she placed her hand in his and followed him into the darkness.

Fayth soon discovered that the trapdoor led to more than a simple cellar, or even a dungeon. There was a place to store food and keep it cool. There were also heavily barred cells for holding prisoners, all empty now. And as they followed the wending corridors cut into the rock that was the foundation of Gealach, they encountered more doors, all locked and barred, leading to more cells and rooms. And more corridors and doors.

He stopped at one that was barred and heaved up the slab of wood. He led her inside, holding the candelabra high. Fayth stopped short and gasped. It was a treasure room, unlike anything she'd ever seen. She stepped forward slowly, gazing around the room in wonder.

"Is this all yours?" she asked, lowering herself into an elaborately carved chair surrounded by bags of gold and silver coins, suits of armor, portraits in golden frames, wooden and metal caskets probably containing more valuables. Spying a loose coin at her feet, Fayth picked it up, inspecting it in the palm of her hand. It was a Spanish ducat.

He shrugged, smiling, and set the candelabra on a stack of crates. "I suppose . . ."

Fayth's eyes widened and she said in a rushed breath, "Is it Prince Shanahan's treasure? That he brought for his fair maiden?"

Alex laughed, hands folded behind his back. "I doubt it. The dates on the coins are from earlier this century."

"Then what . . . ?"

"I dinna ken, really. Pirates, I imagine. I only discovered the door in the larder a few months ago, else I would have used this long ago to ransom Patrick from your brother."

Fayth said nothing, head swiveling, trying to take in everything she could make out in the candlelight.

"No one had lived here in decades . . . so I suppose pirates were using it as a hiding place. But they haven't for a very long time, of that I'm sure. When I found this room, everything was covered in years—perhaps decades—of dust, still is, actually, as I haven't been through all of it. There's trunks of clothes down here, too. That's where your gown came from. If you don't like it, feel free to pick out another." He gestured to several trunks along the wall.

Fayth didn't move. The gown was adequate and there were several more in her room anyway. "So this is pirate treasure?"

"Aye."

"Aren't you afraid they'll come back for it?"

He shrugged. "Not really. Who knows? They might have already come for it and gotten lost in the tunnels." He turned back toward the door, a brow arched. "These tunnels go on for miles it seems, branching off in all directions. I've yet to explore them all." He turned back to her. "There's a story that claims there's a magical spring down here somewhere."

Fayth shook her head, stunned. "If either Ridley or Carlisle knew about this . . ." There would be no pretense of marriage. Ridley would descend in force and clean the place out.

"You won't tell them." It wasn't a question.

She looked at him sharply. "How can you know that? I'm your prisoner, the enemy. What else would you expect me to do? If I can use this information to somehow buy my freedom, why shouldn't I?"

"Because you hate Ridley and would do nothing to further his cause." His voice echoed in the cavernous room. "Besides, you've told me too much. You trust me . . . and I trust you. I think this proves it."

Her hands gripped the carved chair arms as she stared up at him. The darkness around their warm circle of candlelight was complete. Water dripped in the distance. He should not trust her. He should never put his trust in her. She *would* do anything to escape and yet she couldn't stand that he gave her this—something she could use to hurt him. "What do you think I was doing at Annancreag the night I gave you that scar? I was furthering Ridley's cause."

He shook his head. "I used to think that, but I know better now."

She squeezed the wood to hide the trembling of her hands. "You know nothing." She'd never been able to hide her feelings well, but damned if she'd let him see how his words shook her. This wasn't supposed to happen. "You're a fool if you trust me."

He wandered across the room, the darkness swallowing him. Fayth was uneasy with him out of sight, though she heard him moving around, rummaging through the room's contents. A moment later he reappeared, carrying a silver casket.

"I pretended to be a whore," Fayth insisted, "and let a horde of Grahams into your brother's home. They murdered your people and stole Lord Annan's wife." She lifted her chin a notch. She'd refused to contemplate what she'd done for so long, buried it because the shame and regret were too much to bear. But she must take responsibility and what better time than now, when Alex stood there proclaiming her to be something she wasn't.

"That was my doing," she said, holding his gaze. "I am responsible for your people's misery. I am responsible for Lord Annan's unhappiness—*for my own sister's grief.*" She swallowed hard and stiffened her spine. "I nearly ruined her life. And I did it all willingly."

He said nothing for a long time. He opened the casket and began sifting though it. Her jaw clenched tighter and tighter until she thought it would snap. Why didn't he speak? Did he not hear her? Did he not understand what a mistake it was to put his trust in her?

He glanced up at her. "You say you did it all willingly? You kissed me . . . willingly?"

She rolled her eyes. Trust a man to hear nothing but what pertained to his sexual prowess. "Yes, after a fashion. I did what I had to. I needed to let in Wesley and his men. You stood between me and the door."

He nodded absently. "I'm confused . . . You kidnapped Caroline, but then almost immediately released her to a convent. A Scottish convent, where she could easily get word to my brother."

"That's what she wanted."

His brow furrowed. "All that, just to take her to a nearby convent? No one had to die. Rob would have let her visit it."

Fayth sighed. "That's not what I meant. All her life she wanted to be a nun. Papa had promised us both some say in our future. He granted Caroline her wish to take the veil, and me, my wish to marry whom I chose. But then Papa died and Ridley forced Caroline to marry your brother." Fayth tried to find the words to explain Caroline to him, how very exceptional and different she was. "She's not like us . . . she would never run from what she sees as her duty."

"And so you set out to rescue her."

"Yes . . . at least that's what I thought I was doing."

"But it turned out Caroline was quite happy married to my brother."

Fayth raised her brows censoriously. "What I saw of their marriage looked far from blissful . . . but what do I know? He was a beast and she was *crying*." Of course, Alex couldn't understand the significance of Caroline shedding tears, but it had been a shock and a horror to Fayth, who had never seen her sister weep, or rage, or even laugh. "But you're right. She later claimed to love him. I didn't understand . . . I wouldn't listen—after all, he's a Maxwell. And there was Jack . . ." Her gaze dropped to her hands, now folded in her lap. She didn't want to think of Jack. Didn't know why she was telling these things to Alex, things she'd never spoken of to anyone, but it felt good to finally let it out. She didn't want to stop. "And now she hates me. Being Caroline, she'll probably forgive me, but she'll never trust me. Will never look on me in the same manner."

Alex held an ivory-handled mirror in his hand. "Was it your idea, to come to Annancreag and rescue Caroline?"

Fayth nodded, then shook her head. "Well, Ridley sent me for the Clachan Fala. He believed it would be delivered to Annancreag after Caroline and Lord Annan wed. I was to take it if I could and escape. Or let Wesley and his men in to subdue the Maxwells and steal the Blood Stone. But that's not why I went . . . well, not completely. He said, if I did that for him, I wouldn't have to wed Carlisle. But taking Caroline was my idea."

"He didn't want Caroline to be rescued?"

"He didn't care . . . but if I found the Blood Stone, he said we could bring her along."

"Ah . . ." Alex said, rifling through the casket again. He stood just outside the candelabra's light, his expression hidden from her.

"What does that mean?"

"You didn't find the Blood Stone."

"No."

"And you took your sister anyway."

She felt as if she were standing before Ridley again, being interrogated. The same anger and impatience bubbled to the surface. "Exactly! I failed because I'm such a thoughtless fool! I condemned myself to Carlisle."

"The way I see it," he said, stepping into the light and slipping the mirror into her hand, "what you did was completely selfless. You gave up your own happiness and future, to give your sister what you thought she longed for most."

Fayth gazed at her reflection. Her eyes were overbright and there was a tremor to her lips. She tightened her mouth and slapped the mirror facedown on her lap, to hide her weakness.

"Caroline loves your brother. What I did was despicable. Your people died for nothing."

"Maxwells and Grahams have been dying for centuries for less worthy reasons than a woman's happiness." He knelt by her chair, so he could look her in the face. "I have done far worse things than you, in the name of the blood feud between our families. And my father, even worse. And for no more reason than their surname was Graham."

His words seemed to make it worse. His face blurred from the tears collecting in her eyes. He was the enemy. He should not understand. He should not forgive. *He should not trust.*

"You must admit you were wrong and forgive yourself."

She shook her head, tears spilling over her lashes and splashing onto her fists.

"Why not? Do you plan to do it again?"

She shook her head more vigorously, rubbing a sleeve over her eyes. "No, I swear it. I've promised myself I would stop being thoughtless and reckless. And I've tried, I truly have."

"This . . . thoughtlessness and recklessness you keep mentioning . . . perhaps it's merely instinct, such as warriors have, to protect yourself and those you love. It can oft steer us in ways that might seem wrong, but are, in fact, honorable."

Fayth blinked at him, stirred by his words. His face was beneath hers, looking up at her with the shadow of a smile. The deep blue of his eyes held her, almost black in the gloom. She realized his hand rested on her thigh. Heat rushed to her chest, her neck, but she couldn't look away. His smile faded, his gaze moving over her face.

Would he kiss her again? *Oh please let him kiss me again.* Her breath came short, her heart throbbing in her ears. They were completely alone here; no one would interrupt. She swayed toward him.

He blinked, as if waking from a dream, and stood

abruptly. He rubbed a hand over his face, then into his hair, pulling russet locks free from the club at his neck to fall around his face. "There's more . . . I haven't showed you everything."

Fayth wanted to scream with frustration. *Kiss me!* She didn't care about seeing anything else. Her body was alive with quivering desire, all wanting one thing, his mouth. She stood on unsteady legs, too dazed and confused to respond. She took his arm as he led her from the chamber. The tunnels had been leading slowly downward since they left the larder, but now they descended rapidly. Steps had been cut into stone. They became slick as they went deeper. The scent of sea air grew strong and a swift breeze whistled through the caverns.

Fayth hung on Alex's arm, more because she enjoyed touching him than from needing his assistance. He went slowly, warning her to watch her footing. Fayth saw light ahead and as they turned a corner, they were faced with the last set of steps, leading into a sheltered cove. Several boats were moored in the cove, two of them exceptionally long and equipped with oars and a sail. Closer to the entrance was a bark—a three-masted sailing ship. It was smaller than most ships she saw coming and going in the firth, but it could easily carry Alex's entire household and then some to safety. Its size made it more easily maneuverable than larger vessels.

"You're not going to tell me these were here, too?"

He laughed as they reached the rocky shore of the cove. "Well, some of them were."

She released his arm and wandered out of the shelter of the cove, onto a secluded beach. They were surrounded on all sides by cliffs. The only way in or out was the sea, or the steps cut in the cove. She shaded her eyes, gazing upward. The cliff curved over her, but she knew Gealach sat atop it. Eagles soared overhead, circling to inspect the intruders. A puffin ambled along the water's edge, a stack of silvery sand eels in its orange and black beak, white breast feathers ruffling in the breeze.

She felt Alex behind her, though he didn't touch her. Waves crashed against the jagged gray rocks that rose above the water's surface. Fayth's gaze swept the endless horizon before her, breathless from the power and beauty of it. She could almost imagine the ghosts of Prince Shanahan and his Bonny, wandering the lonely beach, searching always for each other.

"I can see why you won't give this up without a fight."

He was silent and so she turned to find him looking down at her, his eyes dark and hooded.

"What are you thinking?" she asked.

He held her gaze a moment longer, then raised his chin to look out over her head. "Things I shouldn't."

He started to move around her. She placed a hand on his sleeve. "Why shouldn't you?"

He looked down at her again, eyes narrowed in caution.

She'd dreamed of him holding her and kissing her. She was tired of waking, flushed and aching with want. She'd caused his people to die, knocked him unconscious, pierced him with an arrow, stolen his horse and sword, and he forgave her. Perhaps he thought it fitting payment for murdering her betrothed. Perhaps it no longer mattered. *Jack.* The named seemed so meaningless now. She couldn't even conjure his face before her, couldn't recall the feel of his arms, the taste of his kiss. Alex had wiped every memory away but his.

"Why shouldn't we?" she asked. The wind whipped around them, blowing hair across their faces, plastering her skirts to her thighs. She thought the wind stole her words, but he shook his head, his expression regretful.

"Fayth . . . you shouldn't—"

"Shouldn't! Shouldn't! I'm tired of being told what I

shouldn't do." She moved closer to him, placed her hands on his chest. "I think I should . . . this once."

His hands went to her shoulders and squeezed gently, his gaze burning over her upturned face. "I thought you were trying to be better. To not be thoughtless . . . or reckless . . ."

Fayth sighed in disgust. "How can it be thoughtless, when all my thoughts are filled with—with . . ." *What was she saying?*

She turned away, but he caught her arm, pulling her against him. He kissed her before she could say another word. She went limp in his arms, surrendering herself to something stronger than her will, more powerful than his resolve. He used his tongue and his teeth, teasing and nipping and sucking, wringing moans of want from her. She clung to him, arms snaking around his neck, pulling his head down to kiss her deeper. She followed his lead, her tongue tracing his lips and teeth, sucking at his tongue, until he groaned and dropped to his knees, dragging her with him.

His hands slipped under her skirts, stroking her thighs and bottom. She ached and throbbed between her legs, damp with desire. She knew how a man and woman came together, had seen servants rutting in the stables and animals mating in the fields—and knew that's what she wanted.

His fingers were at her neck, fumbling with the ties of her shift. When he finally untied the knot, he spread it wide, sliding his palms beneath the collar to cover her chest and shoulders. His hands burned her, big and rough, caressing her skin reverently. He lowered his head to kiss her again, his gaze sweeping over her, devouring her. Then he stilled, his gaze on the juncture between her neck and shoulder.

Fayth had almost forgotten the flogging Ridley had administered what seemed like a lifetime ago, but now shame burned her cheeks afresh. She jerked the collar back over her shoulder, turning away from him.

"What happened?" he demanded, pulling her back and holding her fast.

She didn't try to escape him, burying her face in his shoulder. "Ridley," she said, her voice muffled against his doublet.

His hand slid up her shoulder again, easing the collar back. His fingers traced the pink scar, then traveled to her back, where he tentatively fingered the other lash marks. She couldn't look at him, but felt him lowering his head. The shock of his lips against the scar nearly wrenched a cry from her. A sigh shuddered through her as her head fell to the side.

His mouth moved up her neck to her ear. He pulled the lobe between his teeth, his breath sending shivers through her body. "I adore even your scars," he whispered.

She captured his face between her palms, staring at him in wonder. That he was such a fine man, and she'd thought for so very long he was a monster. She kissed him, her hands slipping over the scar at his temple and into his hair, damp from the sea mist blowing over them and sleek as satin beneath her fingers.

Their tongues swirled and probed, their hands moving greedily over each other. Fayth worked at the hooks on his doublet until it was unfastened. She pulled at the ties of his shirt, slipping her hands inside to feel the hard skin of his belly. Her fingers encountered the puckered skin of scars on his ribs and chest. At his right shoulder the bandage covering his wound halted her explorations. His skin was warm, but not fevered.

She tore her mouth away from his kiss. "Is it better? Does it hurt?"

His mouth moved down her neck and chest, to the swell of her breasts. "Aye . . . nay . . ." he murmured against her skin.

"I'm so sorry," she whispered, her fingers skimming over the clean linen.

"It doesn't matter."

He unlaced her bodice and slipped his hand inside, cupping her breast. She inhaled sharply. No one had ever touched her there. He leaned over her, one arm around her waist, supporting her. His thumb passed gently over her nipple as his gaze traveled over her face.

Her shallow breath whispered between parted lips. She clutched his good shoulder, waiting. He was going to kiss her breast and the anticipation was killing her.

"I've wanted you since I first set eyes on you."

"Even though I'm a Graham?"

"I didn't know . . . then . . ." He lowered his head, taking her nipple in his mouth and sucking at it so her back arched, her arms clasping his head and neck to bring him closer. Heat poured through her, scalding her, centering between her legs. The sensation was sharp, intense, pleasure bordering on pain. His arms circled her, embracing her and holding her close while his mouth worked wicked magic over her body.

He kissed her mouth again. "And you let me do this, even though I'm a Maxwell . . ."

"Well . . . Maxwells aren't so awful, it seems . . ."

He laughed against her mouth and she wanted even that inside her, so she kissed him, swallowing the rough sounds of his amusement. He responded to her ardor, his tongue thrusting, his hands stroking and kneading.

Fayth had no name for what she wanted him to do to her. She only knew the coarse words men used—to swive, to rut—or the odd words the priests used—to fornicate or copulate. And none of those seemed appropriate, so she pressed her hand against his crotch, startled that even through his breeches she could feel the hard length of him.

"Oh bloody Christ," he moaned, gathering her against him again and burying his face in her hair—which he had loosened from its plait, though she had no recollection of him doing so. "We canna do this."

She moved her hand, stroking him, to show him they could if he would just get on with it. But his hand covered hers, bringing it to his face where he kissed her palm fervently.

"I canna debauch ye."

"You can," she breathed.

He shook his head, his eyes still burning with desire. "There are consequences to this act, love." He closed his eyes and took a deep breath as if to brace himself. When he looked at her again, his gaze was firm. "I cannot send you to Carlisle deflowered. If he discovers you're no virgin, I don't know what he'll do. I won't be responsible for harm befalling ye."

It was as if he'd tossed her into the icy sea. She grew stiff in his arms. She didn't know what she'd expected, hadn't taken the time to think of what she was doing. But she'd not expected him to throw Carlisle in her face.

"It's too late for that," she said.

She disengaged herself from him and stood, fixing her shift and bodice. Her hands shook, making the task absurdly difficult. When she had herself in order, she turned, expecting to find him similarly recovered from their impulsive passion and ready to return to the tower. But he sat cross-legged in the sand, his head resting in his hands. His hair had come completely loose from the thong and spilled down over his shoulders, glinting like burnished metal in the sun.

The longer she stood staring at him, the angrier she became. Was it honor that kept him from lying with her? Or simple greed? He wouldn't jeopardize Gealach for a mere rut he could get from any likely lass. She folded her arms under her breasts, staring up at the sheer cliff face. The rational, logical part of her couldn't blame him. Gealach was a treasure. But Fayth had rarely been one to operate on logic. She'd always acted on emotion, giving into it heedlessly. And right now she felt fury—and perhaps a touch of hurt—that she was no more than a tool to men. To this man, that she had expected so much more from.

Even Jack? She blinked at the thought. True, Jack had been landless . . . and marriage to her would bring him land and beasts, but that wasn't why he'd agreed to marry her. In fact, *she'd* asked *him!* It had never even occurred to him that Hugh Graham's daughter would consider wedding him. And she never would have, had Papa not grown ill.

Oh Jack . . . life would be so much simpler if you were still alive.

Sensing movement nearby, Fayth turned. Alex stood, brushing the sand off his clothes. His shirt and doublet still hung open and she could see the dark hair dusting his chest and abdomen. Desire coiled sharp and tight in her belly. She turned away, her fury mounting.

"Fayth . . ."

Her name on his lips made her whirl, hands fisted at her sides. "Do not address me familiar!"

He pulled up short, his face blank.

"I may be your prisoner, but that gives you no leave to maul me like a common whore!"

Uncertainty and confusion marred his brow.

She tried to sweep by him, retaining some dignity, but he caught her arm.

"Pardon, Mistress Graham, but I clearly recall saying we *shouldn't.*"

That he was right was more than she could bear. She yanked her arm away, her anger and mortification galvanizing her, and marched into the cove.

He caught up at the stone steps, his arm slipping around her to lend support.

"I do not need your help!" She tried to shrug his arm away.

He seized her shoulders, swinging her around to face him. "I know you're angry and well you should be. I ken you dinna want to wed Carlisle. I wish I didn't have to send you—"

"Then don't!"

He continued as if she hadn't spoken. "And I had no right to start something I wasn't prepared to finish. But I'll not let you rush heedlessly through these tunnels. They're dangerous and you don't know your way."

"Very well," she said as coolly as she could. He was right, of course. She was being thoughtless as always. She would never escape if she slipped and broke her leg. Damn it all, she hated it when he was right!

She took his arm but refused to speak to him the entire way back up to the tower. After a time he quit trying to coax a response from her. Fayth was so distressed she could not think clearly. It seemed foolish now to have turned shrew on him. She had acted the wanton and now looked ridiculous because of her behavior. And yet, the injury to her pride was too great. She could not look at him without anger and resentment clouding her mind.

They arrived at the ladder where this had all begun, where she'd been giddy-headed in her desire for him. She smirked at her own folly and grasped the rungs as if she could wring punishment from them. Alex sent her up to the larder first, holding the candelabra high so she could see.

When she came up through the hole, she immediately sensed she was not alone. Still poised on the ladder, half out of the trapdoor, she turned. Skelley, perched on a barrel, straightened at her appearance. Biddy sat beside him, whining softly.

Skelley had avoided Fayth since she'd donned a gown and even now stared at the floor, hands clasped behind his back as she crawled through the hole and into the larder.

Biddy came to her tentatively, as if she could sense the waves of furious heat emanating from Fayth. Fayth scratched the dog's head absently.

She was feeling the effects of her afternoon of exercise. Her muscles ached and lethargy rolled over her. She longed to have her former strength back—so she could steal a horse and ride as far from Red Alex as possible!

"G'day to ye, Mistress Graham."

"Greetings, Skelley."

Alex climbed lithely from the hole as if an arrow had not ripped through his shoulder and become dreadfully corrupted, as if the leech hadn't cut his rotted flesh away. The bastard!

Biddy went to his side, tail wagging joyously as he closed the trapdoor and pushed the barrels back into place.

Fayth asked Skelley, "Any word from Carlisle or my brother?"

Skelley slid her a strange look, quickly returning his gaze to the floorboards. "Ah . . . of a sort. Alex? A word?"

He obviously would tell her nothing without first relaying it to Alex, so Fayth turned on her heel and entered the kitchens.

She ignored the stares and whispers, keeping her chin high as she passed through. She knew what they were thinking—a woman, exploring dark corridors, *alone,* with a man like Red Alex. If word of this got out, she was as good as ruined. *So what would it possibly matter now if they lay together?* She pushed that errant thought away, rushing blindly forward. She was almost to the door when a figure stepped in front of her, stealing the air from her lungs.

"Weel . . ." Armless Eliot's black eyes trailed from the top of her head to her toes, and back up again, lingering on her breasts. "If it ain't wee Hugh Maxwell."

15

"ELIOT'S HERE?" Alex said, surprise and relief sending him for the door to the kitchens before Skelley could finish speaking.

"Aye—but wait!"

Alex turned impatiently.

"Laine's dead."

"Dead?"

Skelley nodded. "Eliot says he was killed when they were captured."

Alex paused, his heart sinking to his toes. Laine, dead? He'd been very fond of the boy. They shared a similar history, having both been destined for the kirk. But Alex had never been abused as Laine had. And unlike Carlisle, Alex's father would have killed every last monk party to it and razed the monastery—something Alex had very nearly done himself when he discovered what Father Rae had done to the lad. Skelley, with his usual wisdom, had advised Alex against killing men of God—even the deaths of the ungodly men of Rees Abbey would bring them more trouble than they needed.

And Eliot had been most irritated at Skelley that day. He'd been itching to slaughter the monks. Alex didn't like the niggling doubt at the back of his mind. Eliot hated Laine. That in itself was not unusual, as Eliot hated many men, but Laine had done nothing to earn such loathing. In fact, he'd done much to earn respect and trust. Eliot seemed to dislike everyone Alex trusted. It had taken Eliot a long time to finally accept Skelley.

Alex rubbed his hand over his chin. "Ridley would never intentionally kill Carlisle's son."

Skelley joined Alex near the door, tonguing the gap in his tooth, fingers buried in the tangles of his beard. "It could've been an accident, as Eliot claims."

Alex's eyes narrowed. "Laine was young, but no fool."

Skelley opened his mouth to respond when Fayth's raised voice reached them from the kitchens. "Out of my way!"

Alex raised his brows at Skelley and entered the kitchens. There Fayth stood, hair waving wildly around her shoulders and clothes in disarray, as if she'd just been tumbled well. The ache in Alex's groin returned at the sight of her—and the knowledge of how close he'd been to tumbling her.

Eliot blocked her exit, his gaze raking her covetously.

"Eliot," Alex barked, surprising even himself with the sharpness of his voice. Fayth's shoulders jerked, but she didn't look at him.

Eliot's head turned and he backed away, though his burning gaze lingered on Fayth longer than Alex could bear.

Fayth stalked out of the kitchen. Eliot's gaze followed her until she was gone, then met Alex's. His eyes widened, eyebrows rising knowingly.

Alex approached him. "It's good to have you back . . . but most unexpected."

Eliot looked behind Alex to Skelley, then farther to the larder, an eyebrow cocked curiously. "Aye, weel, I managed to escape. They dinna expect much from a one-armed man."

Alex doubted that. Eliot was well known throughout the west march by many names, not all of them associated with Alex. Neither was Eliot a modest man—but a braggart when it suited him. However, it was also his way to downplay his greatest feats in the interest of building a more interesting tale when he was ready to tell it.

"We lost Laine?"

Eliot's face creased with regret. "Aye, the lad went down fighting, too. He wouldna tell them he was Carlisle's lad and so they didna spare him." He lowered his voice, his eyes slanting around the room. "Carlisle was wi' Lord Graham . . . the lad told me, as he lay there wi' his lifeblood spilling onto the ground, that he'd rather die than go back to his father."

Alex said nothing. He had known Laine well enough to know Eliot spoke the truth . . . and yet Laine did not speak of his father or his time at the monastery with anyone. He'd spoken little of it to Alex and what he did say was revealed only because Alex had been a novice himself once and understood the way things sometimes went among the brothers.

"You sure aboot that?" Skelley asked.

Eliot turned a contemptuous glare on Skelley. "Ye got something to say, man, ye should say it."

Skelley came forward, his normally easygoing expression hardened with suspicion. "The two of ye werena gettin' on last I saw ye."

Eliot stepped forward, going nose to nose with Skelley. "The lad stayed and saved me life when you and the leech ran like cowards."

Skelley snapped out his dirk, slipping it under the thick black waves of Eliot's beard.

"Say that again, you armless—"

"That's enough!" Alex said, stepping between the two of them. Skelley moved back, removing the dirk from its threatening position, but not sheathing it. Eliot didn't budge.

To Alex's surprise, Eliot's notorious temper didn't flare at this provocation. The gaze still trained on Skelley was calculating, as if he planned to bide his time.

"Carlisle was there, you say?" Alex asked.

Eliot nodded.

"They were looking for Mistress Graham?"

"Aye, Carlisle wants her back, so does Graham. Carlisle says no deal wi' oot the lass."

"And yet they're camping in the woods together?" Skelley said scornfully.

Eliot didn't even look at Skelley. "Carlisle insisted on joining the search . . . he's besotted with the lass." He quirked an eyebrow. "He said more than once he'd geld Red Alex if he so much as harmed a hair on her head." Eliot leaned back to look pointedly at the larder again before raising his eyebrows speculatively.

Alex ignored the innuendo. "So, think you Carlisle and Ridley will bargain?"

Eliot nodded. "Oh, aye. I dinna think Lord Graham likes it o'er much, as he kens the value of the Rhins, but Carlisle wants the lass. Have ye sent yer terms?"

"Aye," Alex said, leaving the kitchen with the two men on his heels. "A few days ago. I expect I'll hear back any day now." He stopped suddenly and turned to Eliot. "What did Lord Carlisle do when he learned of Laine's death?"

Eliot's black eyes shifted away, before fixing again on Alex. "He was distressed, but got over it well enough."

Alex held Eliot's gaze. The black eyes didn't waver, didn't blink.

"For your sake, I hope you're not lying to me."

Anger blazed up in Eliot's eyes, his gaze darting to

Skelley and back. He was furious at Alex for scolding him in front of another. Alex was sickened that it had come to this, that a man he had once looked on as brother was now someone he could not trust. But Alex had been very fond of Laine and if Eliot murdered the boy out of spite, Alex would have it from Eliot's hide.

"Ye're one to talk of lies. What of wee Hugh? Ye knew all along she wasna a lad."

"That's my business and not for you to question."

Eliot made a rude noise. "No for me to question, aye? You're the big man, tellin' us all what we must and mustna know?" Eliot took a step closer, raising his chin to direct his dark stare in Alex's eyes. "Ye can play laird, but we all know you're no one. Ye're just a reiver like the rest of us, stealing what ye canna rightfully have."

"If you don't like it, you're welcome to leave."

Eliot's mouth flattened in his beard and Alex knew the blow was unexpected. "Weel, I just might do that." He stalked away.

Alex watched him turn the corner, anger and shame warring in his heart. His father would take a strap to him for treating his favorite nephew so poorly. And yet, Eliot had changed. Alex didn't want him anywhere near Fayth.

"I know not what he's up to," Skelley said, rousing Alex from his thoughts, "but he's a fox and it can be no good."

Alex clasped his hands hard behind his back, thinking. "Aye. If we're lucky, he'll leave of his own accord and that will be the end of it."

"If he doesna?"

Alex sighed, looking regretfully at his friend. "I dinna know. We must watch and wait. I fear he'll not be satisfied until he's made us all as miserable as he is."

"Shall I set an extra watch on the lassie?"

Alex nodded. "Aye, I want her guarded at all times."

He paused thoughtfully. Eliot had friends among Alex's men and though Alex didn't think they'd deceive him, he would take no chances with Fayth. "I want you to personally guard her during the day—I'll take the night watch."

Skelley walked to the door, then turned. "But what of Eliot? Are we to leave him free to do his worst?"

Alex shook his head. "Leave Eliot to me."

Wesley rode into Irvine lands with a score of men. Though he possessed the earl of Dornock's safe conduct, the hair still prickled on his neck, riding into enemy lands in full daylight. Of course, there was nothing to fear. This was no raid. Wesley had become courier, delivering Ridley's missives to Lady Anne and her father. Ridley had insisted Wesley act as messenger—as a sign of goodwill. He claimed that sending his own brother would prove to the earl's daughter how important she was to him. Wesley would have refused and ripped the foolish letter to pieces if not for the opportunity to catch a glimpse of Lady Anne.

He was a fool. It had always been this way. Ridley had always overshadowed Wesley and he'd accepted it. All the lasses fancied Ridley. The men respected and followed him. And it meant nothing to Ridley. He cared naught for what he had, always reaching for what was forbidden. Wesley had grown weary of his brother's devious mind, his contempt for everything. If this war didn't happen soon, he considered leaving to seek his fortune elsewhere.

He might have done so already, if not for Lady Anne. It did Wesley's heart good that Lady Anne saw through the finery to the twisted heart contained inside Ridley Graham. Of course, she didn't like what she saw in Wesley, either, but he could forgive that. He knew he was scarred and awkward with women. It was not her fault and, in spite of it all, she had been kind to him, had not allowed her revulsion to show in his presence. A fine woman.

As soon as Dornock was in sight, Wesley could resist the urge to rush no longer and dug the spurs into his horse's flanks. The horse raced across the heather, his men falling far behind. He thought he caught a glimpse of yellow satin on the battlements, but it was quickly gone.

Wesley was led into the earl's chambers by no less than the earl's master-of-guard. But it soon became clear the knight wanted to speak to him alone. When the doors closed, the knight gave him a conspiratorial smile.

"Pray inform Lord Graham I've worked sore hard to further his cause with the lady, though I dinna ken what good it's done."

Wesley arched a brow in question. "Indeed?"

"Aye. Lord Graham said he would reward me well if I could change her mind. I've been at her meself, as we're friends, and I've paid her maids to talk well of him. Tell him I've worked hard."

Wesley stared at the man until he looked away. "And what was the great reward Lord Graham promised you?"

"I'm not to say."

Wesley forced a laugh. "You can tell me, man. I'm his brother, after all."

The knight smiled and shrugged. "The wardenship of Gealach."

Wesley could barely manage a nod as the man left the room. The wardenship of Gealach and eventually the tower itself was to be Wesley's. Why had he not anticipated this? Ridley was a snake—lower than a snake, a vile worm.

The earl greeted him with great ceremony, ushering him deeper into his private chambers and offering him wine and food. It was all Wesley could do to remain civil. His fury nearly blinded him. What could this mean? Gealach was his! And who the hell was that man? A stinking Scottish knight? Damn it—they were brothers! How could Ridley do this?

The earl was speaking to him. Wesley made a massive effort to set his rage aside long enough to deliver Ridley's letter so he could leave.

"You found no trouble in Irvine lands?" the earl asked.

Wesley shook his head. He liked the earl of Dornock. He was a round, unassuming figure, good-natured and kind to his children. In some ways he reminded Wesley of his own father, though Wesley had a hard time imagining the earl locked in mortal combat with a Maxwell or Carlisle as Hugh had often found himself.

"To what do I owe the good fortune of your visit, Master Wesley?"

Good fortune? Did that mean Lady Anne had changed her mind? Wesley's heart sank, his belly filling with dread. He steeled himself to hear the news. Ridley didn't deserve her, would ruin her. But it was not unexpected. Even the forbidden eventually fell to Ridley's whims. His heart cankered, black with tamped-down rage.

"More missives from Lord Graham." Wesley was aware his voice was tight, curt. He strove for a more friendly tone. "I am instructed to give them only to the lady herself."

The earl raised his frosted brows. "Well . . . she'll not have them, I'm sorry to say."

The tension seeped out of Wesley and he sighed deeply. "Ah, well. I tried." He started to stand, but the earl waved him back into his chair.

"Not so fast, young Wesley."

Wesley did as he was bid, though he sat straight with tension. He wanted to be gone, to confront Ridley and kill him if he didn't like what his brother had to say.

The earl stood and paced the room thoughtfully. "It saddens me that this union is not to be, but I love all my children and cannot bear to see them unhappy."

Wesley nodded, pleased to hear that the earl would at least ensure Lady Anne's happiness in any endeavor.

"I have tried to coax Anne into accepting Lord Graham—this is an important alliance. This strife between our families has gone on for much too long and we both know a truce without a marriage is flimsier than the parchment it is written on."

The earl kept looking at a huge set of antlers mounted on the wall. Every time he did this, Wesley's gaze was also drawn to the antlers, wondering what was so fascinating about them.

"Anne, the simple child, reminded me of our purpose. She said to me, 'Father, if the union is that important, what does it matter who weds, so long as it is an Irvine and a Graham of gentle birth?' "

Wesley cocked a cautious brow. What did he mean? Had he another daughter to offer Ridley? Wesley knew Dornock had many children, both legitimate and of bastard birth, but he'd thought they were all either married or betrothed or far too young to consider. Perhaps one of the children? The idea of Ridley married to a little girl would be amusing if it weren't so alarming for other reasons.

"And what did Lady Anne propose?" Wesley asked when the earl was not immediately forthcoming.

"Well," the earl said, rubbing his hands together and turning toward the antlers, as if addressing them. "Lady Anne has expressed a preference for *you*, lad."

The words were so unexpected they did not register. Wesley turned hesitantly to look behind him. Perhaps Lord Dornock spoke to another occupant in the room Wesley had not been aware of. But they were quite alone.

The earl turned back to Wesley, watching him expectantly.

Wesley pointed to himself. "Me?"

A smile began to grow on the earl's red face. "Aye—you, lad!"

Wesley could form no coherent words. "But . . . but . . . I have nothing." Not even Gealach now, it seemed, as Ridley was handing out promises of the tower like indulgences.

The earl nodded and began pacing again. "Aye—I know this and pointed it out to Anne. Once again, she reminded me that the alliance was paramount. She comes richly dowered, boy. You'll be a laird in your own right."

"Wed to Lady Anne, I'd be a king." Wesley didn't realize he'd spoken aloud until he heard a crash that seemed to originate from the wall behind the antlers. The earl looked sharply at the antlers and cleared his throat.

Wesley stood. "Shall I investigate?"

The earl shook his head, his jowls wagging merrily. "Och, no, lad. 'Tis nothing."

"Perhaps someone has been hurt? It sounded like a fall."

"Aye, well, 'tis no more than she deserves."

"What?"

"Nothing!" The earl crossed the room to slap Wesley's back jovially. "Very well! Then it's settled. So long as Lord Graham agrees."

The disbelieving happiness that had been slowly blooming in Wesley's chest deflated. Ridley would never agree. But Wesley couldn't bring himself to tell Lord Dornock this. Another thought occurred to him. *Who cares if Ridley agrees?* Had he ever intended to bestow the tower on Wesley? Or anyone else for that matter? Crumbs, thrown to keep Wesley loyal, only to be snatched away when his usefulness ran out.

Wesley needed time to sort this out, to decide how to proceed, so he said, "My lord, I will return to Lord Graham and present this proposal to him." He started for the door, his mind whirling with confused plots to convince Ridley to agree. There must be some way to frame the request that would make it sound reasonable. Or perhaps he wouldn't even return to Ridley. If Ridley could forge letters, so could Wesley.

Wesley's mind was churning with possible deceptions when a soft, feminine cough echoed nearby. He turned.

Lord Dornock coughed loudly and boisterously. "Don't leave just yet, Wesley. Would you not like to speak with Anne?"

Speak with Anne? Wesley's face burned with embarrassment, but he nodded.

The earl glanced surreptitiously at the antlers again before walking to the door. "I'll send her along," he yelled.

When the earl was gone, Wesley approached the antlers. They were mounted several feet above him, but up close he could see the small holes in the wood between the antlers.

The door opened and Wesley turned.

The sight of her robbed him of speech, or thought. Her dress was yellow satin and she glowed like the sun. A smudge of dust marred the creamy skin of her cheek and her gloves were dirty and torn. She wore her deep brown hair loose, with ribboned braids at the front. She was so very beautiful and kind and she wanted *him*. At that moment, he knew he was going nowhere. He would not leave Dornock without a wife. A forgery was definitely in order. Once the deed was done, it couldn't be undone.

Anne looked from him to the antlers and back.

They stood staring at each other for some time, until Wesley glanced up at the antlers and asked, "Did you hurt yourself? When you fell?"

She blushed prettily and shook her head.

* * *

Ridley circled the girl Gilford had brought him. He'd found her in a nearby village. She was as different from Mona as fine Merlot from vinegar. Her hair was long and white blond. She was perhaps sixteen or seventeen—far younger than he preferred them. However, her skin was unmarked and her teeth very nice.

"What's your name?"

"Alice, my lord." She was properly respectful, keeping her eyes downcast.

Ridley stopped in front of her. The plaid wrapped around her shoulders hid her bosom from him, so he grasped the edge of it and pulled. She gasped, making a move as if to stop him, then halted, hands balled at her sides. When the plaid lay in a mound on the floor, Ridley inspected the woman's form and found it pleasing.

They were alone in his tent and he could do with her as he pleased. He approached her and touched her chin, raising her head so she looked at him. Eyes blue as the sky. He caught the scent of lavender, his favorite. She had been bathed and garbed especially for his pleasure.

"Do you know why you're here?" he asked.

She nodded.

"You're no whore."

She shook her head.

"Were you kidnapped?"

She shook her head again.

He took a step back, frowning at her. "Then why did you come?"

She licked her lips, swallowing hard. "Because . . . my da is verra ill. He said—the man who brought me—he said if I pleased you there would be a great reward in it for me, that perhaps he could even cure me da."

"Gilford is a liar."

The girl began babbling so it all ran together in a flood

of gibberish. Ridley closed his eyes, rubbing his temples to ward off the headache forming. The depths Gilford was willing to sink, just to find Ridley a suitable woman, repulsed him.

"Are you a virgin?"

She couldn't stop blubbering long enough to answer, but Ridley didn't care. He touched her shoulder, leading her to the tent flap.

"Go home to your father, Alice."

The girl's face was stricken as she stumbled from the tent. As soon as Gilford saw them he rushed forward, his face creased with misery. He took the girl's arm, turning her back toward Ridley. Her cheeks were streaked with tears and her trembling lips turned down in an extremely unappealing manner.

"She does not please you? Tell me why and I'll do better next time."

"Pay her and remove her from my sight—and pray do not promise women magical cures to coerce them into compromising themselves."

He returned to the tent and paced the floor. Damn it all if he wasn't dead inside. The lass was beautiful, young, fresh, and yet she'd stirred him not a bit. It was Mona. She'd bewitched him . . . ruined every other woman for him. He kicked the brazier over, scattering charred wood and embers across the carpet. He quickly stepped on them before it ruined the expensive weave. It was her—his stepmother— who made him do these things. She drove him to it.

He dreamed of her still. Before, they'd been dreams of lying with her, sinking himself into her soft white flesh while she moaned and writhed beneath him, the black silk of her hair twined about his wrists. But now . . . it was that Maxwell knight she'd run away with. He rutted on her and Ridley was helpless to do aught but watch. He would kill them all—every last Maxwell—for trying to thwart him.

But first Alexander Maxwell. He snatched the missive off his table, reading the infantile request again. Fayth for the deed to Gealach. As if that piece of baggage was worth it. Carlisle was becoming something of a hindrance, wanting to at least discuss the possibility.

Ridley still hadn't decided how he would respond to Alexander's letter, but soon enough he would answer it with a sword in the bastard's throat.

He turned at the scratching on the tent flap. Gilford entered. Ridley was prepared to give him a tongue-lashing and perhaps even line his back, but Gilford was followed by another man bearing a familiar crest on his tunic.

"I come from His Grace, the Duke of Norfolk. The king has ordered troops assembled at York and your presence is required." The messenger stepped forward, unrolling a parchment bearing the king's seal. Ridley's eyes skimmed it, unseeing. The man rolled it up and stepped back.

It was as if he were dreaming. He'd planned and worked, made alliances with scum not fit to lick his boots, was to marry a fat Scotswoman, all in preparation for this day. This event.

Ridley stared at the messenger in disbelief, the blood quickening in his veins. *It begins.* The Clachan Fala was not yet in hand, but that mattered not at all, as it soon would be. Ridley had no doubt of it. There was still time. Negotiations would begin in York. They would drag on for weeks. Yes, he still had time to finish this business. He must have the Blood Stone before the invasion—it would keep him from harm and bring him glory on the battlefield. With it the king would refuse him nothing.

"Tell His Grace I will be along as soon as I collect my men who search for my lost sister and send word to my brother."

The messenger left. Ridley went to his writing desk. Wesley had been overlong on his latest task. Ridley quickly wrote his brother, detailing the situation and ordering him to wed Lady Anne by proxy and then return posthaste with his bride so he could bed the pig and be done with it. He then wrote another to Laird Johnstone. The Maxwells had many enemies, both English and Scottish, but besides the Grahams, their most vicious foe was their Scottish neighbors, the Johnstones. The Maxwells had been locked in deadly feud with them nearly as long as they'd been feuding with the Grahams. Because of this, Ridley had cultivated extremely useful friendships with several Johnstone clans.

When his letters were off, he left his tent and ordered camp to be broken down. He was being dressed in his raiding attire when Carlisle burst into his tent.

"What's this business of attacking Gealach?"

"I am required in York and so the games must end."

"No deal without the woman."

Ridley whirled around, grabbing the old man by the front of his doublet. "I have the matter in hand. She will be yours, as I've promised. Question me no more." He released Carlisle with a push.

The man stumbled back, his face purple with indignation.

Ridley turned away from him. "I have a man inside Gealach, working to free Fayth. Fash not."

Carlisle grunted, momentarily mollified. "Red Alex has more than enough men to defend Gealach."

"I have the situation in hand."

Carlisle's temper flared again, but he left, the strange fevered light still in his eyes. Ridley felt an unusual pang of unease for his sister, but pushed it away. It was no more than she deserved. She'd come uncomfortably close to ruining some of his plans. It was fitting punishment.

As Gilford dropped a shirt of mail over Ridley's head, and strapped on his greaves and shoulder plates, the tension began to build in his chest. Action. Finally, he could get on with this. Once he secured Gealach and bedded Lady Anne, he would head north, where the Clachan Fala—and Mona—waited for him. It would take the duke weeks to conscript and assemble an army. The Scottish king would send representatives to try and negotiate, but it was formality. The situation had festered too long and King Henry would not be easily mollified. They were only buying time, and little did they know, giving Ridley the extra time he needed. He would be back at the border, Blood Stone in hand and alliances secure, in time to invade Scotland.

He smiled to himself as he left his tent and strode to his horse. Yes, he had everything in hand.

16

FAYTH SIFTED through Alex's horde in one of the rooms below Gealach. She'd claimed she didn't like the gowns chosen for her and wanted new ones. Alex had given her permission to choose more—with Skelley guarding her, of course. Skelley rested in a chair near the door, Biddy at his feet. He'd tried to keep the dog in the larder, but she'd leaped through the hole, determined to follow Fayth on her adventures. Skelley grumbled about having to carry the dog back up the ladder later, but Fayth thought he secretly enjoyed Biddy. Skelley's hand dangled off the chair arm, toying with the dog's fur, and he chatted with her as if she were human. When he addressed a question to the dog, she stopped panting and looked up, as if listening intently to whatever he said.

The pair had become a fixture in Fayth's life the past few days. She knew that something was wrong. Why else would Alex set his closest friend to guard her all day, every day? But Skelley was tight-lipped about it and Alex had made himself scarce. Well, during the day he did. At night he sat on a bench outside her room, guarding her himself. He was more vigilant than Ridley. She would never escape from Gealach. She'd tried to devise ways to distract him, but had thus far been unsuccessful.

Fayth set aside another box that she'd hoped contained jewels. But it had contained naught by pearl necklaces and earbobs. It had seemed a clever idea at first. So far as Fayth knew, no one alive had ever seen the Clachan Fala—if it even existed. Fayth had heard stories and knew it was a ruby in a gold setting. If she could find something fitting that description, perhaps Ridley could be fooled.

Now, however, it didn't seem like such a fine idea. Though there were many coins and baubles and clothes, there was little valuable jewelry. Fayth looked around the room, hands on hips.

She was covered with filth, her hands, dress, and face. She'd found the mirror Alex had handed to her the last time they were down here and had decided to keep it. Fayth pressed her hand against her bodice, where she'd hidden it when Skelley wasn't looking.

"I'm hungry, lass," Skelley said, coming to his feet. It was a hint that he was ready to leave the dank darkness.

"There's more than this, isn't there?"

"Just what are you looking for? I thought you only needed another gown?"

"I don't like any of these." She snatched up the pearls. "They have to go with pearls."

Skelley sighed and paced out the door. His steps echoed along the corridor before coming back. Biddy hardly moved, lifting her head to watch him go, then stretching longer on the floor, her paws twitching.

Skelley reappeared. "There's more down here. Can we not come back after some dinner? This cold seeps into my bones."

Fayth nodded guiltily. Skelley's youthful days were

long past, his thick beard streaked with gray, his eyes lined
with age.

"Yes, let me just have a look in the other room. Maybe
we won't need to come back at all." She took one of the
candles and hurried past Skelley before he could stop her.
He didn't follow, pulling his chair into the corridor and po-
sitioning it so he could watch the doorway. Biddy got to
her feet and trotted at Fayth's side.

Fayth held the candle high as she entered the room.
Trunks, chests, cabinets . . . there was even a bed frame, its
massive oak posts reaching into the darkness. Fayth wandered about the room, opening chests to survey the contents. This was plunder Alex had seized on raids, not pirate
treasure. Her shoulders slumped. She would find nothing
useful here.

At the doorway Biddy whined, low and uneasy. Fayth
turned. The dog was poised on the threshold, staring into
the blackness, the fur on her nape bristling. Fayth shivered,
holding the candle before her and watching the shadowy
figure of the dog.

"Biddy? What is it?"

The dog looked quickly over her shoulder at Fayth, then
returned her attention to the door. She took several tentative steps forward. Fayth followed. By the time she
reached the door, Biddy had advanced deeper into the passage, a low growl rumbling from her chest. Fayth looked
down the opposite way, where Skelley sat idly in his chair.
When he noticed Fayth and Biddy he came to his feet.

Biddy's rumbling growl turned to a snarl threatening vi-
olence. Fayth jumped back as Skelley hurried to join them.

"What's wrong with her?" he asked.

Fayth shook her head, peering into the dark. She could
hear nothing but far off dripping and a whine of wind
through the tunnels. Biddy was almost out of sight when

she sprang forward, melting into the darkness. They heard nothing for a full minute, then the corridors were filled with the guttural snarl of an attacking animal. Skelley seized Fayth's arm, dragging her back the way they'd come.

"What is it? What about Biddy?" Fayth cried, struggling to keep up. He'd grabbed her injured arm. It was all she could do to hold it steady so he didn't wrench it in his fervor to get her away.

At the ladder, Skelley shoved her up, his hands on her bottom, urging her to climb faster. Fayth was going as fast as she could, when she heard a horrible, high-pitched yelp, then nothing. Fayth remained poised, hand gripping the opening to the larder, eyes staring sightlessly into the dark. She'd lost her candle and the only light originated from the square of light above them.

Skelley too had frozen. "Jesus wept," he murmured, then sprang to life. "Go on, lass!"

Fayth tried to reverse directions and climb back down. "Biddy's hurt, we must go see—" Her wrists were grasped from above and she was hauled through the opening. Alex set her on her feet and immediately turned away, facing Skelley as he climbed into the larder.

"What happened?"

Skelley shook his head, the skin above his thick brown beard pale. "I know not. Something, or someone, is down there. They got Wolf."

Alex hopped into the hole. Fayth grabbed a taper from the candelabra and stepped forward, offering it to Alex. He took it and their eyes locked briefly. There was anger and determination in the set of his firm mouth, but the eyes that burned her heart were worried. He disappeared, leaping from the ladder to the ground below. Fayth was shaken, her stomach fluttering, a clammy sweat coating her forehead and neck. If Alex was worried, what could that mean? She'd come to think of him as a pillar of strength, always knowing how to act, and possessing the strength and resolve to accomplish it.

"Maybe you should go with him," Fayth said, staring at the black hole anxiously.

Skelley looked from Fayth to the hole. His decision was made when Wynda and her husband appeared. He jerked his head at Fayth to indicate they were to watch her. Wynda came to stand beside Fayth, a small frown marring her tanned brow, and watched Skelley climb down into the caves.

"Whot happened?" the older woman asked, her hand coming to rest comfortingly on Fayth's shoulder.

Fayth shook her head. "I don't know. Biddy—er, Wolf— saw or heard something and attacked it."

No more was said as they waited. Fayth's heart still raced. Both Alex and Skelley were absent—the significance of this jolted her. She hadn't had such an opportunity in days. She could pretend to be ill and say she wanted to go to her room and lie down. Then she would steal a horse and escape. Arguments against this course of action quickly presented themselves. Men guarded the gate, they wouldn't just let her ride away—and even if she did get away, Alex would be notified immediately and set out after her. In the past, Fayth would have tried anyway, but of late, she found herself reluctant to rush into the unknown. She told herself that it was her newfound thoughtful, cautious nature. But sometimes, when she lay in bed, unable to sleep, she acknowledged that she wasn't finished with Alexander Maxwell. Not yet.

And now, faced with an unexpected and wholly unwelcome fear for his safety, she was forced to admit that she might not be finished with him for a while. She chewed her nail, images of the unimaginable flitting through her head. A dragon, living in the bowels of Gealach, ripping all trespassers to shreds. The pirates, returned to reclaim their treasure, set on murdering anyone in their way. The ghost of the fair maiden who threw herself from the walls of Gealach, guarding her treasure. Or worse, something else, something she couldn't fathom.

The moments ticked by. The apprehension and fear built in Fayth's chest until she could no longer bear it. She grabbed the top of the ladder, prepared to go after them.

"Just whot do ye think ye're doing?" Wynda asked, rustling forward.

"Someone has to go after them. What if they're hurt?"

"Stop her," Wynda said.

Her husband caught Fayth around the waist and plucked her off the ladder.

"They be just fine, lassie." He set her on her feet and placed himself between Fayth and the ladder. "Dinna fash on Red Alex, he can take care of himself."

Fayth was about to argue when she heard men's voices below. Alex and Skelley joined them in the larder, tight-lipped and somber.

"Well?" Fayth said, when they weren't forthcoming with information.

"I don't want you down there anymore," Alex said, as he pushed two casks over the closed trapdoor. He straightened, surveying his work with dissatisfaction. "We need something heavier to block it, but something we can move quickly if necessary."

"Block it?" Fayth circled Alex's tall form, enormous in the close confines of the larder. "What are you trying to keep out? Where's Biddy?"

Alex looked at her for the first time since he'd gone below. He took her elbow, leading her into the kitchens. "I don't know." He called over his shoulder, to Skelley, "Gather up as many men as you can and take them below.

Search every room and corridor you discover, all the way to the cove. I'll join you directly."

When they were through the kitchen Fayth said, "You don't know . . . ?"

He led her into the hall and up the stairs. When she realized where they were going she halted stubbornly halfway up the staircase. "I don't want to go to my chambers."

"I'd feel . . . better, knowing where you are."

"Then I'll simply tell you—"

His hands cupped her shoulders, turning her to face him. Fayth had been trying to ignore how close he was to her, the feel of his hand, burning through the thin material of her sleeve, but this she couldn't ignore. She purposefully averted her eyes, looking at the wall behind him.

"I don't know where Wolf is. She's just gone. Perhaps she found some prey and is pursuing it. Perhaps not. But I'm taking no chances with you. I have no idea where those tunnels lead and I'll not have you wandering about down there, lost."

"Do you think it's Ridley?"

"I don't know."

"Maybe we should look for her. What if she's hurt?"

"She's a braw lassie and can take care of herself. I've had her since she was a pup. Her mother had been killed and she was starving, but full of fight. All her brothers and sisters were dead, but she hung on." He squeezed her shoulders. "She reminds me of you, refusing to give in to death, or anything else contrary."

His hands kneaded her shoulders and Fayth steeled herself. She wanted to melt against him. It suddenly seemed so unfair that he was a Maxwell, and she a Graham; that he was responsible for Jack's death; that Ridley must try and take from him the one thing he would not concede; that Alex was hero to so many, but jailer to her.

She raised her gaze, across broad shoulders and strong

neck, a mouth firm and uncompromising, but so soft to kiss. When their gazes locked his hands stopped their kneading, tightening slightly.

"You've rescued everyone it seems . . . Eliot, Laine . . . Wolf. Why can't you rescue me?" She hadn't meant to say the words aloud, to concede how much it hurt her. But she couldn't take them back and didn't try.

He searched her face, visibly disconcerted. But he did not speak. She knew the answer, it was clear in his eyes, in his actions. Gealach was all he cared for. He could never care for her in the same way. She knew from experience the importance of land and titles. It was what drove men, sustained them.

Besides, it was wrong for her to want him. It was a poor way to honor Jack's memory. Wesley would curse her as he had Caroline. Her father would have been shamed.

Fayth grasped the hands gripping her shoulders and pushed them away. He didn't follow her up the steps and her heart hardened. She supposed she couldn't blame him. Given the choice between Gealach and Fayth Graham, well, not many would choose the woman.

But Fayth had wanted him to and she felt such a fool for losing her thoughtless, reckless heart to a man who would not have it.

Alex's arse hurt like hell. His shoulder ached, his legs cramped, and he was so tired he could barely keep his eyes open, even sitting on the stone bench. This was the third night he'd sat here, in the corridor outside Fayth's chambers. *Why can't you rescue me?* He tried not to recall her words, the bleakness of her dark eyes.

But still, it rankled. *Why can't you rescue me?* As if she'd lost faith in him. As if he'd let her down. But damn it all, he hadn't known she'd expected much of anything from him. He was a Maxwell. What could she expect? According to Grahams, naught by thievery, rape, and lies.

And now she'd stopped speaking to him. She wouldn't join him for a meal, or walk with him. Skelley said she showed no more interest in digging through the treasure in the tunnels. Alex still wondered why he'd shown it to her. Had he meant to impress her? Put himself in a worthier light? He wasn't sure. Perhaps he only wanted to share some secret with her. Whatever he'd intended hadn't worked. She was not swayed by his horde nor by his trust.

He longed for her smile, her laughter, for her to acknowledge him, but since he slept half the day, he only saw her in the evenings when she wandered the tower and the grounds, pointedly ignoring him. It was for the best. It would be difficult to send her away, to the arms of another man. No sense making it harder.

Why can't you rescue me?

Alex ground his teeth, determined to put her words, her face, from his mind. It was useless to dwell on it.

Wolf had not returned and Alex feared the worst. No one had been found in the tunnels, and when Alex interrogated Eliot, his story was solid. Alex was beginning to wonder if he'd been wrong about his cousin. Eliot had not attempted to speak with Fayth, or even approach her. And neither had Eliot left. Alex didn't know what Eliot wanted from him or if he simply had no place else to go.

He buried his face in his hands, trying not to groan audibly at his quandary. Both Alex's father and his uncle had trusted him and Rob and Patrick to look after Eliot's welfare. What would Red Rowan do? His father's trust never wavered. And if his trust were broken, then he punished mercilessly. Alex had always thought he was very much like Red Rowan, not just because of his coloring, but his temperament. He was beginning to doubt that assumption, as he couldn't remember his father ever being so indecisive, about either a woman or a friend.

He shifted on the bench, trying in vain to get comfortable. Crossing his arms over his chest, he leaned his head against the wall. He had received word from Carlisle today. The laird expressed his willingness to discuss the matter but Alex suspected it was no more than a delay tactic or perhaps a trick. He had not yet responded to it.

Movement near Fayth's door interrupted his thoughts. Whoever it was must think him asleep, by his position. Alex tried to see, but the only candle in the corridor rested on the bench beside him, illuminating him clearly, but hiding the intruder.

Alex waited until he heard the creak of the hinges before springing to his feet. The shadow came to life, fleeing in the opposite direction. There was another staircase, for servant use, though no one used it, as the boards were rotting and dangerous. The figure entered the darkened staircase and disappeared.

Alex stood at the head of the stairs, staring down into the inky blackness. There was no crash, or sounds of falling, but Alex didn't have a candelabra with him. He would not chance breaking his neck in pursuit of a phantom. Damn it all. It was someone within the keep. He had hoped that Wolf's disappearance was an isolated occurrence, that someone had gained access via the cove and had their revenge. But the culprit was still here and he'd been after Fayth.

Eliot. It had to be.

Alex went to the main staircase and whistled softly. Two men appeared from the darkness. He instructed one to search the lower floors for anything unusual and posted the other at the bottom of the unused servants' stairs.

When they departed, Alex returned to his candlelit bench. He started to sit when he noticed the gray rectangle of Fayth's doorway. The intruder had unlatched the door and it must have swung open. Alex walked quietly to the door and reached for the latch to pull it closed.

Moonlight streamed into the room from the open shutters, illuminating the room with a soft silver glow. The air left him at once when he saw her, standing an arm's length away, beside the open door.

Her hair floated around her shoulders, partially hiding her face. Her nightshift covered her from wrist to toes, but the neck gaped, exposing soft collarbones and neck. He recalled having his hands against that skin. His palms itched, hungry for the feel of her.

The eyes that gazed up at him were luminous, unblinking.

"What are you doing, standing there?" His voice sounded strange, raw and broken.

"I thought it was you."

His mind raced forward, trying to find hidden meaning in her words. "It is me."

"I mean . . . I thought it was you at the door . . . coming to me."

His heart slammed a painful rhythm against his ribs. Blood rushed loudly in his ears. *I thought it was you . . . coming to me.* She hadn't moved; neither had he. He still leaned forward awkwardly, his hand grasping the door latch. *Why can't you rescue me?*

"Were you going to send me away?"

She shook her head, curls brushing her shoulders.

Alex gripped the latch so fiercely the metal bit into his palm. "Fayth . . ." He didn't know what he meant to say. He hadn't the strength to tell her no again.

She wore nothing beneath her nightshift. Small toes peeked at him. When she stepped toward him, he glimpsed tiny, arched feet, the ankles so delicate he could snap them with one hand.

"You sit out there every night." She gazed up at him, her skin limed in moonlight. "And I can't sleep, knowing you're there . . . so close."

The muscles in his arm trembled from how hard he gripped the door latch. He released it, flexing his cramping hand. He wanted to touch her, but knew if he did, it wouldn't be enough. Still, his hand rose, sliding over soft skin, to cup her cheek. Her fingers gripped his wrist and she lifted her chin, waiting for his kiss.

He lowered his head, until his mouth hovered over hers. "If we do this—"

She closed the distance between them, pressing her lips to his and silencing his warnings. He pulled her into his arms, words forgotten in the warmth of her mouth, the stroke of her tongue.

Fayth tried to pull him closer. He was so tall and she, so much smaller. She wanted him over her, around her. She couldn't believe he was here, in her room. Every night she prayed he would come to her—and here he was. She would not let him walk away. When he held her and kissed her, she could forget who he was, who she was, and that's all she wanted tonight. To be man and woman, not Graham and Maxwell.

His hands slid beneath her arms, lifting her above him. She gasped, but understood readily. Her arms snaked tightly around his neck, her thighs gripping his waist. She laughed at his power, his strength, as he shut the door and carried her to bed.

He smiled back, wicked and knowing, before capturing her mouth again. He sat on the bed, so she straddled him, and she kissed him and kissed him, until she could hardly breathe from the pleasure of his mouth. His hands were beneath her nightshift, sliding over her back and waist, and lower, to cup her bottom.

She moved against him. Her body ached and throbbed, and pressing her groin to his sent ripples of excitement deep in her belly. He groaned into her mouth. His arms circled her so tightly she felt the rumbling timbre of his voice in her bones. Then his hands were at the neck of her shift, inelegant and eager. When he could not untie the knot, he yanked, ripping the material open and exposing her breasts. She gasped, then laughed.

The hands that pushed the material from her shoulders were gentle, trembling slightly as they slid over her back. She was bare from the waist up, shivering in the breeze from the open window. He lowered his mouth to her breasts, his tongue swirling over the peak, while his hand slid down her belly, between her thighs.

She gasped his name between panted breaths; his fingers seeking, pleasuring. She clutched his shoulders, mindlessly receiving all he gave. He lifted her off him, laying her on her back. He spread her thighs, and to her profound astonishment, replaced his fingers with his mouth. The protest caught in her throat, her hands poised to push his head away. Her head fell back, her hands grabbing handfuls of sheet. He held her firmly as her hips writhed and jerked, his tongue and fingers working in rhythm with the pounding of her heart. She thought she would die. She could barely draw breath, her body coiled and tightened, the ache building inexorably to some climax she could not fathom. And then it burst over her and she heard her own disjointed cries and whimpers.

Her body was limp as a rag and she thought perhaps she'd gone blind, as she could see nothing but splotches of light and color. But her sight slowly returned, along with her hearing. Alex moved about nearby, but his hands and mouth were gone. She became aware of her undignified position: shredded shift bunched about her waist, her breasts bared, arms limp at her sides and thighs spread wide, exposing herself completely to him.

She summoned the energy to close her legs, but before she arranged her shift, he leaned over her, arms braced on either side of her head, and gloriously naked. She could only stare at him, illuminated as he was in the moon's pale light. His broad shoulders were cloaked in corded muscle, veins stood out on arms thick with sinew. Dark hair covered a heavy chest, leading down a flat belly, and farther . . . Her eyes jerked back to his, her cheeks flaming.

"What you did was wicked," she said, as his head lowered, eyes shining in the moonlight.

"Ye didna like it?" he whispered, his tongue tracing the lobe of her ear. He stripped away her shift and tossed it over his shoulder.

She shivered, hands sliding over his arms. "You know I did." Her hand stopped at his ravaged shoulder. The bandage was gone and it was scabbed over. He lifted his head at her tentative touch, frowning slightly.

"I'll put my shirt on, if ye'd rather."

His Scots grew thicker with emotion, and she kissed the corners of his mouth, loving the knowledge that she, and this act, moved him.

"No, I want your skin against mine."

A sigh shuddered through him and his eyes closed as he slipped his arms beneath her, pulling her against his chest. He kissed her, long and slow, his knee pressing between hers. She opened her legs to him, her body tender from his mouth, but warm and throbbing again, ready for him to fill her.

The tip of him pressed against her and she shifted her hips to take him. He gazed down into her face, the muscles standing out on his neck and shoulders, as if he were under great strain. He pushed into her slowly, and she gasped at the invasion, her eyes widening—afraid she couldn't take him, that he would rip her apart. But then he was in, their bodies pressed together tightly, and the pain abated. She tightened around him, her body rippling with sudden pleasure that he was inside her; his skin, damp with sweat and smooth as silken steel, pressed to hers. The crinkly hairs of his chest abraded her nipples. The scent of him, the taste of him, filled her.

He was so very still, his broad, muscular hands framing her face. It was as if he were afraid she would shatter.

"I'm fine, Alex," she whispered, kissing his neck and chin. "I'm a strong lass."

He withdrew slowly and she hissed at the loss. His brow furrowed until her hips rose to take him again. His eyes shut and he began to move inside her, slowly at first, then faster at her little cries of pleasure and urgings.

He groaned loudly, his sweat mingling with hers and said, his voice hoarse, "Jesus God . . . I'm sorry lass, I canna stop."

She had no idea what he apologized for, she'd never felt anything so fine. She was frantic to have him deeper; he stroked something inside that sent her body coiling and shuddering all over again. He thrust deeply again and again.

"Fayth . . . Oh God, Fayth . . ."

She sunk her teeth into his arm to muffle her cries of pleasure. He throbbed inside her, but his body was still, except his heavy breathing. His heart raced against hers.

She lay there, covered by him, her arms and legs still wrapped tightly around him as they calmed, and wondered at what she'd done. She'd ever been heedless of consequences when she wanted something. And she'd wanted him so very badly. He'd warned her there were consequences to this act.

Alex rolled onto his side, resting his head in his arm and looking at her. Her eyes went to his ravaged shoulder and her brow creased. It would be a brutal scar, even now that it healed it looked violent and painful.

"I promise it doesn't hurt."

She met his warm gaze and smiled uncertainly. "I wish I could take it back."

"Well, you cannot." His eyes darkened. He pushed a curl from her forehead, his hand coming to rest on her shoulder. "We cannot take this back either."

What did he mean? She didn't want to take it back. But as she gazed at his troubled expression her heart chilled. He was worried about Gealach. He was afraid by lying with her he'd ruined his chance to use her for a trade.

He stared blankly at the sheet covering her breasts, his brow furrowed with thought. How could it hurt so much? Tears burned at the backs of her eyes, fighting to free themselves, but she wouldn't cry—not in front of him.

"Don't worry about it," she said, rolling away from him and leaning on her elbow. She clutched the sheet tightly to her breast. His fingers trailed absently down her bare back, tracing a pattern. She shuddered. "I can handle Carlisle." It would never come to that, but no use telling him that. She would never marry Carlisle.

He gripped her arm and pulled her onto her back. "What are you talking about?"

"I'll hide a vial of chicken blood beneath my pillow and I'll cry out when he ruts on me, as if I'm in great pain. When it's over, I'll open the vial beneath me."

The way he stared at her—as if she were speaking another language—stoked her growing anger.

"And if I should bear a redheaded child? Well, what matter? It'll be too late by then, eh?"

He sat, his face darkening with anger. "Fayth—"

"Don't touch me!"

He reached for her, but she moved away, gathering the

sheets closer about her. She saw the blood on the sheets. Her blood, evidence of what she had given him. Of what she'd trusted him with.

"You would let Carlisle rut on you? After what we did?"

He sounded angry! She threw a pillow at his head. "You fool! Do you think I'll let him put his head between my legs? Do you think I will scream and cry for more? He'll not be pleased with me! I promise that!"

She struggled to get off the bed, but he caught her about the waist, easily stopping her and dragging her back. He held her tightly, her back pressed against his chest and belly. She tried to pry his hands loose, but he held her fast, his cheek against hers.

"Listen to me," he said sternly. "You're not going to Carlisle. There will be no trade."

She went limp, staring blankly into the gray light.

"I thought you understood," he said, turning his face so his warm breath caressed her neck and his whiskers scraped her skin. "I would not have done this if I meant to give you up."

"But Gealach . . . what about Gealach?"

He sighed deeply, his face buried in the juncture between her shoulder and neck. "I don't know."

She shook her head slowly, disbelieving. "But it is . . . you love this place. You can't just give it up, not without a fight!"

He shushed her, his mouth warm against her skin. She shivered, her body rising again, quivering inside. How could she want him again, so soon? She'd thought once she'd lain with him, it would be over, the longing. But here it was, sharp and urgent, ripe with the knowledge of how well he could assuage it.

"You have my protection until I can see you to safety." His arms wrapped tightly about her waist. "I'll take you to Rob and Caroline. There, you'll be safest—"

"I can't go to Caroline," she whispered. "She'll never trust me again . . . and I cannot live like that."

"I'll speak for you. I'll explain to her what happened."

Fayth let out a breath of disbelief. "You'd do that?" She wanted to see his face, but he held her so firmly she couldn't turn.

"Aye."

Fayth contemplated this gift in silence. He offered her protection, reconciliation with her sister. But he did not offer himself or marriage. Fayth found she did not want to leave Gealach, not yet. But she would not tell him that.

One of his hands slid up to cup her breast, toying lazily with the nipple. Her eyes fluttered shut and she let her head fall back against his shoulder. His mouth moved to her neck, sucking, licking. No, she didn't want to leave. Not yet. His hand burrowed beneath the sheet, sliding over her belly, between her thighs.

Perhaps now that things had changed between them he would help her find Mona. He'd offered to reconcile her with Caroline, surely he would give her this. And in return she would help him keep Gealach. Yes, she thought, her body loosening under his explorations, things were finally going her way.

Alex woke, more from the hand on his chest than the light behind his eyelids. He opened one eye a crack. Fayth lay on her side beside him, sheet pulled over her breasts. She inspected the bead he wore about his neck. Even with her lying next to him, her body warming his arm and thigh, he could not believe what he'd done—and that she'd consented.

When she saw he was awake, she asked, "You'll help me find Mona now?"

"If that's what ye want." He took the bead from her,

closing it in his fist, as if that's all that held her there with him and he had to guard it.

She smiled, self-satisfied, and pulled at his fingers. He opened his hand readily, surprised at how familiar she was with him, as if they'd been lovers for much longer than one night. There was no awkwardness, no strangeness. His heart seemed swollen, aching, every time he looked at her.

She fingered the stone thoughtfully. "We might find the Clachan Fala, too."

He slid his hand up and around her, urging her closer. "Aye."

She resisted, leaning against his hand, her head bent over the bead, her hair brushing his chest.

"If Mona really is the keeper, then she's worked very hard to keep it out of Ridley's hands. If it's real, then it will give him great power."

"That's a lot of 'if's,' lass."

"I know." She looked at him earnestly, her dark eyes wide and appealing. "But it seems foolish not to even consider it . . . right?"

Alex smiled, rubbing his hand over the soft, bare skin of her arm. "But first we must separate the legend from the fact. It's a piece of treasure shrouded in myth." He flattened his palm on her back, pushing her down. "Remember the tale of the Irish prince? There's another told in the village of a ghostly pirate ship that sails by Gealach on nights when the moon is full, searching for its lost treasure." She didn't resist him, her eyelids lowering so her gaze was fixed on his mouth as he spoke. "The Clachan Fala that has caused so much bloodshed is no more than a bauble, likely of great material value, but possessing no magic."

Her sheet slipped as their lips met, the firm round globes of her breasts searing his skin. She teased him with her mouth and the tip of her tongue, staying just out of reach, until he gripped the back of her head, forcing her to deepen the kiss.

She slid her leg over his waist, so she straddled him. His hands were buried in her hair, his erection throbbing against the heat of her bottom. He would never let her go, but he couldn't tell her that. She would balk at being held, even by a man who adored her, but nevertheless, he would not relinquish her to anyone. He must somehow convince her that the only logical thing for her to do now was marry him . . . unfortunately logic wasn't the way to appeal to Fayth.

She rubbed against him, purring deep in her throat. He slid her up his body, so he could take a dusky nipple in his mouth.

"That's what I was looking for, you know," she murmured.

"Hmm . . . ?"

"Below . . . when Biddy disappeared."

Reluctantly, he released her nipple with a kiss and looked up at her. "What were you looking for?"

"Something that looked like the Blood Stone, something that would fool Ridley. Then he would give you Gealach and leave Mona alone."

Alex considered her plan as she stared down at him, hands braced on the bed on either side of his head, red-brown hair falling forward to frame her face.

"He's not stupid—"

"But he's never seen it! Don't you see? At the very least he'll come and investigate, bringing the deed with him in case it's true. And if you show him the bead and tell him where you got it, I just know he'll believe you."

"You've a cunning mind, but I cannot take such chances."

"What chances? Have you a better plan?"

"No, but I'd rather you not be involved."

"Not involved! This is about me, remember?"

She was a fighter, he knew, and would want to be there for the battle—and the victory. Every day that passed Alex began to doubt he would ever own Gealach outright. He would not have her near if things turned ugly.

"Not anymore."

Her words reminded him of all he had to do. It was light out and soon Skelley would come to relieve him and wonder that no one was outside Fayth's room, guarding her. He lifted her off him and sat up, swinging his feet over the edge of the bed.

She grabbed his arm. "You're wrong. Gealach is not Ridley's unless I marry Carlisle. And Carlisle is not the kind of man Ridley can push around." She became gravely serious. "You must use me. I *want* to help you."

Alex searched the floor for his breeks. "What are you suggesting, lass?"

"I could go with them . . . pretend I'm glad to be escaping from you—"

"Bloody hell—no!" He found his breeks and yanked them on.

"I would escape from them and come back—"

"No!"

She was on her knees on the bed, the sheet wrapped haphazardly about her body, her jaw set mutinously. "Why? I owe you!"

Alex grabbed his shirt off the floor and shrugged into it. "You owe me nothing. I kidnapped you!"

"I was escaping anyway."

"I meant to rape you!"

"But you didn't!"

He waved his hands at the bed. "I've ruined you!"

Her cheeks reddened indignantly. "I wanted you to ruin me." She said it like a queen, delivering a verdict.

He was inflamed with lust at her bold declaration, but

he would not risk her. And he would never tell her why. "We are enemies."

"We *were* enemies."

By God, she was stubborn! He crossed to the bed, placing his hands on her bare shoulders. She glared up at him, challenging him to keep her away. "If we're not enemies, lass . . . then what are we?"

Her lips trembled and she swallowed hard, but she squared her shoulders, tilting her chin up slightly. "After last night, I'd say lovers." She leaned toward him, emboldened by the unmistakable evidence of his lust. "You're the only man I've ever lain with. I'm your mistress now. Doesn't that mean we're in this together?"

She was defiant in everything she did, even taking a lover. He wondered how much of it was calculated to gain his cooperation and how much she truly felt. Was he another Jack? A wild grab at freedom? But he was not a fool like her Jack had been.

She held his gaze, her hands sliding inside his shirt. "What are you thinking?"

He stared down at the wide eyes, gazing up at him with earnest trust, and found he didn't particularly care if he was nothing more than a tool. Hell, she would have married Jack, had he lived. Of course, Jack had been a Graham. She would never wed a Maxwell.

The sheet slid down to drape about her hips and as she struggled to cover herself again, he knew he'd take whatever she deigned to give him. He caught at the sheet, pulling it up around her and using it to drag her against him.

She exhaled in surprise, but her eyes glowed with passion, as unquenchable as his own. "I'm thinking, lass, I'm safer as yer enemy."

17

THEY SPENT THE DAY in the tunnels below Gealach, picking through treasure. Alex searched with her, surrounded by many heavily armed men. Biddy had not been found and Fayth was saddened by what this meant.

Fayth suspected Alex joined her in the search for a ruby pendant for no other reason than to humor her. But that was reason enough for Fayth. This was important to her. Whether he had intended to or not, Alex had saved her from the fate she dreaded more than aught else and now he had agreed to help her find Mona. Fayth *must* help him keep Gealach. She knew he didn't believe there was much she could do, but Fayth wasn't convinced she was helpless in the matter. She knew Ridley well—the Clachan Fala had become his life.

It seemed amazing, too, that her companion in all this was a Maxwell—the very Maxwell that had killed Jack. That was still difficult to contemplate, but this was the border. Men died here every day. It was not an easy life—she knew this. Jack had known this, as well. Jack had probably provoked Alex, or done something unacceptable—after all, he hadn't been perfect—he'd been a borderer, too. For now, however, Fayth was content to remain ignorant of the circumstances of Jack's death. This thing with Alex could not last forever and for now she wanted to enjoy it.

Fayth slid a look at him and found herself gazing into cobalt eyes, smoldering as they had last night when they . . . fornicated. It rose in her again, the lust, as if it had never been quenched but stoked hotter. The air seemed to crackle, thoughts of Jack dissipating like wisps of fog in the morning sun until Skelley's voice broke through.

Alex left to converse with the older man in the doorway and Fayth bent back to her search, warmed by what happened when she was near him.

Alex glanced over his shoulder, catching Fayth's eye, and gestured for her to join him. She crossed to Alex's side, watching the men curiously.

"It's finally happening," Alex said.

"What? Have Ridley and Carlisle come?"

He shook his head. "The English are massing troops in York under the duke of Norfolk. King James is assembling an army in Edinburgh."

A fist closed around Fayth's heart. "You're leaving?"

He held her gaze, hesitating. She knew her feelings were laid bare for him on her face, she'd ever been incapable of hiding them, but at the moment she could not feign indifference. Ridley was set on massacring every Maxwell should there be a war and Fayth was beginning to fear he would be successful.

"Aye, but not to Edinburgh."

"Then where?"

He took her arm and led her away from the others clustered at the doorway. "My brother, Lord Annan, has already answered the king's summons and taken men and horse to Edinburgh. He would never leave Annancreag undefended, of course, but the majority of his men must serve the king. And the Maxwells have many enemies."

He fell silent, staring at her. His eyes were so intense, so full of regret that Fayth became agitated. "What? What's the matter?"

"I received a missive from Caroline. The Johnstones have attacked Annancreag in Rob's absence."

Fayth's hands flew to her mouth. Caroline—in danger! "You must go, of course. I will go with you."

"I cannot take you."

"You must! It's my sister!"

He shook his head and started for the door.

Fayth followed close on his heels. "Why can't I come? I can ride and use a latch—"

Alex turned abruptly and she crashed into him. "You've been recently wounded. We'll be riding hard and likely not stop until we arrive."

Fayth made a rude sound. "You've been wounded, too!"

"Fayth—"

"I'm fine. Look." Fayth darted forward and snatched Skelley's sword, yanking it from the scabbard before he could stop her.

"Hey!" Skelley cried.

Fayth wielded it until Alex caught her wrist, plucking the sword from her grasp and returning it to its disgruntled owner. He slid an arm around her shoulders, leading her through the torchlit corridors. "I can't have you there, in danger. You'll be safe here. Ridley cannot ignore the writ of his own king. He'll have abandoned his talks with Carlisle and his threats on me, and even now be journeying to York."

"What about Carlisle?"

"Lochnith isn't far from the border. Though not in the direct line of invasion, should they enter from the west, it's still a possible target for the English if they fanned out. He will return to Lochnith to fortify his tower in case of invasion and possibly even to join the king in Edinburgh, though I'll not lay wagers on it." They stopped at the ladder. "Gealach is safe for now. From Ridley, Carlisle, and the English. We're too far for anyone to concern themselves with. If the English prevail, well, that's quite something else." He grinned and winked at her. "But we're not that far yet, aye?"

Fayth caught his arm. "After you relieve Caroline, will you go to Edinburgh?"

He hesitated, the smile fading. "I will send you word."

There was no more to say, unless she wanted to confess things she was not even sure of herself. Words pressed at her chest, traitorous words that betrayed Jack and her surname, but instead of voicing them she climbed the ladder, following him as he strode across the keep.

She'd never been in his chambers. His rooms were quite different from Ridley's and Carlisle's or even his brother, Lord Annan's, at Annancreag. It looked more like an armory than a place of comfort. Half a dozen breast and back plates lined the walls, some propped up on stands, others on the floor. Two shirts of mail hung from wall pegs. Shields, swords, crossbows, Jedburgh axes, and lances lined the walls. Some hung neat and shining as if just polished, others lay in piles in the corners.

As he quickly unhooked his doublet to dress, without the aid of a squire or servant, Fayth was reminded of what Alex was. He was no knight or lord, had no code of chivalry binding him, no oaths of fealty to honor. He was a reiver. An outlaw. A killer. He was responding to the call of blood. The Maxwells and the Johnstones had been at feud for a hundred years or more. Both Scots clans, but steeped in hate despite their shared nationality.

She had been fooling herself, trying to convince herself he felt regret for what he'd done to Jack. But Jack had been a Graham and it was unlikely he felt anything but satisfaction for eliminating another enemy. And what of her? Did he care for her? He'd wanted to rut with her when he thought she was a whore. He'd meant to punish her when he learned what she'd done to his people. Perhaps he'd scored another victory over the enemy by ruining one of their women.

He slid the fine linen shirt over his head, and then the padded vest, followed by a gleaming shirt of mail. Fayth was motionless in the doorway. He'd forgotten her, intent on preparing for battle. But then what was he doing, but rushing to defend Fayth's sister—a Graham? Hadn't he freed her from Carlisle and Ridley? Promised to help her find Mona? Cared for her when she was near death? Fayth's head swam with these contradictions.

When he was fully arrayed, leather breeches, boots and spurs, sword belt strapped on, latch and quarrels hanging from it, he finally faced her, helm dangling from his long fingers.

"I'm leaving you Skelley and a dozen men. Eliot is gone. It must've been him last night, at your door. We've found no sign of him in the tower or below it. You'll be fine until I return."

Fayth said nothing, arms folded hard under her breasts to stop herself from touching him. She wanted to hold him to her, keep him here—keep things from changing again.

He crossed the room, coming to stand before her. "You'll be here, when I return. Together we'll find Mona and Patrick." When she didn't answer he caught her arm. "You will not go after them on your own. Stay here and wait for me."

Though he framed it as an order, she knew he sought confirmation from her. She could not lie to him. There was no way to know how long this war would go on—he could be gone months before there was even fighting. And what if he didn't return? Though her feelings had changed, her situation had not. She must find Mona. Ridley was probably frantic for the Clachan Fala now—Mona's danger had never been greater.

She returned his gaze silently, promising nothing.

He searched her face, his mouth a flat grim line, then stepped around her. She didn't turn, listening to his steps echoing off the floorboards, muted by the fragrant rushes. Her heart ached, hollow and wanting.

Alex swung onto Bear's back, his men mounting their horses and gathering around him. Skelley stood at Bear's head, holding the horse's bridle.

"Do not leave her side. Sleep in the hall outside her door."

"Do ye really think that's necessary?" Skelley asked. "No one will bother with Gealach until this battle is fought."

"I'm not worried about the Grahams. She'll try to run." He gave his friend a hard look. "I expect her to be here when I return."

They streamed out of the gates, taking the steep and treacherous road leading away from the castle at a gallop. When they reached the bottom of the incline, Alex turned in his saddle, to look back at Gealach and saw a figure on the battlements, hair gleaming in the sunlight, yellow cloak billowing out from her shoulders. She raised a hand in farewell. Would she be there, waiting for him, when he returned?

He dug in his spurs and headed for Annancreag.

They rode hard, resting only briefly and sleeping not at all. They traveled the rest of the day, through the night and all the next morning. They reached Maxwell lands noon of the second day.

Alex called a halt at the edge of the forest. His men clustered around him. "It is possible the Johnstones know of Lady Annan's missive and allowed it to pass. They could be lying in wait to ambush us."

His men knew the wood almost as well as he did and needed no more than his warning to understand what must be done. They split into three groups, one of the groups, with Alex at their head, traveled openly on the main track through the forest.

Alex had grown up in this forest. It was part of the extensive holdings that Red Rowan passed to Robert. The local people believed fairies and elves inhabited the wood. Alex had never seen the little folk and he and his brothers had combed every inch of the forest. They'd done nothing to dissuade the tales, it kept many of their enemies away, as the only way to conduct a protracted siege of Annancreag was to camp near the forest. Eventually one must venture into the wood to forage. The only enemies bold enough to attempt taking Annancreag in spite of the fantastic creatures were the Grahams and the Johnstones. Hate, it seemed, overrode fear. Annancreag had never fallen to a Johnstone, but, like the Grahams, they had breached its defenses on occasion.

This would not be one of those occasions. The familiar fury that had once been such an integral part of Alex's person returned full force. It had deserted him in the past weeks, leaving him vulnerable to Fayth and her charms. It bolstered him now, enabled him to put her sweet face from his mind. That the craven Johnstones dared to attack his sister-in-law, the good and pious Caroline, while her husband was away serving the king set Alex's blood to boiling. He would teach them not to trouble Maxwell womenfolk.

He whistled a tune as they trotted down the road, to be certain the Johnstones didn't miss his coming. His latch rested casually across his thighs, loaded. Bear's ears pricked and swiveled. They had traveled a mile when Alex knew the ambush was near. The birds and squirrels fell silent. The only sounds in the wood were the creak of saddle leather, the snort of horses, the jangle of bridles, the crunch of leaves and twigs under hooves, and Alex's whistling.

A bush shuddered to Alex's right. He swung his latch around as shrieking battle cries filled the air and John-stones dropped from the branches onto the track. Alex leaped from Bear's back and sent a bolt into one's chest. He pulled his sword from the scabbard secured to the sad-dle and engaged the nearest Johnstone.

The fight was over as quickly as it had begun. Alex's men exploded from the trees behind the Johnstones, swords drawn. The Johnstones not already bristling with arrows dropped their weapons, surrendering. Alex didn't have time to take prisoners. He stripped them of their armor and weapons, leaving them their undergarments, and tied them to trees.

They continued their approach to Annancreag. As the trees began to thin near the forest's edge, Alex signaled his men to stop. He crept forward alone and climbed a stout oak to get a view of the castle.

Situated on an upper branch, Alex surveyed the scene before him. Annancreag sat on a natural rise, craggy on one side, gentle slope on the other. There were no secret ways in or out as there were in many border towers such as Gealach. Maxwells manned the battlements but at the mo-ment there was no fighting. Alex climbed higher, until he swayed gently in the top branches. Johnstones clustered around the edge of the forest. A group was currently tun-neling beneath the wall and another cutting the branches away from a felled tree. Alex surveyed the area to the south, noting the loch was lightly guarded.

He climbed down and gathered his men about him. "They outnumber us and appear to be alert. Our best chance is surprise. They'll not expect to be attacked at night. We'll come at them from all sides, remaining near the line of trees to mask our number, as well as provide cover." He pointed to three men. "I must let Lady Annan know we've arrived and secure her aid in this. I will slip into the keep by way of the loch." He waved his hand at the rest of his men. "The rest of you, conceal yourselves until I give the signal. Do not fall asleep. We'll attack when the moon is full and the fog conceals our movements."

They melted into the trees. Alex led the three men south. They walked for an hour, then headed east, catching the river before it emptied into the firth. They followed the river until it branched off, following an estuary that emptied into the loch that lapped the castle wall on the southeast side. Alex couldn't get any closer as Johnstones guarded the loch. However, they were guarding against escaping Maxwells, not someone trying to enter.

Below the surface of the loch, water flowed through a grate-covered channel in the wall, emptying into a stone pool. It would not be a pleasant swim. Not only was the water frigid, but a scummy, bubbly film lapped the shore and the castle walls from the waste that had once been liberally dumped into the waters—a practice Caroline had put a stop to.

Alex shrugged out of his armor and jack, stripping himself down to shirt and breeks. "Make sure I get in, aye? Then join the others."

He waded into the foul-smelling water. The rocky bottom quickly gave way to deep waters and Alex sunk beneath the surface. He glided through the water, swimming against the current, until he was near enough that the guards would see him, even though they weren't watching the water. He dove below the surface, swimming along the bottom until he reached the grating. The bars of the grating were not wide enough for a man's body to pass through, but the Annan Maxwells had been in this situation many times before and had sawed off two bars, allowing a large man to squeeze through.

Alex pulled himself through the dark channel cut in the thick curtain wall, his lungs straining. He restrained the urge to burst forth once he was through. He slowly broke the surface. The Maxwell standing beside the wall started at the sight of him and raised his latch.

Alex held up a hand. "It's me—Alexander Maxwell."

The color drained from the young man's face and he quickly dropped his weapon. "Thank the Lord! Red Alex has come!"

He helped Alex out of the water and led him into the keep. The great hall was filled with villagers that sought refuge from the attack. A golden head rose above them all, floating through her people like an angel of mercy. Caroline, Fayth's sister and Alex's sister-in-law. She saw him standing in the doorway and gave a quick order to her maid, Celia, before joining him.

"You came," she said. Her expression was serene, as always, but he saw the relief in her eyes, the lines of strain in her face. The braid that was customarily wound about her head hung down her back in a thick rope, as if she'd not taken the time to groom herself properly, and likely she had not.

"Aye, have you sent word to Rob?"

She nodded as Celia reappeared with a bath linen. Celia's nose wrinkled in disgust and she backed away. Alex knew he stank, though Caroline gave no indication she smelled aught foul. She took the linen from Celia and draped it around Alex's shoulders. Caroline's Graham priest, Father Jasper, separated from the villagers. He was long and thin as a stick, his face gaunt, but kind.

"You have brought men?" the priest asked.

"Aye, we'll send the Johnstones scattering with their tails between their legs."

Caroline gestured for him to follow her. "When?"

"Tonight, when they least expect it. The fog will aid us."

"And it will hide them as well." She led them into Rob's chambers.

Celia reappeared, bearing hot spiced ale and a bowl of barley stew.

"I apologize for the poor fare," Caroline said, "but we must ration our provisions until the siege is lifted."

Alex took the meal gratefully, sitting behind Rob's large oak desk. Other than the fire, a single fat candle illuminated the room. The priest sat nearby and Caroline tossed more peat on the fire. As Alex regarded her, he thought how unlike Fayth she was. He couldn't imagine such calm serenity ever befalling the younger sister. He wondered what had made them so different.

"Have the Johnstones made any demands?" Alex asked.

Caroline turned, brushing her hands off on her skirts. "Only that we quit Annancreag."

Alex snorted. *Fools.*

Caroline approached him, a pale eyebrow raised slightly, hands clasped at her waist. "I've received word you're holding my sister."

Alex set his spoon aside and wiped his mouth. "Aye." He normally would prepare himself for a tongue-lashing, but Caroline was not one to become shrewish, so he waited cautiously.

"And is she well?"

Alex hesitated, remembering how close she was to death at one point. "When I left her she was in good health."

Caroline didn't miss the significance of his words and her lips tightened. "I hope you don't expect her to be there when you return?"

Alex averted his gaze to his ale. Wisps of steam rose from it. He drank deeply, the strong liquid warming him. He was cold from his swim in the icy loch. He could smell the loch stench on himself. Celia returned from the adjoining room with clothes belonging to Alex's brother.

"Did you accomplish what you wished?" Father Jasper asked.

"What's that?" Alex asked, turning gratefully to the priest. A nervous sweat had broken out on his forehead and upper lip under Caroline's clear gaze.

Father Jasper slumped on a bench against the wall, his robes dirty and torn. "You had some purpose in kidnapping Fayth or was it simply vengeance?"

Father Jasper bore a disturbing resemblance to Caroline, Alex noticed. It was more than his height and eye color, for they were both exceptionally long and had unusual pale green eyes. But more than that, it was their manner. The priest now addressed him with the same placid persistence as Caroline had. Most disconcerting. Alex couldn't imagine how Rob managed with the two of them standing in constant judgment. Of course, Rob was thoroughly besotted with his bride and now viewed all the world with a rosy hue.

"She is unharmed." He wasn't about to discuss his plans for Fayth with her sister and a priest when he wasn't even certain what those plans were. All he knew was that she was his now and he would not let her go—he would work out the details later.

The priest frowned. "That's not what I asked."

Alex sighed, leaning back in his chair. "No, I did not achieve my purpose. I might have, if not for this war. But I suppose I'll never know, now."

"And what's to be her fate?" Caroline asked. She folded Rob's garments neatly on the desk, pushing them toward him.

"Well . . ." Alex held Caroline's gaze. Now was a good time to argue Fayth's innocence. "That's up to you."

Caroline straightened. "Me?"

"Aye . . . when it's safe, I thought to bring her here until the war is over, but she fears you will never forgive her."

Caroline lowered her gaze and turned partly away.

Alex stood, circling the desk to confront her. "She thought she was helping you." Alex grasped Caroline's elbow, turning her back to face him. She didn't pull away, though he felt the shift, the slight straining of her body to escape him. Alex was not going to let her block him out. "She thinks so highly of you. She thought you wanted to be a nun. She did it for you."

Caroline shook her head, still not looking at him, her brow furrowed slightly.

"I will not have that on my conscience," Caroline said, meeting his gaze finally. "I forgive her but I cannot accept that people died *for me.*" She pulled her elbow firmly away and moved to the fireplace.

Alex felt the frustration rise. She was so like Rob. Rob could never understand why Alex pursued the blood feuds. Why Alex couldn't set it all aside, pretend as if it never happened. Rob had always been quick to forgive, slow to bear a grudge, ever willing to hear both sides of a story. Alex thought this the way of fools and dead men. He trusted no one until they earned it and was ever suspicious.

"You think what she did was thoughtless, cruel even, but she sacrificed everything to save you. She valued your happiness above all else—even her own. She was motivated by love."

Father Jasper had been listening, one arm crossed over his chest, the other rubbing his mouth. He spoke suddenly,

"And what motivates you, lad, to defend her so fiercely. To beg forgiveness and understanding in her stead?"

Alex was appalled by the flush burning his neck. What answer could he give? That he'd debauched her? That he loved the impulsiveness she cursed, as it was what sent her into his arms? That he had become so attached to her he could not bear the thought of another man handling her? They both watched him expectantly.

"What do you mean?" Alex managed to say. He turned to the clothes on the desk and gathered them up.

"When you left here last," Caroline said, "you were out for blood. You vowed to make Wesley and Fayth pay. I believe you said of her . . . she is 'the spawn even Satan won't claim.' Now you plead Fayth's case to me as if you were her barrister."

Alex grunted.

"And he is red," the priest said, pointing at Alex's ears. "Look, he's turned crimson to the tips of his ears!"

Alex was gifted with one of Caroline's genuine smiles as she crossed the room, intent on his ears.

Alex ground his teeth in annoyance. "Well? What say you? Will you accept her?"

Father Jasper and Caroline glanced at each other, exchanging an infuriatingly knowing look.

"What's the matter, lad?" the priest asked. "Will she not accept you?"

Alex sputtered a vigorous denial and headed for Rob's bedchamber.

Caroline intercepted him at the door. "Alexander, have you compromised my sister in your revenge?"

"What? I— What do you mean?" He'd never been so mortified in his life. He held Caroline in high regard and hadn't considered how he'd feel when she discovered what he'd done—Christ! If she told Rob . . .

"Did you rape Fayth?"

"No!" The word exploded out of him. "I would never hurt her."

"I see. So it was consensual."

Alex turned away abruptly. "I need to change and ready myself for the attack."

Father Jasper stepped forward as Alex opened the door. "It's not for hours—"

Alex slammed the door on the priest's words. This was a disaster. He would have to speak with Caroline of this sooner or later and then be confronted by Rob when she told him. Bloody hell! Rob would thrash him. There was nothing for it but to offer for Fayth. He'd wanted to ask her to marry him ever since they'd made love, but he'd feared she would laugh in his face, just like Diana. He was only a third son—and a Maxwell, at that. She might willingly lie with him, but she would never willingly wed the Maxwell that had ruined her life. He needed time to convince her otherwise, but it looked as if time had run out.

He thrust his arms into Rob's shirt. The sleeves were a bit too long, as were the breeks. Of the three brothers, Rob was the tallest and Patrick the biggest. Alex was somewhere in between.

When he was dressed, he lingered in the bedchamber, reluctant to go out and face his sister-in-law and the priest. There was another door out of the bedchamber, leading to Caroline's chambers. Alex opened that door cautiously. Finding the room empty, he slipped through and was crossing the room to exit the chambers when he heard a strange gurgling moan.

He turned, scanning the candlelit room for the source and saw a pallet had been set up before the fire. A gray-haired old man lay on the pallet, linens wrapped thickly about his neck. He was trying to raise himself up, his hand reaching toward Alex, his bloodless face straining with the effort.

"Jesus wept," Alex breathed, recognizing the man—boy. He rushed to his side. "Christ, Laine! What happened?"

Laine's hand went to his bandaged throat and he shook his head.

Alex looked around the room, spying the desk beneath the high recessed window. "I'll be back." He found paper, quill, and ink and returned to Laine's side. "Can you write?"

Laine lifted his arm and flexed his hand. The painfully thin limb trembled with the effort, but Laine nodded. As Alex was trying to determine a way to prop Laine up, the door swung open and Caroline and Celia swept in.

"What are you doing?" Caroline came swiftly to Laine's side and knelt, hovering protectively over the boy. "He is grievously wounded. You must not disturb him."

Laine grasped Caroline's wrist and shook his head slightly, his face distorting in pain.

Caroline held his hand between hers and said to Celia, "Get him water."

"I know him," Alex said. "His name is Laine. He rides with me."

Her eyes narrowed disapprovingly. "This *boy* rides with you?"

Alex forced away the urge to fidget under her steady gaze. She made him feel the worst sort of lout.

"Where did you find him?" he asked.

"The villagers found him stumbling about the woods." She held Alex's gaze and a silent message passed between them. *I don't know how he's lived this long.* By God's graces, surely. Her hand passed over Laine's chest, parting the blanket momentarily so Alex caught a glimpse of the thick padding strapped to his chest, stained with blood.

"I've been able to communicate with him very little," she said, "as he is weak and can only answer yes and no questions." Her lips thinned. "I've tried to have Father Jasper comfort him, but the priest seems to distress him."

Alex could well believe that. Laine hated priests, but that fear came from one man, Father Rae of Rees Abbey, a man Alex wished he'd killed when he had the chance. His throat thickened as he stared disbelievingly at the boy. That Laine had come to this.

Alex held up the paper and quill. "He can read and write."

"But he hasn't the strength," she said firmly. *It will kill him,* her eyes said.

Alex looked at the lad and knew he would die anyway. And he was the only one who could tell him what had happened between Eliot and the Grahams. Still Alex hesitated. He would not cause the boy any more pain. His life had been miserable enough.

But Laine still possessed his own will and grasped the quill, tugging it from Alex's hand. The eyes that burned into Alex's understood that death was but a breath away.

"Let him write," Alex said. "I'll hold him up and you get something firm for him to write on."

Caroline nodded and stood. She returned with a slate for lessons and a piece of chalk. "This will be easier."

Alex lifted Laine gently. He smelled death on the boy— rotting skin, poisoned blood. Laine's breath was ragged and tortured, his pallid skin had a slightly gray hue up close. Caroline slipped the chalk into his hand and held the slate in front of him.

Laine's hand shook as he sketched out an E, then an L.

"Eliot," Alex finished.

Laine nodded. He scratched out BETRAY.

"Eliot means to betray me?"

Laine nodded again.

"How?"

FAYTH.

The slate jerked when Caroline realized what he was writing, causing Laine to trail a jagged line across the dark slate. Laine's hand dropped. Sour sweat darkened his hair, almost completely gray now.

A calm fury fell over Alex. "Did he do this to you to keep you quiet?"

Laine nodded again.

"What was it worth to him? I hope the prize Ridley offered was equal to his betrayal."

Laine's eyes were full of anger and sadness. He raised his hand unsteadily and wrote GEA. Before he could finish Alex whispered, "Gealach."

Laine's hand dropped. The chalk rolled away. The lad's eyes closed.

"I'll get Father Jasper," Caroline said, starting to rise.

Laine's eyes sprang open, his cracked lips parted, baring his teeth. "Nooo . . ." It came out a breath, rattling frighteningly through his chest.

Caroline froze, her eyes wide on the boy.

"No," Alex said, his voice strange and raw. "He would not want to go that way—with a strange priest giving him his last rites."

Caroline frowned, but didn't get up. "His soul must be commended to heaven."

"I know," Alex said. "I will do it."

"You? You're not a priest."

"No, I was never ordained. But a true priest will be of no comfort to him."

Caroline stared at him defiantly, obviously opposed to this latest bit of blasphemy.

Alex held her gaze, his resolve growing stronger. He'd turned away from the kirk since those years at the abbey, when he'd foolishly thought God dwelled inside a building, or manifested Himself inside the vestments of so-called holy men. What Alex meant to do now was God's will. It was right and good and he felt it to his bones.

"Get me the oil."

She held his gaze, and seeing he could not be swayed, called for Celia.

Laine slowly opened his eyes, his hand rising to grip Alex's, and mouthed, "Thank you."

18

NIGHT FELL AND STILL Fayth stood on the roof of the tower, watching and waiting. *Like the lady of the keep, watching for my lord's return. Or the fair maiden, waiting for her moon prince . . .* Why should she think such fanciful thoughts? She sighed, the cool breeze blowing at her back, snapping her skirts around her. She hadn't yet attempted to escape. She wanted to give Alex time to return. *No reason to be rash . . . give him a few days, at least.*

"Are ye no ready to go down now?" Skelley asked. He stood beside her, sheltered from the bracing wind behind a merlon, cloak wrapped tightly around him and cap pulled low over his ears.

Fayth sighed again. It was becoming a habit with her, as if she could somehow expel the emptiness inside her heart. She was not ready to leave, but felt sorry for the poor man, having to follow her about all day on her wanderings.

"I don't know what's wrong with me. When I'm not up here, watching, it's the only place I want to be. And when I am here, I become so frustrated because there's naught to see."

"Ah, lass. It's yer lad ye long for." Skelley's voice was wistful, dreamy almost.

"He's not my lad."

"So ye both say . . ."

She slanted Skelley a sharp look. "What do you mean?"

Skelley shrugged, his gaze respectfully turned downward. "I know what I know."

"And what do you know?"

"That he fretted o'er ye when yer wound festered, though he was just as feverish. And that he spent many a night, diligently keeping you from harm—"

"He mistakenly thinks I am worth a great deal. That was the reason for his care and diligence."

"Och, lassie, there's no mistakin' yer worth." He glanced up at her, eyebrows raised.

Fayth felt herself blush. "That's very kind, Skelley. I have enjoyed your company as well." She paused, gazing through the crenel at the setting sun. Mists rose in the distance and would soon billow out to meet the fog rolling in from the sea, blanketing the Rhins in a ghostly shroud. "I find myself at ease here, among Alex and you and the others. It's not like Graham Keep."

"If ye've never had a home, it's hard to ken what it feels like."

The dull ache began in her chest, only to curl and settle in the pit of her stomach. *Home.* Would she ever find one? She could not stay here. The longer she stayed, the harder it would be to leave. And if Alex returned and took her to his bed again . . . she might never break away, at least of her own will. He would eventually send her away and she would grieve for him. Perhaps even hate him.

The thought brought a smile to her face. Wasn't that how it began? With hate? How she'd loathed the Maxwells and Red Alex in particular. And now everything had changed. The anger, the hurt, the hate, were gone. Perhaps it was only buried by infatuation, or misplaced loyalty. But when she searched her heart, she could find no trace of the old emotions, even toward Ridley. She pitied him, knowing now how his unrequited love for Mona cankered his heart.

Fayth turned slightly, facing the older man. "Have you ever . . . loved another. A woman, that is?"

"Och, aye," Skelley said, straightening, suddenly impervious to the cold. "My Jennet. She's been gone some ten years now. She died in childbirth and took our daughter wi' her. They're buried together."

"I'm sorry."

"Dinna be sorry, I'm not. Well, that she died, of course I am, but I was blessed to have her at all." He paused, gazing out at the misty sea. "And the babe . . . she was so verra bonny, not quite of this world. Methinks the Lord wanted her."

Fayth regarded Skelley curiously. "You're a Musgrave?"

"Aye."

"And yet you sound very much like a Scot. Oh, I know, on the border, sometimes it's hard to tell, we all sound the same. But even so, you seem more Scots than English."

"I was raised in Scotland. My mother was a Maxwell, so when my father got in a spot of trouble with the English warden, the Maxwells took us in. I've been in Scotland, most of me life—'cept when we're making forays into England, that is." He looked down at his hands. "My Jennet was a Maxwell."

Fayth turned back to watch the now obscured horizon. She should go in. Even if Alex climbed the steep track to the tower she would not be able to see him. She sighed, deep and heartfelt, then turned from the crenel.

Skelley watched her. "You never know how much time ye have, lass. Dinna forget that."

Fayth knew he spoke of Alex, but it made her think of Jack. She'd had so very little time with him. She knew now she'd never loved him. She'd hardly even known him.

"How did Jack Graham die?"

Skelley became very still. "If he hasna told ye that, then it's no my place. But I will say this, lass, ye canna blame him for what happened."

Fayth grasped his arm. "Then Jack instigated it? Did he attack Alex?"

Skelley's lips thinned in his thick grizzled beard, but he only shook his head. "I wish I could say but I canna."

Fayth nodded dejectedly. The mist had crept over the rooftop while they spoke and now swirled around them. "Come, let's get out of the cold."

Skelley went down the ladder first. Fayth stared into the fog a moment before following him. She knew something was amiss the moment she passed through the hole. The corridor was dark, no torch or candle lit it, though Fayth still smelled the burning fat, as if the light had been recently extinguished. Beneath the smoky smell was another, one of rotting fish.

She paused on the ladder, halfway to the ground, and peered into the darkness. "Skelley?"

When he didn't answer, Fayth began to panic. He would never leave her. Something was wrong. There was no escape if she went back up and yet the darkness about her was complete. Her only hope was surprise. Rather than finishing her descent, she swung to the side and leaped to the ground. Only it wasn't ground beneath her feet, but something soft and lumpy. Fayth stumbled and fell, her shoulder connecting hard with the stone wall.

"Christ! She jumped."

Fayth jerked toward the male voice, even as pain stabbed her shoulder. She scrambled to her feet, trying to remember which way to the stairs. Movement and muttering was all around her and before she could move, arms encircled her. Quite suddenly she recalled where she was and that she had only to scream to bring help rushing. She opened her mouth, but before she could let loose, a hand clamped hard over her lips.

"Hush now, lassie," a voice breathed in her ear.

Fayth struggled—his hand was too big, too filthy—covering not only her mouth, but her nose as well. She couldn't breathe. Her lungs strained and she bucked, moaning pitifully.

A flint struck and the corridor was illuminated by candlelight. She could see little, but someone hit the man holding her.

"She cannot breathe, fool!"

His hand slid down incrementally as Fayth's vision fragmented. Air rushed into her nostrils, burning on its way down. The stink of old fish surrounded her, emanating from her captor's clothes and body. When she could think again, her gaze darted wildly about at her other captors. Armless Eliot, accompanied by two Grahams she recognized as Ridley's men and another she suspected belonged to Carlisle. The man holding her was not a Graham. He would not be groping her breasts if he were.

One of the Grahams quickly took note of his roaming hand and hit him. "She is to be unharmed!"

Her captor grunted, but lowered his hand, gripping her tightly about the waist.

"Gag her," Eliot said, handing a filthy rag to a Graham. The hand was replaced by the rag, stuffed in her mouth and secured around her head with another. The rag tasted of oil and rancid meat. Fayth's tongue receded to the back of her mouth as she willed herself not to retch. She was turned so her hands could be bound, and that's when she saw Skel-

ley, sprawled at the foot of the ladder, blood streaming
from a wound on his forehead.

The cry stuck in her throat, tears pricking her eyes. They
yanked her arms roughly as they tied them. When they
turned her back around, Eliot's black eyes stared into hers.

"Dinna fret," he said softly. "I'm here to rescue ye. I'm
takin' ye back to yer betrothed."

Her eyes widened and she shook her head vigorously.

He chuckled. "Oh, ye're going. I'm no so much a fool
as Alex. Ye may be bonny but you're no that bonny."

He turned away from her and she kicked out with her
feet, knowing her captor would not drop her. Her foot connected squarely with Eliot's back, sending him stumbling
forward several paces. He caught himself before he tumbled down the steps. Her satisfaction at hurting him quickly
evaporated as he turned around, his face thunderous.

"You stupid bitch. Ye think it amusing to push the one-
armed man?"

They stared at each other for a long time. His normally
well-groomed beard was gnarled and matted with filth, his
clothes caked with dried mud. His fury abated and he
scanned her body dismissively. "You're no worth it." He
jerked his head at one of his men. "Bind her at the ankles
and knees. We'll roll her in a rug and carry her down. If anyone sees us, I'll claim to be taking the rug as payment due."

Fayth struggled in earnest, fear blossoming in her chest.
She scissored her legs wildly so they couldn't get them together. The tower was practically deserted with Alex gone.
He'd taken more than half his men, and surely Eliot had
killed or disabled the guards on duty. Fayth kicked out forcefully, catching a Graham in the nose. Blood spurted forth.

Angry now, they fought her to the ground and onto her
stomach. Eliot sat on her legs, his muscular thighs clamp-
ing her legs together. Pain shot through her hands, trapped

awkwardly beneath her, and she ceased her struggles. She tried to scream when groping hands slid up between her legs. But they did no more than sneak a feel before binding her securely so she could do little more than wiggle about like a worm.

Alex. The thought comforted her. She prayed Skelley wasn't dead, but even if he was, someone would send word to Alex and he would come. He would see Eliot dead for this. Eliot yanked her to her feet and as she stared into his black eyes, she let him see her fury.

His mouth, full and sensual in the waves of his beard, quirked at the corner, acknowledging her unspoken threat. "If ye knew it all, lass, ye'd want to geld me yerself."

They were in a boat, that much Fayth was cognizant of. She'd fainted for lack of air, wrapped so tightly in the musty rug they'd yanked from the wall of an empty room. She'd wakened to the salty air pricking her nose and the rocking of waves. Water sloshed as someone wielded oars. They'd taken her below, through the honeycombed corridors beneath Gealach to the sheltered cove to escape by sea. They'd likely been below all along, waiting for their opportunity, hidden in some undiscovered chamber or corridor. They'd probably killed Biddy, too.

Fayth tried to move her arms and legs as her mind teetered at the edge of another swoon. She could not lose her wits or she'd never escape. She jerked her arms, bent awkwardly against her stomach, until the pain in her wounded arm brought her to full, excruciating consciousness. She heard voices nearby, but the rug and the surf muffled their words.

Her mind was filled with Alex. What if he went straight to Edinburgh, to join the king? How long would it take a messenger to reach him with the news of her kidnapping?

With war imminent, would he come for her? Her heart sank as she realized how unlikely it was that he would rush to her rescue. Using her as ransom had failed to work. She held no value there. She was a Graham and marriage to her would bring him nothing but trouble. He would cut his losses and try a different tack to secure his home. It was the only logical thing to do.

As the boat wallowed in the water and the misty cold penetrated the rug and set her to shivering, she knew she would have to save herself.

Alex left the keep and Maxwells gathered eagerly around him. A bell had tolled compline hours ago. Dark had long fallen and fog had finally seeped from the nearby bogs to blanket the castle. When Alex left them, Caroline and Celia had been sewing a shroud for Laine. Alex inhaled deeply, steeling himself for the battle ahead. The infernal waiting was slowly driving him mad. A terror had seized his soul, unlike anything he'd ever known. Fayth would not be there when he returned. Eliot was at this very moment hurting her, taking her to Ridley and Carlisle, where the most sickening and horrifying acts would be administered to her as punishment.

He *must not* think of Fayth. To think of her in the coming conflict would fragment his concentration, cause him to falter, to fail. He could not fail. Not now. Not when he had to get through this and back to her. But Laine's information pressed down on him. Eliot was in league with Ridley, which meant it was unlikely he had truly left. In fact, Alex leaving with more than half his men was probably the very opening the bastard needed.

His stomach lurched yet again with the sickening realization that he had played right into their hands. The men all watched him expectantly. He wanted to take them all and rush to Gealach, but they were trapped. One man might get through the loch grate, but not a small army. His only hope was to secure Annancreag as quickly as possible and ride home as fast as Bear could go.

Father Jasper joined them. He'd insisted they join him in prayer and that he bless each one of them, commending their souls to God. They all knelt and bent their heads. Father Jasper went down the line, stopping before each man.

After praying, Father Jasper turned to leave, but Alex caught the priest's robes. "Shrive me, Father. It's been ten years since my last confession."

Father Jasper's brows arched, but he nodded. Alex swallowed hard. He'd put God and the church behind him long ago. But he feared he couldn't do this alone and he would not return to Fayth with his soul burdened with avarice and hate. When this was over he would go to her as a man, not a Maxwell, or a landless, titleless third son. What filled him when he was with Fayth went beyond land or towers. She was more than that to him and he could not lose her. Ridley could have Gealach, but he could never have Fayth.

Father Jasper was making the sign of the cross over Alex when he heard splashing and a cheer went up from the men. Alex turned to see his brother, Robert, emerging from the river entrance, just as he had. He jogged across the bailey, his hand raised in acknowledgment, water flying from his clothes and hair.

Alex chased after him as he burst into the keep, bellowing his wife's name. Alex found them in the great hall, clinging to each other, heedless of Rob's current state of foul saturation.

"All is well," Caroline was saying when Alex approached them, her voice hoarse with emotion. "I sent word to Alexander and he came."

Rob released his wife and turned to Alex. Alex was stunned to see his brother was close to tears. He took

Alex's hands and gripped them so hard Alex swore his bones creaked. "You came."

"Of course I came. What would you have me do?"

"I will not forget this."

Alex pulled his aching hands away. "Aye, well. It's hardly over. Don't bother drying off, we'll take out the Johnstones guarding the river entrance. You brought men?"

"Aye," Rob said. "I brought a score. They wait in the forest for my signal."

Alex nodded, turning to leave Rob with his wife, but his brother caught his arm. "Any word of Patrick?"

Alex shook his head regretfully.

Rob swore. "The king sends for him. Few men have his fighting experience. He wants him to advise Huntly."

It wasn't the first time King James had sent for their brother. He'd even written to Ridley once, pleading their case, but even the king of Scotland didn't have the kind of coin Ridley was asking for Patrick's release. Perhaps that was the reason Ridley had held him for so long. Though many Scots served as mercenaries on the continent, few had such wide experience as Patrick, who'd had great honors bestowed on him by foreign rulers. He was very valuable to the Scots army. Ridley must have known that.

"The king will have to make do without him for now."

Rob nodded, grim-faced, and turned back to his wife. Seeing Caroline and Robert reunite only made the ache for Fayth more acute, though he was glad for his brother's presence. There was no one he'd rather have beside him in the coming fight than his brothers. They were fierce and strong and single-minded in a fight, protecting their own like lions. Aye, with Rob here, they would finish this quickly.

A short time later, Rob joined Alex. They slipped into the black, freezing water near the wall and disappeared beneath the surface.

19

By dawn, Fayth's abductors had abandoned the sea for land. Her legs were now free, but as she straddled a horse and was doing everything in her power to stay mounted, her legs did her little good. It was necessary, as her riding companion was Eliot and he gripped the reins with his only hand. Fayth's hands were bound before her and she clutched the horse's mane, swaying precariously as the horse clopped over the dangerously craggy terrain. Fayth did want to escape, but not by tumbling headfirst into sharp rocks, only to be trampled by a foul-tempered stallion. And Eliot's horse was in a nasty temper. It was no doubt due to his rider sawing angrily on the reins and digging his spurs into the horse's flanks until blood was drawn.

Fayth had never seen such abominable treatment of a horse and when the rags were finally withdrawn from her mouth and she'd drunk nearly a skin of sour ale, she said so.

"Shut yer mouth," was Eliot's only response.

But Fayth wasn't about to shut her mouth, not now that her ability to speak had been regained. "You are a bastard and a blackguard and I vow you will be dead in a sennight."

Eliot laughed loudly. "Oh and will ye do the deed yerself?" They had stopped at the edge of a small stand of birch to rest the horses and eat.

Eliot stood and came at her, pushing her so she stumbled, grinning all the while.

When Fayth regained her balance, she stepped forward boldly, her chin held high. "If Alex doesn't kill you first."

He snorted, shaking his head, and pushed her again, this time sending her reeling into a tree trunk. "You're aboot as threatening as yer betrothed was."

Fayth righted herself, furious. "Who? Carlisle?"

Eliot looked at her from beneath thick black brows. "Och, no, lass. I mean yer Graham lad."

A strange prickling heat infused Fayth's skin. She leaned back against the tree, afraid her legs would buckle beneath her. She couldn't take her eyes from the empty black ones, from the grinning face.

"He meant to see me dead, too." Eliot made a mock angry face. "Vowed on it, he did."

Fayth slid down against the tree, until she was sitting, her knees to her chest, her mind a maelstrom, her stomach nearly heaving. Eliot—that one-armed bastard—had murdered Jack. And Alex had lied to her . . . why? To protect Eliot? Or to keep Fayth at a distance?

Her head came up, staring again into Eliot's evil visage. Yes, she saw it, the sharp, arrogant nose, the chiseled cheekbones. He was a Maxwell, Alex had told her that. Cousins. Alex had trusted him, as Caroline had once trusted Fayth. And he had betrayed that trust, and still Alex tried to recoup his losses, allow Eliot to earn back his trust. And look where it got him.

Eliot stood, stretching. "Aye, he said I cheated him at

cards. Why, he was the one cheating. But he was a vicious wee bastard, just like yer brother, Wesley—"

Fayth surged to her feet, tree bark scraping her back. "What about Wesley? What have you done to him, you devil!"

Her outburst elicited no more than amused laughter from the men, Eliot most especially.

"Lord, they said you was a wildcat. Good riddance, I say. I like me women meek." Eliot went to his horse, still laughing and shaking his head. When he was mounted he held out his arm.

As Fayth was thrust into the saddle before him she wished for free hands and big dirk. She trembled with ill-contained rage, her thoughts murderous. His face was in her hair, his mouth near her ear. She jerked away and almost tumbled from the horse. He guffawed as she fought to right herself.

His mouth was there again. "Alex never told ye, lass?"

"Told me what?"

He spurred the horse forward. "That I was the one that did the deed." When she didn't respond, he murmured, "Fancy that."

Why Alex would protect the bastard behind her was a mystery, but he had and this was how Eliot repaid his friendship. It sickened her.

"Alex is your kin, your friend. How can you do him such a turn?"

"My friend?" Eliot spat. "He's naught but a thief, an outlaw. No better than me or anyone else and yet he thinks he deserves Gealach, that it should be all his."

"That's what Ridley promised you, isn't it? Gealach?"

"What if it is?"

"Then you're a bigger fool than I thought. He's using you."

Eliot smacked the back of her head. "Shut up. I'm sick of yer prattle."

Fayth pressed her lips together, staring blindly ahead. There must be a way to escape. She wiggled her wrists, but the hemp tying them was secure. She couldn't believe she'd thought Alex a murderer and all along it was the loch-scum behind her who'd killed Jack. Everything she knew of Alex proved he wouldn't kill indiscriminately. She had seen that, had been confused by it. She wished he'd told her that Eliot was the one who'd ruined her life and murdered Wesley's best friend. The will to revenge swelled in her, near to bursting. She must act or she would faint from the pressure.

Fayth's anger and desperation was such that wild schemes began to fill her mind. She tried to school herself for calm, to think and consider each move reasonably. But reason had fled. She was captive of the monster who had murdered Jack. She was being taken to Carlisle to wed. She refused to suffer any man but Alex's touch. She considered nothing too drastic to extricate herself from this situation.

They had skirted the trees and were traveling near the coast. The road was high above the shoreline, descending sharply into a rocky shore. Fayth gauged how badly she would be hurt if she threw herself from the horse. How far could she run, before they caught her? The possibility of breaking an arm or leg—or neck—was high. Or smashing her face up. She would chance a broken arm or a marred face if it meant success.

Eliot's arm brushed her fingers as he adjusted his grip on the reins. Her hands curled into fists. Of course. She wouldn't go down alone.

The blood pumped furiously through her veins, her heart hammered against her chest, but she remained still, watching for the right place to execute her plan. Ahead there was a break in the sharp rocks—a trail—leading to the beach below. In one swift movement Fayth grabbed Eliot's arm and threw herself back and to the right. He inhaled sharply, sliding off the saddle, but to her horror he managed to catch himself, yanking his arm easily from her grip. Fayth kept going, headfirst, the ground rushing up to her face, then she was jerked to a halt. Eliot caught her around the knee.

His horse, however, did not appreciate this new fashion of riding and reared up angrily. Eliot released her to grab at the reins and Fayth crashed headfirst to the ground. She couldn't get her hands up quickly enough to protect her head. Lights burst through her skull, her shoulder jarring painfully as she rolled onto her back. The horse screamed and Fayth forced her eyes open in time to see flailing hooves near her face. She jerked her head back just as Eliot spilled to the ground beside her.

Pain wracked her body, but she had to move. Eliot was clearly dazed. She rose to her knees and snatched his dirk from his boot, clutching it tightly in her hands. She struggled to her feet. Without looking back, she ran for the break in the rocks, gripping the dirk tightly in her bound fists.

Though she didn't hear immediate pursuit, she knew they would not be far behind. She must find a place to hide. She staggered along the path, her knee nearly giving way, her head pounding dully, her filthy and torn skirts catching on the jagged rocks. On the beach she stayed close to the rocky outcropping, so no one could see her from the road. A cluster of boulders was ahead. Fayth hurried into them, sinking down to her knees behind one. Her kneecaps throbbed brightly and she noticed a crimson stain midway down her skirts.

Fayth manipulated the dirk until the blade was pointed toward her body, sliding it beneath the hemp rope. She began to saw awkwardly, her hands shaking so she almost dropped the dirk.

Calm. She must remain calm. If she did not succeed, she might never see Alex again. That one thought sustained her. She must race to Annancreag—to Alex.

The dirk sliced her fingers and palms, poked at her forearm, but she kept at it, even as blood slicked her hands, making it more and more difficult.

"Come out, wee lassie," Eliot called and not but a hundred feet away. "If ye dinna come out, I'll beat ye senseless when I find ye."

In her panic, the dirk slid from her wet fingers and clattered to the stones. It sounded like glass shattering to Fayth's ears. She yanked hard at the bindings and felt them give. The surf roared, obscuring any sounds of approach. Fayth tried to force her arms apart with all her might, pain stabbing through her wounded arm. The rope snapped and coiled to the ground around her knees.

Fayth twisted around just as Eliot ventured into her hiding place. His eyes lit on her, noting the cut rope and bloodied dirk. Fayth lunged for it. He ran at her. Fayth's hand closed around the hilt, but his boot kicked her hand, sending pain radiating up her arm and the dirk scuttling across the rocks.

Fayth leaped for it again, scrabbling across the pebble-and rock-strewn ground like a crab. She grasped the hilt again just as his boot connected with her rib cage. The air whooshed out of her as she rolled away, still clutching the dirk. She moaned, her vision black, trying desperately to breathe and get to her feet. He grabbed a wad of her hair and hauled her up.

Fayth stabbed at him, but he easily evaded her. She had an advantage. He couldn't hold her and disarm her at the same time, not with only one arm. Until his men appeared, she still had a chance.

He held her at arm's length, dragging her out of her hiding place. Fayth swung the dirk at his chest, but the blade missed its mark by inches. On impulse she thrust the blade into his biceps. He howled with pain, releasing her. But she didn't release the dirk, she yanked it from his arm and came at him again, this time burying it in his chest.

She stepped back, her entire body quaking. He slid down a rock, grasping the hilt in his hand. She had stabbed a man and it had been much easier than she'd anticipated. Her stomach churned, threatening to bring up the ale. She pressed her hands to her forehead, willing her senses to return. His men might have heard him yell. She knew she should retrieve the dirk, she would need it, and yet she could not approach him. Her stomach roiled with fear and revulsion at what she'd just done.

She ran into the rocks, until she reached the embankment. She climbed upward, rocks showering down around her, never looking back until she reached the road. The horses had been hobbled and were untended. Fayth looked back and saw the four men on the beach, searching for her. One spotted her on the road and yelled, pointing. Fayth removed the rope from the horses' legs. She slapped four of them on the haunches and sent them racing into the trees. She mounted the fifth, digging in her heels just as the men gained the road, and raced away, leaving them in her wake.

Fayth stopped in a village to beg food and drink. She had no coin. The tavernkeeper was a fat, sweaty woman. A film of coarse black hair coated her upper lip and her thick black brows met in a point over her nose. She looked Fayth over shrewdly. Fayth was uncomfortably aware of her disheveled appearance. She was dirty, her fine clothes were ruined and blood spattered, blood clotted her hair and her hands were mangled. She'd lost her shoes at some point, though she had no recollection of it, and filthy toes peeked out from beneath her skirts. Her hair bushed wildly about her scratched and raw face.

The tavernkeeper went to the door and stared out at Fayth's mount. Fayth stood quietly against the wall, waiting for the verdict. Her muscles quivered with fatigue, her head buzzed, every cut and scrape burned and throbbed. She wanted food and a bed. She prayed the woman would not make her work for a meal. People milled about, having their dinner or drinking and gaming. Fayth raised her eyes to none of them, her gaze fixed either on the floor or the tavernkeeper.

The tavernkeeper came back. "The saddle."

Fayth blinked at her. She would have to ride the horse bareback. She'd done that before. She should be angry— what the woman asked was larceny—but Fayth found her head bobbing forward in agreement.

The tavernkeeper's expression softened. "Here. Ye sit. I'll send me girl down to wash yer cuts and bring ye dinner."

Fayth sat on the low stool offered to her. Her hands lay limp in her lap and she stared down at them, shocked at how ravaged they were. Her palms were laid open like raw meat, her fingers lined with deep cuts. Fayth's shaking grew violent. She pressed her hands into her bodice and stared out at the milling bodies filling the tavern.

She had to think hard to even recall where she was. A small fishing village, just past the Machers, on Luce Bay. She had ridden as long and hard as she could, wanting nothing more than to be at Annancreag with Alex, siege be damned. But she could not go on, not without food and sleep. She was close to collapse. Though she could forage and sleep in the woods as well as any reiver, she was exhausted and wounded. When she saw the little village it was like a vision, beckoning her closer.

A girl of about twelve approached carrying a basin and

rags. Fayth said nothing as the girl knelt before her, taking her hands and uncurling them. She muttered something in thickly accented Scots and set to cleaning out the cuts. Fayth stared down at the dark head bent over her hands. The girl was not gentle and Fayth hissed and jerked as she dug dirt and tiny pebbles from the wounds. Fayth wondered what they thought, a woman traveling alone and in such a state. Laughter bubbled in Fayth's chest, inappropriate and unstoppable.

The girl looked up, an eyebrow arched in question. "Are ye well, miss?"

Fayth smiled wanly. "I know not."

Fayth slowly became cognizant of the room and people around her. The interior of the tavern was dim and hazy from candle smoke. It smelled of ale and meat and sweating bodies. The people were indistinct forms in the murk, their voices a loud drone, punctuated with shouts and laughter. A flash of raven hair caught Fayth's eye. Her first thought was that Eliot lived and had followed her. Her feet were braced on the floor, ready to bolt, when she realized it was the back of a woman's head, moving toward the door.

Fayth stared after the woman, recognition jolting her. She knew that walk, that shape. She surged to her feet, but before she could shout her stepmother's name, a hand clamped over her mouth, the clean scent of lavender soap filling her nostrils.

"Shh . . ." Ridley whispered in her ear, "We can't have her know we're here, now can we?"

20

BY THE TIME Gealach was in sight, Alex and his men were near collapse. They'd slept little since they left their home four days ago. They'd fought a battle, sending the Johnstones scurrying home, and left immediately, riding hard to return to Gealach. Alex prayed he wasn't too late, but his heart was heavy, knowing a great deal could occur in four days.

The sight of Gealach was not a welcoming one. Gone was Alex's banner from the tower's walls. In its place an enormous green silk banner snapped in the wind, bearing a white serpent, coiled and ready to strike.

Alex didn't know what it meant. Had Ridley merely taken the tower? Or was the deed done—Fayth wed to Carlisle and the tower legally in Ridley's possession? Alex surveyed his weary group of men, no match at their best for Ridley's hundreds, but now, wounded and exhausted. Despair edged his anger. He supposed he should not be surprised Ridley ignored his king's summons, but he was. He had underestimated the opposition, believing even Ridley must answer to someone. And he must . . . eventually, but he would obviously do it in his own time.

Alex's men gathered round, watching him expectantly, waiting for their orders.

"We'll go to the village and get news," he said. "Perhaps we can gain access by the cove, if they haven't already discovered that." If Eliot had a hand in this, they already knew.

They took the long way to the village, to ensure they weren't sighted by the Graham guards on the walls of Gealach, and entered the village at dusk. There was a great deal of activity for so late. The shops were all open and bustling with business. Wagons were trundling slowly up the tower road leading to Gealach. The villagers knew Alex well, and as he and his men straggled onto the main road, they were greeted and blessed by many.

They stopped in front of the alehouse. A wagon was being loaded with casks of ale and wine. Alex called to the driver.

The man approached him. "Aye?"

Alex paused, unsettled by the man not addressing him as "my lord." Though Alex didn't hold Gealach legally, the people had nonetheless taken to addressing him as the laird.

"Where is this wine going?"

"Lord Graham has ordered it for the wedding tomorrow. A Graham lass to Lord Carlisle."

A mixture of panic and relief washed over Alex. He nodded mutely. So the deed was not done, but it would be tomorrow. That left him little time. He entered the alehouse and sought out the owner. He was directed to the back where he found the young blond man pointing out casks to be carried to the wagon.

"Sandy, what happened?"

Sandy's brown eyes widened in surprise. "Ye're back, my lord!" His thick, pale brows then lowered in consternation. "I'm supposing ye're wantin' to take the tower back?" When Alex just stared at him incredulously, he nodded briskly. "I see ye do. Could ye but wait 'til after the wedding? Business hasna been so guid in years."

"That's a fine welcome."

Sandy shrugged sheepishly. "He's paying in gold coin, my lord."

Alex's gold coin, likely. Alex no longer held out hope that Ridley hadn't found the tunnels beneath the tower. "Whatever Lord Graham has sent for, I will pay double. There will still be a wedding, but it will be mine."

Sandy rubbed his hands together, a genuine smile spreading across his ruddy face. "Very guid, my lord. What can I help ye wi'?"

"When did Lord Graham take Gealach?"

"The day afore yesterday. It happened sae quick-like we didna hear of it till the deed was done."

"When is the wedding to take place?"

"Tomorrow noon, followed by a feast."

"Did he bring a priest? Who is to wed them?"

Sandy gestured through the doorway into the tavern. "He sent to Rees Abbey for yon priest. They stopped for a dram afore climbing the tower road."

Alex went to the doorway and peered out. The alehouse was crowded, but he spotted colorful vestments and tonsured heads seated near the wall. Alex's eyes narrowed in recognition. Father Rae's shiny pate bobbed in boisterous conversation. Two monks accompanied the priest. Long suppressed anger rose in Alex. Father Rae made his home at Rees and had been responsible for much of Laine's religious instruction. He'd also been solely responsible for Laine's abuse, though the brothers were guilty of ignoring what went on in their sacred halls.

Alex crossed the alehouse, coming to stand before the priest's table. Father Rae glanced up briefly, returning his gaze to the bowl of stew before him. His head jerked back up, eyes bulging. His chair scraped as he stood hastily. "I—I'm here under the abbot's orders—to—to—"

"I know why you're here," Alex said.

The two cowled monks stood—a nefarious-looking pair, low browed and hairy. One reached surreptitiously into his robes and came out with a gleaming dagger.

"Sit." Alex pointed to the benches.

Father Rae seemed to consider his options, his gaze darting about the room.

"I let you live once, Father. I'm not in a generous humor today."

Father Rae swallowed hard and resumed his seat. The other monks followed suit.

Alex slid in beside Father Rae, so close their arms touched. Alex's men hovered nearby, hands on sword hilts.

"Well, Father . . . going to a wedding, eh?"

Sweat sheened the priest's high forehead and long upper lip. "You cannot intimidate me."

Alex smiled with no humor, fixing the priest with his most threatening stare. Better men than Father Rae had quailed under such a look and the priest was no exception. He quickly lowered his eyes, folding his trembling hands on the table.

"I recall telling ye once, never challenge me."

"What do you want?" Father Rae said to his hands. "I haven't touched . . . since Laine. There have been no others. I swear it."

"I'm glad to hear it. And now, I need something from you."

The priest exhaled loudly. "Why should I help you?"

"Because your soul is nearly lost."

Father Rae turned his head slightly to frown at Alex. "I have cast that life aside, I told you."

"Laine died cursing your name till the end."

The color drained from Father Rae's face. He licked his twitching lips. "Laine's death has naught to do with me."

For days now Alex had refused to dwell on Laine's haunted life and senseless death but the rage surfaced as he stared at the perpetrator. Heat swept up his neck and he wrapped his hand around Father Rae's wrist, squeezing so hard the priest's fingers spasmed. "Laine's death has everything to do with you. If not for your depravity he would be a novice, preparing to take his vows, rather than an angry boy that cursed God." Alex held the priest's gaze. "You'll answer for it, you ungodly bastard, when you meet the Maker, but for now, you'll make amends. Starting with me."

Father Rae tried with little effect to extricate his wrist from Alex's grip. "I have done no wrong. I owe you naught."

"Aye, you do owe me. I spared your life. Had I killed you, you'd still be stuck in the circles of hell. But you're alive and given the chance to mend your ways, to earn back God's grace."

Sweat beaded the priest's upper lip. "I've done no wrong," he said weakly, as if trying to convince himself.

" 'If thou wilt have true and everlasting life, keep thy tongue from evil, and thy lips from speaking guile; turn away from evil and do good.' "

Father Rae's forehead furrowed, his breath panting between thin lips. He opened his mouth as if to speak, then apparently thought better of speaking more guile.

Alex leaned closer, pinning the priest's wrist harder onto the tabletop. "Is that you, Father? Or have you still a ways to go?"

Father Rae sighed finally, his shoulders slumping. "What do you require of me?"

Once again, Fayth found herself confined to a room, waiting for her impending doom, or in this case, her wedding. Carlisle had visited her. She'd told him with relish that she had lain with Alex, that she might even carry his child. Unfortunately, this information did not infuriate him as she'd hoped. Rather than call the betrothal off, he sent for the midwife to examine her. He threatened that if any evidence of pregnancy was found he'd lance the spawn out himself. Fayth prayed she was not with child. She'd heard how midwives and witches rid women of unwanted babies. It was not a process many women lived through.

Fayth sat on her bed, her hands and ribs and head throbbing. But all of her new bruises and wounds seemed trivial to what was to come. *Oh Alex, please come for me.* She stared down at the bed. They'd lain here together. She'd become his wife in all but name and she held that to her breast, hoping it meant as much to him as it had to her. He would come, she didn't doubt that, but would it be for her, or for the tower? That she didn't know the answer hurt her worse than she'd believed possible.

Her shutters were thrown wide. The dawn quickly burnt off into a blazing afternoon sun. How could the sun shine on such a day? It mocked her despair, belittled it. Soon she would be wed and though she might later run away, the vows could not be undone.

The door to her chamber opened and Ridley entered, followed by two Graham men and three large, muscular women. He held a small parcel wrapped in velvet.

Fayth stood.

"I wish you to make the acquaintance of the goodwife Gunna, the local midwife."

The oldest of the women stepped forward. Her nose was long and pocked as old cheese, her lips fleshy, her eyes hard black stone.

"She's come to verify your virginity. She brought friends, to hold you down, if necessary."

Fayth looked from the women to Ridley. Her mind raced, but for once, no solutions presented themselves. There were too many of them and she was hurt. Hopelessness washed over her in waves, her bandaged hands clenched tightly at her sides.

Ridley regarded her curiously, stroking the golden brown hairs of his pointed beard. He turned to the women and the guards. "Leave us."

He watched the door until it closed behind them, leaving the two of them alone. Ridley turned back to her, his gaze assessing. "I care little if you fucked the red reiver but throwing it in Carlisle's face was unwise."

Fayth winced at his crude term.

Ridley's brows raised. "Ah, I see how it is." He shook his head, smiling slightly. "These Maxwell brothers must be sorcerers, the way they ensnare women."

"There's no sorcery involved. Only honor and truth, courage and loyalty. Things you know nothing about."

Ridley laughed, slightly incredulous. "Jesus God, you've been seduced. I didn't think it possible."

Fayth knew there was no point in arguing or reasoning with her brother. He would be neither swayed nor inclined to grant favors. He was visiting her for a reason and would come to it sooner if she remained quiet.

"You see that I speak the truth now? I've known where Mona is since she left Graham Keep, she and her fatheaded knight."

Fayth darted a look at him, not remembering seeing Sir Patrick, but then she'd been in no condition to observe much. She would be sure to tell Alex when she saw him again. *Please, Lord, let me see him again.*

"Oh, aye. He was there. Sniffing after her like a hound." Ridley's lips curled as he turned inward. After a moment he seemed to shake himself and crossed to the cabinet beneath the window. He set his velvet-wrapped parcel on it. "This is for you to wear to the wedding. I found it below in Alexander's little treasure trove. Did you know of that?" When she ignored him, staring straight ahead, he said, "I see you did."

He approached her with a bemused frown. "You're unusually subdued." His gaze dropped to her hands. "Are you in pain?" He paused, visually inspecting her. "There are things that will dull the pain. Those things will also make your wedding night more bearable."

Fayth could take no more. "Enough! Why are you here? What do you want?"

He threw his head back and laughed. "That's more like my wee sister." He crossed his arms over his chest. "I do want something."

"No?" Fayth exclaimed in mock surprise.

"I want no trouble from you. Go through with the wedding ceremony, say your vows, and lie like a dead fish in Carlisle's bed tonight. You cannot escape your fate—as even you should understand by now. Just cooperate, for once, and be done with it."

"And what do I get?"

"If you comply, it's less likely your husband will beat you." His gaze darted to her hands, his brows raising meaningfully. "It appears you've been brutalized enough. Save yourself some unblemished skin."

"Is that all?"

He shook his head. "I will send the midwife away— after she reports to Carlisle that you were lying. That you're still a virgin. I trust you can fake virginity tonight? I will supply you with blood for the sheets."

Fayth shuddered, choking down the miserable sobs that rose in her chest. Ridley's choices were not choices at all, but one horror in exchange for another.

"Ridley, please," Fayth said, doing that which she'd sworn to herself she'd never do—beg. "I love Alex. Don't make me do this. I ask you as a brother, have you any love for me at all?"

Ridley came to her, his brow furrowed, and placed a hand on the top of her head, smoothing it over and over her hair. Fayth resisted the urge to jerk away from him.

Finally, he dropped his hand and shook his head. "No, I think not."

Fayth closed her eyes, her shoulders slumping. She moved away from him. How she hated him. "Mona will never have you, you know. You can follow her to the ends of the earth. The best you could hope for is to rape her." The words were out before Fayth could stop them. The fury that flared in Ridley's eyes brought her no satisfaction as it had in the past. Her barbs had always been fashioned to wound him deeply, but now she wondered if twisting the knife also hurt Mona. Did Fayth feed his resentment? When he finally laid hands on Mona, would her step-mother pay for all the pain Fayth caused?

But she could not take the words back now, so she returned his glower impassively, her mouth shut tight against the other invectives straining to spew forth.

"Shall I send in the midwife?"

Fayth shook her head. "I will cooperate."

Ridley took a deep breath, smoothing his hands over his silk doublet. "I will send two maids to dress you for the ceremony. The priest has arrived. You will be sent for in two hours."

Ridley was not gone long when two women entered the room, laden with an elaborate pink gown, encrusted with jewels. Fayth recognized it. It came from the treasure room in the tunnels beneath Gealach. Fayth didn't think her heart could hurt any more, but it did. How dare he rummage through Alex's possessions? How dare he set himself up like master of Gealach? And where was Wesley in all of this? He hadn't accompanied Ridley to the village and neither was he among the men Ridley used to infiltrate Gealach. In fact, she'd seen nothing of him since she escaped Lochnith weeks ago.

Not that Wesley would be of any help. He'd shown himself completely under Ridley's sway. In fact, that's certainly how Ridley was managing to evade King Henry's summons—he wasn't. He'd probably sent Wesley in his stead with a host of men, promising to follow soon with more.

Fayth allowed herself to be dressed. They laced her up in wooden stays that creaked and groaned every time she moved. Her hair was pulled away from her face so tightly her mouth and eyes felt stretched. Silk slippers, gloves, and a veiled headdress completed the ensemble. The only part of her body revealed was her breasts, overflowing the bodice thanks to the suffocating stays. The heavy necklace Ridley brought her was clasped around Fayth's neck like a collar.

One of the women held her ivory mirror up and Fayth gazed at her reflection. A laugh was torn from her throat as she focused on the necklace resting just above the swell of her breasts. A large ruby in a gold setting, surrounded by a cluster of smaller rubies. Fayth nearly choked on the irony. Had Fayth found this first, they might have succeeded in passing it off as the Clachan Fala. Ridley would have given them anything they wanted. Fayth wanted to scratch it from her neck and hurl it away. What could have been freedom was now just another shackle.

Alex had forced Father Rae and his small retinue to spend the night in the village where he could watch them. Father Rae might fear for his immortal soul right now, but Alex doubted that it was enough to stop him from turning

Judas on Alex the moment they stepped foot inside Gealach.

The next morning, Father Rae and Alex, wearing monks' robes and cowl, left for Gealach. The robe was too short by several inches. Alex was forced to stoop like an old man so it covered his boots. He kept the cowl pulled over his head, hiding his face. In the company of Father Rae, he was admitted through the gates with no more than a cursory glance.

Gealach was even busier than the village, though there was no gaiety in the people's faces. No traces of excitement for the upcoming feast. Graham and Carlisle men filled the courtyard. Sweat trickled between Alex's shoulder blades. He walked beside Father Rae's mule, hand wrapped firmly around the priest's ankle in case he decided to try something stupid.

In the main hall, Alex noted Wynda's daughters, sullenly sprinkling fresh herbs into the rushes. Several Carlisle men harassed the eldest, poking her sides and saying crude things to her. From the looks she gave the men they'd suffer plenty for their unwelcome advances.

Many villagers had been brought to the tower to help prepare and serve the vast amount of food. If anyone recognized Alex, they gave no indication, so busy were they with their tasks. Other than his servants, no one else from Alex's household was in sight. Not Eliot, Skelley, Davie, or any of his other men. Alex hoped they'd escaped. Otherwise they must be imprisoned or dead.

They were presented to Lord Graham after their arrival. Ridley regarded Father Rae with thinly veiled distaste and quickly dismissed them, giving Alex several hours to set things in motion. His first stop was the kitchens, under the pretense of blessing the food. Alex would not let Father Rae out of his sight, lest the priest decide to inform on him. While Father Rae recited prayers in a bored voice, Alex wandered over to stand beside Wynda. She turned several birds on a spit. Her brow was puckered with dismay and damp with sweat. She was pointedly ignoring him. This told Alex more than anything else that Ridley's presence was upsetting to his people, for Wynda had never been one to ignore any irritant.

After hovering some time with no acknowledgment, Alex said, "You never slave over my meals in such a fashion."

Wynda jerked, her hand going to her ample bosom, eyes wide with shock.

"Shh," Alex hissed, giving her a meaningful look.

She scanned the kitchen nervously before turning back to her birds, wide-eyed. "It's pleased I am to see ye," she whispered. "Yer puir lassie is aboot to meet an ugly fate."

"How has Lord Graham treated everyone?"

"He's an angry man and hard to please. He . . . sent for the midwife . . . for Mistress Graham."

Alex's belly clenched. Damn. He'd hoped to save her the worst of it. He moved closer, as if inspecting the birds. "I have men, they are sailing around to the cove as we speak. What of Skelley?"

"That maggot, Eliot, beat him fey, but he's recovered. He hides in the tunnels wi' yer men. Lord Graham knows of the tunnels but like you, he's no been able to search them all."

"Good. I need yer help. Graham has men guarding the cove?"

Wynda nodded.

"I need them taken out. Skelley and the others can handle the rest. Can you do that for me?"

"Not to worry. We've the situation in hand. I sent all the guards some of me *specially* spiced ale this morn, just to be spiteful, see, as they wilna leave me lassies alone. But I'll send down more straightaway."

Alex grimaced. He'd had some of Wynda's "special"

ale before and found himself unable to stray far from a closestool or garderobe for several days for fear of ruining his breeks.

"Aye, thank you. That'll do fine."

"They won't notice a thing, too busy squattin' in the rocks, they'll be!"

The guards near the kitchen door roused themselves to wander over by Alex and Wynda. Alex made the sign of the cross over the birds turning on the spit and moved away, to join Father Rae who still droned on and on.

"That's enough," Alex hissed.

Father Rae stopped abruptly and cleared his throat. "Ah . . . Amen." He turned and gave Alex an expectant look.

He urged the priest out of the kitchen and back into the great hall. "Now you will offer to hear Mistress Graham's confession before her wedding. I cannot go with you. At the very least Lord Graham will have us searched, I cannot chance it. So you must do this."

Father Rae nodded.

"Tell her I am here. Give her this." He reached under his robes and into his shirt, yanking the bead from around his neck. He pressed it into Father Rae's palm. "Tell her to be ready."

The priest started to turn away. Alex caught his shoulder. "When I took Laine from the monastery he told me everything. I swore to him I would never tell a soul so long as I lived. But I wrote it down. It's safe for the moment, but if aught happens to me, it goes straight to the abbot of Dunfermline. Do you understand?"

Father Rae swallowed hard, his Adam's apple bobbing, and nodded. Alex released him and watched him cross the room to address one of the guards. A moment later the guard led him up the steps and out of sight.

Alex turned away, surveying the hall. Now he must find

a way to get into the tunnels below the larder and speak to Skelley.

Fayth didn't acknowledge the knock on her door. She stood at the window, staring down into the bailey. A cloud of dust billowed through the gate, followed by a score of mounted riders, bearing Ridley's crest. Fayth recognized the rider at the front. Wesley. Her heart leaped, only to drop sickeningly. He would not help her.

She turned away as the door opened. A priest entered wearing a shabby alb and tattered vestments. He had a long face and close-set eyes. He tried to close the door behind him, but Ridley shoved the door open and followed.

The priest frowned. "It is not seemly for you to be present."

"Nevertheless, present I am."

The priest seemed genuinely flustered by Ridley's insistence on staying.

"Can I not give my last confession in private, Brother?"

Ridley rolled his eyes. "It's hardly your last confession."

"It's my last as a maiden woman. My last before this evil deed is done."

"I suspect you've not been a maiden for some while," Ridley sneered. "Get on with your papist rituals! It's time to get this over with. I cannot tarry here another day."

"Hot on Mona's trail, eh?"

The priest cleared his throat and stepped forward. "Come to the window, child."

Fayth followed him. She instinctively didn't like him and wished for Father Jasper if she must be shriven.

"Give me your hands."

Fayth held her hands out, one eye on Ridley.

The priest covered her hands with his, pressing something small and hard into her palm. Fayth instinctively looked downward, but the priest whispered, "No. Just listen."

Fayth froze, her gaze locked on the silver enameled rosary around his neck. "He is here. Be ready."

Then he drew away from her, making the sign of the cross over her bent head and mumbling incoherent prayers.

Ridley stepped forward. "What was that?"

The priest stumbled over an excuse while Fayth dropped her hands, burying the gift in her skirts.

Ridley pushed the priest aside. "What's in your hand?"

Fayth shook her head blankly. "Nothing."

Ridley came at her. Fayth backed away, but was unable to move quickly due to her massive gown and bruised state. He grabbed her elbow and jerked her around, yanking her fist up. Fayth fought him, kicking at his ankles and jerking her arm away. He knocked her feet from beneath her and the next moment her face was pressed into the floorboards, her brother sitting on her bottom like she was eight years old again. He twisted her arm behind her back while she screeched her fury and indignation, and pried her fingers open.

Then the weight was gone. Fayth rose slowly to her knees. The veil that had been pinned carefully to her hair dangled from her ear, pulling wisps of hair from the tight knot at her nape.

Ridley stared into his palm in disbelief. Fayth was becoming desperate to discover what the priest had given her, but before she could get to her feet Ridley struck the priest across the face. Blood sprayed from the priest's mouth.

Fayth was stunned. What had Ridley become, that he would strike a man of God? The priest cowered near the door, arms shielding his head, babbling something about the knave threatening to kill him.

Ridley yanked open the door and shoved the priest out, calling over his shoulder, "There will be no more delays!"

The door slammed shut, leaving Fayth, utterly bewildered, still kneeling on the floor. She stood, fumbling to remove the veil from her hair. She'd hardly smoothed her hair back when the door opened and two guards entered.

"Mistress Graham? Your groom awaits you."

With a sickening sense of doom and fate nearly averted, Fayth let them usher her from the room.

21

SOMETHING HAD GONE terribly wrong, though Alex had yet to determine exactly what. He'd returned from the larder—Wynda's daughters had managed to thoroughly distract the Grahams in the kitchen—to find Wesley Graham had arrived with even more armed men and the wedding already in progress.

He tried not to panic as he slid along the wall, toward the dais where a dozen people clustered. A rather pathetic wedding party, made up of Ridley, the bride and groom, and no one else. Fayth was there, one arm held by Ridley, the other by Carlisle, though from the look of her it seemed they supported rather than restrained her. Her face was wan, her eyes round and bleak, her slight body completely obscured under the armor of silk and jewels adorning her.

Didn't she know? Alex pulled his gaze away from her to settle on Father Rae. Sweat leaked down the sides of the priest's face and thin trickles of blood tracked his chin. His hands were clasped tightly in front him, but still shook. A guard stood beside him with a naked sword.

Jesus God, they'd been caught.

Alex was frantic. She could not say her vows. His men were not due to burst through the larder for another half hour, at least. And yet, by Fayth's expression of utter defeat, she'd given up hope of rescue. Was Father Rae discovered before he delivered the bead?

Alex was armed to the teeth beneath his monk's robes. But what use was it all in a nest of Grahams and Carlisles? Regardless, he had no choice. Ridley would waste no time. Once the words were said, Carlisle and Fayth would be closed up together to consummate. *That could not happen.*

He quickly surveyed the scene. Though Father Rae was obviously under duress, he was managing the service with distressing alacrity. Wesley and a dozen men descended the stairs. Ridley's head swiveled around to his brother. He raised his brows questioningly. Wesley shook his head and Ridley pointed to the kitchen. Damn. They were searching the tower for him. Wesley disappeared into the kitchen. Alex hoped he was going to the tunnels below where Skelley and the others would take care of him.

Alex would have to act fast. Clutching his sword beneath his robes, cowl pulled low, he staggered forward as if wounded. "Maxwells!" he rasped. "Ootside."

Ridley turned, his face thunderous, and gestured to his men. "Go! Stop them."

Alex stood aside as most of the Grahams rushed through the double doors. Ridley's servant shut the doors behind them. Fayth's wild and hopeful eyes were fixed on the door. She thought he was out there. Alex's chest constricted, recognizing the expression. She was about to do something foolish and impulsive. Carlisle had released Fayth's arm to confer with Father Rae. Fayth stepped forward and grabbed the candelabra, even as Alex began to run, throwing back the cowl and fighting to yank his sword from beneath the drape of his robe.

Ridley felt her move and turned, his brow furrowed angrily. Fayth thrust the candelabra in his face, wax splattering him and fire singeing his beard. She succeeded in freeing herself and ran for the double doors, effectively putting Ridley between her and Alex.

"Fayth, no!" Alex yelled. As there were no Maxwells to be found in the bailey, she was running straight into the arms of the Graham men.

Ridley roared with pain, his servant fluttering excitedly about him. Carlisle came at Alex with sword drawn. Fayth swiveled around in astonishment, but Alex could see no more, as his vision filled with Carlisle's sword, arcing through the air at his head.

Alex ducked, the blade cutting empty air, and brought his own sword up. He struck. Carlisle parried. The robe hindered him, tangling his arms and legs. Bloody Christ, he'd always hated the habit! His attention was fragmented when Fayth's shrill scream reached him. He jumped to the side, anxious to see what befell her just as Carlisle's blade burned into his arm.

Fayth snatched up another candelabra, with the intention of setting Carlisle's hair on fire. Though Alex acquitted himself admirably, Fayth sought to speed things along. Soon Wesley and the others would return, then there would be no hope for them. She rushed for the pair when Ridley loomed up beside her, his face red and blistering, the skin already weeping. Half his beard was blackened and smoking.

Fayth screamed at the sight and thrust her candelabra at him again. More wax splattered his face. Screaming, he struck the candelabra aside. It crashed into the rushes. Before they burst into flames, Father Rae rushed forward and stamped them out. Fayth backed away, trying to keep one eye on Ridley and one on the couple engaged in battle. Alex was wounded, but he had shed the monk's habit.

Though his arm bled profusely, he beat Carlisle back with furious blows.

"I will kill you for this," Ridley spewed the words out, part shriek, part wavering cry.

Fayth's heart lodged in her throat. She'd never seen her brother so crazed. Terror coursed through her, immobilizing her. He reached for her and she jerked away, stumbling backward and falling inelegantly, skirts flying up, stays cutting into her hips and ribs. She fought desperately to right herself, but Ridley had her.

"You will never interfere again, bitch!" He yanked her to her feet only to smack her back down.

Fayth had been through a great deal in her life—and a great deal more of late—but she had never been struck so hard. Light burst behind her eyes as her face hit the floor. She tried to push herself up, but could not. Buzzing, like a swarm of angry bees filled her head. Her stomach lurched. Ridley's hands were on her again, but her head was so mixed up, she couldn't even panic. Dimly, she heard Alex call her name.

Alex saw the blow—Ridley striking his sister down so hard blood splattered Father Rae's vestments. The priest shrieked and ran from the hall. Ridley stalked toward his sister, crumpled on the ground, motionless. Something exploded in Alex's head, edging out rational thought. Ridley must die.

Carlisle was at him again, sword bearing down. With a roar of fury, Alex parried the blow and sent his next strike home, under Carlisle's guard, slicing into his shoulder. Carlisle's sword clattered to the ground. Alex yanked his sword free and drove it home again, piercing the heart. Carlisle crumpled to the floor, gray eyes glittering in shock.

Alex strode by the dying man, advancing on Ridley, who

crouched over Fayth, trying to wake her with vile words and threats that he wasn't through with her yet. Alex kicked him hard, his boot connecting solidly with ribs, and sent him sprawling in the rushes. Ridley was on his feet, whirling toward Alex, ruined face distorted with hate and the naked steel of his dagger gleaming.

Alex pulled back in time, the blade nearly clipping his nose. He swung his sword, but Ridley ducked, freeing his own narrow blade from the scabbard. Ridley lunged forward, brandishing sword and dagger. In his rage, Alex fell for the feint. The sword blade sliced into his shoulder. Ridley immediately redoubled, coming at him again, jabbing with the dagger. Alex deflected the blow, sending the shining blade skittering into the rushes. Undeterred, Ridley struck again and their blades caught as Alex surged forward, locking them at the hilt. Alex rammed his elbow into Ridley's face. Ridley's hold slackened and Alex hit him again with his sword hilt.

Bone crunched and Ridley staggered back, hand to his nose. Alex took the opportunity to kneel beside Fayth. He slid his hand around her throat. It was warm and her heart beat strong against his fingers. The doors burst open. Grahams returning from their fruitless Maxwell hunt. They streamed through the double doors, most pausing to take in the scene before them with considerable confusion.

Alex lifted Fayth, tossing her over his shoulder.

Ridley had recovered, blood streaming from his misshapen nose, but didn't attack. He held his sword in a defensive position, his face a lumpy horror. "You've lost everything," Ridley said, his voice lisping through a chipped tooth. "All for a stupid little whore." He smiled, his flesh stretching unnaturally in its new mask. He motioned for his men to apprehend Alex, his sword dropping to his side with relaxed confidence.

Alex raced for the kitchens.

Wynda and one of her daughters stood in the doorway to the larder. "Oh, hurry, my lord!"

Alex pushed at her shoulder, shoving his sword into her hands. "Come, we must all go." He slammed the door shut behind them, dropping the heavy bar in place. That would not hold them for long.

When he swung around, he froze reaching to retrieve his sword. There, blocking his escape, was Wesley Graham and a handful of his men. Alex bit into his lip until he tasted blood, frustrated anger nearly consuming him.

Wesley stepped forward. "Here, I'll lower her down to you."

Alex blinked stupidly at him. Pounding began on the door behind him, shaking the entire frame with the force of it.

"Goddamnit—go!" Wesley gripped Fayth's waist, pulling her from Alex's shoulder.

Alex didn't relinquish her, still imprisoning her under her arms. He shoved Wesley back. "This is a trap."

"It's not!" Wynda cried. "He's spoke to Skelley—Skelley believes him."

Alex frowned at Wesley, still uncertain.

"It's no trap," Wesley said, stepping forward, the twisted scar Alex had given him standing out red against his pale skin. "Ridley has been cozening me all along and I'm finally wise to it. He'll pay for it—and I'll start by letting you go free."

"He'll kill you for this."

A shadow passed over Wesley's face and his mouth flattened. "He can try." He tugged at Fayth gently, nodding his chin at her inert form. "Don't worry about Ridley—I'll deal with him. You deal with the shrew."

"How do you know I won't hurt her?"

"She told Ridley she's in love with you and it's clear she means more to you than this tower. That's enough."

She's in love with you.

The pounding on the door stopped abruptly, only to begin again with enough force to knock things off the walls and shelves and to set the casks shuddering.

"Go!" Wesley said. "Before it's too late!"

She's in love with you. Alex relinquished Fayth to her brother, still stunned by his revelation, and climbed quickly down the ladder. Wesley and another man lowered Fayth into Alex's waiting arms. Wynda and her daughter quickly followed, bearing candles.

"Where are the others?" Alex asked.

"Below. Waiting."

Alex looked up, at the trapdoor, to give a final farewell and thanks to Wesley, but the door slammed shut, drenching them in darkness but for the faint circles of candlelight.

Fayth slowly became aware that she was on water. She could hear it lapping forcefully against the sides of a boat, the roar of surf, the rhythmic slice of oars through water. The vessel wallowed and rolled over the waves. She panicked until she realized she was not bound and rolled in a carpet, but held tightly in someone's arms. A strong heart beat against her ear.

She moaned and tried to lift her head. The sun stabbed her squinted eyes and she shielded them. Every bone in her body ached. A hand smoothed over her hair and Fayth looked up.

It was Alex's arms that held her. Fayth blinked up at him, dazzled by his countenance, smiling down at her. He'd never looked at her so—with a mixture of relief, hope, and . . . love?

"Welcome back," he said. "I feared you would not wake."

Fayth tried to smile, but the whole left side of her face felt swollen. She winced.

Alex frowned with concern. "Aye, that hurts."

Fayth ran her tongue over her teeth, relieved to find them all intact. Her lips were raw and stinging.

"I was afraid you wouldn't come," she said.

"And leave behind the greatest treasure in all of Scotland?"

Fayth straightened, looking behind her. Skelley and Davie rowed them away from Gealach in a long boat. They were heading straight out to sea, to avoid being smashed against the rocks. Gealach stood sentinel on the cliff above. On the beach Grahams were just arriving, nocking their arrows and firing. But the arrows fell short. Fayth looked around and saw three more long boats, filled with Alex's men and servants, all rowing away.

"I don't understand. Ridley still has Gealach. Did you get the treasure out, at least?"

Alex caught her chin, turning her to look at him. "Aye, lass, the only one that matters."

Understanding was slow to dawn on her, but when it did, her eyes widened. "Me?"

He nodded. "If ye'll have me, I'll make this one thing official. I haven't much to offer . . . though I'm sure I'll manage some—"

Fayth threw her arms around his neck and kissed him. She winced, her lips stinging, and pulled away. He wrapped his arms around her and pressed his mouth to her temple. "I love ye, Fayth, and Gealach means nothing without you."

Tears gathered in Fayth's eyes. "I love you. And we'll get Gealach back. If it's the last thing I do, I'll make Ridley pay—"

Alex laughed shortly, pressing his fingers gently against her lips. "Enough of vengeance, for now. I've a brother to find and a new stepmother, as well. And there's a war coming."

Fayth's heart fluttered in her chest with new fear. Alex would rally to the king and they would be apart again. She might lose him in battle. She pulled away from him. "How did we get away? Ridley had hundreds of men. You were alone in the hall."

"Wesley helped us."

Fayth's mouth dropped opened. "Wesley?"

Alex nodded. "Aye, it seems he's had a change of heart."

Fayth looked back to the tower, new worry growing in her heart. "Oh, Wesley . . ."

"Shh, lass. He's a fighter, like you. He'll be fine."

His lips were against her skin again, pressing reverent kisses to her forehead and temple, the only part of her body not battered and bruised. His hands trailed over her back. Fayth closed her eyes, her heart swelling with love and hope. She would wed him and they would never be torn asunder. She would have his children and they would get Gealach back. She vowed it to herself.

She smiled, imagining their sons and daughters, roaming the tunnels beneath, and she and Alex, on the roof, gazing up at the moon.

EPILOGUE

HAND-IN-HAND, Alex and Fayth wandered around the curious group of standing stones, stopping to inspect each one in minute detail. They finally stopped before an oblong stone with a hole in the center, through which they could stare straight up the west coast of the Scottish highlands.

"This is it," Alex said, running a hand through his hair.

"What does it mean? It doesn't bear the markings that were on the bead."

They no longer had the bead, but Alex claimed to have memorized its shape and markings.

He shook his head, releasing her hand to circle the stone. He scuffed his booted toe over the ground in front of the stone, but it was undisturbed. He planted his hands on his hips and stared around at the group of stones again, as if they held the answer.

"Damn," he said. "I thought I'd come here and the answer would be clear. But if you saw Mona near the firth, they've certainly already been here and gone."

Fayth came around the stone, sliding her arm around her husband's back. He'd been most distressed when Fayth told him she hadn't noticed a large blond man with Mona. She'd tried to assure him it meant nothing; she'd caught but a glimpse of her stepmother at the tavern. Ridley had said Sir Patrick was still Mona's traveling companion and Ridley certainly appeared to know a great deal more than she'd expected.

Fayth pulled Alex back around to the opening and pointed through it. "Maybe it's simply a marker, telling them to go that way? She had a whole necklace of these beads. Perhaps they were a map of sorts."

This had also distressed Alex when she'd told him. He'd thought the bead a lone landmark. But if there were scores of them they'd never be able to track down his brother. In the week since they'd escaped Gealach and Ridley, they'd sailed to Ireland, married, and sailed straight for the Highlands, to this group of stones Alex was desperate to seek out. Their next stop was Annancreag—and Caroline.

With a sigh, Alex slid his arm around Fayth's shoulders and turned her back toward the track leading to the village. Seeing they were leaving, Biddy heaved herself to her feet, limping along beside them down the hill. Skelley had found her in the tunnels, badly wounded, barely able to walk. The dog had found the rumored spring beneath the tower and had lain beside it, lapping at the cool water to stay alive. Davie had tended her wounds and she was healing fine, though she looked dreadful, with linens wrapped thickly around her ribs and right leg.

This far north the air was turning chill with coming winter. Fayth remembered Gealach with a pang of longing. On the Rhins the weather would still be mild. Though they suffered from frequent and heavy rains—more so than the rest of Scotland—the cold was slow to come and quick to leave.

Fayth glanced at her husband. He gazed up at the sky.

The moon was still out, though it was full daylight, a faint white globe in the horizon.

"They're fine." Fayth squeezed her husband's arm reassuringly. "If Patrick is anything at all like his brothers, Ridley doesn't stand a chance."

Alex stopped and turned her toward him, hands on her shoulders. "And if Ridley is anything at all like his sisters, we're all in trouble."

Before Fayth could muster a sufficient rejoinder, he silenced her with a kiss.

CAPTURED BY YOUR KISS

JEN HOLLING

Turn the page for a preview of
Captured by Your Kiss. . . .

PROLOGUE

West March, England, 1531

MONA MUSGRAVE GAZED out over the crowd on unforgiving faces, her lips threatening to quiver with the strength of her terror. She stiffened them, refusing to weep or beg. She'd done enough of that already. If she were to die, she'd die with dignity.

Her hands were bound tightly behind her back, the hemp rope coarse against her throat. They'd dragged her to the gallows on a litter full of holes; her gown was torn and her arms and thighs chaffed raw from the ground. The drying juice of rotten vegetables and fruit matted her hair to the sides of her face and stained her clothes. A fiddle and a flute played a wild reel that made her head spin. Children danced to the tune, singing *The witch is dead! The witch is swinging by her neck!*

Even now, moments from the end, the villagers hissed at her, called her a witch and a murderess. They believed a dead man over her, these people she'd cared for, healed, helped. Her chin quivered again and she clenched her jaw against it, her vision burning and blurring.

The priest bellowed prayers at her, the *slap, slap* of the

back of his hand against his open palm punctuating his sermon on the dangers of the devil and how women are so much more susceptible to his wiles. The boards creaked beside her as the executioner stepped forward to kick the stool from beneath her feet.

A bright blob swayed and jiggled before Mona's eyes, distorted by her tears. She blinked rapidly, sending tears cascading down her cheeks, but clearing her vision. It was Arlana Musgrave, a white witch and the rumored keeper of the Clachan Fala—the Blood Stone of legend.

Mona inhaled sharply. The priest fell silent with a final slap. The fiddler stopped on a screeching note. Parents hushed their children's singing. The crowd turned away from the spectacle of Mona to view Arlana with awe. They parted to allow her fat pony to pass, bearing its enormous burden.

No one knew what Musgrave grayne Arlana sprung from. Many people in this area bore the same surname and had no blood attachments, so this was not unusual. Mona had not seen the white witch since she was a child and had never spoken to her. Arlana looked no different than she had a decade ago.

Hugely fat, her bulk was draped in bright, rich cloth. Yellows, reds, greens, painted with odd shapes and symbols. Silver chains and colorful beads draped her thick neck, bangles clinked on her wrists. Her gray hair hung loose down her back, flowing wildly over her shoulders and mingling with the pony's mane. Her face was beautiful. Round and pale as a moon and for all her many years—no one knew exactly how old she was—she had not a wrinkle. Her blue eyes were penetrating and bright, framed by long black lashes.

Her pony, its sides heaving and lathered with sweat, stopped before the gallows.

Mona remembered to breathe and the air whooshed out of her. Dizziness nearly overcame her, but she steadied herself—Arlana was looking right up at her. Why was she here? Had she come to watch the execution? That would be Mona's luck—the notorious recluse emerged from her hermit hole for a bit of diversion.

Arlana's gaze fastened on Mona, assessing, judging. The silence drew out interminably. Mona could hear her heart pounding against her ribs, her breath laboring with fear. The villagers were similarly quiet, everyone waiting with bated breath for Arlana to reveal her reason for venturing out of the wood.

"My apprentice is dead," Arlana called out, her voice cracking as if she hadn't used it in years, never taking her eyes from Mona. "I need another. She'll do."

A soft murmuring began in the crowd and washed through them like a wave. Mona stared at the old woman incredulously. Though Arlana was much revered by the village she couldn't seriously expect them to just let Mona go because she said so.

The priest stepped forward, distressed. "B-but she is a murderess—"

"I know what I know and you're wrong." Her sharp gaze pinned the priest. "She was telling the truth. Her husband was possessed."

The crowd gasped and the priest swung around, wide eyes on Mona. His lips flapped but nothing came out. Without orders the executioner swiftly removed the rope from Mona's neck and cut her bindings, helping her gently down from the stool.

Mona looked out at the crowd, confused, trembling from the sudden reprieve. They eyed her differently now. She'd always been known as a healer, and yet all knew she was human, fallible—and of late, they believed her depraved. Arlana was viewed as something else, something otherworldly, beyond understanding. And she was *good*. A *white* witch. This is what Mona saw in their eyes now as they gazed at her. Wonder, as if seeing her for the first time.

Legs shaking, Mona descended the gallows steps. No one tried to stop her. As she neared Arlana, the villagers reached out to touch the old woman's skirts and her pony. Mona reached Arlana's side and gazed up at her. A small smile curved the witch's lips.

Mona shook her head slowly, unable to give voice to the emotions welling up in her chest, choking her. "Thank you," she whispered.

Arlana let out a short, breathy laugh as she tapped her pony's sides and gestured for Mona to follow her. "You'll be cursing me afore this is over."

It was a fine cottage—bastle house, really—with a spacious upper floor and the lower floor devoted to livestock. It was precious few that didn't live intimately with the cows and chickens. The floor was not dirt but clean wooden planks. The wood creaked and groaned as Arlana walked on it and Mona feared it would give way under her bulk. But it held and the old witch lowered herself slowly and painfully onto the rug before the hearth. She waved a fat-fingered hand for Mona to build the fire back up. The silver rings on her fingers glittered in the dim light, shafts of weak sunlight from the open windows catching the cut edges of her jewels.

Arlana had spoken little to Mona on the long ride into the woods. Mona had tried to question the white witch about why she'd been chosen as the apprentice, for Mona had always thought Arlana's apprentice had to be a virgin. But Arlana only shook her head and bade her to be patient.

They'd had to stop frequently to rest the pony and Mona had been forced to help Arlana from her perch on the poor creature's back. Mona had never seen the like—Arlana's ankles were as big as Mona's thighs—and her feet were small, plump things, encased in silk beaded slippers. Mona knew well where all the finery came from. Scots and English alike traveled to her for healing remedies and fortunes. So far as Mona had heard, Arlana was never wrong. Though she never asked for a penny in payment she was always well rewarded.

"You should have come to me long ago," Arlana said as Mona piled logs onto the dying embers.

Mona turned, frowning. "Come to you?"

"When you first suspected your husband was . . . not right in the head."

The slithering returned to Mona's belly as it always did when she was reminded of Edwin Musgrave. "I couldn't. He wouldn't let me out of his sight."

Arlana nodded sagely.

Mona leaned forward. "Is it like you said? Was he possessed by the devil?"

Arlana scowled. "How should I know? It isn't like the old horny ever showed hisself to me." She cocked a dark brow. "Not the Almighty, either—and me a white witch. Don't you forget it."

Mona shook her head. "But you said . . ."

"Never mind what I said. What's the matter with you, girl? Have you never told a lie?"

Mona placed her hands firmly on her hips. "I don't lie."

"Aye—that much is clear. That's why you found yourself on the gallows with a noose about your neck." She snorted, shaking her head and pulling a wooden bowl near. "She doesn't lie! Imagine that!" She pointed the pestle at Mona before smashing it into the bowl. "Thank the good

Lord that I do lie, or you'd be swinging in the breeze, lassie! Swinging in the breeze!"

Mona's hand crept up to her neck and she grimaced, massaging the suddenly sensitive skin. "I am to be your apprentice . . . ?"

Arlana glanced meaningfully at the cold logs. "Not if you cannot get a fire going."

Mona leapt into action. Once the fire was blazing, she lowered herself onto the floor beside Arlana. "I owe you my life. I will do anything you wish, but please tell me what it is you want from me."

Arlana set the bowl aside, the contents—herbs or roots Mona was not familiar with—now ground to a fine red powder. Her round cheeks were flushed from the exercise of pulverizing the substance. "I have long watched you, Mona Musgrave."

Mona put a surprised hand to her chest, but didn't speak. Since she was a very small child she'd heard stories about Arlana. She was the keeper of an ancient stone, the Clachan Fala. She was a white witch, immortal. She'd been alive forever. She was feared and respected in the village, her name spoken in hushed whispers. That Arlana had been watching Mona Musgrave was a shock.

Arlana's penetrating gaze took in the play of emotions across Mona's face and she nodded slowly. "Yes. I had my eye on you when you were but a wee lassie. I'd marked you as the one to take my place. But then you fell in with that foolish Edwin and ruined my plans."

Mona had the strangest urge to apologize, but held her tongue. How could she be sorry for something she'd never even been aware of?

"But now he's gone and I see that he was part of the plan."

Mona blinked. How could being married to Edwin be

part of anyone's plan? Visions of his twitching face, his fierce eyes, his impassioned outbursts—him holding her under the water until she went limp—all these things bombarded her and she shook her head incredulously, her face twisting with the effort to shut the memories away.

Arlana's lips only pursed and her eyebrows rose. "Oh, yes. It is a solitary life I lead, you see that. But it must be that way. No men are allowed to know the secrets of the Clachan Fala—except the chosen one. You . . ." Arlana waved a hand, gesturing at Mona's body. "Men are drawn to you. You would have eventually been tempted and then all would have been lost. But now, after Edwin, I suspect you want nothing to do with men."

Mona shuddered, a trembling revulsion filling her. But it was accompanied by a deep ache. She desperately wanted a child. Just one. And for that, she needed a man. But Arlana was right, after Edwin, she'd come to the conclusion it wasn't worth it.

"You're right. I am . . . afraid to be with another man."

Arlana smiled and nodded, content. "Ah, good. You are right to be afraid." She pointed a fleshy finger at Mona. "Men are responsible for slipping a noose about your neck. Men fear a woman strong enough to take matters into her own hands and rid herself of a worthless, abusive husband. You terrify them—so they tried to kill you. If there is a devil, it lives in the hearts of men. Oh, they don't know it and some of them look to be angels in the flesh, but they will suck your soul away and throw it out like trash. To be the keeper, you must have your soul intact. Is your soul intact?"

Mona frowned, unsure how to answer. She searched within herself, feeling certain that Edwin took nothing but her innocence and trust, and they were not her soul. They were only remnants of the child she once was. "Yes, my soul is intact."

"Good. Do you want to be my apprentice? To one day be the keeper of the Clachan Fala?"

Mona opened her mouth to give an affirmative answer, then closed it, confused. The gratitude she felt toward Arlana was enormous, but she wasn't even sure what the Clachan Fala was, or what, as the keeper, she would be expected to do.

Arlana gave her a cynical smile. The fire, now blazing, cast her face in a red light, making her resemble a grinning goblin. "Not so grateful now that the noose is gone."

Mona's head snapped up, deeply insulted that Arlana would doubt her integrity. "I will be the keeper. I will do all that you teach me."

A cold smile spread over Arlana's face and her eyes grew flat. "Good. Now forget everything you've ever learned about right and wrong. It no longer matters where I will take you. It is a world that only women can understand. Men have no place in it. The men of this world think only they understand loyalty, courage, honor, duty—but they know nothing. I've given my entire life to protect the Clachan Fala and if I had my life to live over again, I would repeat it."

Mona leaned forward, entranced by Arlana's words. "The Clachan Fala . . . what is it?"

Arlana smiled and leaned back, settling her enormous bulk about her, adjusting the colorful skirts over her round knees. "This is how it begins. My master, Merry Musgrave, first told me the story and now I pass it on to you. There are two rules you must never forget. The first is that nothing I tell you is to ever be written down." Arlana tapped a finger against her forehead and Mona noticed the nails were stained bright red. "It all must be in here. You will commit it to memory, every word, and when I'm gone, you will find an apprentice and begin anew."

Mona nodded. "What is the second rule?"

"You tell no one but your apprentice what I teach you."

"No one?"

Arlana's eyes narrowed. *"No one.* There are many who think they already know a great deal and they'll want to know more. They'll try to make you tell them. You mustn't give in."

Mona nodded, chilled by these rules.

Arlana reached into her bodice and brought forth a beaded necklace. She cradled it lovingly in her palms, gazing down at it with soft eyes.

"This, my child, is your new lover. The *iuchair.*"

Mona was surprised to find herself reaching eagerly for it. As the cool beads slid between her fingers, she closed her eyes and saw things—the mountains and valleys of the Highlands. Heather-covered peaks, standing stones . . . a bleak and unforgiving island blasted by wind and the sea. The crumbling arches of a ruined abbey. Mona gasped, an inexplicable longing welling up inside her. She'd been there, a thousand times, though she'd never left the West March in her entire life.

Mona opened her eyes and met Arlana's knowing gaze.

"Do you now understand?"

Mona smiled slowly, realizing she'd finally come home.